Praise for the futuristic fantasy of

Robin D. Owens

Heart Journey

"Unexpected tragedies, critical family issues, ar ... ex- plained thefts add gravity and suspense, while ... nd sentient spaceships and houses offer a touch of fa ... hat series fans will enjoy. Verdict: Sexy, emotionally ... ced with humor, Owens's ninth book in her Celt ... nce again draws readers into one of the more imagi ... ldly cultures."

...rnal

"The suspense woven into the background of the passionate struggle between HeartMates is contrasted by the moments of light humor, balancing the book into a skillfully crafted read for any lover of futuristic or light paranormal romance." —*Fresh Fiction*

"A captivating fantasy filled with love, magic, and suspense. A delightful read."

—*Smexy Books*

"What is a ten-letter word for *Heart Journey*? Phenomenal!! . . . If it is a Celta Heart story, you really can't go wrong. Highly recommended, along with the rest of Robin Owens's series."

—*CK²S Kwips and Kritiques*

"[A] delight to read. I loved seeing more of the planet Celta. Seeing how wild and unsettled, how dangerous and uncertain life is first-hand was exhilarating and intriguing . . . If you love romance and adventure then I highly recommend you set your sights on the Heart series."

—*Night Owl Romance*

Heart Fate

"A superb romantic fantasy filled with heart."

—*Midwest Book Review*

"A touching tale of learning to trust again . . . Even for readers unfamiliar with the Heart world, Owens makes it easily accessible and full of delightful conceits." —*Publishers Weekly*

"[This] emotionally rich tale blends paranormal abilities, family dynamics, and politics; adds a serious dash of violence; and dusts it all with humor and whimsy . . . Intriguing." —*Library Journal*

continued . . .

Heart Dance

"The latest Heart fantasy is one of the best of this superior series . . . retaining the freshness of its heartfelt predecessors."

—*The Best Reviews*

"I look forward to my yearly holiday in Celta, always a dangerous and fascinating trip."

—*Fresh Fiction*

"The world of Celta is amazingly detailed, and readers will enjoy the bits of humor that the Fams provide. Sensual, riveting, and filled with the wonderful cast of characters from previous books, as well as some new ones, *Heart Dance* is exquisite in its presentation."

—*Romance Reviews Today*

Heart Choice

"The romance is passionate, the characters engaging, and the society and setting exquisitely crafted."

—*Booklist*

"Character-driven story, brilliant dialogue . . . Terrific writing with a very realistic and sensual romance make *Heart Choice* a fantastic read."

—*Romance Reviews Today*

"Well written, humor-laced, intellectually and emotionally involving story which explores the true meaning of family and love."

—*Library Journal*

Heart Duel

"[A] sexy story . . . Readers will enjoy revisiting this fantasy-like world filled with paranormal talents."

—*Booklist*

"With engaging characters, Robin D. Owens takes readers back to the magical world of Celta . . . The characters are engaging, drawing the reader into the story and into their lives. They are multilayered and complex and grow into exceptional people."

—*Romance Reviews Today*

Heart Thief

"I loved *Heart Thief*! This is what futuristic romance is all about. Robin D. Owens writes the kind of futuristic romance we've all been waiting to read . . . She provides a wonderful, gripping mix of passion, exotic futuristic settings, and edgy suspense." —Jayne Castle

"The complex plot and rich characterizations, not to mention the sexy passion . . . make this a must-read." —*The Romance Reader*

"Owens spins an entrancing tale . . . A stunning futuristic tale that reads like fantasy and is sure to have crossover appeal to both SF and fantasy fans." —*Library Journal*

"Owens has crafted a fine romance that is also a successful science fantasy yarn with terrific world building." —*Booklist*

HeartMate

**Winner of the 2002 RITA Award
for Best Paranormal Romance
by the Romance Writers of America**

"Engaging characters, effortless world building, and a sizzling romance make this a novel that's almost impossible to put down." —*The Romance Reader*

"Fantasy romance with a touch of mystery . . . Readers from the different genres will want Ms. Owens to return to Celta for more tales of HeartMates." —*Midwest Book Review*

"*HeartMate* is a dazzling debut novel. Robin D. Owens paints a world filled with characters who sweep readers into an unforgettable adventure with every delicious word, every breath, every beat of their hearts. Brava!" —Deb Stover, award-winning author of *The Gift*

"A gem of a story . . . Sure to tickle your fancy." —Anne Avery, author of *The Bride's Revenge*

"It shines, and fans will soon clamor for more . . . A definite keeper!" —*The Bookdragon Review*

"This story is magical . . . Doubly delicious as it will appeal to both lovers of fantasy and futuristic romance. Much room has been left for sequels." —*ParaNormal Romance*

Titles by Robin D. Owens

HEARTMATE

HEART THIEF

HEART DUEL

HEART CHOICE

HEART QUEST

HEART DANCE

HEART FATE

HEART CHANGE

HEART JOURNEY

HEART SEARCH

Anthologies

WHAT DREAMS MAY COME

(with Sherrilyn Kenyon and Rebecca York)

HEARTS AND SWORDS

Hearts and Swords

Robin D. Owens

BERKLEY SENSATION, NEW YORK

THE BERKLEY PUBLISHING GROUP
Published by the Penguin Group
Penguin Group (USA) Inc.
375 Hudson Street, New York, New York 10014, USA
Penguin Group (Canada), 90 Eglinton Avenue East, Suite 700, Toronto, Ontario M4P 2Y3, Canada
(a division of Pearson Penguin Canada Inc.)
Penguin Books Ltd., 80 Strand, London WC2R 0RL, England
Penguin Group Ireland, 25 St. Stephen's Green, Dublin 2, Ireland (a division of Penguin Books Ltd.)
Penguin Group (Australia), 250 Camberwell Road, Camberwell, Victoria 3124, Australia
(a division of Pearson Australia Group Pty. Ltd.)
Penguin Books India Pvt. Ltd., 11 Community Centre, Panchsheel Park, New Delhi—110 017, India
Penguin Group (NZ), 67 Apollo Drive, Rosedale, Auckland 0632, New Zealand
(a division of Pearson New Zealand Ltd.)
Penguin Books (South Africa) (Pty.) Ltd., 24 Sturdee Avenue, Rosebank, Johannesburg 2196,
South Africa

Penguin Books Ltd., Registered Offices: 80 Strand, London WC2R 0RL, England

This book is an original publication of The Berkley Publishing Group.

Cover illustration by Tony Mauro.
Cover design by George Long.
Interior text design by Kristin del Rosario.

PRINTING HISTORY
Berkley Sensation trade paperback edition / December 2011

Library of Congress Cataloging-in-Publication Data

Owens, Robin D.
Hearts and swords / Robin D. Owens.
p. cm.
ISBN 978-0-425-24341-1 (pbk.)
1. Life on other planets—Fiction. 2. Love stories, American. 3. Fantasy fiction, American.
I. Title.
PS3615.W478H48 2011
813'.6—dc23

2011033329

PRINTED IN THE UNITED STATES OF AMERICA

10 9 8 7 6 5 4 3 2 1

To my readers who've asked for these stories.
I hope you enjoy them.
And to Cindy and Deidre who gave me a chance
to tell them all at once.

Contents

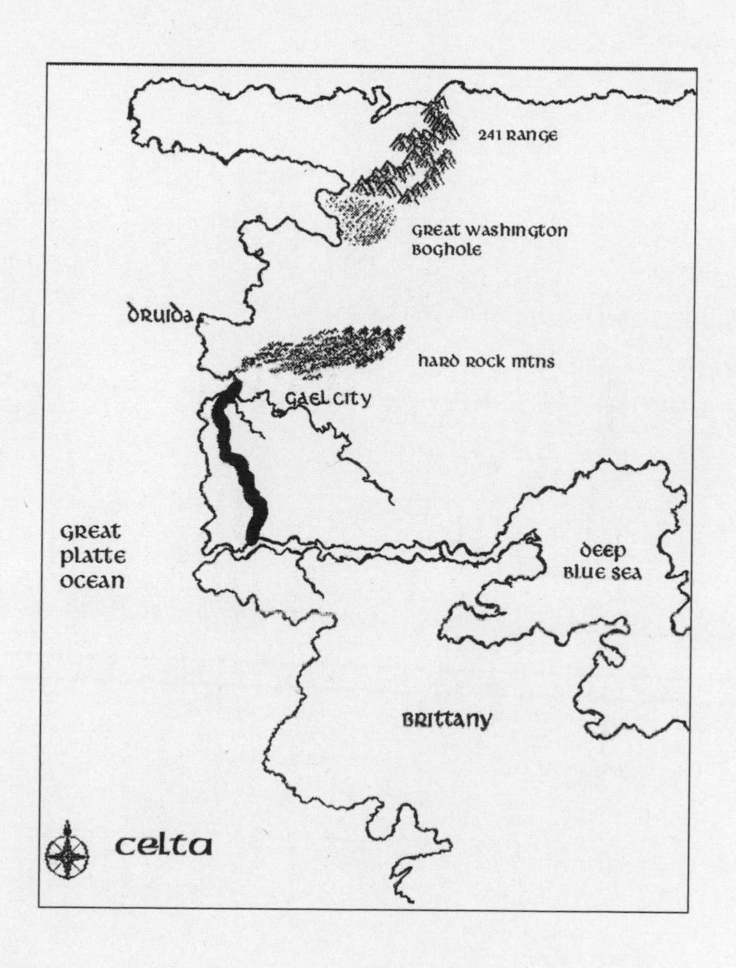
241 RANGE
GREAT WASHINGTON BOGHOLE
DRUIDA
HARD ROCK MTNS
GAEL CITY
GREAT PLATTE OCEAN
DEEP BLUE SEA
BRITTANY
CELTA

Heart and Sword

To my critique buddies, without whom I would have been drifting through space without a life pod.

Note: The events of the discovery of Celta are sprinkled throughout the series but most notably appear in *Heart Thief*, *Heart Journey*, and *Heart Search*.

One

On Board *Nuada's Sword*
Generational Colonist Starship
from Earth
Currently in Outer Space
the Month of May/Oak

The mist of deathsleep cleared before Kelse Bountry's eyes, and he saw a woman's dark brown eyes set in a raisin-wrinkled face peering down with an anxious expression. His long-motionless chest compressed and he coughed.

"Wake up, Kelse!" the woman snapped. "I started your Awakening process this morning. Your indicators show the drugs have cleared enough for you to be conscious, so wake up!"

He blinked and blinked again. The foggy stuff in the cryonics tube was dissipating into the dimness of the starship's bay. He flung out his hand, more muscle memory than true thought, the emotional need to feel his wife lying beside him. Of course his knuckles banged on the forceglass tube surrounding him, and pain was more than a dreamy memory; it was real.

He convulsed, moaning. His muscles ached, required to move after the long sleep, his nerves twanging throughout his nude body.

The tube opened and slid into the sides of the platform. He coughed as oddly scented air fired his lungs.

The old woman's soft hand patted his chest. "Hurry!"

"What? Who?" he muttered.

"Chloe Hernandez, the Captain's Executive Officer," she said in a strange, clipped accent. Her thin shoulders wiggled. "Something bad's coming, worse than what we already have. I can feel it. So I started your Awakening process this morning."

He stared. Something must be wrong. She shouldn't be so old.

She'd been slated to be Awakened during the last quarter-decade of the century starship journey to their new home planet.

He remembered her at twenty-three. Now she looked more like ninety.

And he wasn't supposed to be Awakened until the ship had landed, when he'd walk out onto a new world hand in hand with his wife.

His heart pumped faster. He jackknifed up, suppressed another groan as his body swayed, then steadied above his pelvis. "What's going on?"

"I had a bad feeling about the mutineers, so I woke you."

"Mutineers!" He could barely think. His blood pounded excruciatingly in his head. He lifted his fingers and rubbed his temples, slid his fingers along the scar at his hairline.

Mutineers. The word rattled in his brain until he could put a meaning to it. Rebellion. He knew rebellion, had been inside that. Now he was outside of a mutiny.

Rebellion on a ship. Where there was no place to go.

Icy horror slid through his veins like sleet. He kept his face impassive, not hard to do; those muscles were stiff, too.

"Have mutineers taken over the ship? Who? What are their numbers? Where's security?" He'd authorized and trained eighty top-notch fighters for the eight-hundred-head crew. "Where's Captain Whitecloud?" The man wasn't a fighter, like Kelse was, but he was an excellent leader.

Draping a thick robe over his shoulders, Chloe said, "Take this, first. I need you clearheaded." She thrust a bottle of revitalizer in his hand. He wanted to throw it across the room.

"I'm surprised you can even sit after being so long in the cryonics process. You're not supposed to be able to move much." Her gaze locked on his. "Something bad's happening. I'm sure of it, but I need your help to find out what it is and how to stop it," Chloe said.

Through the mist in his head he recalled Chloe's psi powers had included dead-on hunches.

When he tried to speak again, nothing came out so he glugged the damn liquid, hand shaking and spilling it down his chest. He racked a cough, sucked in a breath, spit out words. "Not going anywhere if the ship has been captured."

Narrowing his eyes he considered the place as a defense headquarters, if he had to fight to regain control of the ship. Terrible.

He nearly heard his neck creak as he turned his head to see his beloved wife, his Fern, lying in the cylinder on the next dais. Her tube was filled with fog, showing occasional thin patches. One was at the curve of her hip. He longed to squeeze her there. He saw her cheek, the short ends of her black hair, but not her eyes. Of course her head wasn't turned to look at him. Her violet eyes wouldn't be open.

Some of the acid in his stomach subsided as he saw all her life-indicator lights were a bright green. She was fine. He managed another breath. His woman, the person he'd lived for instead of dying fighting the government troops or anti-psi mobs. The reason why he wanted peace and a family.

But it didn't seem as if peace was here and now. No, this cryonics bay couldn't be a headquarters.

He swayed. Get a grip. They couldn't fight from here. Fern was here, all his friends.

Adrenaline surged through his body, as much from seeing his wife as the effects of the revitalizing agent. He felt woozy, but he had to think fast and sharp.

"Here's what I know," Chloe said. "The mutineers don't hold the ship quite yet. They're a cadre of young men who want to abort our plan to colonize another planet and take a wormhole that they think will lead back to civilized space and Earth. We don't know their exact numbers. They're agitating for people to join them and have a lot of popular support, about seventy percent of the crew. I had this terrible feeling . . . so I woke you."

Again he looked at the tubes. He and his wife were rebels back on Earth. If Chloe was so old, time had passed. Kelse wouldn't know these mutineers, but he should be able to work with their parents. "We're all dead if we return to Earth. The crew knew that when they signed on." He set down the drink and slowly stretched out his right arm, stuck it into the robe sleeve. That hurt. He threaded his left arm through the robe. "So, as far as you know it's just some kind of conspiracy."

"I suppose that would be the word," she snapped out.

He wasn't relieved. Sounded like he was in the minority and having to fight mobs—again. Only this time on a ship. "Where's Captain Whitecloud and our men?"

Her face folded into inscrutability. "Whitecloud is . . . gone. We don't have as many men as you think."

His head continued to ache. "How much violence?" That would give him clues, he knew all about violence, quantity and quality.

"Mostly against this chamber, the cryonics bay. Ramming the door to get to the sleepers. The mutineers know if we're all gone, they can take over the ship."

His ears cleared with a pop of pressure and he heard yelling and pounding at the door. His lungs squeezed tight. "We have control of the ship?"

"Yes, the nose bridge and the console in the Captain's Quarters. Come *on*, Kelse." She hopped down from the platform and scuttled away. That sent more anxiety coursing through his muscle fibers. Chloe was—had been—a tall, Amazonian woman, easily able to see into the tubes. She'd always moved with stately grace. Now . . .

She hadn't told him everything. But he was better with action, himself. And the first thing he needed to do was secure this room his Fern and his helpless friends were in.

Every muscle shaking with effort, he rocked forward to hands and knees, biting the inside of his mouth to keep from crying out in pain.

On Earth, he'd lived and worked with the underground psi movement before they'd put the money together to buy their own starships. Before they left for a new home they would shape better than Earth.

He was no stranger to pain, but his vision was blurry, his hands trembled, his muscles quivered. This, he was not used to.

"So many bad feelings." Chloe rubbed her hands up and down her skinny arms. "The mutineers . . . conspirators . . . here aren't our worst problem. They've been ramming the door every week, but it's solid. We must go!" She pushed an anti-grav pallet to him. "Get on the cot and we'll head to the Captain's Quarters where we can plan. It'll take a couple of days for you to adjust and be able to walk."

Chloe glanced at the main door, still being battered. "That entrance should hold for another day or two. Come on! Something else is wrong. I feel it in my bones. That's why I woke you."

"No cot, and I'm not leaving yet." He had to protect his wife and his friends from the conspirators. He slid, centimeter by painful centimeter, off the platform. Leaned on it and hauled in heavy breaths. He stood, hunched and hanging on, forcing his feet to take his weight, his blood to pump vertically and not horizontally. He refused to moan again.

The bay was lit dimly, as if only enough stingy power to keep the cryonics going was allowed. There were no techs. His nose twitched and he thought he scented the odd tang of cryonic nano machines working without supervision.

Chloe said, "We closed this room down for security reasons years ago to ensure there were no threats to the sleepers."

Slowly, slowly he straightened, put his teeth in his cheek again, and let pain sharpen his eyes and stared at Fern's tube. The roundness of her thigh was visible. He swallowed hard. How he loved her.

"Come *on*!" Chloe demanded. "The past is gone. We must see to the future."

Turning away from Fern was a hard, hard thing to do. His eyes focused on *red* lights. The module next to the main security doors showed four red lights indicating failure of defenses and one green, indicating good. He staggered toward the door, robe flapping. The room seemed kilometers long; each step he swayed, caught his balance, and moved on. He had to protect the sixty . . . fifty-nine . . . other sleepers. Fern. His friends.

"By the Lady and Lord, you're walking! Eh, your reflexes were always good. Going in the wrong direction, though." Chloe caught up with him, her bony fingers curved around his biceps. Throwing him off balance. He stumbled, plowed on.

"We can't deal with the security door now!" she whispered.

"We *will* deal with the door's defenses now," he croaked.

His ears cleared enough to hear echoing voices outside the door. "Get the sleepers; they suck *our* energy. Us or them!" A wild laugh.

Shouts of agreement. Pounding.

Kelse fell against the door. Now he felt the punishing vibration. He had to protect. Somehow. Protect. He felt a small drain of energy, his head went muzzy. Blinking away the fog, he angled to straighten and saw that the security indicators had gone from four red lights and one green to three red lights and two green.

A harsh intake of breath from Chloe. "You augmented the shields with your psi power!" She passed her hand near the door and he could almost see forcefields—tech and psi. Which he couldn't before. He didn't understand it, but he'd felt it. Panting, he decided to think about that later.

When Chloe turned back to him, her face was grim. "Please, Kelse, we need to go. The doors will hold. You've given them enough energy for a week." Staring into his eyes, she waited three beats and said, "You're needed elsewhere for other problems. I *feel* it."

Always the same, he was needed to fix problems.

He pivoted, reeled away. The pounding seemed to lessen on the door.

As he wove toward the emergency access hatch where Chloe stood, he saw her slump, shake her head. She leaned against the wall.

"What's happened?" he asked. "What did you foresee?"

"Nothing. I'm not a prophet. Just follow hunches now and then, is all. I'm the ship's Exec. The Captain's Exec."

"Yeah, yeah," he said. For a moment her phrasing tugged at his memory—ship, intelligence—then it was gone.

She stowed the anti-grav cot, gestured to the emergency hatch and the dark hole leading to the guts of the ship.

He hesitated, but there were no more blows against the door. Yells were fading. Staying here wouldn't bring him the information he needed to counter any threats. He had to act. He wasn't a sleeper now, someone helpless and at the mercy of a mob. Nothing he hated more than a mob hunting psis.

"The Captain's Quarters is secure and runs the ship?" he asked. He could get answers there, check on the conspirators, wring info from a less distracted Chloe.

"Yes. We'd be there by now if you hadn't lingered."

His steps went *thump, thump, thump*. He wasn't walking well, couldn't summon the grace to prowl as he had in the alleys of greater NJNY when he lived off the grids.

Chloe slipped a strand of her short white hair behind her ear. Tear tracks silvered her cheeks. "Whatever's happened has happened. Too late now," she murmured. "We must focus on the future."

Her narrowed gaze swung to him. "I was right to Wake you. I know it. You're walking well. You always had good psi—Flair, we call it now. And we've found it increases while in cryogenic stasis. We all get a boost in personal psi."

"Nice," he croaked, but his mind was clearing and zooming in ten different directions. The adrenaline reaction to threat—kicking in too late as far as he was concerned. His physical reactions were off. Unsurprising but unwelcome. He'd always prided himself on his reflexes.

Though she pretended calm, anxiety tightened Chloe's aged skin, sharpened her rounded features. She stood aside as he approached, whispered, "Now that they know they can't break in, they'll leave soon, probably to one of the entertainment lounges. Battering the door is just fun for most of them."

He gritted his teeth against fury. Liking to wreck things was fun. Threatening helpless lives was *fun*.

There were thrumming footfalls near, running people—away

from the cryonics bay door, along the corridor beyond this space. Retreating!

With infinite, silent slowness he lifted one foot over the low bottom sill of the panel, drew in the other foot, slipped sideways behind a foam metal girder, around a huge tube that radiated heat. Chloe pulled the panel close, and Kelse angled, watching the faint shine-under-dust of the cryonics vanish, straining for the last sight of Fern. Then it was dark and the only sound was Chloe's shallow breathing and his own less even breaths.

He was Awake and without his woman.

Fern was asleep, maybe dreaming of their life together, unknowing of danger.

He hurt. "What happened?" he asked. His words were barely a breath of sound.

Her smile was more a mouth-turned-up rictus. "You want to read the histories, they're available. But I always thought you were a bottom-line guy."

"I am. Give me the short version."

"Something harmed the ships after we exited the second wormhole. We think either the hole vortices or space warped our fuel cells. Or our fuel might have been substandard." Her smile was vicious. "We wouldn't be around to complain to the seller, would we? We couldn't make our original planet, and that section of space had been mapped. There were no Earthlike planets within reach of our drives. But there was a relatively close wormhole and our main astrophysicist had heard that the space beyond was very promising for colonization. And unpopulated by Earth assholes. We decided to risk it."

Kelse frowned. "A wormhole screwed with the ships—we still have three ships?" They'd all been refurbished, all different designs. What the Colonists could find and afford.

Chloe nodded.

"Good. So a wormhole screwed with the ships and someone decides to go through another wormhole?"

"Kelse, you've been in situations of certain death and risk. That's what we had then. That's what we have now."

Everything in him chilled. "And that's why *I* was Awakened."

"Yes!" Chloe said, as if she'd just realized that herself. "You never give up," she said simply.

He'd believed with all his heart when he'd entered the ship hand in hand with Fern that they were on their way to a bright new future, a green planet where they wouldn't have to fight other people, only nature.

He'd been wrong.

Fighting was his life. Why had he thought he'd ever escape that? Chill slithered through him. "How long has it been?"

She looked back over her shoulder. "Two hundred and fifty years."

He lost his balance and bumped into girders. They gave off low, hollow sounds. Fear pitched in his gut like biting poison.

They'd planned for the journey to take, worst-case scenario, a century and a half. Had hoped for seventy-five years. With seventy-five years, even a century, they'd have had elders in the crew who'd lived on Earth.

Chloe said, "We've passed by ten star systems that had unviable or marginally habitable planets. No other spacefarers. Maybe because of the bad wormholes." She shrugged. "Maybe not."

He managed to weave around the next few girders. His muscles were warming, working, moving more smoothly than jerks. He was thankful. Chemicals and cryonics, psi and magic had kept him well. That had gone right, at least.

Finally Chloe and he reached another emergency access panel. It had security features, a keypad, DNA scan, retina scan. All looked clean and functional.

Chloe jerked her head at the setup. "I programmed it for you when I left the Captain's Quarters."

He swiped his finger, stared into a blank panel. "Kelse Bountry recognized," said a flat metallic voice. Then the keypad lit.

"Code is the day you proposed to Fern." Chloe gave an old woman's cackle. "Not in any of our records, but you won't forget the day."

No one who'd fought the mob out for psi blood in NJNY would forget that day. He'd nearly lost Fern. Had decided that he must speak after all, though loving and marrying was crazy under the circumstances. He'd never forget the bruise on her cheek, or the feel of blood running down his face from his scalp, when they finally reached safety and he asked her to marry him.

Yes, he remembered the day and he entered the date. The door panel glowed and Chloe pushed it. "Only you and I and the Captain are authorized." She went into the room and gasped.

He stepped through the door and smelled blood and death.

Two

Chloe rushed to a large red stain on the rug before the command center. Stooped and brushed the fibers, lifted bloody fingers, and began keening. "Kiet! The Captain!" she wept.

"Hang on for a minute and let me think," Kelse said.

The main door of the Captain's Quarters was slightly open. Memory clunked in Kelse's mind. This door wasn't a double metallic one that could be short-circuited or jammed. His glance went to the hinges. The reinforced shielding around them was still good. Someone inside had opened it.

Walking toward the door, he looked into the dim light of the corridor indicating night hours. No one. The security pad next to the door showed no forcing. Where were the cameras?

He shut the door and moved back to Chloe, who was rocking and whimpering. Again foul scent wrapped around Kelse, the first was the odor of poison, usually delivered by dart. Then he smelled the fragrance of a man he'd known. A tall, elegant man, beautiful in the way of so many mixed-race people. "Kiet Moungala."

Chloe nodded, tears trailed down her creased cheeks. She shuddered, pulled a cloth from a hidden pocket, and wiped her fingers. She circled the command center, touched the surface panel, wheezed out a breath. "The console locked down." Her fingers flew across the glass. “I’ve opened it with my code.” She tapped the large screen. “Locating Captain Moungala immediately by his geo wristband.”

Kelse joined her to view the map on the console in time to see a human icon show up, colored black.

“Black! He’s dead!”

Kelse stepped close. Put an arm around her waist. “I’m sorry.”

Her hands fisted. “They did this. They killed him.” She trembled with rage. “Mutineers,” Chloe said stubbornly. “They may not have taken over the ship,” her voice broke. “But they killed the Captain.”

As they watched, the icon blinked out, leaving only a tiny orange glow.

“What does that mean?” Kelse asked.

Chloe hunched a shoulder. “They put his body in the decomposer. They couldn’t turn off or destroy the Captain’s wristband.”

“That’s the orange glow?”

“Yes.”

“Where’s the security force?” Kelse asked.

“Show Moncrief, Rye, and Beranik.” Nothing happened. Chloe paled. “They’re gone, too.”

“Gone?”

“Disappeared, probably also dead and composted.”

“What of their geo wristbands?”

“Show security wristbands,” she ordered the computer. The screen split in two, on one side there were two bands close together, the other showed a single one.

Kelse could read the map well enough. “Two are right down the hall.” He wanted to get them, do something active, but if there was any physical threat, he couldn’t handle it. Not yet. He had to get in shape. And get a weapon. And discover who his enemies were.

“I’ll send a cleaning bot to get all three.” Her fingers tapped and dragged on the console.

“Why are there only three security people? What happened to the other seventy-seven?”

Her face set in furious lines. "Until the latest trouble, we didn't need many. We were a good community, not the psi barrio or NJNY. So as they died out, they weren't replaced. We only needed three for decades."

"How many crew do we have now?"

"We capped the birthrate at twelve hundred. That's what we have." Then her face went immobile. "No. We have eleven hundred and ninety-six."

"And you don't know the numbers of the core conspirators?"

"No. Like I said, the majority of folk trust them, born on the ship. Not us. And most don't try to break into the cryonics bay. Don't do that violence."

"Can anyone locate anyone by their geo bands?"

"They have privacy settings. Only this computer and the nose bridge can locate security officers. Only this computer and my and Captain's handhelds can locate the Captain." She swallowed hard and her mouth tightened; she placed both palms on the console and closed her eyes. More tears dribbled down her face.

He held her close and she smelled of powdery old woman, and his image of her as young vanished. Not much he could say would make her feel better. "I never give up. I promise I won't give up on justice for Kiet and the guards."

His knees began to tremble. Up too long, too much drugs and psi spikes and natural adrenaline flowing in his bloodstream. He stepped away from Chloe, half fell into the chair behind the command console. It felt good.

Chloe nodded. "Thank you. We've had a little fighting. Not much; the morale is bad, but this goes beyond."

"Killing always does." He'd had to kill to defend himself and Fern, and a lot more than four people. It marked you. Marked and scarred an honorable man.

Chloe cleared her throat, opened her eyes, and her fingers danced across the console. "This is Exec Officer Hernandez. Note that Captain Moungala is dead and I am transferring command to the recently Awakened Kelse Bountry, who formerly occupied cryonics tube twenty-one. His stats are already coded."

"Done," the computer said.

His pulse leapt. Captain of a starship. Nothing he'd ever anticipated being. And if these were good times and Fern was with him, he'd like it, he supposed. But if these were good times, he wouldn't have been Awakened.

"So as far as everyone knows, the Captain and the security force have disappeared," he said.

"That's right."

"Will the conspirators claim responsibility for the deaths?" he asked.

Her forehead furrowed. "I don't know."

"Because violence has been rare. Wonder how much they've studied the past or if they're making it up as they go along." He grunted. "Attack on the cryonics bay." He couldn't think of that now, of Fern being helpless. Move on. "Killing Moungala. Pretty obvious that they don't want the sleepers in power. Two hundred and fifty years." He shook his head. "They've all grown up here. Who else alive now were sleepers?"

"On *Nuada's Sword*, only you and me. You know the Captain of *Arianrhod's Wheel*, the astrophysicist Julianna Ambroz. The Captain of *Lugh's Spear* is Umar Clague, who ran a cell of the rebellion on Earth. Who else they woke, I don't know. They don't have a conspiracy on their ships." Chloe whimpered, drew herself straight. "We can say Kiet's heart failed," she offered in a broken voice.

"I'm not lying to my people." He remembered the continual lying of the USTATES government. No, he wouldn't start down that road. "Too easy to be caught in a lie." He considered the angles. "Best if the crew knew there were dangers. Better that I do some sort of address."

"We'll transmit it live for this shift, but also record it and send to individual computers, quarters, and handhelds as a special notice for people when they wake—it's about midnight. We'll send the speech to the other Captains."

"All right. What do the conspirators want?"

Chloe rubbed the back of her neck. "We're heading toward two systems with planets. Great potential according to our astrophysicist, Julianna Ambroz, but we'll burn the last of our fuel to get there. One of our young scientists, a genius—now co-opted by the mutineers—located a wormhole in a different direction. He extrapolated that it would shoot us back into civilized space. Where we could refuel—"

"No!" Immediate denial, then thought followed. "The government issued an order confiscating our ships for the good of the nations. We outran that. But I don't see any government giving up something it wanted, even"—he swallowed—"centuries later."

"It's an option." Her smile was a travesty, her eyes seemed to have sunk into her skull. "The crew doesn't have the experience with the USTATES government and the mobs they directed against psis, like we do. They don't believe in the mission. The mutineers think we're liars." She blinked rapidly.

Too much data for his fuzzy mind to sort. Kelse straightened. If he leaned back, he'd fall asleep.

"Let's do this statement. It'll be preliminary. With morale down, we'll need to generate a sense of purpose, get the majority believing in the mission again."

Chloe let out a quiet sigh that seemed to deflate her thin body, but this time her smile was real. "And I believe in you. If sheer determination can get us through, you'll do it."

"Damn right."

She went to the closet and pulled out a long cape. It was red. With gold epaulettes.

Kelse stared.

"You must look authoritative."

He supposed so, and the bathrobe and his hairy brown and gray chest wouldn't do it. But he hated military trappings. Too many of them had tried to kill his friends, him, and Fern. He could do this for Fern.

Chloe draped the cape around him, showed him how to access the vid programs and recording. He'd recalled that vocal orders should have been available, but that was an extremely low-priority issue.

He tapped the console to record, stared a few seconds at his own grim and scarred face on the screen in front of him. His image was surrounded by the golden aura that resulted from the mix of his psi and the cryonic drugs. "Greetings. I am Kelse Bountry, duly appointed by Exec Officer Hernandez as the new Captain of this ship. I am saddened to report that Captain Kiet Moungala was murdered and the security force is missing and presumed dead.

"I *will* find those who killed Captain Moungala and Security Officers Moncrief, Rye, and Beranik and bring them to justice. I *will not* tolerate violence on my watch. Anyone who has information about the deaths of Captain Moungala and Security Officers Moncrief, Rye, and Beranik, please contact me. Investigations are under way and progressing." He drew in a breath, had on his fighting face so was impassive. He hoped he looked scary. "Men and women wishing to apply for the posts of security officers should present themselves to me—"

"The day after tomorrow, MidAfternoonBell, Gym Two," Chloe murmured. He didn't want to wait that long, but saw no way around it, so he repeated what she said.

"I will brief you again within the day, and will be touring the ship." He ignored Chloe's noise of protest, struggled to find a good closing, recalled their new culture. Wiccan.

"We still Wiccan?" he whispered to Chloe.

She nodded.

"Blessed be," he said, then cut the vid stream.

"You did very well, under the circumstances," Chloe said. For a moment her face tightened, then her shoulders slumped. "We have to get back on mission, Kelse." Walking over, she patted his shoulder. "I know you'll get us out of this mess. We *will* find our planet and our future."

Kelse nodded. It was the only thing he could think to do.

With a last wave that was partial salute, she pushed the door button. It opened and she stepped into the hall.

Then the door slid shut and he was alone.

Alone in a room he didn't know, in a ship going nowhere he knew.

In a life he no longer understood. All he wanted was to go back to the cryonics bay and look at Fern. Wake her up and hold her in his arms.

But his muscles were stiffening into stone, he couldn't sit for long. His whole body was . . . off. He'd been active all his life. He'd had to be, fighting the corrupt police of NJNY, fighting the mobs the government incited. But now his body wasn't how it should be. Too much to think about. Too much to feel if he let his emotions out of the inner box he'd stuffed them into the last hour.

Some tendons made popping noises as he stood. The map on the black glassy console had shifted to a real-time map of the Captain's Quarters and the hallway outside it. No one was around.

The conspirators had gotten Moungala to open the door, killed him, but there was no vacuum of power for them to fill. Thanks to Chloe, Kelse had already taken command. The conspirators' plans must be trashed.

Leaning on the desk he studied the mainspace with enough room for visitors. There was a small bathroom. His shoulders were tense and he rolled them. Then he realized his legs were trembling, so he shook them out. He turned toward the bed. And stared at a large marmalade cat who sat on the mattress. The cat tilted its head and scrutinized him with light green eyes.

Greetyou. You are the new Captain, once a sleeper.

Kelse heard the words in his head and fell against the desk, propped himself up. Not many of their community could use telepathy. He'd never heard such a strong projection, and something in the tonal quality was odd.

There was no one around to speak with him. Was he overhearing someone? But who? Where?

He glanced at the cat. It had lifted its white forepaw and was grooming it. Before he could quite turn his head back, he heard another sentence.

You look like a tough man.

Kelse froze, stared at the cat. *Are you talking to me?*

Who else would I be talking to, Kelse Bountry? You have the psi power, the magic, the Flair to hear Me.

Flair?

The cat twitched his white-tipped tail. *Psi power. Is too long to always say. Some call it magic, most call it Flair.*

"Flair," Kelse said aloud.

A ripple rolled down the cat's body. *We Cats have Flair, always have, but now We can talk to humans. We have changed in that way. You, who lived in the-then, are stronger than many who live in the-now.*

This had to be the strangest thing that had ever happened to Kelse. He didn't know how much the cat knew, how intelligent it was, but figured he'd need every ally he could get.

Though many humans in the-now are getting stronger in Flair.

"One of the best qualifications for crew members for the journey was psi power, or genetic indicators of psi power. Why are you here and what can you tell me about the conspiracy?"

I just wanted to see you. To see if you would talk to Me. Maybe we will talk again when I know you better.

"Yeah?" Kelse said. He was supposed to be flexible, able to think on his feet, even after being blindsided by fate or circumstances or a stick to the temple. But a telepathic cat?

We are Fam animals.

"Fam animals."

Familiar Companions to humans.

Kelse still grappled with the telepathic part. "I see." A good, common answer.

You don't, but you may, said the cat. It sauntered toward the door.

Kelse noticed it was a male.

The cat looked back. *Yes. I am as male as you. My name is Peaches.*

Kelse nodded. *Right.*

At the entrance, Peaches's ears flicked and rotated. *You may open the door for Me. Quickly, there is no one in the hall now. I don't want to be seen with you!*

Kelse hesitated, needing more data. But when did a cat ever do anything a human wanted? He leaned over the desk, propping a shaking arm on the glassy surface and swiping the door control.

The cat shot from the room and was out of sight before Kelse thought to ask who Peaches was a companion to. Kelse's gut told him it was important.

He staggered to bed, leaving the cape in his wake, flopped onto a different surface than he'd experienced for two and a half centuries.

He didn't want to sleep, struggled to marshal the facts of his new situation, but finally sleep sucked him into a hole of darkness and threatening dreams. Worse than the cryogenics tube.

He awoke to a shrieking alarm.

Three

He leapt from bed. Stood a few shaking seconds getting his bearings. Warehouse? No. Wait, the tube . . . No! Ship. Captain of the ship. Hell. He ran to the console. "Ship, report on the alarm." The noise sent pulsing knives to his ears. "Ship?" Hadn't the ship answered before?

Two and a half centuries before, maybe. Slapping his hand on the console top, he ordered, "Pinpoint the alarm." Nothing. Dammit. He banged his fist on the desk.

A flat, generated voice said, "Security breached in the cryonics bay."

Adrenaline flooded him.

"Show all routes from here to the cryonics bay."

Instead of the top clearing to show the map, a projection beam widened and focused beyond him.

On the glassy wall that was a porthole he hadn't looked out, he saw a map of the ship. The drawing showed a fast trail with two turns down the main corridor, a snaking path the way he and Chloe had come last night.

"Status of security of cryonics bay."

Numbers flickered on. All sleepers' health indicators were fine. A frisson of a hunch skittered between his shoulder blades.

Kelse yanked on a pair of pants he'd found in a drawer and exited by the emergency access hatch, locked it behind him. Running lightly along the path he and Chloe had taken the night before, he reached the emergency door to the cryonics bay and keyed himself in. Again he locked the panel behind him.

There was no banging against the door, and the security lights looked just the way he'd left them. Two green and three red. He strode to the security station on one side of the room. That was familiar, something he'd worked with before. He checked everything. All seemed secure. Which meant the alarm in his room was fake, the voice sent to his quarters false . . . to lure him out? Maybe.

His blood was slowing. He walked to the main doors. Still no sound outside them. Rolling his shoulders, he stretched, then set his hands against the doors, braced himself, and *sent* his psi energy into the shields. Once again he noticed they weren't only tech, but also psi, and the psi had layers . . . from the very first Captain to himself. He spared as much energy as he could, then staggered back. The door lights now showed four green and one red.

Good enough.

Panting, he scanned the room, dimmer and cooler than his first memories. A few of the sixty tubes were empty. Some of those would have been the previous Captains. He needed to study the history of the ship, its current culture. There was only so much he could do relying on his own memories of a past time and society.

His feet took him to his old tube, and Fern's. His tube was dark, decommissioned, giving him a gut jolt. He couldn't go back. What the hell, he wouldn't trust anyone to put him back into the cryogenic stasis.

For one year or another century, he was stuck. Unless he died.

He'd make sure the ships got back on track. He could focus on only the future, holding the image he planned on making come true; he'd learned that a long time ago. If he considered failure, he was already lost. Sweat dried on his chest and back, itching.

Turning to Fern, he watched the fog swirl in her tube. This time he was allowed a glimpse of her lips and her neck, and he couldn't stop from remembering their kisses, the scent of her as he nibbled along her jaw. How she smiled. He waited to see her eyes but it didn't happen.

There was a creak, he dove for a tool cart where he'd noted a long steel wrench. Rolled, came up with it in his hand.

To see Chloe entering the room. Her frown eased at the sight of him. "I went to your quarters. Heard the alarm." Her lips tightened. "The mutineers grow more bold and clever."

Kelse put down the wrench where he'd found it. "Did you have any trouble on the way?"

"No. I am seen as an ineffective flunky."

Grunting, Kelse said, "Seems to me that you're the real Captain. You run the ship."

Her mouth quirked in amusement at the compliment. "We gained some time; most Awakened need at least a full seventy-two hours before they can function well. You should still be in your bed."

He considered that. "I don't think I looked too well in that speech to the ship—"

"You looked like hell. You could have been propped up in your bed with Moungala's cape around you."

"Or I could have been sitting in the command chair, having walked from here to the Captain's Quarters, as I did. Maybe the alarm was a test to see how recovered I am. Easy to guess that one of my main priorities would be protecting the cryonics bay." He thought of the cat, wondered how discreet Fam animals were. Did Peaches let something slip? Lady and Lord, another subject he'd have to learn about.

Chloe's gaze went to the security hatch, then returned to him. Her glance held reproof and her eyes narrowed as she noted his weariness. "I'm sure the mutineers have a tech who is monitoring the status of this door."

"Well, now they know it's been reinforced."

"You need food," Chloe said. "The other Captains have been notified of Moungala's death and want an inter-ship conference in half an hour." She turned and stepped back into the dark hole.

The other Captains, Julianna Ambroz and Umar Clague. Kelse's pulse picked up again. He'd probably be junior to both of them now. Julianna had been younger than he, Umar a few years older. Strange times.

Kelse walked by Fern's tube. Once again mist parted and showed him her lips, her unsmiling mouth. He ached to kiss her.

Too many things prevented him.

He touched the forceglass surrounding her. "I wish you were with me, Fern Bountry, able to give me your advice. I'll always need you."

Her lips parted, and he thought they formed, *Kelse*, then *love*. Fog enshrouded her face again, and he knew he'd imagined her words because it was what his heart wanted.

When the ship-to-ship video revealed the faces of his compatriots, Kelse kept the surprise of seeing their aged faces behind an impassive mask. Every hour a new shock.

Julianna Ambroz of *Arianrhod's Wheel* smiled at him. She was wearing a dress of natural fabric with an embroidered front. He envied her. He was dressed in some slick material. Couldn't find any nice-feeling shirt in the closet. Most of them had insignia, and he wouldn't wear that.

Clague appeared sour.

"Good morning, Julianna, Umar," Kelse said.

"Greetyou, Kelse." Julianna's smile became wider. Inside Kelse, a sliver of hope began to bloom under a pile of detritus that they might be able to pull off the mission.

"Greetyou, Kelse," Umar Clague said.

"How close are we to finding a planet?"

"We're close. I'm hopeful about the two systems with fourteen good-looking habitable-type planets," Julianna said. "Good odds."

Kelse didn't think so. "And we can definitely make these with the fuel we have?" he asked.

Julianna hesitated.

Umar grunted.

Julianna's gaze dropped, then lifted. "We on *Arianrhod's Wheel* have modified our solar sails and have deployed them. We have the power."

He should have felt good knowing that at least one ship would make it. But it wasn't the ship that Fern and he were on.

"Umar?" Kelse asked.

"We need food and energy. We are on strict rationing and our solar sails were damaged in the wormholes. We repaired them, but the repairs are failing."

"Julianna, can you ferry something over to Umar?"

She shook her head. "I'm sorry, we don't have shuttles. Both our crews have tried to figure something out, but it would burn more energy than provide."

"*Nuada's Sword* has shuttles." Kelse was sure of that.

"*Nuada's Sword* has life pods and fighter dagger ships," Umar said. "But if you're like us, you don't have the energy to spare for them or trained Pilots."

Kelse glanced at Chloe. Face set into a melancholy expression, she shook her head.

"Do we have any solar sails?" he asked her. "Any food we can dropload?"

Her fingers swept over her computer console. She frowned, but when she looked up, hope glittered in her eyes. "*Nuada's Sword* doesn't use solar sails, but we have some in storage, and they can be fitted to *Lugh's Spear.* That was the reason we bought them. We also have grain and seeds we can send." She made a face. "And two tons of subsistence sticks, guaranteed to last for three hundred years."

"Better than nothing," Umar snapped.

"Our relative coordinates are such that we could drop cargo that you can intercept," Chloe said.

"Can I check those figures, please?" Julianna asked.

"Transmitted to you both," Chloe said.

Julianna opened her hand to show a shiny pink square. "They look good. What do you think, Umar?"

His eyes flickered as he scanned the data. He swallowed hard enough that Kelse noted it. "Looks good." His voice cracked. "I'll shoot you the specs needed for our ag sector."

"We'll get something to you, Umar," Kelse said. "Chloe will coordinate with you."

Umar stared at him. Then his video went black. He said in a choked voice, "Thank you. You think you can?"

"Good chance."

"Best drop time is in a couple of hours," Chloe said. "I'll oversee it. We have enough loyals to stock and pack the dropcube."

Umar's video came on. His face appeared damp, he was blinking spiky lashes. "You know, Kelse, I don't think I ever appreciated you before."

"Thanks." He looked back at Julianna. "Is there anything closer than those two systems?"

"The wormhole," Umar said.

"You want to take our chances with another wormhole." Kelse kept his voice expressionless.

"No!" Umar and Julianna said at the same time.

"No!" Umar's face contorted. "If we reached civilized space again, they would take my ship. They would take my wife and the other sleepers for who knows what. Experimentation. They'd shoot me." He reached for his glass with a trembling hand, and Kelse knew it was from fury.

When he glanced at Julianna, her face was hard. Her words were crisp and bitten off like the professor she once was. "If you will recall, I was declared a *treasure* of the USTATES. Which meant I was kept under lock and key. I don't see the government we left progressing into a higher morality toward individuals. Not their own citizens and definitely not anyone they perceive as different."

"Mutants," Umar said. "That's what we psis were considered and we still would be."

"We're agreed that we don't take the wormhole," Kelse said.

"It hasn't been charted, none of this space has, since Earth liked keeping all its resources on planet. Our starfaring years were a very short time period," Julianna said.

"We know that," Kelse pointed out.

She drew in a breath. "As I said, this area is not charted, the wormhole could go to anywhere." She hesitated. "The energy emanating from it *does* appear like that near the last Earth outpost. But that doesn't mean—"

"Understood," Kelse said. "I'm asking if there's anything more viable *for us*. A planet to colonize."

"There's a little system closer, but I don't like the looks of it. White sun, two planets that might possibly support life. My calculations put them slightly too far from the sun." She shrugged. "As well as other considerations that indicate a poor choice for colonization."

"Launch probes to the near system," Kelse ordered.

"We only have a limited number of probes, and fourteen potential planets we'll need to scan in the future," Julianna said. "*Arianrhod's Wheel* has five probes and no labs."

"*Lugh's Spear* has two probes. We had a planetary laboratory station, but it was dismantled before my time for parts," Umar said.

Chloe said, "*Nuada's Sword* has two probes and one lab." She cleared her throat. "We don't have a trained scientist to deploy the lab and analyze the data. Chung was Awakened on time and died of old age." She looked down at her handheld. "Fern Bountry was trained as backup."

"Fern is *not* being Awakened, under any circumstances, until we land," Kelse said, rising. She could die in her sleep.

The thought that she'd die, they'd never have that future they'd fought for, made him wild inside; panic slid on his nerves. He could not let that out. He'd known fear and panic and loss before and withstood it. "That's my price for handling this conspiracy for you." He'd said the word they'd all been avoiding.

Julianna's face tightened. "It's a bad situation, but Moungala wasn't you." Trained in craftiness and fighting, she meant. "You have a small violent minority. Just infuse the majority with purpose, Kelse. You were always good at that."

"Or cull out the youngsters and build an army," Umar said cynically. "You're leader enough to do that."

Kelse realized that was exactly what Umar had done. It had worked for him.

"I intend to improve morale first." A side of his mouth lifted in a half smile. "Then they will be infused with purpose. Before I sign off, Julianna, what are our real odds of finding a habitable planet and making it there considering all our problems?"

She stared aside. "*Arianrhod's Wheel* has a sixty percent chance of making landfall if an acceptable planet is found. Our survival after that will be in question if the other ships, particularly *Nuada's Sword*, does not survive. Currently *Lugh's Spear* has a twenty percent chance of landing. If the drop goes as expected, *Lugh's Spear* also has a sixty percent chance of reaching a planet."

"And *Nuada's Sword*?" Kelse pressed.

Julianna's stare met his. "That's why I am glad you are Awakened, Kelse. Currently, not taking into consideration your talents—"

"Bottom line, Julianna," Kelse said.

"Thirty percent chance of reaching a planet." She smiled brightly. "But we're sure you can improve that."

Four

I'm launching probes at the white sun system." There was protest, but he cut the signal, ending the conference.

Chloe looked as his shaking body, the sweat rolling down him, and tsked. "Take a shower and get some sleep."

"I want to address the crew as soon as you're done with the drop," he said.

She glanced up from her handheld. "No."

"That's not the correct response," Kelse said. He sat back down. "There's only one Captain on a ship."

Turning, she put her hands on her hips and stared at him. He stared back. She flushed, uncurled her fingers around her mini computer, and looked at it. "All right."

"Trust me to know my own limitations."

Again she looked up. "You're tough."

"Damn right."

There was an audible click. "Captain Bountry will address the crew at FirstAfternoonBell. Any work not of an essential nature is suspended at that time." Chloe's voice came through the speakers of his cabin.

"Thank you."

"Get a shower and some sleep."

"I'll need to tour the ship after the address."

She let out an exasperated breath. "You just push your luck, don't you?"

"The only way to get things done."

"Right." Her gaze was serious. "You'd better look healthy when you do that."

"Or I'll draw assassination attempts."

She winced.

"The conspirators made a mistake in escalating to violence. They couldn't break the shields to the cryonics bay or get into the Captain's console. Though they killed Kiet, they had no time to follow up on that coup because you had Awakened me. They've made the majority of the crew nervous."

"My hunch was good, but not soon enough to save Kiet." Despair passed over her face. "If only I'd had the hunch earlier you might have been able to save him." Her hands fisted. "Just a few hours earlier to start your process."

He rose and went to her, wrapped his arms around her, and set his feet so she could lean against him. "We can't live our lives on *if onlys*; if we do, we go bitter or crazy." If only he hadn't believed in this journey. If only he'd taken Fern away to a nice, calm country on the lower side of the world instead of fighting for psi rights.

They'd be dead by now, fighting or living in peace.

"And you expected me to need seventy-two hours to recover. Didn't know I'd be functional," he said.

She stayed silent against him for a minute. She was so much more frail than he'd expected. Her spirit masked that. The conspirators had underestimated her. How long would they do so?

As long as he commanded their attention.

She straightened. "Right now I need to launch the probes and initiate the cargo drop for *Lugh's Spear*. Good thing the emergency cubes were all stored together."

"Thank you." He kissed her forehead.

"For what?" she asked, stepping away.

Fern had taught him the answer to that question. "Just for being you."

Chloe flushed, waved a hand. "Yeah, yeah. Shower. Get some sleep. Eat." She left.

Kelse paced the room. He was tired of all this hiding. But showing himself outside his quarters wasn't wise.

He'd asked Chloe about the cameras focused on the Captain's Quarters last night and was told they'd had a glitch. Pulling up the recording anyway, he noted it was fuzzy, and nothing he or the computer could do could clear it up.

He hadn't interacted with his crew, the people he wanted to save. All right, Fern was the first on that list, and himself and his friends. The sleepers in the other ships, then the crew. But he was used to being responsible for people.

And he missed young faces. The youngest face he'd seen recently was his own, and that was far too grim.

After he showered, he spent a while watching the ship's cameras.

His crew appeared . . . soft. And pale. Very pale. Even the obviously mixed-race people seemed to have skin lighter than what he'd expect their natural color to be. Mutation due to living on the ship? Genetics? Flair? Who knew, and that didn't matter a damn.

He ate. Terrible food. That was one thing he could fix as long as the crew's stomachs hadn't gotten as tender as their bodies. If they were going to colonize a planet, they'd better get in shape physically. He'd set up required exercise. Yeah, that would make him popular, but maybe Fern would have an idea—

Then came the shock that he'd thought Fern was with him as she had been for the last four years. He'd already grown accustomed to this job, a portion of this life. How could he have forgotten she might be in jeopardy?

The alarm pinged. Ten minutes to his address. The crates for *Lugh's Spear* should have been dropped. He accessed the view outside. The comm stated, "Captain's Quarters porthole transparent." Slowly he turned, braced himself. The vastness of space, the huge sweep of spangled stars, nearly overwhelmed him. Somewhere in the back of his mind a little voice wailed that he should not be here. Space was no place for him. He breathed through his nose to keep calm, though the hair on his skin rose.

His eyes focused on some big cubes floating away to other sparkling lights in the distance that outlined *Lugh's Spear*. It was a prettier ship than *Nuada's Sword*, built with the romanticism of dreamers who thought people would actually go into space instead of war on Earth. He focused on the crates. Those were tangible results of human effort, unlike the cosmos, which was beyond his understanding.

The door to his quarters opened and Chloe said, "Wonderful, isn't it?"

Kelse made a sound, couldn't say himself what it meant.

"There are those of us who love space. And I speak for most of the crew, too. Viewing rooms are always open and always full. I suspect that what the mutineers really want is to refuel and continue on an endless journey."

At that instant the crates vanished. Kelse blinked. Stared. Shut his eyes and opened them. But they weren't in sight.

Chloe sucked in her breath, then cackled in satisfaction. "Umar said that they would have a Flaired circle translocate the drop. I didn't think they had the strength, but that proves me wrong."

"Have him send me everything he has about this," Kelse said, still expecting the crates to be there and a bot or machine to snag them.

"He already has. Some of our older folk are practicing power circles, but not the younger."

"You?" Kelse asked, still staring at a whirlpool of stars, far, far away. It seemed less intrusive of her privacy.

"Yes. Opaque portal," Chloe ordered. "There are uniform shirts in the closet in several colors. Get one and wear it. Like it or not, you're the top authority on this ship. Unlike on Earth, you don't have a rep here, so you need symbols of authority."

"I will never turn into a dictator or a tyrant," he said, remembering the uniforms who'd always spoken for the government.

"You won't have the time," Chloe said. "And I wouldn't let you."

Kelse stared at the shirts. They were all of a shiny fabric. Nothing he'd seen on the crew. The least offensive was a black one with a mandarin collar with oak leaves on the throat and golden buttons. He wasn't sure about the buttons, but it beat the red shirt with epaulettes, and the green multicolored design—

"Time, Kelse," Chloe said.

He shrugged into the shirt and took his place behind the desk. The video panel showed him looking unusually stern. He loathed uniforms. They represented a corrupt authority. He was all too aware that *he* might be seen as that. But he was uninterested in power. He wanted only to save lives. Fern's. His own. Everyone on the ships.

He still radiated a goldish aura that would mark him as different. Well, he'd been different all his life. He ached deep inside to think that these people, his people, might consider him a freak and mutant, too.

Authoritative. He straightened his shoulders into an even tighter line. He wasn't going to pretend that all was well, and he damned well wouldn't be the fatherly figure the prez of USTATES had projected.

He watched the blinking light of the camera as it counted down the seconds to broadcast.

Chloe was watching her handheld. "Say, *greetyou*."

Three. Two. One.

He stared into the camera. "Greetyou, fellow travelers. I am Kelse Bountry, succeeding Kiet Moungala as Captain of *Nuada's Sword*. I am here to tell you the status of our journey. First, Captain Moungala has been killed, and the three security officers have disappeared. If anyone has information on these matters, please contact me or Exec Chloe Hernandez. That is the most immediate issue that threatens all of us, violence against us on our ship.

"Second, *Nuada's Sword* is on the way toward two star systems with fourteen prospective habitable worlds. We are launching probes to a world even closer to measure its viability as a place to land.

"Our resources are strained, but we *can* make planetfall. I want to live, as I'm sure all of you want to live. I was Awakened to ensure that we *all* live. That means coming together with purpose to ensure our lives on the ship are good ones, and more, to make sure that we continue our mission. You all are descended from courageous men and women. People who believed in a better life on a planet of our own. Believe in our mission.

"In the meantime, I want suggestions from you as to how you think we can make life on the ship better.

"We are a great people, with intelligence and ingenuity and vision. We can succeed in our mission. Believe."

There was a slight hiss and the vid wavered and Kelse's torso was replaced by another man's. His face was narrow but quite beautiful, his skin pale, his hair black, and his eyes piercing blue. Kelse recognized men like these, lean, lithe, with a quickness of mind and body. And he became aware of every scar on his face, his hands. Would the crew see those scars as strength or detriment?

"But there can be a better way," the newcomer said with a flashing smile. "There's a wormhole much closer. One that will take us to civilized space where we can refuel, where we will be welcomed."

Kelse stared. The guy was literally selling pie in the sky. "I doubt that. You are?"

"Dirk Lascom."

Nodding, Kelse replied, "Wormholes damaged our ship once. I wouldn't risk it again. But you will. Risk damage to everyone in the ship."

"As for resources, didn't you just send some of our very valuable resources away?" Dirk asked.

Kelse wondered how he knew. The screen split, showing them both. Kelse let his held breath filter out.

Dirk's eyes glittered. Drugs? Psi—Flair? Or pure natural vitality? He grinned and showed perfect white teeth.

Kelse answered, "I sent some solar sails we stored for *Lugh's Spear* to that ship."

"And food!"

Kelse smiled easily, saw the irritation simmer under Dirk's skin. "I sent standard meal bars nearly three centuries old to *Lugh's Spear.* They are life-sustaining, but not tasty. In fact, we still have enough for everyone to try. I'll have them available in the cafeterias, should you wish to have one. Then you can tell me whether it was a good jettison or bad."

Dirk's eyes narrowed. "You sent seeds."

"Also true. They, too, were excess, something that we would have recycled and will not be missed. Did you have another purpose for those?" He looked over to Chloe. "Can you post the manifest of the goods we dropped for *Lugh's Spear*?"

Once again the screen split, adding a sheet with a list of the drop.

Dirk hissed through his teeth. "I need time to study this."

"Surely," Kelse said. Then his tone hardened. "Are you so selfish that you would have others starve when you could help?"

"I'm not the selfish one here. The sleepers draw too much energy. You and yours are selfish."

"No."

"Care to defend that statement with more than words, *Captain* Bountry? Or will you hide in your quarters like Captain Moungala did, never showing his face?"

"I don't like how you refer to a man who has been murdered. It shows a lack of respect for human life, same as being uncaring of wormhole dangers. I'll show my face and the rest of me," Kelse said. "Sounds like you're challenging me to a bout of sparring."

Bright glee shaped Dirk's features. "Sure, come on. Let's fight, oh golden one."

So the guy knew how long it usually took for someone recently Awakened to recover from the experience. Probably figured a man who fought on Earth wouldn't acclimate to the ship fast, either.

Surprise. Kelse inclined his head. "Done."

A flicker of wariness showed in Dirk's eyes, then his same cheerful grin. A grin Kelse had seen on others that masked mania.

"Top of the pyramid," Dirk said. Emphasizing that he was a man of his people and knew the slang and Kelse wasn't and didn't. That Kelse was the past, not the present or the future?

Kelse would show everyone differently.

"Sporting Room One," Chloe murmured. She stared at Kelse, fury in her eyes, but scanned him ruthlessly. "In an hour."

"Sporting Room One in an hour," Kelse said.

"No weapons," Chloe murmured.

"No weapons," Kelse said.

Dirk's mobile brows rose up his equally mobile forehead. "Of course not."

Kelse knew he lied.

"Now I'll continue with my address to my people."

"*Our* people," Dirk said.

"Do you wish a command position?" Kelse asked.

Another charming grin. "You might say that."

"Come see me."

Dirk shook his head. "Oh, no. I don't trust you and your old ways." He lifted his hands, gazed straight out of the screen. "*Nuada's Sword* should be ours, we who lived on her all our lives, not some outdated mission forced upon us. Let us take her back and through the wormhole to refuel and decide our own lives." His image faded.

The screen filled with Kelse's torso. He looked solid. Good.

"Fellow travelers, I'll tell you what I will do for you. I will protect you from violence caused by others. Who benefits from Captain Moungala's death? And I will listen to you. Believe in the mission." He smiled. "And try the new spices and sauces in the cafeteria. Blessed be." He cut the broadcast.

"Kelse, how could you agree to a challenge?" Chloe demanded.

He raised his eyebrows at her. "I can take Dirk Lascom in a fight, Chloe. I spent thirty-seven years learning whether I can win a fight at a glance. Do me the courtesy of believing in that." He rolled his shoulders; the shirt was too tight and strained. "And, primitive reaction or not, Dirk will lose much face and authority and believability when I win."

She scowled. "I need to set this up. I think you have the energy now, but don't know how long it can last. Prepare." She strode from the room speaking on her computer.

Kelse searched the quarters and found a stained but acceptably fitting gi. He did a kata or two to balance his muscles, energy, and psi power. Then he sank to the floor and entered a light trance.

Fifty minutes later he was walking down empty corridors with

Chloe. Occasionally there was an open door and people standing there, but they said nothing.

He was being judged, and not too favorably. Since he was eyeing the dull curving metal walls around him, walls that didn't even have water stains or small mouse turds or the hint of scum growing on them, Kelse wasn't surprised. Helluva thing, missing the decrepit signs of the ghetto and the warehouses the underground had lived in. But there had always been signs of life.

Now most of the signs of life he noticed were in the recycled air. "This is a dreary place," he said.

Chloe flushed red.

"We always knew it would be a dreary place, whether the metal shone or not. But we thought we could live in it for seventy-five years." Kelse grimaced. "I'm sure we did as well as could be expected. We must improve the quality of life. I want to look at that great Greensward of yours." He skimmed his memories. "A third of the ship, right?"

"Correct." Her voice was tight.

"I think you had an excellent idea to have the whole crew visit it more. I haven't seen a twig or leaf in fifteen hours and am feeling the lack."

"We'll have to develop plans to facilitate the preservation of the Greensward. Twelve hundred people is a lot."

"Some will need more time in the green than others." Kelse thought of Fern. She'd be like that. She'd loathe the ship as it was. She'd made accepting noises when they'd toured, but the metal and the lack of natural materials had displeased her. She'd spent time in the Greensward. He'd barely given it a glance.

He and Chloe reached an omnivator and slanted down several stories. The air got denser and smellier. Too many humans on the ship for too long.

Chloe said, "The lowest level of techs are the ones most inclined to favor the mutiny."

"They have the least to lose, the most to gain." He'd been like that once.

Then Chloe pushed through some double doors, and Kelse stepped into a small arena.

The sporting area was round with white spongy mats covering the floor. The space was encircled by a three-meter-high wall. Above the wall were tiered seats, every one of them filled. In the center of the chamber, Dirk Lascom was limbering up. Pitiful.

At the top of the wall sat an orange cat. Peaches.

The bad man lies and cheats! Peaches said.

Five

Telepathy still bothered Kelse. I know! He shouted back to the cat mentally.

Peaches winced, whiskers quivering.

Then Dirk Lascom strolled toward Kelse, proud. The emotional resonance of the crowd supported him.

Kelse moved to the center of the circle and projected his voice. "First blood?"

"If you insist." Lascom smirked. His voice seemed to carry without effort.

"Good." Kelse summoned his psi—his Flair—and let it prime his muscles, slide over his skin. Faster reflexes, extra strength. He studied his opponent, who wore a reckless grin. Then Kelse projected his voice. "Any rules?"

"No!" Dirk kicked at Kelse's groin.

Hand blurring, Kelse caught Dirk's foot, wrenched it, and flung him over, caught hold of the young man's clothes, and tossed him toward a padded wall. His head thumped against it satisfactorily. Kelse heard no crack of a neck breaking. He'd gauged right then. The guy shouldn't be out more than a minute or two. A tingle riffed his inherent defensive shields and he dropped and rolled. Green blazer fire singed the floor mat.

Screams erupted. People shoved to get away.

"Don't panic." Kelse snapped the order. No psi here, just years of experience. *"Sit down in the nearest chair."*

"He's gone," someone yelled, and that helped. People calmed. They found seats and sat. Kelse wondered how many had been hurt, saw Chloe speaking into her handheld. Then calm people garbed in white—Healers—entered the room through the doors at the top.

"Thank you, friends," Kelse said. "I promise that incident will be added to the crimes we are investigating. We are considering motive, now."

Dirk was twitching, raising himself on his elbow. Kelse strode over and yanked him to his feet, released him before he gave in to the urge to punch. "You want to say anything about an ambush?"

The young man rubbed his head, then shook it. "I don't know what you're talking about."

"You've got blood on your lip. That makes this bout mine," Kelse said.

There was a ripple of applause, a few shouts of approval. The crowd seemed to have settled down to watch the show.

Dirk's glance darted around, anger emanating from him. Kelse could guess what he was feeling. The guy wanted to hit Kelse, would really like to take him down, and wouldn't care if he did that from the back. But of course he was aware of people around him, judging him. Judging Kelse.

Kelse planted his feet, again projected his voice; the acoustics in the chamber were perfect. "First we fought. Next we'll talk." He held out his hand, and Lascom raised his.

Kelse didn't like the gleam in his eyes. Kelse slapped Dirk's arm, curving his fingers just under the young man's elbow. He didn't look at what made a tiny clink as it fell to the ground. Dart probably. He stepped forward and crunched it under his foot.

Smiling, he said to Dirk, "Now you clasp my arm in the same manner, and it will look like a greeting or an agreement, not like you meant to poison me."

"Not poison," Dirk said under his breath. "Just a blood gauge to see how you were doing. You shouldn't be this active so soon. What did you take?"

Kelse didn't believe Dirk's easy excuse and didn't reply. Let the man pursue his drug idea. Kelse evaluated his blood and energy himself. He didn't have long before he'd collapse. He'd used a lot of psi today.

Dirk clasped his arm. Kelse stepped back.

Again Kelse spoke to the crowd but didn't take his attention off Lascom. "As I said in my address, I welcome suggestions. Gentle-Sir Dirk Lascom and I will set a time to confer."

Chloe and two husky guys showed up. The larger of the two gestured for Dirk to retire from the center of the arena. Kelse felt safe enough to focus on the crowd. "Lascom and I will speak together. But I have consulted with the astrophysicist Julianna Ambroz, the Captain of *Arianrhod's Wheel.* She is doubtful that the newly discovered wormhole would lead us to civilized space and more provisions." He paused. "And she has the calculations and analysis to back her up. Ask and I'll forward them to you."

A young man, no more than eighteen, leapt from the wall down to the floor. "I'll take you up on that."

Kelse turned to him, saw that Dirk was walking toward the guy, hand out, grinning. Probably wasn't going to dart him.

The newcomer was in his late teens, thin, and didn't move like a fighter. He had a slight olive skin tone, blue eyes, and black hair like Dirk, but didn't appear to be a relative. Kelse got no intent of threat from the guy.

A few seconds later, Kelse recalled that the conspirators had a scientific genius. Should have remembered that sooner. Yes, he was slowing.

Did the young man know Dirk had murdered the previous Captain? How could he overlook that?

The bad man lies, Peaches said. The cat's gaze was concentrated on Dirk.

Kelse said, "I will be glad to provide you with Captain Ambroz's information. Exec Hernandez, please forward—"

"Randolph Ash," Chloe said in suppressed tones.

Randolph gazed at her with sad but determined eyes.

"Please forward the data to GentleSir Ash." Following instinct, Kelse spread his arms wide, turned slowly in place, meeting the eyes of one or two crew members in each section. "Thank you for coming. I welcome your input." When he reached his original spot, he finished, "I remind those of you who wish to apply for the position of security officers to meet me in Gym Two tomorrow at MidAfternoonBell." He glanced at Chloe and the two large men. "Let's go."

They exited the arena to a buzz of voices that filled and echoed around the room.

The walk back to his quarters passed in a blur. People were lined up to see him—only to see him. Occasionally a projectile was lobbed at him and he caught it. That was natural reflex, but he could feel his strength fading with every step.

Chloe opened his door while he mumbled thanks to the men who'd accompanied him. They'd both be at the gym the next day. He hoped they had more than their size to recommend them. Basic fighting skills would be good.

He stripped and fell onto his bed.

A slight chiming woke Kelse and he lifted his eyelids to peer around groggily. The emergency hatch door was open, showing a dark hole.

Fern stepped through and the portal closed behind her.

Couldn't be.

"Kelse," she said huskily, as if she hadn't spoken in a long time.

He sat up. She glided a pace into the room, then to him. Her fingers brushed his cheek. *She was real.* She smelled like chemicals and *Fern*, his woman.

He was suddenly and completely awake. His chest ached with unsteady breaths.

He saw her tremble. As he was trembling.

He didn't care.

It didn't seem like a day since he'd been with her. No, there were those ages of lonely dreams in the tube. It felt like the full two hundred and fifty years since he'd experienced her touch.

He was unbearably aroused just looking at her naked, thinking of her and how they'd come together, loved, before. He hoped she was the same, because he knew the next moment their skin touched, he'd have no control. He would want only to claim his mate, ensure that she would know him, never forget him for any amount of time. Always be his. Forever.

Even in the dim light, he saw the scar on her chest where the bullet had penetrated. He'd have lost her if an excellent Healer hadn't been next to her when the mob had found them, turned on them.

"Fern." He didn't think he actually said her name, might not even have mouthed it. But she heard.

She choked and tears glistened on her face. Then she jumped on him.

He grabbed her close, held her hard, and knew he'd been wrong before. Holding her, not sex, was important. Using his embrace to show her how lonely he'd been, how he'd missed her, how he could never let her go. The feel of her, her soft breasts against him, her skin, overwhelmed him. Now her fragrance enveloped him, sank into the pulse of his blood.

He'd heard, knew, that smell was the most emotional sensory trigger. His Fern was in his arms, he smelled her skin, Fern-musk. His senses filled with her. His throat tightened. No, he couldn't speak.

They rocked together back and forth.

Finally he heard something. Little whimpers from Fern.

Low moans from himself.

Hurt animals finding love, finding their mate.

They fell back onto the bed. Then she was atop him, and the feel of her body rubbing against him removed all thought. Her tongue touched his lips, and he opened her mouth and he tasted her and she tasted him. Fern! Woman! His!

Her lips were soft. He felt the caress of her fingers on his cheeks, sliding down his shoulders to his arms, the flutter of her right hand along the long scar he carried there. She took her mouth away and was over him, and wet salt fell on his face, on his lips.

"Kelse, Kelse, Kelse." It was a chant, and from outside his head because he never thought of his name. Then a long sigh and a squirm from her, and he was in her and nothing in his whole life had ever been as good as this moment. Huge hunger exploded in him and his hands clamped around her butt. He'd forgotten how good her ass felt in his palms, his woman, his. Right for him as no one ever had been or would be ever . . . ever . . . ever.

And they were crying each other's name, and they were riding together, and they were zooming high, high, high to the top of the universe, then shattering in bliss and sending bits of themselves sparking and sparkling throughout time and space.

Long minutes passed as his mind coalesced into thought and settled back into his brain, and his brain was in his skull, and his body felt fabulous and was on a good bed and his woman was on him.

His arms were around her, but lightly. He stroked her back. There was dampness between them—tears and sweat and sex. That felt good, too. Life affirming. He was alive and so was his Fern.

And he would do anything to make sure they stayed that way.

Would do anything to fulfill the dream they had, the dream they still shared.

She moved, and emitted a small scream.

"Wha?" His thick tongue formed the fragment.

Her hand and arm curved in a gesture that he spent seconds admiring before he saw what had torn the sound from her.

The great window wall of the room was transparent, showing space. Blackness beyond imagination with the sparkles he'd thought were himself and Fern. Brilliantly white, bright blue, pinpricks deep and glowing red.

Space.

What was outside the ship they were in.

The doomed ship.

It was beautiful.

It was terrifying.

It wasn't what he'd promised her before they'd stepped into the tubes.

He'd failed.

* * *

Kelse let himself stare at his woman. She had a heart-shaped face and short black hair. Her misty violet eyes, the eyes that had snared him, were closed. He'd see them again soon. Her skin was soft, softer than anything in his life before he'd met her. Her roundish chin belied the sheer determination of her. In that they matched.

Fern didn't give up, either.

She was with him.

"I don't understand it," Kelse said. The bed was large enough for her to roll away from him but they'd been separated too long. He wanted her in his arms. "Chloe didn't Awaken you."

"No. There wasn't anyone there when I woke except a little bot."

"Automatic then." He didn't like that. So much could have gone wrong.

"Nothing went wrong." She slid her fingers through his hair, and he simply closed his eyes and felt her skin against his and breathed in her scent. It should have felt like only two days since he'd held her hand, but somewhere in his brain, maybe in his psi magic, he knew it had been centuries.

"I saw your empty tube." Her voice hitched. "And knew you'd been Awakened. I checked on the stats and found it had only been sixteen hours. I was glad." She kissed him, her body sliding against his sinuously to arouse, her tongue parting his lips and sucking on his tongue. When she lifted her mouth, she said, "You're supposed to tell me that you're glad to have me with you."

He rolled her under him, slid inside her, loved the little whimper of pleasure she gave when he was snug. "I'm glad to have you with me. To be with you. To be in you." Then he began the slow, teasing thrusting that pleased them both. He closed his eyes as her legs wrapped around him. This was the very best of all worlds.

He ached for her, still.

He feared for her more.

An hour later the main door opened and a woman walked in, working on a handheld. If she hadn't been giving off such I'm-all-about-business vibes, Fern would have been suspicious of her motives.

Fern and Kelse sat up.

"It's time you meet the nose bridge crew." The older woman glanced up and her mouth dropped. So did her computer. "Kelse!" It was a near shriek.

Then, *"Fern."* She stared at Fern, swung her head back at Kelse. "Your fear for her is a weakness. You shouldn't have Awakened her," the old woman snapped.

Fern draped a sheet around herself. It wasn't as warm as Kelse's muscular arm at her waist. And he was here, with her, solid, and the wispy dreams had vanished. His lower body was covered by a sheet, too, and that was good.

She studied the woman, trying to place her. A small shock hit as she realized this small, thin woman was Chloe Hernandez.

"You misremember," Kelse said in those hard tones that allowed no doubt. "I was never taught how to Awaken anyone. I don't have those skills."

He'd always been so focused on the end result of this mission, colonizing the planet, building a house and a city. Awakening before the ship had reached their planet must have been like a bombshell. She leaned against him, giving her support, as always. The tension in him lessened.

"She's not glowing," Chloe said.

"What?" Fern asked. Then she blinked as she noted a visible golden aura around Kelse.

"No," he said thoughtfully. "We believe she was Awakened automatically."

Chloe scowled. "That shouldn't be possible."

Kelse shrugged. "We don't know how it happened."

Head tilted, Chloe continued, "And she obviously doesn't need the standard seventy-two-hour recovery period." She shifted to gaze at Kelse. "I accepted that your Flair would help you out—"

"Flair?" Fern asked.

"Psi power," Kelse said.

"Your psi has always been of a more physical nature. But I wouldn't have expected Fern to have recuperated already."

The woman was right. Fern blinked. She'd been trained in the Awakening process—one of every couple had. She shouldn't have been able to enjoy fabulous and energetic loving with Kelse.

She shouldn't have been able to walk. "We don't have answers for you."

Still frowning, Chloe picked up her computer. Her dark brown eyes focused on Kelse with the intensity of a tractor beam. "It is imperative you meet the nose bridge crew. They are completely loyal and dedicated to our mission." She slid a quick look of a woman appreciating a well-built man along his torso, something that Kelse didn't notice. "And, after that fight, they consider you an idol."

"Fight?" Fern asked. There shouldn't be fights on the ship. Anxiety trickled like cold rain through her. She recognized the place, now. She and Kelse were in the bed of the Captain's Quarters. Which made him the Captain. If Kelse was Captain, it meant that the ship needed a strong leader accustomed to fighting for what he wanted. Choking dread filled her throat, made her swallow hard against fear.

"It wasn't a fight," Kelse said.

He meant that, but his definition wasn't the same as many others'. Fern's gaze collided with Chloe's. The older woman was obviously weighing Fern, considering how much she'd interfere in Chloe's manipulation of Kelse. Kelse wasn't a man who was easily led, but these certainly weren't regular circumstances for him—them. The large wall of space edged her vision. They were Earth folk—planetary people—surrounded by the hostile environment of space.

Chloe nodded and Fern realized that the older woman confirmed that, yes, indeed, Kelse had been in a fight. Sliding her gaze toward her husband, Fern didn't see any new bruises.

"How much damage can the nose bridge crew do if they want?" Kelse asked.

"You can override anything at your command console." Chloe nodded to the huge desk.

"But I don't have the scientific knowledge to navigate the ship, and neither does Fern," Kelse said. "So we'd better make sure the nose bridge crew is on our side."

Sides? That didn't sound good. Fern needed to figure out what was going on, fast. She and Kelse were a team. They shared their concerns and they stood as one. But she could make mistakes if she didn't know the situation.

He shifted and Fern knew he was seconds away from heading to the shower. She put her hand on his thigh and he stilled. "If you'll excuse us?" Fern asked. "Kelse will accompany you in fifteen minutes. Just as soon as he brings me up to speed." She smiled.

Chloe didn't like it, but she nodded and left.

"You'd better tell me everything," Fern said.

"Opaque wall," Kelse said instead. Outer space disappeared and Fern suddenly realized how small the room was, just a medium-sized room for Earth, though luxurious by ship standards. Well, she and Kelse had lived in tight quarters before.

"I'll tell you in a minute," he said, striding over to a small door in the opposite wall from the bed, opening it, and shutting himself inside. The sound of a shower came.

It wasn't like Kelse to avoid problems. No. He wasn't avoiding problems. He was avoiding talking to her. If it wasn't obvious that the head couldn't accommodate two, she'd be in there with him, though the water had a heavy scent she didn't like.

She couldn't comprehend his behavior. Except when they'd first met, he'd never shut her out. They'd lived on the edge of desperation, and they'd relied on each other totally. Now he wasn't talking. Or he was figuring out exactly what he wanted to say.

The water clicked off and an awful air-whirling noise came. A minute later he emerged dry from the air tube. He didn't like those and was frowning.

"What's wrong, Kelse? Why were you Awakened?"

Six

Kelse said, "Chloe had one of her hunches and Awakened me."

He was dressing fast in black clothes that didn't fit. They weren't his clothes and they weren't something he'd like wearing, especially the shirt with insignia of command.

Kelse gave Fern a meaningless smile. "I haven't figured out when she was Awakened. Maybe you can get her to tell you how old she is."

Fern snorted. Yeah, that would happen. Like never. She trolled her memory. "She was scheduled to be Awakened near the end of the voyage to help the Captain and the Pilot run the ship while we were all preparing for landing." Something about the ship snagged at Fern's recollection, but she didn't catch it before Kelse spoke again.

"That didn't happen. We're over schedule."

Fern's mouth dried. "Lay it out, Kelse."

He grimaced. "There's a mutiny on board." He shrugged his excellent shoulders. "Not much of one, and I've got a handle on it."

Truth.

She stood and walked over to work on his shirt cuff tabs. He wasn't looking at her, but a ruddiness showed under his skin, and an interesting bulge in his pants, so she figured it wasn't because he wanted to mislead her.

There came a hard knocking at the door. "Gotta go," Kelse said. His arm came around her to yank her to him. Take her mouth, remind her that she loved him and desired him. Then he set her aside, and she was relieved to see an old gleam in his eyes.

"I'll be back soon. We'll have dinner." He grimaced. "Such as it is. I need help with menus for the crew, the food is atrocious, but I don't know how they'll react, or how their stomachs will."

"So the mutineers aren't a big problem."

"More like conspirators." He hesitated and the gleam died in his eyes and he changed from lover to fighter. "They killed Kiet Moungala, the previous Captain. But they misjudged the timing and me. I'm in control of the ship, Fern."

She sat abruptly on a nearby chair. This made no sense. Kiet wasn't supposed to have been Awakened, either. He had a natural charisma but a dislike for space. Who didn't know that? Her memory was buzzing, but her concern for Kelse was too much to pay attention to it.

"Will you stay in the cabin?" he asked.

"Sure. If you allow me access to your console, so I can understand our circumstances. And you tell me the worst of it. So I hear it from you instead of figuring it out for myself."

The skin tightened on his tanned face, accenting his eyes, making them seem silver instead of gray. That expression she knew. The mission wasn't going well . . . and could be fatal. If this was Earth, she'd insist on accompanying him. She stood. "Live and die together, that was our original deal before we got married."

He winced as if he hadn't wanted to be reminded.

Chloe opened the door, stormed in, took a glance at them, and faded back out.

"How dangerous is it out there, Kelse?"

He snorted and she relaxed a bit.

"Not much. I think it's a small cell but had some general support. They got away with taking out Moungala and the security officers. That's all the killing they'll do."

"You weren't here when they died."

"No." He strode to the desk console, jerked his head for her to join him. When she did, his nostrils flared. She must still smell of sex. Taking her hand, he placed it on the desktop. "This is Captain Kelse Bountry giving full authorization to Fern Bountry for any and all accesses and actions on this ship."

"Recognizing Fern Bountry," the ship said in a flat tone that bothered Fern.

Kelse took both her hands and she naturally turned to him. This was going to be bad.

"We're lost."

She stilled, panic rooted in her stomach, sent thorny tendrils through her, whipping her mind to gibber. She shuddered and managed one word. "And?"

"And we're running out of fuel." He squeezed her hands. "It isn't hopeless yet. Believe that."

If he said so, it was true. She drew a deep breath. "All right."

"We have one close star system we've sent probes to that might have two viable planets. Julianna Ambroz is Captain of *Arianrhod's Wheel*. She doesn't like the looks of that system, but they're possibilities. We can reach two more systems with a total of fourteen potential habitable planets before our fuel runs out. Probably."

"All right." But she could see there was more. She angled her head, waiting.

"There's a wormhole that might be to civilized space—"

"No!"

His smile was faint, though his brows were still low with worry. "That makes it unanimous." He glanced at the console. "I haven't had time to do any research." He opened his hands. "On any of this. I know what Chloe has told me."

Fern nodded. "I can look at the analyses."

"Thank you." A kiss on her forehead, the warmth of his body reassured her. "Last . . . brace yourself."

He'd only ever said that to her once, when they'd had news that her family had died in mob violence in the Northeast Area. Targeted because of her and her relationship to Kelse. He hadn't lied. She sank into her balance.

He nodded. "The ships have been traveling two hundred and fifty years."

Incomprehensible.

He kissed her cheek and left while the words and a faint hint of the concept behind them circled in her mind.

She stood there until she became aware of the cold, then shambled to the head and a shower under strange water that had been recycled many, many times. Other water that must have come from the ship's collectors, or somewhere, she didn't recall the science. Not from Earth.

Then she dressed in one of the shirts in the closet and sat down at the console and began reading Moungala's log. Recent history was most important.

The young nose bridge crew—none of them in their thirties— welcomed him like they were acolytes and he a high priest. The golden aura that surrounded him might have had something to do with impressing them.

Apparently over the sixty years they'd been sequestered, this crew had become their own society, with the elders retiring to a tiny section of the great Greensward that was kept for them.

For fun, the crew had modified the search-and-find-and-colonize-and-build program Julianna Ambroz had written. Long and scientifically titled software had become *Our Mission.*

The crew had already focused on the relatively near white star and the sixth planet revolving around it—they'd begun the moment they'd launched the scientific probes. Since their voices held a false cheer when they talked about it, Kelse avoided asking how often the Colonists in the program survived.

Kelse had occasionally seen a war game or the popular *Mob vs. Psis* at an arcade. Always destroyed the machine. It had been nothing like gritty reality.

Maybe science games were different. He could only hope.

While he was with them, he kept his own belief in the success of the mission high, along with his enthusiasm. He had little in common with the youngsters but could show approval and pride in them and their accomplishments.

Yet when he and Chloe left the bridge by a labyrinthine back way as secret as they'd gone there, he once again felt tired to the bone. Maybe he hadn't recovered as much as they'd believed he had.

Or maybe he was expending energy short-circuiting his constant worry about Fern. It had been bad when she was in the cryonics bay. But she hadn't known of the danger and he'd liked sparing her that.

Now she would be openly with him—and no way would he be able to keep her in the Captain's Quarters—she would be a target.

"Fern can make a real contribution," Chloe said. She'd rapidly accepted the change in circumstances.

Kelse had been better about doing that on Earth, but he'd never coped with such strange circumstances as the last day.

"No," he said. He'd shut Chloe down on the walk to the nose bridge on the same subject.

She sniffed but said nothing more.

He figured the women would do what they wanted. Somehow he'd have to keep Fern safe. He didn't know how.

When they neared his quarters, they stepped from a wall access panel and into a quiet corridor. The next turn brought them into a busier hallway.

People quieted. He got a couple of greetings.

Then a man staggered toward him, red on his shirt and pants. "Cap'n!"

Kelse lunged at him to help before he realized the red wasn't blood.

"Sure do like this ketchup, Cap'n."

Kelse laughed and people turned, wide-eyed. "I can see that."

With a goofy grin the man passed them. Kelse said to Chloe, "Anything in the ketchup that would make people act strange?"

"We did a sensitivity test on volunteers before we introduced it," Chloe said primly. She'd already told him that he'd created a lot of work. "Fresh ketchup as requested, made from ingredients grown in the Greensward. Also several chutneys and various spices."

"Thank you again."

Chloe turned and looked back over her shoulder, then permitted herself a small smile and a little sigh. "It was a good idea. Though I've never liked ketchup."

"Me, either." Always looked a little too much like blood to him. But he'd gotten a small adrenaline boost when he'd thought the crew member was hurt.

Then they were at his door. Chloe nodded at the temporary security guards and walked on. Kelse acknowledged them, too, then entered his code, his heart bumping hard. Soon he'd have Fern in his arms again.

The room was dim and he locked the door behind him. Fern was asleep at the console. So beautiful, his Fern. The most beautiful being in the universe.

How he wished she was in the cryonics bay, away from all these problems.

How glad he was to have her with him. He picked her up and she snuggled against him, murmuring, "Kelse."

Since she didn't like to sleep raw, he left her in the shirt and put her on his bed. There was no sight as wonderful as Fern in his bed. She rolled over and the shirt hiked up, revealing her excellent ass. His body tightened and thought vanished as he stripped. But when he lay down beside her, he had time only to hold her before sleep crashed on him.

When he woke in the morning, Fern was watching him. The first thing he saw was her face, lips curving into a smile. "Missed you," he said hoarsely, "so much."

"Me, too."

They made slow love and even managed to squeeze in the tiny shower cubicle together, bodies bumping.

Fern placed his clothes and her shirt in the cleanser, and put on a red one with gold epaulettes that barely reached her thighs and made Kelse's mouth dry.

Before he could jump her again, Chloe knocked on his door. This time the older woman waited for his, "Come in." She nodded to him and smiled at Fern.

"Fern, the clothing you ordered will be ready by this afternoon." Chloe's stance relaxed. "The buzz about Kelse is good. The crew involved with the food and clothing issues are excited and passing that on to others. I think we'll have a good crowd for the security officer tryouts. I've moved it to Sporting Room Two."

"No," Kelse said.

"No?" Chloe frowned.

"I don't want this to be a spectacle, or seen as entertainment. Three guards have already died."

"I know that!"

"I want the applicants to understand that, and I don't want a crowd belittling them or making comments about their skills." He slid a glance toward Fern. She'd obviously heard about the fight yesterday. "I also want to ensure that the room is safe for the applicants. No guy with a blazer."

Chloe grumbled but began tapping her handheld as she answered him. "We'll push the exclusivity factor then."

"Good idea," Fern said.

"Any suggestions from the crew?" Kelse asked.

Studying her computer, Chloe smiled and said, "All shifts in sector twelve want to repaint their cafeteria."

"Approved," Kelse said.

Chloe grinned and the green comm light on Chloe's computer lit as she flicked the message out.

"Some of the widest corridors had garden boxes that have been stashed. There have been requests to open them again and restock."

"That will be approved on a sector-by-sector basis." Places that might not be interesting to the conspirators could be okayed. "I'll need to know the dimensions." He didn't want to fight around boxes, wanted a clear view of corridors, with no place for ambushers to hide.

"I'll have the crew submit the dimensions to me—"

"I believe I know Kelse's concerns regarding that," Fern said coolly. "I'll check them." She was irritated with him. Probably thought he was hiding a lot from her. He was. All his fears.

Expression sober, Chloe said, "No one came forward with any information on Moungala's or the security officers' deaths."

"I didn't expect anyone to. I'm still an unknown quantity, and not of the ship culture, yet," Kelse replied.

"I'm going to the security guard tryouts," Fern said.

Kelse clenched his jaw against denial. She wouldn't accept that from him. Instead he said, "I don't want to make a formal announcement of Fern's Awakening. I'd rather rumor circulate." The more confusion around Fern, the better, as far as he was concerned. Made her less a target.

Both women stared at him. "Why?" they asked together.

"I think it's best."

Both frowned, but since they considered it minor, they'd let him have his way.

"All right." Chloe jerked a shoulder, then a slightly mean smile touched her lips. "Dirk Lascom, the head of the mutineers, wants to speak with you at MidMorningBell this morning."

"Fine."

"I'll set it up in the conference room on the opposite side of the ship, where we can see the star systems we want to reach," Chloe said.

"Is that all?"

"For now." Chloe eyed Fern as if she knew his wife was simmering, though Fern kept an easy manner.

Chloe left.

"Are you ashamed of me?" Fern asked.

Anger buzzed in his ears. "You know better than that."

"I'm not sure I do." Her expression was stormy, her violet eyes deepening to purple, her cheeks taking on color.

"I want you safe."

"And I've always wanted you safe, too, but you were the head of the underground in NJNY when we met so I knew it was futile." She walked up close to him, into his personal space. He'd never liked anyone in his space but her, and even with her, it had taken time. She knew that and used it.

Tilting her head back, she said, "I'm going to the security guard tests with you."

"I heard that." His face and manner closed down. He tried to roll his shoulders, and the shirt constrained him, so he ripped open the front tab strip. It made a long, tearing sound.

He shucked his pants. They were too tight, also, and he went to the chair behind the console. When he looked down, he saw Moungala's words . . . they'd been handwritten on a pad program. Kiet's penmanship was beautiful. Kelse's was crap.

"He didn't talk much about the conspirators," Fern said. She came up and laid her fingers on Kelse's shoulder. "He called the group *irritants*."

She was too close again. He wanted to take her and love her. In the chair, on the rug, back in bed.

And he couldn't.

There had never been enough time for them, then they'd slept away two hundred and fifty years, and Awakened to face death again.

Breathing in deeply—her scent, the faint odor of Kiet left on the leather of the chair, himself—Kelse just plain ached with inner pain at threats that he'd thought he'd never feel again.

Fern lifted her hand from his shoulder. Her fingers hovered over the red "book" of Kiet's diary that showed on the screen. "He didn't passcode it. We'll keep it, and all the other diaries, right?"

"How many Captains were there?" Kelse asked.

"You're the sixth. All of them were Awakened, and some of them have left descendants in the crew . . . mostly the nose bridge."

His stomach clutched. They'd been able to live full lives, have children. "Six in two hundred fifty years, long time spans of command."

"That's right. Kiet was going on his twenty-first year."

Kelse took her fingers, squeezed them, then slid open the crew biog program. "Dirk Lascom," he said.

The man's vid came up, eyes sparkling, hands gesturing as he spoke to the tech recording him.

"Greedy. Power hungry," Fern said.

Kelse jerked. He'd seen the greed, the need to be admired.

"The ship would be in a world of hurt if he'd succeeded in killing the Captain and the rest of us in the cryonics bay and took over," Kelse said.

"He doesn't have good leadership qualities," Fern agreed. "Not for a community this size. Small groups, sure."

"He's an ambusher." Kelse met his wife's eyes. "Which is why I want you to wear body armor."

"Kelse!"

He rubbed the back of his neck. "I'll have a hard time concentrating on my job if I know you're in danger. Wear the armor."

The slight moment of agreement between them vanished. She moved away and he missed her closeness. "If you will."

"Hell. I don't even know where mine is."

"I'll find our belongings in the ship's stores and have our armor delivered and will check it out before the security officer selection." She frowned. "There must be sparring clubs."

The alarm chimed and a monotone voice said, "Five minutes before leaving for Conference Room A."

Kelse stood, aligned his shirt tab and slid his thumb up the front, and grabbed his pants and put them on. "You check into those clubs. See which members are trying out for the security officer position, note if any might be with Dirk. See where and when the clubs have a schedule."

She nodded. "We can join." She went to the closet.

"I can. And I want you to stay in these quarters until our armor arrives."

Seven

She turned on her heel, brows down, hands on hips. "Since when have you become such a coward regarding me, Kelse Bountry?" She flung out her hands. "I fought by your side. I can take care of myself." She tapped her chest with her fist.

"I always knew you could run if you had to, outside NJNY, to the sanctuary overseas, if necessary. Had that escape hatch. There's no escape on this ship."

She stared at him. She'd had no idea he'd harbored such a fantasy. "What happened to *live together, die together*?"

He glowered. "I always thought you could run," he repeated.

Shaking her head, she said, "The only running I've done is to you, Kelse."

"We don't know these people or culture. We can only guess."

She lifted her brows. "More reason for me to look through the records?"

"Yes. And you have more formal education, scientific education. Can you study the ship specs and see what the hell happened in the wormholes and what the fuel situation is?" He rubbed the scar on his scalp and his hair actually looked better afterward. He always looked great in "rough-and-ready" mode. "Lord and Lady know that I tried, but even the summaries were over my head. See if the other Captains understood what happened. Dammit. I should have that info for this meeting. The conspirators want to take a chance on the wormhole. They have a scientific genius."

They shouldn't have taken time to make love, he meant. "I'll do that," she said.

"I'm outside your door," Chloe said over the intercom. "I'll brief you on the way on the people and events."

More irritation unwound within Fern. She stared at Kelse. "So I'll be doing busywork."

Kelse snorted. "You know I hate data from only one source."

That was true.

He strode to her, grabbed her, and lifted her from her feet to kiss her hard, and she was surrounded by him, by the pulsing tension of arousal, the desire between them. He thunked her to her feet against the wall, out of blazer fire from the door. And banged a fist on the "open" button.

Dragging in a breath, Fern said, "You look like shit in black."

His shoulders tightened, the fabric showing strain at the seams.

The door opened. "You should wear a cape or cloak," Chloe said.

"No cape." Fern muttered the words as Kelse said them. After the door closed, she went back to the console to check on their clothes and their body armor. A few of their other belongings sifted through her mind, precious mementos they'd packed to recall their old life when they'd reached a new planet.

No, she didn't want those. Not now. Irritated, she shook tears away.

Kelse sat in a beautiful conference room with one whole side a large window into space—that unnerved him. Gorgeous but awful. He didn't think the view would engender the same emotions in the people he was meeting with.

But, to him, the vastness of inimical space burning with beautiful stars underscored their plight. Extraordinarily breathtaking from the inside of the ship. Literally breathtaking outside. No place for a human.

He found himself rubbing a thumb over the lovely grain of the huge slab of redwood that was the table. He had no recollection of seeing money go to purchase the thing but hadn't often looked at the expense sheets sent around to the Colonists. He'd let Fern tell him if there was anything that seemed dubious. He didn't think he'd seen such a table in his life, but as a reminder of home, it was unbearably beautiful. A polished red, with a satin grain under his hands. Wood. So much warmer, richer than the cool metal of most of the ship's furnishings.

He was impressed. He hoped his adversaries would be, too.

The double doors opened silently and Chloe, in a new uniform—dark green with a lot less gilt braid and buttons—walked in. "The Ships for Ourselves party members," she announced brusquely.

Only three men walked in. The first was Dirk Lascom, the second Randolph Ash, and the third a hulking guy with the blank eyes and stolid expression of a man who has given all his loyalty to another. Who would die for him.

Who would kill for him.

Kelse nodded to them. "Greetyou." He stared at each one in turn. "Is this all of you?"

"We have seventy percent of the people behind us!" Randolph said.

"And the core group?" snapped Kelse.

"Twe—"

"Enough," Dirk said loudly.

Had that been twelve or twenty or twenty-some?

"I wasn't introduced to the third of your party," Kelse said, nodding at the blond tough—muscle guard.

"Jeremy Stinson." Dirk smiled.

"Greetyou," Kelse said.

The man nodded.

"Please be seated." Dirk and Randolph glanced at each other, Dirk sat at Kelse's left . . . his back toward the window looking into space. Randolph sat to Kelse's right. The guard sat next to Dirk and fixed his stare on Kelse.

Chloe took her seat at the far end of the large table, becoming, again, the "flunky." Randolph glanced at her, at Kelse, and scowled.

Kelse turned his attention back to Dirk. "Tell me what you want."

Dirk laughed. "Our party says it all. The ship for ourselves."

"To do what?" Kelse asked.

The other flung his arms wide. "To *live*. Not to follow outdated jobs, do tasks that make no sense."

"Ah," Kelse said. He sat in silence until Dirk and Randolph gave him cues that they were uncomfortable. "But you will need most of those tasks to be done if you want to continue to travel, which I understand is your underlying goal."

Once again the men shared a glance. Randolph leaned forward, pale under his olive-toned skin. "We've had an excellent run, but though the ship is nanotech, and built for centuries, the fuel cells are depleted."

"And you don't believe in the mission."

The younger man met Kelse's eyes squarely. "I don't think we have the fuel to reach the star systems." He waved at the huge window on space; a hungry, hopeless expression molded his face for an instant. "I examined those analyses I was sent." He shook his head. "We still can't make it."

"But we have the resources to reach the wormhole," Dirk said smoothly. He nodded to Randolph.

The younger man's eyes lit. "Yes, it's much closer!" He pulled out a memory button and slid it to Kelse. "And I've studied the composition of its waves extensively. There are traces of molecules that belong to starship fuel in it! That indicates that beyond the wormhole is civilized space."

Kelse tapped the button on the table. "And did you scrutinize the figures for how the previous wormholes affected this ship? When it was much younger."

Randolph's expression clouded. He stiffened and his nostrils flared. "I don't—"

"We believe the public figures and analyses are incorrect." Dirk shrugged, opened his hands.

Not looking at Chloe, wanting to keep her profile low, Kelse said, "I'll double-check the public data against that I have." He gazed at Randolph. "And if there are any discrepancies, I will forward the information to you. Tell me about the white star system that we launched our probes at."

"I think that Captain Julianna Ambroz is correct. The system and the planets in it are marginal for our colonization."

"I see," Kelse said.

"What has happened," Dirk said lightly with a sharp smile, "is that the previously Awakened Captains squandered the resources of this ship. And you continue to squander them." Still smiling, Dirk said, "And if we make . . . adjustments . . . we can arrive at those potential planets."

Kelse knew what he was intimating. Kill the sleepers in the cryonics bay. He stared straight at Randolph. "I didn't take you for a man who would be easy with killing."

"Of course we wouldn't kill anyone!" Randolph's eyes went wide. Then he met Kelse's hard stare and swallowed heavily. Not looking at Kelse, he said in a low voice, "I . . . uh . . . postulated that we could reduce the energy to the cryonics bay."

"To my friends and the people who launched this enterprise," Kelse said. "I recall enough of my personal briefing regarding the stasis state to know that we chose to be moderate in the use of such energy."

"There are redundant systems," Dirk said.

"Yes," Kelse agreed.

"For the good of the ship, for us *all*, we need the energy for our standard systems," Dirk said, mobile brows raised. "With that energy we can reach those star systems that you want."

"But it's not your brain and body on the line, is it?" Kelse stood. "You can go now. But be aware of this. I don't negotiate with murderers. And that seventy percent of the people you claim support you? You might have had them before you started killing people."

"We didn't kill anyone!" Randolph protested.

Dirk gave one twitch, then was unaccustomedly quiet. The guard rose slowly, threateningly. Kelse ignored him.

"There aren't other suspects," Kelse said. "Kill the Captain, kill the people in the cryonics bay, and the ship is all yours. A good and daring plan. But it didn't work."

Dirk stood, gave Kelse another false smile. "Oh, but you might have wanted the Captaincy."

"Moungala had other enemies," Randolph said uncertainly.

"And the security officers?"

"You have no proof, and I promise you, my people would be in an uproar if you did anything to me," Dirk said, walking confidently to the door, followed by his guard and Randolph, who shambled a bit.

Kelse said, "Soon you will make a mistake. Then I'll let the crew, our people, decide what to do with you."

The door hissed shut behind them.

Chloe cleared her throat. "The boy was right; the public docs regarding the warping of our systems by the wormholes don't match the engineering analyses."

"The public documents aren't as frightening, are they?"

"No."

"Transmit the engineering specs before and after each wormhole occurrence to Randolph Ash."

She tapped her handheld. "Done." Her dark chocolate gaze met his. "You think you can save him?" she whispered.

"Randolph? Yes." Kelse stretched his arms and shoulders as much as his shirt allowed. "And I think we need him."

She wet her lips. "Something you should know."

"That he's your grandson?"

"I'm his Father's Dam, FatherDam." She closed her eyes. "And I hope you can save him. You're handling him right, at least." An ironic smile raised one corner of her mouth. "Not like I did. Completely alienated him. But that's not what I wanted to tell you."

"What?"

"Fern watched the whole meeting."

"I don't have secrets from Fern."

Chloe snorted.

"Window opaque, replace with view of the hallway outside Conference Room A," Kelse said.

As he'd suspected, the guard, Jeremy Stinson, lingered outside the door. There were five other large men in the corridor, too. And a lack of other passersby. Kelse shook his legs out, then sank back into his chair, attached the small memory button to his handheld, and watched as figures scrolled.

He would rather try to take the six thugs in the hallway than pound his mind against these stats. He sent them to Julianna Ambroz instead.

He leaned back and watched the hall, sure he could outwait the men. And the corridor was a busy one, people wouldn't avoid it for too long. Dirk wouldn't want witnesses.

Fern's heart thumped as her window changed from the view of the conference room to the corridor outside and she saw six men waiting to pounce on Kelse.

He wouldn't leave, would he?

No, of course he wouldn't. They were all younger than he, and he didn't know how well they were trained.

For the next hour she kept an eye on the view outside the conference room as she continued to skip back in time for data. When shift changed and the hallway teemed with people, the six men moved along and Kelse exited the room, greeted and spoke with people as he returned to her.

Just as Kelse left the conference room, a knock came at her door. Screening, she saw two young women. One carried a stack of folded garments in forest green. That color was particularly flattering for Kelse and Fern didn't look too bad in it, either.

The second woman carried a small box. Fern could read the panglish tag: *Bountrys' armor, casual clothes, and sweats.* She recalled there wasn't much in there. Glancing down at herself, she knew she'd lost some weight and the clothes would be too big. Kelse's might be, too, and she was sure his "sweats" were rags. She'd hide them in the far corner of the closet.

By the time he returned, she'd checked and double-checked their body armor. The mesh unders were large on her, but the molded chest and back plates were adjustable and fit well.

He glanced at her armor and his gaze became cool. Her heart

picked up a beat. She wasn't used to chill looks from him. "You're insisting on going to the security officer application session," he said.

"I haven't changed my mind." She didn't like being at odds with him and had to keep her voice steady in the wake of his disapproval. This new situation was affecting their relationship. But they were a couple and she wouldn't let him forget that.

His jaw flexed, then he turned away and stripped. He pulled on the new gi of dark green with a grunt of satisfaction. "Thanks," he said.

"You're welcome."

"I don't want you sparring today."

"What!"

He did a few lunges, then segued into a short pattern. Almost, watching him diverted her from their conversation—another one that was becoming an argument. He paused and bowed to an invisible opponent. His chest was rising and falling more rapidly than it had a week—two and a half centuries—ago.

Glancing over at her with his hard face on, he said, "You aren't fully recovered from the cryonic stasis sleep."

She'd have liked to deny that, but she'd done a couple of katas herself and didn't like her shape. "I bet I could beat a few."

"We don't know that. We don't know who trained them and whether that training has stuck. We don't know their moves or how their fighting has changed."

She chuffed a breath. "I saw your 'fight' with Lascom."

That surprised a smile out of him, but it was all too brief. He came over and put the edge of his hand under her chin, tipped her head up. Not something he usually did or she usually allowed. "I want them to think of you as an unknown quality."

She grimaced. "They will." Then she pointed to the console with her chin. "There are two fighting clubs, and they seem to be based on ship class structure. One is for tech levels ten to five—lower class. The other is first level through fourth. And of both clubs there are only two women, both in the upper level." Women had fought long and hard for equality on Earth, and the ship wasn't such an environment that brute strength would be a predominant need. Fern wasn't sure what went wrong, but something had.

"Is that so?" Kelse asked.

"So."

"Then they will definitely underestimate you." He dropped his hand and stole a kiss.

"You're not going to get around me by sex."

His laugh was short, and he began moving again. "I never have. I should get so lucky now."

She sighed. "I'll observe the tryouts."

"Good. The best thing you can do."

"All six of the men in the hallway outside of the conference room were in the higher-level sparring organization."

"Of course they were. Along with Dirk Lascom and Randolph Ash?"

"Ash is lower class."

That stopped Kelse. "The hell he is. He's Chloe's grandson."

"He's illegitimate."

Kelse just stared at her. "That matters?"

"Yes."

He shook his head and swore.

The timer pinged. "NoonBell," said the flat tone.

Fern took off the gi she wore over her armor and put on her loose sweats. She gave Kelse a hard hug. "Come on, I hear they have some wonderful chicken noodle soup in Cafeteria A."

"Show mobile route to Cafeteria A," Kelse said. The tiny cameras along the route flickered in real time. There were no threatening men, the walkways were busy. She and Kelse left.

"If anyone comes up to us at lunch, I'll introduce you," Kelse said. They weren't touching now, both free to deal with any threat. "But I don't think that will happen."

It didn't. They ate solitarily, but under the gazes of many . . . and more arriving every minute. The soup wasn't bad, but it was blander than Fern had expected, and she knew it was better than usual.

The winnowing out of the men for security detail took hours. No women applied. One of the toughs who'd waited for Kelse after his conference with the mutineers was there—and sat with another muscular man in intent conversation. *Stupid*. Now they knew one more of Dirk's cadre. Kelse dismissed them both.

Fern got a hinky feeling about two other men, and though Kelse seemed to be fine with them, and their skills were as good as the rest, he sent them away, too.

Finally, they ended up with ten men. All of whom were close to becoming Kelse loyalists.

They all escorted her back to the quarters, then went to a gym, where Kelse would begin forming them into a squad.

She was left out and she didn't like it.

There was sex and loving that night, but despite that, Fern thought the day had ended overall on a low note.

Kelse wasn't the same hopeful man she'd last seen smiling down at her before the cryogenics mist weighted her eyelids. She'd loved the change in him once he'd discovered the colonization project. For that, more than anything else, she'd gone along with the plan. She'd wanted to leave NJNY and the USTATES for the Southern Confederation. Kelse had been sure there was no place on Earth that the USTATES assassins couldn't find and quietly kill them—just in case Kelse decided to return. And Kelse's stature was such that people would want him to mix into politics. The colonization scheme had been a perfect plan.

Now they were Awakened before the ship had landed, and Kelse was back in "battle-hardened warrior" mode.

The next morning they awoke to a bouncy jingle and a vid of Dirk Lascom.

"Greetings, friends and supporters!" Dirk flashed a gleaming, cheerful smile. "It's me, Dirk Lascom of the Ships for Ourselves party." His expression saddened, but there remained glee in his eyes. "Our meeting with Kelse Bountry didn't go as well as we wished yesterday."

Kelse cursed and rolled from bed. "Gotta see if I can break his speech like he broke mine." He stomped to the closet and yanked on his uniform, took a brush from a drawer, and pulled it through his hair. Then he was behind the console, muttering low commands and fingers jabbing programs to tie in with Dirk's vid.

Eight

Bountry revealed that the public records regarding the wormhole events in our ship's past were falsified." Now Dirk Lascom's hands fisted. "We have been lied to all along." He shook his head. "But we must recall that those who funded their precious mission to colonize another planet were criminals. They *can't* return to Earth. But other Earth colonies and ships waiting through the wormhole would welcome *us*. We'll be able to pick up more fuel, more food, live on a planet or make *our ships* exactly as we want them—colony *ships*." Lascom spread his hands. "Let's consider all our options." Another shake of his head. "The options they've left us with after burning our resources." His eyes flickered to the left. "Signing off."

Kelse missed the hookup by two seconds. When his image flooded the screens, Fern winced. He was in fearsome mode. "Greetyou, friends and fellow travelers. I will be courteous and respond to Dirk Lascom as he has styled himself, the leader of the Ship for Ourselves party." Kelse's voice scraped roughly from him. No, he wasn't nearly as charming.

"Yes, we were outlaws. Every one of us was with the psi underground. We were born with Flair and we used it. For that we were persecuted. How many of you have Flair now? Would you chance to go back to a place that may have wiped out every person who had psi? Government-approved persecution of people with Flair had begun. Mobs were organized against us. We wanted peace, not violence. But violence has found all of us here on our ship." He drew a breath and his chest expanded. The dark green shirt with minimal insignia—two golden leaves on the upright collar—suited him. He looked solid, authoritative. A man you could trust.

Fern was pretty sure that even as the dimmest crew member, she would trust Kelse over Dirk.

"As for the falsification of records, I would remind you that two hundred forty-five years ago most of the people on this ship did not consider it home." Kelse's silvery glance met hers. Were they the only people alive now who didn't consider *Nuada's Sword* home? She thought so. "We are on a starship. If those people panicked, there was nothing but their home to wreck, their very livelihood. So less dire records were given to them."

"Offer them Captain Whitecloud's log and journal notes about the event and situation," Fern said. "They're touching." She'd found them so. His worry for his community, the son he'd convinced to come with him. The Captain's line still lived, and she was glad of that, because she'd liked him. A wisp of memory touched her, but Kelse was speaking again.

"I will make Captain Whitecloud's log and journal public regarding the first and second wormhole events." He paused. "Also a translation of panglish and cursive handwriting." A line grooved between his brows. "I am pleased to announce that I have chosen ten fine men as new security guards." He reeled off the names. "They are here to protect you. To protect us all. But since the disappearance of Jose Moncrief, Altai Rye, and Sid Beranik, I hope that you will protect them, too. If you see them being provoked and attacked, notify me via the ship intercom or photo them with your handhelds. We do not want any more people vanishing on this ship." He'd cautioned the new men against being arrogant, and to be aware of the people around them, and not to go off with anyone they didn't know. "That said, I hope you are enjoying the new menus of the cafeterias and your visits to the great Greensward.

I've approved the requests for painting the cafeterias and private quarters. Blessed be to each and every one of you."

The vid faded and Kelse cursed again, scrubbed his face. "A fliggering propaganda war."

"Looks like it," Fern said. She walked over and put her arms around him. He held her and rubbed his chin on her head.

"Did I do wrong in answering him?"

"He's one of them, born and bred. You're the outsider. I don't think you can afford to ignore him. You have to be seen and accessible. Kiet Moungala wasn't."

Kelse grunted. "Sooner or later Dirk and his men will slip up and I'll pounce. I'm not forgetting the dead."

"No, of course not."

"But this word war is a damn nuisance." He stepped away and looked down at her, smiling, and her heart simply turned over. "I found my old sweats in the corner of the closet."

"You mean your rags?"

"I knew you'd unpacked them because you had yours." He glanced at the time on the console. "We have an hour before breakfast in the cafeteria, let's work out."

They'd made love twice in the night, but that had been slow and easy and aching.

"How are you feeling?" he asked.

"Fine," she said, lifted to kiss him on the mouth. "Fine."

He searched her face and nodded. "We were always good at living in the moment."

"Yes."

For the next week, every day, at some part of the day, Dirk Lascom would broadcast allegations against Kelse and Fern, the sleepers, the other Captains, and the mission.

Usually Kelse tapped into the agitator's vid before he was done—and Dirk rarely answered Kelse.

The ship was energized by the messages, and the crew viewed them as prime entertainment. Which was dangerous because they were enjoying Dirk and didn't think of him as a deadly threat.

On the whole, though, Fern believed Kelse's side was winning. Julianna Ambroz, with her grandmotherly look, her sharp scientific mind, and especially the dress she wore, made a good impression.

The youth, Randolph Ash, also appeared by vid one morning after Dirk spoke smoothly about wormholes. He glanced often to the side of the vid, as if needing encouragement. Again he stated that he believed the current, ever-nearing wormhole could lead to *civilized* space. But he didn't have the same passion for the notion as previously. Fern wasn't surprised. Randolph and Chloe were speaking again, and she could have translated the engineering specs and Whitecloud's log easily for him.

That led to Fern's particular favorite response of Kelse's. He'd looked out of his vid with a mocking smile, and asked, "What makes you think we won't all go *boom*?" Kelse had mimicked an explosion, closed hands flying apart, with excellent sound effects.

The wormhole wasn't mentioned after that.

Her Kelse had never been a speaker, but Fern found herself impressed with him. At least on the vid. He continued to shut her out, which led to her own irritation and anger at him . . . a nasty cycle. She'd ask about his feelings, minimize her own, and they'd hold on to each other with despair and make love with desperation.

Then the first results of the probes they'd sent to the planets of the white star returned.

Fern and Kelse consulted with the other Captains in the large conference room. All her nerves shivered under her skin, and the hair on her nape rose as the opaque window was filled with the white star's solar system, and almost straight ahead, the other two systems they were headed for. Those seemed very far away.

Kelse had invited a representative of the Ship for Ourselves party to the meeting. To Fern's surprise, Randolph Ash showed up. He appeared more pale than ever, with dark circles under his eyes. Confronting hard truths did that.

She and Kelse shared a look, then Kelse's eyes narrowed and he smiled. Dirk had made a mistake in sending a man who was having doubts about his cause. Kelse would capitalize on that.

"Preliminary shots of the planet appear good," Umar Clague, the Captain of *Lugh's Spear*, said. He was old now, but just as stern. He and Kelse had never gotten along because Umar had been in the military. It appeared they'd resolved their differences.

"We've received the mini samples from the sixth planet. They're . . . acceptable," Julianna said gravely.

"What's your concern?" asked Kelse.

"The atmosphere seems fine. The gravity measurements very close to Earth normal, slightly more than one grav." Her face relaxed in a smile. "If we land, those who are Awakened could tell no difference."

"But?"

"I don't like the looks of the mixture of soil and atmosphere and sea. There are combinations that concern me."

"In what way?"

"There could be effects upon us that aren't noticeable at first but could be cumulative."

"Looks beautiful to me," Umar said truculently.

Julianna drew in a breath. "I vote we don't risk it. We want a home, not a planet that will kill us. The other solar systems are more promising. We've got probes back from them, too. Definitely fourteen worlds considered in habitable zones."

Fern wanted to fiddle with something, square the sheets of the reports, pick up the writestick and roll it in her fingers. She didn't. She'd learned stillness from Kelse. But she spoke, "Fourteen planets," she agreed. "But the farthest ones are the most promising."

"And that's close to being too far for our fuel reserves," Kelse said softly.

Randolph spoke for the first time. "I would like to see the probes' data." His jaw firmed and he stared at each one of the Captains. "All the data, and unfiltered."

"Sure," Kelse said. "Streaming our data to *Lugh's Spear*, *Arianrhod's Wheel*, my console, nose bridge, and Randolph Ash."

"Same," said Umar.

"Ditto," said Julianna. Then she turned to stare at Kelse. "Surely you don't think we should change course for the white star, take such a chance. We only have one shot at this—the white star or the good systems."

"I think we should launch a lab," Kelse said.

Fern's spine stiffened in surprise. He hadn't spoken to her about this, and he should have. As far as she knew, she was the most experienced person with a planetary laboratory.

"We only have one lab. I forbid—" Julianna stopped, but her face had flushed and gone hard. "I strongly recommend saving the lab for later."

"I'll consider it," Kelse said.

Julianna inclined her head.

Umar cleared his throat. "The anticipated time to reach the new systems for close scrutiny is two years?"

"For optimal testing, twenty-two months, nine days," Julianna said.

"And we would land shortly after, say within another six months?" Umar pressed.

An uneasy expression passed over Julianna's face, but she said, "That was always the timetable, though I believe that eight months might be a better schedule for an unknown planet, and that was agreed at the beginning of my term."

"That's two and a half years. I have an announcement. I plan on Awakening our Pilot, Netra Sunaya Hoku. He will take the title of Captain, though I, of course, will still consult."

Julianna shifted. "You're anticipating that we will find a good planet to colonize."

"I'm expecting that we will find home. Our Celta." Umar stared at her a full ten seconds. "Julianna, you may have other alternatives, but neither I nor Kelse do, our fuel will run out. That's a fact." Umar looked at Kelse. "Though I will say that I, personally, like the idea of less time on the ship, and wish the news about the sixth planet was better." He gave a sitting bow. "Merry meet."

"And merry part," Fern echoed along with Julianna. Kelse lagged; he'd come late to their spiritual beliefs and the culture they'd create on their planet.

If they ever made landfall.

* * *

That night Kelse couldn't sleep. He'd made tender love to Fern, and she had responded, but he knew there was distance between them. He wasn't sure why that was, only that it existed and he didn't know how to breach it. If he had the time. He'd never had so many lives resting on his shoulders. He didn't like it. Especially since they were civilian lives—soft, regular people . . . with psi power.

Everyone who joined the psi underground knew they would be a soldier, knew they were fighting for their people. Knew their lives could be forfeit.

Not here in the ship. This morning he'd officiated at a Naming—and had been appalled that he'd had to hold a newborn. He was sure that hadn't shown, and Fern had watched on, smiling, but the event had twisted something inside him.

That baby's fate rested in his hands.

He wasn't sure he could bear the thought, and it seemed to him that he was shoving too many thoughts and emotions away until the box they were in would soon burst.

So he gazed down on his love, his Fern, for a moment, then put on his raggedy sweats and walked the hidden way to the gym. He wasn't too surprised to see Peaches in the walkway.

He's making a mistake, the FamCat said.

"Randolph?" Kelse asked.

"Yessss." The cat actually hissed the word. Kelse was impressed.

Peaches thrashed his tail. *I am Randolph's FamCat. I am loyal to him.*

"Of course. But he's making a mistake."

He wanted better conditions for all. Others who pretend to be friends don't want this. Don't believe in the mission or a new planet. They only want power and chaos here.

A scenario Kelse was all too aware of. Time and again, the psi community would splinter, with others leaving in anger to find and found "a better way."

Yet the more they splintered, the less power and community and sense of common destiny they had. And those who hated the psis found them weak and easy prey. That had been going on for a good century until the plan to emigrate evolved and Kelse and the others jumped on it. Even then, they'd had to fight to buy the ships and supplies, hire the crews, launch.

"You want me to help Randolph Ash."

He is not listening to Me. The cat sniffed. *The Bad Ones hide what they want from him but not from Me. They talk when I am around. Make fun of Randolph.*

Dirk wants power, to rule. But sees too little. He does not have the skill or Flair or knowledge to make things better. Only to rule until we all die. More tail thrashing. *I do not want to die. But We must fix things soon!*

"I agree. The time will come when Randolph and I need to trust each other. Be there."

I go now.

Kelse bowed to him. "Later."

Peaches rose and swaggered off. He glanced over his shoulder and licked his whiskers. *I like the new fish in sauce.*

"Good to hear." That's what would win him the crew. Providing better food, more motivation.

Kelse only hoped it would be enough.

Nine

The next morning the vid bleeped on early. Again.

Fern figured Dirk and his supporters knew her and Kelse's schedule somehow. Usually they would be making love. Unfortunately that wasn't the case. Kelse was already gone and she was alone.

Dirk's cheerful face gave way to a somber Randolph, who appeared as if he hadn't slept, eaten, or changed clothes since he'd received the analyses from the probes. His black hair stuck up, and he read from a prepared statement.

"Yesterday I was privileged to be in a consultation with the other Captains of the starships when we discussed the results of the probe to the two planets of the nearby white star." He gestured a little limply. Tired and worn. The background behind him showed the star system. "One planet is not habitable. The other showed signs of acceptability. There were soil and plant samples that indicate the First Ones who seeded the galaxy visited the planet."

He coughed. "But they seeded many planets and some do not match with humanity. I have concluded after long study of the analyses of the probes that planet six, too, is not habitable."

Fern went cold, pulled a cover over herself. She wanted Kelse. He was in the gym working with the security team.

Randolph's gaze slid to someone off camera. "The Ship for Ourselves party wants to continue our journey, not colonize any planet." He bit his lower lip. "Yet we need more resources to fulfill that goal. We need fuel." His young voice rasped. "But we have the technology to make more fuel. Or will." He lifted red eyes. "There is a large asteroid field just before we reach the two star systems. We can mine the asteroids."

His hands trembled. Fern stared. No one had done much more than their usual jobs on the ship. No one had the skills to move in space, to use whatever tools *Nuada's Sword* carried to mine asteroids.

"But, by my calculations, we will need a . . . trace . . . more energy to reach the field." He licked his lips. "We will be working on options to develop this energy."

Fear slithered through Fern like an army of snakes, making her tremble. Dirk had just upped the stakes, and targeted the sleepers. Now that the crew was wary of wormhole travel, he would be pounding on the amount of energy the cryonics bay drew.

Randolph stared away from the camera and ended with, "Whether we wish to mine the asteroids or find a planet to settle, we need more energy."

Kelse replied immediately, calm, controlled, in command. "I do not accept that we should mine the asteroid fields for fuel to continue fruitless travel. I still believe in the mission. However, if the Ships for Ourselves party are contemplating resources and mining asteroids, I suggest they consider who has experience with such things. Which would be people in the cryonics bay. All our people in sleep stasis have skills to help build a colony. Otherwise they wouldn't be here. There are also experts on our fellow starships, *Lugh's Spear* and *Arianrhod's Wheel*, but they, of course, will only help if they believe the overall mission is being followed, and no one is harmed here. Blessed be."

A minute later Kelse slammed through the access panel that led from the gym to their quarters. "Lord and Lady, I *hate* that Lascom." His hands fisted. "If this was Earth I'd challenge him to a deathfight."

"It's not Earth," Fern said.

"He dances around me," Kelse said, frowning. "Like I danced around the prez of the USTATES. Never thought I'd have an ounce of sympathy for that man."

"We can't censor him or stop the broadcasts."

"No. He'd gain too many followers. Rumor would warp everything we did. And it isn't right to stop him. Except he's a liar and murderer." Kelse flung off his clothes and headed for the shower. "Politics," Kelse snarled. "Now I have to waste my time soothing every-damn-body today."

It took Kelse two days to reassure the ship's crew enough that they once again believed in him, despite Dirk's daily rantings.

Neither Kelse nor Chloe nor Fern could deny that the cryonics bay used a lot of energy. There'd been an attack on the door again, and she and Kelse had reinforced the door with psi power—Flair. She didn't know how he did it, but she loaned him some of her strength. It seemed as if the bond between them was almost tangible, as if it could be seen. For all too few minutes.

Fern had the idea of playing vids of each sleeper for the crew. Short pieces showing an individual happy, laughing—then their tube. "Helpless and dependent upon the ship, and you, whom she trusts." Fern only hoped that individualizing the sleepers was the right thing to do.

Yet the next afternoon she walked into their quarters after weeding in the great Greensward, and Kelse was sitting on the bed, head in his hands. Or he was for an instant. The moment he saw her, he rose and put on that impassive expression she was beginning to loathe. He'd never used it on her before . . . before this hideous time.

"Tell me what's wrong," she asked.

He went to the console and punched at an icon. The window changed from wall to a view of the white star system and the two other systems beyond. They still looked too far away. All of them.

And too cold.

She still didn't like looking out at space. Had to concentrate on not hyperventilating. But Kelse seemed to need the view, especially when he was brooding. The wall was space most of the time.

This wasn't a panorama that they would see from the ship, since the white star system was actually on their right, but a visual if all the systems were lined up.

Kelse's jaw flexed a couple of times, then he said with suppressed anger, "The two systems with the fourteen planets are too far. I know it in my gut." He waved at the burning white star. "That's our best chance. It isn't the one I'd choose, but it's our best option if we want to live. If we want our mission to succeed." He prowled along the wall, and she noticed with a jolt that he'd lost weight. He'd fined down to pure muscle.

When he turned to her, his eyes burnt as intensely as the sun. "It's wrong to continue on. I know it. We need to take the chance we have."

"The First Ones who seeded the galaxy, Earth, also seeded that planet. That's a good sign," she said softly.

He cast her a cynical look. "I know. But like Randolph said, they seeded many planets and many aren't compatible with ours." Kelse snorted. "They had more than one packet of seeds." He rubbed one of his scars. "I could fight Julianna, convince her to believe me. Umar would go along, too. But I. Can't. Fight. My. Own. People."

"And they believe Randolph."

"And Randolph wants to be sure. There *are* no certainties in this matter. None. There are only gut feelings and I don't trust Julianna's or Randolph's gut."

Fern moved close to him, was afraid if she put a comforting hand on his arm he'd flick it off as he'd been doing, and that fact made her eyes sting. But she kept her lashes lowered so he wouldn't see that he was hurting her. Kept her voice steady. "Go talk to Randolph."

"That won't work."

"Take him the probe samples."

Finally he looked her in the eyes. "What?"

"He's seen statistics, data. Let him see soil, dirt like he's seen in the great Greensward. There were a few plant samples, let him see and touch green." She made her mouth smile. "There was even a minuscule turd. Give him the samples."

Kelse's eyes went distant as he considered, then he nodded to her. "Good thinking." He went to the door. "I'll give him ours, and if he needs more, I'll make Julianna send a packet and Umar translocate one." The corners of Kelse's mouth turned up. "But if the samples hurt him, we're doomed," Kelse ended almost cheerfully. He walked out of the door with an absent greeting to the guards.

And no kiss for her.

They were doomed already.

A few minutes later she'd gathered her ragged emotions and cobbled them together. Somehow she and Kelse might find a way back to each other when this was over. But anger flared. She was supposed to be his support in the bad times, too.

She hated that they'd been Awakened. Hated that these problems had come between them. Hated that she was angry at him and was hiding her own emotions—fear and anger—from him.

So she sucked it all in, the fear and anger, the distress. And decided to work on a plan of her own.

Kelse sent a message to Randolph that he wanted to meet him in the conference room. To ensure good faith, Kelse asked that Peaches join him as his escort.

First Kelse took a personnel folder and tucked it under his arm. He stopped by the landing bay that held the probes. Here, too, the crew was more educated, dedicated. They wanted to give him *the best* samples from the probe. Rumor circulated fast through the ship and Kelse didn't want word to reach Randolph that the samples were chosen.

As soon as he left the bay, he saw the cat and crew members. "Thank you, Peaches, for meeting me."

He glooms. Peaches finished a last lick on his chest hair, then stood and began strolling toward Conference Room B.

Kelse nodded to the watching crew members and said, "I'm meeting with the FamCat's companion, Randolph Ash." He lifted the bag he carried. "Actual samples from the probe of planet six of the white star."

That caused enough buzz in the small crowd that he knew the

info would spread through the ship in minutes. Tightening his hand on the grip of the heavy bag, he watched for trouble, as always. The bag could be a weapon.

But they arrived at the conference room without incident. A security officer was stationed at the door.

Kelse opened the door for the cat, then followed Peaches in.

The eighteen-year-old slouched in his chair. He still wore the clothes of the day before. Uniform pants of red, something that looked like a white T-shirt.

"You're making things worse. Not better," Kelse said.

"I know." That was barely a whisper.

Kelse wanted to pounce on the boy and shake him hard, but that wouldn't help. Instead he sat across from Randolph and studied the youngster in silence. Randolph didn't seem to know or care.

The door opened and Chloe stepped in. Her expression was worried.

"Welcome, Chloe," Kelse said.

"I want to take notes," she said.

"Of course," Kelse said.

She looked at her grandson, hesitated, then went to the end of the six-person table and discreetly turned her recorder on.

"There was an attack on the cryonics bay two nights ago. You don't know anything about that, do you?"

Randolph jerked, looked up, shook his head. "No."

"I didn't think so. The alarm rang, but the cameras were mysteriously blurred. So, once more, we can't identify the culprits."

Has bad friends, Peaches said.

Randolph winced.

Kelse let the silence stretch, but it had little effect on Randolph. The cat was right, he was drowning in gloom.

"Here's the woman you want." Kelse slid him the hardcopy.

"Woman?" Randolph said blankly.

"Woman. You should know from your grandmother's example"—Kelse nodded at Chloe—"that women can be of formidable intelligence, organization, strength." He thought of his own Fern and ached. The problems of the ship and his people kept his mind spinning, never quiet, an experience that hadn't happened to him since he was the age of the youngster before him. Kelse had proceeded gradually up the ladder of the psi underground, learning as a follower what would be expected of him as a leader. After he was solid in his life, he'd met Fern, could handle the distraction of love. That was then, this was now. Trying to be a good Captain was screwing up his relationship with Fern. He pulled his mind back on task.

"The good news is that she's had a great deal of experience, including setting up an asteroid mine, as well as mining remotely. She's with us because most of the areas of Earth had decided to forego any further space exploration. As you know, there are great resources in space—but the governments didn't find them cost effective." Kelse used his knife smile. "The bad news . . ."

"More bad news," Randolph said dully.

"Yes. The bad news is that Lydia Herda is not aboard *Nuada's Sword*. She is in the small cryogenics bay of *Lugh's Spear.* Also bad for the Ship for Ourselves party is that Umar Clague, the Captain of that ship, runs the *Spear* on military principles. He is not, nor ever will be, sympathetic to your cause. And if you begin killing people in the cryonics bay, he'll see you in hell before he'd cooperate with you. Me, though, he understands. We share the same values." Different methods but same values.

Randolph looked at the folder, the pretty woman with platinum blond hair. He didn't pick it up. "Doesn't matter."

Kelse stilled. "And why is that?"

The youth-becoming-man stared at Kelse with a hopeless expression. His eyes appeared even more red-veined in person. "I . . . fibbed . . . the other morning. We don't have the fuel to get to the asteroid belt. I don't understand it. It's not only the wormholes effect on our fuel cells. Something else happened when the second Captain took over. I don't know what, but it significantly slowed all our systems, particularly repair. We don't have enough energy." He tossed a red and glowing memory button on the table; it activated and scrolled pages of columns of figures.

"No?"

"Even . . ." His gaze glanced off Kelse's. "Even if we . . . uh . . . disable the cryonics bay . . . um, Awaken everyone—"

"Is that what Dirk said he'd do? He's lying to you, Randolph."

"No!"

Yes! said Peaches, and Chloe said, "Yes!" at the same time.

Time to shake the boy out of his funk. Kelse had to infuse his own sense of purpose into Randolph. And Kelse could do intense determination all day. Every second of every minute of every day. He'd been determined all his life. He wouldn't let anyone take his dream from him, even if he gasped his last breath here.

He leaned close. "I don't think we're doomed. Not yet. I want to live, and I want my friends to live. And I want your help."

"You've hoarded the resources. You've squandered them!" Randolph burst out with the standard phrase of Ship for Ourselves. "You don't know what it's like—"

Kelse cut him off with a gesture. "From what I've seen, the resources have been managed well. You can judge. You're now in charge of them."

"What?"

"I will give you everything you need to figure out the fuel problem, help find a viable planet for colonization." If his eyes could burn from the inside, they were. They felt hot enough. "And since you think we're doomed, if there's a trade-off of years on the ship versus a great effort to find and colonize a planet, I want the new world."

"The energy to keep the sleepers safe . . ."

"Will continue to be used. If we're doomed on the ship, we need to get off. You know the ship and its life and its people. But what do you know about living on a planet? Those people in the cryonics bay were chosen carefully. They *know* how to survive on a planet." Kelse's mouth twisted. "Hell, even I might survive. But you've never even been outside the walls of this ship. Imagine that."

Randolph shuddered, and Kelse wondered how many of the crew were agoraphobes. How many would he lose from madness once they landed? He needed some way to accustom them to life outside the ship. If there was a chance.

"What information do you need?" he asked.

The youngster looked dazed.

Kelse grabbed the youngster's upper arms and pulled him to his feet, went to the wall where an aux center was stowed. He opened it, swiped his hand over the system board. Picked up Randolph's limp fingers. "Randolph Ash is now authorized to access all databases. Randolph, you can see exactly what our resources are, and all the starcharts."

"I can't. We can't."

"We *will*."

Peaches hopped onto the fold-down computer and stared at Randolph. *You are not thinking right. You are feeling instead of thinking and that is bad for you. You can't fix things when that happens.* The cat wrinkled his nose. *You smell.*

Randolph flushed.

"Go to your quarters and sleep, Randolph," Chloe said. "Things will look better then."

Kelse lifted the bag to the table. "These are the actual samples from planet six of the white star. Check them out."

Randolph stared. "You don't want to go on to the two systems."

Kelse rolled a shoulder.

"You're mad."

"I'm Captain. We need all our resources to save us all, that includes your hard head. Find a way, Randolph."

"I can't—"

Kelse put his hand on the young man's shoulder and squeezed. "What you can't do is think negatively."

Captain is right. Come ON, FamMan, Peaches said.

And Chloe was there, putting her arm around Randolph. She flicked her fingers at the bag and it rose on an anti-grav spell. "You'll eat, then sleep. Then we'll *live*, right, Kelse?"

"Right," Kelse said, trying not to look at the memory button and the figures that blurred and blackened, then winked out.

Fern sank to the middle of the carpet in front of the comm console, breathing deeply and letting her tumultuous emotions calm, then sift away from her. There was something deep in her mind that fear and hurt had prevented her from recalling. Now was the time to find it.

Ten

Nuada's Sword had only one functioning lab station.

But they had another that had a glitch. Some flaw that no one now understood or could fix. It was nanotech and should have been able to mend itself, but it hadn't. If only some other entity . . . A wisp of a memory beckoned, and she followed. Spiraled in on words she'd heard . . . "Most are but this one is male . . ."

Such an odd sentence.

Then she recalled the day she'd toured *Nuada's Sword*. She'd hated everything except the great Greensward, and the first Captain, Anthony Whitecloud, had understood that. He'd taken time from his own duties to show her a tiny grotto in the Greensward. He'd pressed her hand. "I'll be fine, Fern." He looked around him, waved a hand. "I have a wonderful place."

"I'm sorry Sylvia couldn't have seen this," Fern said. His wife had died the year before, right after they'd decided to become Colonists, defending her home.

"I am, too. But she'd be glad that I was going. That I'd be the first Captain. My son will be in stasis sleep like you, but I have the Ship."

"What?"

"The Ship, *Nuada's Sword*, for company."

She stared at him. “The Ship!”

“He’s a nanotech Ship and has the capacity for intelligence.”

“He? Aren’t ships usually considered female?”

“Most are, but this one is male. Deciding that proves intelligence. Is that right, Ship?” Whitecloud winked at Fern.

“Yes, Captain Whitecloud.” A hollow voice, which sounded like a multitude of voices, said from nearby.

Whitecloud chuckled. “There’s a speaker installed by the bench. Ship, this is Fern Bountry.”

“Greetings, Fern Bountry. My data says that you are assisting Chung with the planetary lab.”

“Yes,” she replied cautiously.

“And your husband is a warrior of renown.”

Fern glanced at the Captain. He wiggled his brows.

“Yes,” she said.

“Kelse Bountry is on board now, making suggestions for My defense at dock. This is well done.”

She blinked at that. “Thank you.”

“You will be in berths twenty and twenty-one in the cryonics bay.”

She shivered. “That’s right.”

“We will have a good trip,” the Captain said. “Like I said, I have the Ship.”

Time faded back from the beauty of hope to the scariness of now.

Fern couldn’t risk the only good laboratory station. But if she could activate the other . . . if she could activate *the Ship* to instruct the planetary lab on how to repair itself . . .

She knew now what had been bothering her. The Ship should have been intelligent. Instead it seemed as if it had slept, too. “Ship?” she asked.

No response.

She marched to Kelse’s command computer. Two hours later, Fern found out what had happened. The Ship’s autonomy function had been turned off when the first Captain had died. Which was a hideous shame because it could have warned more loudly of problems, warned in voice instead of other ways that had been overlooked.

In fact, now that she studied the records, the speed had begun to deteriorate after the Ship's Autonomous Intelligence Module had been closed down. Terrible.

It made sense to awaken *Nuada's Sword*. Surely in the Ship itself, they would have an ally.

"Display the manual and step-by-step instructions for reinitiating the Autonomous Intelligence Module," Fern ordered.

And it was all there, and there was an auxiliary switch . . . in the Captain's Quarters.

It was a long and irritating process that had her swearing and pacing and swearing and banging her fist against the wall as she fumbled through the codes and manually opened panels and slide doors and flicked tiny nubbin switches. Had her sweaty.

Finally she'd done all she could and closed everything up and lay on her back under Kelse's desk.

There was a new hum around her. Kelse wouldn't like it.

"Who is in the Captain's Quarters?" came the multitude of voices that deepened into one malelike tone.

"Fern Bountry and Kelse Bountry. I suggest you scan all your systems reports."

"We have been unconscious for two hundred and ten years!"

Fern didn't doubt the Ship lived now. "I know how you feel."

"We are proceeding slowly."

"We have problems. Furthermore, we are trying to determine whether the sixth planet of the star system of the white sun is acceptable for habitation."

"We did not make landfall on the original planet."

"No."

"You are right, We must check all Our systems and understand what has transpired."

Clearing her throat, Fern said, "I would like you to also check out planetary laboratory station two, and whether you can repair it or instruct it how to repair itself."

"Our stores are not acceptable. I will begin—"

"Wait! The morale of the crew is low. We—you—must proceed carefully. I order that you divert only the most minor amounts of energy possible to any systems."

"If We divert more energy, We can repair and recondition systems faster."

"Not if the crew stops you again. Not if I'm forced to turn the AIM off again."

"You wouldn't do that!" it whispered, and Fern thought she almost heard fear.

"I may have to. Umm, consider this a secret between you and me. Unless there's an emergency."

A low buzz, then, "Very well, Fern. You turned Me back on. I will trust you."

"Good," she muttered as the doors opened for Kelse. "Because I am trusting you."

Something was different about the ship . . . and about the crew. Kelse couldn't put his finger on it except that there seemed to be an additional, nearly subsonic hum. A hum that increased his vitality.

And for the first time in a week and a half, there was no broadcast by Dirk Lascom and the Ship for Ourselves party. He did note a gathering of some of the public members and another sort of buzz—anger—from them. They'd requested privacy, so he couldn't turn on vid or audio monitoring of their room, only watch little icons move. He thought about spies and whether he'd be able to squelch the conspiracy before it turned into a real widespread mutiny.

Chloe knocked on the door, then entered and glanced around the room. "Where's Fern?"

Kelse gestured to a tapestry and the portal behind it. "In the Greensward." As usual. He'd anticipated that she would gravitate there, but not having her close . . . ruffled his aura.

"Ah," Chloe said and actually slipped her handheld into her pants pocket. She clenched her hands together. "I wanted to thank you for being . . . lenient with Randolph."

"I can't afford to be hard on him. We need him. But other than that, I like . . . his FamCat."

Chloe frowned. "Peaches."

"That's right. And anyone with a brain, such as Dirk Lascom, would keep Randolph in the dark about violence. I think you did a good job on his morals."

"He doesn't want to think his friends would do such things," she said sadly.

"He hasn't learned of betrayal," Kelse said. His shoulders shifted; he didn't want to recall that lesson of his childhood.

"No," Chloe said, shrugging. "They lie to him and he believes." Her voice sank. "I worry for him, now that he is with us."

"He has a friend in one of the security guards. I've told the man to protect Randolph."

"Thank you." She inhaled deeply. "You really think we can get out of this mess?"

"You're the one with hunches. What do you think?" he shot back.

She looked startled, then answered immediately, running with her Flair, "I think I woke you just in time."

"There it is, then."

She searched his face, but another thing he couldn't afford to do was show any of the hideous doubts that gnawed on his gut and made his heart beat quickly. To no one. Especially Fern.

His love believed in him and what he could do. He didn't want to tell her he secretly thought they'd all die.

It was late, and Kelse was asleep. He wasn't holding her and tears coated Fern's throat, threatened to overflow her eyes and dampen the bed she shared with him—apart.

She'd been aware that Kelse had slipped from bed last night and had stopped pretending to be asleep after he'd left. He hadn't been gone long, and when he'd returned, she knew he'd been working out again. She didn't know what demons drove him because he wouldn't say, even when she asked.

Did she look that frightened to him? Did he feel her fear?

Thinking back—a month or two hundred and fifty years, and she shuddered at that—he'd especially opened up when he'd heard of the colonization project. So enthusiastic, full of hope. Until then, she hadn't realized he'd lived without hope, had considered he was fighting a rearguard action to survive, and have his friends, his people with psi, survive.

He'd been the one to believe in the colonization idea first. She had been more cautious. Could that be ripping at him? Of course.

This was not what they had planned. They'd boarded *Nuada's Sword* hand in hand, walked with their friends in triumph to the cryonics lab. That had been daunting, but cryonics had already proven itself if done well and expensively. There, in a small cubicle dressing room, she and Kelse had undressed each other and shared a last wonderful kiss.

She had been the one to be processed first, because she was the most fearful. She'd wanted Kelse's hand on her arm as she fell asleep. And when she was barely conscious and the tube had slid shut and the fog of the chemicals had begun to fill it, she still had the last sight of Kelse's gray eyes, his loving gaze fixed on her face.

Now she was Awake again, and not because the Ship had made a jubilant landfall and they were all at their new home. No, they were lost in the blackness of space, stars of many hues whirling by.

Whatever toughness she'd had in the psi underground—which she'd understood—was eroding away here. She'd have to find it and grab it and pull it back inside her.

Kelse had changed. He'd been strong when she'd first met him, a leader in the underground psi community, striving to stay alive. But he had never been so closed down, so uncommunicative, as he was today.

Now it was time for her to sneak out, and act.

She moved through the back ways of the Ship to the space where the planetary laboratories were. The storage area was large and dark and empty. She summoned a spell-light.

The lab itself was about the size of a small house and loaded with instruments. There was room inside for two people to stand. Fern and the Ship talked through the problems, then she worked both inside and out for several hours. Finally she hooked it up to the Ship for additional corrections. "When can I launch it for the white star?"

"I'll give it coordinates. For the best trajectory and course, I anticipate the launch to be best done at six bells."

"Six A.M.?"

"That would be the time you're familiar with." Ship sounded irritated. Probably because it couldn't launch the lab itself.

Fern sighed. "You'll move the lab to the landing bay, then wake me twenty minutes before I should launch it?"

"Yes."

"Thank you, Ship."

"Thank you, Fern," it whispered in its multivoice.

When she returned, Kelse reached for her and said, "Where have you been?" He nuzzled her, and she wanted nothing more than to be with him. "You smell slightly . . . metallic."

"Come with me," she said instead, and rose again and took his hand. "I have a place in the Greensward I want to show you."

"Oh?" His voice was light but held an undertone of arousal. He left his shirt, but slipped on his pants.

They went to the access passage and down to the Greensward. It was night there, too, most of the enormous mirrors hidden, just enough to simulate Earth starlight. Dim starlight now by all her new standards. She'd worked on the grotto today, clearing out the hanging streamers of green that had hidden it and trimming the circle of grass. She'd cleaned up the bench and verified the speaker worked.

But the pathway was still rough, and she hoped she could find the grotto, hoped it was as beautiful as it seemed.

Hoped Kelse would like it, too. He didn't spend much time in the Greensward.

"Spell-light," she murmured, and a fuzzy yellow globe coalesced and lit their way.

"Yes." His hand was strong on hers, his feet certain on the trail. He was awake, and once again she sensed a tangible bond between them. Was it only in the night when they were more vulnerable that they could feel such a connection? She wanted it always.

Then his fingers dropped from hers and his arm came around her waist as the path led up the artificial hillside that was close to one of the Ship's walls. They wound along the trail and then, before them, was the arch of the entrance, covered so heavily in vines that it appeared natural.

With waves of her free hand, Fern lit tinier spell-lights, more like busy fireflies. The area wasn't large, only about four meters by four, and circular.

Kelse bent under the branches, eyed the bench, and drew her away from it. "Beautiful. Beautiful place for my beautiful woman."

His words vibrated through her. The bond between them pulsed with yearning.

Eleven

She turned to him and put her hands on his shoulders, felt his tensile strength. The contours of his body were so familiar to her hands. She could see only a gleam in his eyes, not the color or the shape, but knew his gaze was fixed on her. She lifted her hand and brushed a thumb over his lips and he went still, waiting. Her body knew this kind of waiting. Her breath came faster, her thigh muscles loosened. Then, through that pulsing golden bond between them, she realized that their hearts beat in the same rhythm. Miraculous.

His hands came up to cradle hers. He took one and kissed the palm, his tongue tickling the hollow of her hand and sending fire to her sex.

"Kelse." There was so much she wanted to say, and she could find only the form of his name on her lips. "Kelse." Then, "Love."

"Yes," he said huskily, "Love."

His fingers touched her shoulders, trailed over her collarbone to her throat and the opening of her shirt. He slipped his thumb down the front tab, and her clothing parted noiselessly. Just his feather touch along her skin had her moaning. Her shirt fell to the grass and its slight disturbance sent the fragrance of newly cut greenery into the air.

Kelse's chest rumbled with satisfaction. Slowly she traced the length of his torso with her fingernails, was rewarded with a low groan. He'd always liked that, and pleasuring him pleased her.

He cupped her breasts, finding her nipples with his thumbs, stroked, and she arched. Her lower body pressed against his and dampened as she felt the length and thickness of his sex. She couldn't keep her eyes open, her need was so great.

So she let herself go, let him hold her. Let him lower her to the grass and strip her of her pants.

His fingers went to the seat of her desire, parted, played, thrust until she was moaning and twisting. Vaguely, she remembered that she'd wanted to give him the gift of loving seduction, but it was he . . . he . . . Kelse, caring for her.

Yet, she needed the touch of him against her hands, needed her own hands filled with him. She reached and she found him, hot and hard and thick, and the remembrance of passion past and the anticipation of pleasure, always new, always consuming, had her panting. Stroking him, placing him against her and then just inside her, and enjoying each tiny slide of him into her.

Her hands went to his shoulders; her fingers pressed against hard muscle. Hers. Her Kelse. No other, ever.

The golden bond between them pulsed red desire.

Then he was all the way in her and they breathed together, unsteady. Hanging on the edge of ecstasy.

He withdrew slowly and she felt cold. He penetrated again and she was full and fulfilled.

They snapped and let the wild out to rule. She yelled and dug her fingers into his shoulders, rocked her hips, needing more, more, *more*! He pounded into her and she lived in a firestorm of sensation, all nerves plucked, all the tunes of the universe smashing together in glorious sound. That was her scream and his moaning release.

She swore the universe revolved around them. They were the center of it, of everything. Their love was all encompassing and would survive forever.

He kissed her mouth, then he kissed her wet cheeks, and he held her close and twined his legs in hers and they soared into the velvet darkness of sleep.

* * *

Morning came too soon, with the speaker near them chirping an annoying six times, pausing and doing it again. In a multitude of various bird notes. Fern woke groggily and realized it was time to launch the planetary lab. She scrambled into her clothes. She didn't want to leave Kelse. Especially not sleeping so vulnerably in the grotto.

She moved her fingers in a pattern to raise a spellshield. It wasn't nearly as strong as Kelse's, but it would alert him if disturbed. "Can you watch him?" she whispered. She blinked as a shine of light hit her eyes.

"I have a working camera," Ship said in satisfaction. "Repaired by me last night." Fern only hoped that Ship was uninterested in human mating habits.

But it hadn't been only mating. It had been lovemaking.

She shook off the thought. Time to make sure that their future would be good. If Kelse believed the white star's planet was the right one to settle, Fern would do everything to support him.

She leaned down and brushed his thick hair from his face, looked at the warrior planes of it. They *would* make it through everything. She had such hope this morning. She believed in the essential goodness of life. The Lady and Lord would bless them with a new home . . . and children. Fern wanted children.

She'd never dared believe that she and Kelse could have children. It would have been impossibly tragic on Earth. And she hadn't believed in that since Awakening. But during the long-drugged dreams of the stasis sleep, children had run through, laughing.

"Guard him," she ordered.

"How?" The Ship sounded curious.

"If anyone comes near him, wake him."

"How near is near?"

"If they reach the top of the rise."

"Agreed." There was a note of satisfaction in the Ship's voice, as if it, too, wanted to be useful.

Fern moved quietly to the passage that was the back way to

their quarters, then to the landing bay. She double-checked the lab and the instrumentation. Then she fumbled her way into a space suit, shut the airlock behind her, and counted down.

Knowing she could infuriate her husband, alert the crew to secrets being kept, and anger the other two Captains, Fern pushed the button to launch planetary laboratory station two.

Immediately lights began to flash and a claxon blared through the Ship. "Object launched from Landing Bay Two! Object launched from Landing Bay Two!"

"Ship!" Fern yelled as the airlock closed and atmosphere equalized and she struggled from her suit. The alarm continued to pound at her ears.

"I am sorry, Fern Bountry, many of my responses are set on automatic that I can't override without human manual control," Ship said. It didn't sound too happy, either.

"Well, hell." No use sneaking around. "Please invite the Captain, Exec, and Randolph Ash to Conference Room B."

"I am receiving signals from the other Captains. Captain Ambroz requests information on the launch of a planetary laboratory to the white star system," Ship said even as Fern's handheld marched with Kelse's comm tune.

"What's going on!" he snapped. Then, "Yes, I will meet you in Conference Room B."

"Be right there," Fern said, overly cheerful, mouth drying. She walked fast and garnered wide-eyed looks from the crew as she moved through the corridors. And picked up two security guards on the way who stationed themselves outside the door.

When she strode into Conference Room B, chin lifted, Randolph flicked his glance at her and hunched his shoulders. Chloe scowled at her. Yes, she was in trouble. Kelse moved to her side in support.

On the large screen, split for Captains Julianna Ambroz and Netra Sunaya Hoku, along with former Captain Umar Clague, heads turned to see her enter. Better looking at them than space.

Ambroz's disapproving visage stared down at Fern. "You sent out the only planetary laboratory we have—"

"No."

"No?" snapped Julianna.

"No," Fern replied. She moved to the beverage dispenser and poured herself a mug of coffee, gestured to Randolph, who was sitting at the small table, to help himself. He rose and tiptoed toward the dispenser.

Kelse grumbled and went to get his own coffee.

"The flawed planetary lab was fixed. I deployed that."

"You're sure?"

"Yes."

Julianna switched her gaze to Kelse. "You authorized this?"

Kelse slipped his arm around Fern's waist. As always, he was solid. "Yes."

"We have limited resources," Julianna scolded.

"I am well aware of that." Fern sipped her coffee and looked at the Captain over her mug. "But I believe that the sixth planet of the white star system was dismissed too easily as a home for us, based on only a couple of probes. I sent the lab out to record everything and orbit the planet. New information about the system, and even the planet, should be coming in now."

Umar grunted, looked down at his handheld. "It is."

Hoku glanced at his handheld, raised his brows, but said nothing.

Kelse looked at Randolph. "Have you had time to check the previous samples?"

He reddened and bobbled his coffee. "I rounded up a couple of old friends." He flushed even more. "And asked them to help."

"Study group friends," Chloe murmured. "Not Ship for Ourselves party members."

"And?" Kelse prompted.

Randolph glanced at the screen. "They're working on the samples. My friends are excited." His brows lowered. "Optimistic."

Kelse clinked his mug against Fern's. "Always pays to be optimistic and determined."

The bond that had sprung between them the night before was still there, though she knew he wasn't as calm as he sounded.

"We'll be studying the new results," Kelse said, glanced at the screen. "Anything else?"

"Not us," Umar replied. The vid from *Lugh's Spear* winked out.

Julianna sighed heavily, a twisty line between her brows. "I'll examine the findings, too. Later." Her image faded and the screen became wall again.

Kelse's arm dropped from Fern's waist and he glanced at Randolph. The youngster looked longingly at his mug.

"Take it with you," Fern said.

Randolph nodded and slipped from the room. Lips compressed, Chloe shook her head at Fern and left, too.

Kelse stared at her. Anger pulsed through their bond. "You aren't wearing armor and you're running around the ship. We agreed you wouldn't do that."

"You're right. I used mostly the back ways, but I violated our agreement. I'm sorry. The optimal time to launch was at six bells."

"You left me alone and asleep in the grotto."

"I raised a spellshield."

His gaze was dark. "Don't do it again." He turned on his heel and left, without touching her.

The constant stream of information from the planetary lab, and data from Randolph and his friends and the nose bridge crew, kept Kelse busy for the next week. Too busy to spend much time with Fern.

Who was keeping some sort of secret from him.

Of course she wouldn't endanger the crew or the ship or him. But she might endanger herself. Since she wasn't talking, and he'd been too damn quiet since being Awakened, it was easy for her to avoid him. She spent most of her time in the Greensward, or the Earth DNA storage unit, checking on all the species the ship carried.

The Ship for Ourselves party had been too quiet, too. Randolph had heard through the grapevine that their prime tech hadn't been able to use the ship's intercom or broadcast system. That would be frustrating for Dirk Lascom, and could make him more dangerous.

Kelse had a security force of twelve by now, well trained because he'd spent a great deal of time with them. Their first priority was to protect the crew and the ship. No violence. The second was to protect Fern. Their third job was to note and observe the members of the SFO party. Kelse was sure of the eleven who'd conspired to kill Moungala and break into the cryonics bay. Dirk, his tech, and nine guards. Too many to cover up the situation, but they'd planned on being in power. Kelse still didn't have any proof.

Randolph was still extremely nervous about the fuel cells and reserves. At the rate they were going, they could barely make the solar systems and asteroid belt. He was also depressed when the final results of probe samples remained equivocal. He and his friends spent too many hours studying how to eke out the fuel to the two star systems that held the Colonists' best chance. And, somehow, the ship's energy had become more efficient.

Kelse felt unusually indecisive. His gut told him the white star system was the way to go. But that might just be because he wanted off the ship. Fourteen prospective habitable planets were surely better than one marginally viable one, even if that was closer.

The decision point, the point of no return, was upon them. Either way they chose, they would be set on a course that couldn't change.

That night, Kelse tossed and turned in bed. He'd let Fern hold him, or he held her, dozed, then dreams or his running mind would wake him and he'd struggle with the choice. He sweated through the linens, woke and noted the undertone of gray in his skin. Then he called another Captains' conference to inform Ambroz, Hoku, and Clague of his decision.

He'd dressed in his dark green uniform. He and Fern hadn't spoken much, but she knew his mind. When he reached for her hand, she let him hold it, and they walked to the small conference room with fingers linked. The restraint between them had subsided . . . for the next crucial moments.

Again he sat at the head of the table. Fern was at his right. Chloe and Randolph sat at the other end. Peaches had accompanied Randolph and settled near the food and beverage dispenser. A small screen showed the grouped nose bridge crew.

"Contact the Captains of *Arianrhod's Wheel* and *Lugh's Spear*," Kelse stated. He was relieved all the thinking was over and he could move into action.

As soon as Julianna Ambroz's, Netra Sunaya Hoku's, and Umar Clague's faces appeared on the screen, Kelse made the announcement.

"I have decided that *Nuada's Sword* will head for the sixth planet of the white star system."

Julianna squawked, "No!"

He met her eyes, felt his face harden. "Yes."

"It's marginal! And if we go there, we'll have no resources to find something else!"

"We know," Fern said calmly beside him, and he'd never loved her more.

"We could die off in three generations," Julianna pointed out.

Twelve

That's three more generations than we will see on this ship," Kelse said. "Nose bridge crew of *Nuada's Sword*, your input?"

There was a hesitation, then a clearing of several throats, murmuring. "I'm waiting," Kelse prompted.

"With all due and *great* respect to Captain Ambroz, we believe the planet to be more than viable. We consider it quite habitable," a young, quavery female voice said.

Another one chimed in. "It appears to be perfect for terra forming and city building." Another small cough. "Or so all our programs show."

Ah, now he knew why they were enthusiastic. They were those who would run the machines to build the cities—or, rather, one city to begin with. They'd played/practiced with those during games, too.

"Good land and water masses. We should land well," added a third.

"What do you base this on?" asked Julianna.

"Your programs," someone replied.

"Which programs?" snapped Julianna.

"Why, the ones you designed and sent to us and *Lugh's Spear* just before you became Captain."

"Ah," Julianna said, appearing slightly mollified, though she yet had lines in her broad forehead. "How many times have you run those?" she asked.

"Oh, um, oh," said the breathy youngest voice. "One of us has been running it continuously since we launched the first probes."

"Since. You. Launched. The. Probes."

"Yes, our colonies died quite a bit when we first began." A strained, nervous giggle. "Especially those from *Arianrhod's Wheel*."

"My ship," Julianna said.

"But we started living past the sixty percentage point after the first data came back from the probes, and after the info from the lab . . . well, we usually make ninety-seven or ninety-eight percentile. Even when we add rougher parameters . . ."

"Could you send me a summary of data on these runs?" asked Julianna.

"We'll spurt it to your transnow." There was the sound of activity in the background, then a loud whisper. "If we might recommend something to the great Ambroz," someone said.

"I'm listening," said Julianna. She was leaning forward.

"We think that, due to the size and configuration, *Arianrhod's Wheel* should land at a certain point."

"I see." Her gaze had gone to a monitor that showed a rotating world. One of her assistants—dressed in a long gown with sleeve pockets like a kimono—pulled an electronic tablet from her sleeve and gave it to Julianna. Charts and figures flashed on it. The games summaries.

Randolph cleared his throat. "Could I have one, too?" He was staring sourly at the screen. Kelse thought he was both envious and feeling superior.

"Surely," a young woman from the bridge said. "We'll spurt it to your handy and your desky."

"I, too," said Hoku.

"On its way to *Lugh's Spear*!"

"My thanks," Hoku said and lapsed into silence. He was still looking pretty golden from the Awakening.

"Randolph, your input?" Kelse asked.

The young man jerked his mind back to the business, flushed as if caught daydreaming at a vital meeting. He squared his shoulders. "We take the chance."

"Fern?" He took her hand and squeezed.

"I don't have the great scientific knowledge that these others have." Her lips quivered. "And I haven't played the game—I mean, I haven't run the programs. But I know that I still believe in founding a society, the culture that we want. Of fulfilling our dreams."

Peaches hopped onto the table. *The four Famdogs say yes.*

Turning red, Randolph repeated what the cat said.

The six FamCats say yes. We are tired of Ship. And Ship says yes, too.

Again Randolph stated the Fams' position.

There was silence as everyone stared at Peaches. Finally he hopped from the table and strutted to the door. *Time for food. Steak bits in Cafeteria Three A today.*

Chloe let him out, saying, "I have a good feeling about this."

"I still don't think . . ." Julianna began stubbornly.

Damn. Kelse hadn't wanted to bring this up. He squared his shoulders. And looked directly into Julianna's eyes. "Julianna," he said softly, "throughout this seventy-year journey of yours"—and she still appeared more like fifty—"we have come across six planets that you did not consider viable."

She flinched.

"And you don't consider the one circling the white star viable."

"I'll check the new data," she said stiffly. Her fingers were trembling.

"Julianna, I can't afford to base my decision on your advice alone, no matter how estimable your credentials. We have to act, and act now. *Nuada's Sword* is taking the chance." He stood. "Because we cannot risk any farther voyage. We will be diverting to the white star and the sixth planet from it."

"I will follow Captain Bountry's decision," Hoku said. "With the vids I've scrutinized of the planet from the lab, I am confident that I can make a good landing."

Julianna had paled. "I still think the other star systems would have been better. Despite what everyone says, what everyone believes, this is a huge risk."

"It's the only one we can take. Sooner, rather than later, we've come to our last chance," Kelse said. He leaned over the console, tapped a sequence.

"This is nav, Captain."

"Launch Planetary Lab One to land on the planet and stream data back. Engage the nano engines and steer for Celta."

"Yes, sir! Nose crew back to our duties! Signing off."

Julianna looked down.

Randolph squirmed in his seat and Kelse nodded at the young man. He escaped. Chloe's raised-brows glance at him, then at Kelse, indicated that she wanted to follow her grandson. He nodded.

Hoku scanned their room, then said, "Those young idiots on your nose bridge aren't expecting to land *Nuada's Sword* because they've been practicing in simulators, are they?"

Fern flinched beside Kelse.

"No," he said. "You're our best and most experienced Pilot, but we have our own who has landed starships as large as *Nuada's Sword*."

"Good." Hoku's expression was somber. "Because games are just that. Games."

"That's right," Kelse said.

Hoku nodded. "We'll make it there, and I'll land *Lugh's Spear*, then we'll see what we'll see. Later." His image vanished.

The last sight Kelse had of Julianna was with her head bowed, her chest rising and falling with weeping. She couldn't go it alone. He'd forced her to follow him, and he hated that. He hated that he had no choice about anything.

He hated that, at the beginning of this trip, so long ago, he'd thought that everything would go well. He and Fern would be out of the escalating violence against psis. They'd sleep, they'd find a new home, build a new city, a new culture.

Everything had looked great on paper. The science programs and all the other analyses they'd studied more than two centuries ago had been fine. He'd believed in experts.

He'd had hope.

Nothing was as horrible as when hope crashed.

He'd brought Fern into a dreadful situation. All his insides squeezed, sweat spread on his palms. He dropped Fern's hand.

There were measures to be planned if worse came to worst.

They'd changed course. They were committed.

Vids of "their" new star system and planet sent from the planetary labs—one in orbit and one on the way to the planet—were updated every hour and had become the main entertainment.

Fern lingered on the path to the grotto. She'd come the back way from their quarters, as usual.

She'd thought that after the great decision, Kelse would loosen up. She'd been wrong. He'd narrowed the bond between them, and she could think only that he was too sensitive to the link. That he believed it might make him weak in some way. She was learning more about her husband under these circumstances, and fear crawled through her, gnawing. Her breath quickened as she considered how fragile their marriage was. She swallowed and bit her lip, tasted blood. She hadn't been able to reach him and their marriage could break. The worst fear of all.

That morning, knowing they both had a full day, she'd whispered an invitation for a romantic break in the grotto instead of dinner. Maybe that would be enough to keep them going.

Meanwhile, keeping the secret that the Ship was awake and alert wore on her. She didn't know why she hadn't told Kelse, except that it seemed like he would want to share it with others and she didn't. A confrontation avoided. No way to run a marriage.

Now she was striding up the trail, stretching her muscles for more flexible sex, when she felt the sting in her neck, clapped a hand to her throat to rub it, and wondered muzzily about bees and wasps. Then she was falling, and the last thing she saw was Dirk Lascom's gleeful face. Fear, even concern, was oddly absent.

Kelse was late to his rendezvous with Fern, and as much as he wanted to think about loving and touching, irritation whipped through him and had him gritting his teeth.

The minute he reached the grotto, he realized something was wrong. There was no scent of Fern, no sign. He'd left footprints in the soil along the top of the rise, she hadn't.

His heart began pounding, knowledge trickling through him that she was in danger. He brushed away a swath of blossoming vine to reveal the aux computer screen. "Show the location of Fern Bountry," he ordered, his voice too harsh.

At the bright green icon, the searing breath that had stuck in his lungs pushed out, and he dragged another deep one in. The icon was motionless.

The screen went from a map to the pulsing red of an emergency—her locator was being removed. Randolph's face appeared on the screen. He was panting and fear lived in his eyes. "Fern's been kidnapped."

"I know. Split screen," Kelse ordered. But he was too late, her locator wristband had been pulled off. It showed steady and orange.

"Dirk doesn't trust me anymore, but I know their meeting places. I'll find out where they're holding her."

"Be discreet."

"Yes, sir."

"If you find her, report to me. Do not try to handle this yourself." He didn't know what Dirk had in mind for her. Torture. Rape. Terrible things. Kelse prayed that the man wanted her alive to bargain for something and not for pure vengeance.

Kelse hadn't told her he loved her lately. Not for days. He hadn't been tender to her. He sure hadn't been able to talk to her.

He could hear the blood rushing through his temples, knew he'd been a stupid fool.

He only hoped he wasn't too late, that he wouldn't lose her.

That he hadn't screwed up their marriage permanently.

He couldn't lose her. It would break him. Just the thought had him running on pure adrenaline, heightened his senses, kicked in all his Flair.

Randolph's guard said, "We'll get her, Captain. I'll alert the other guards."

"Discreetly. Do not converge on the area, proceed with your usual duties until I give any orders."

"Yes, sir."

Kelse turned and ran back to his quarters, drew up the map on the command console, stared at it.

Twelve against the eleven core Ship for Ourselves members if he took in the new guards who'd never fought in a real battle. So easy for Fern to get dead.

"Dammit to fliggering hell!" He slammed his fist on the console.

"Captain?" It was a tentative whisper.

He drew his blazer, spun around. No one was there. Glancing at the life signs of his quarters, he saw only his.

"Who's that?"

"It is We."

Something was wrong with the voice, like there was more than one, like it was a chorus of ghosts. An atavistic shiver whipped along his spine.

"Who. Is. That?"

A metallic tinkling, almost as if someone ran nervous fingers through a jangle of bracelets. He was alone in his quarters.

"It is We, the Ship. *Nuada's Sword*."

Kelse's mind went blank. "What?"

"Fern reactivated Our Autonomous Intelligence Module. We've been alive and Awake since the night before the lab launched."

"Alive and Awake," Kelse repeated.

"Yessss." There was a few seconds' pause. "Our sentience was originally initiated just before undocking by Captain Whitecloud. When he died, his successor . . . sent Us into hibernation. We had only enough slight awareness to initiate one or two actions."

Things fell into place. "Like Awakening Fern."

"Yes. You wanted that. Fern wanted that. An automatic Awakening had been programmed in Us during Whitecloud's Captaincy, should it be necessary."

"Hibernation," Kelse repeated. Something about the way the Ship had said the word made Kelse think it was more like murder.

"But Fern brought you back to life, and I now have more assets than I thought. I suppose you are the reason the refurbishment of some of the systems are going so well?"

"Yes. But We wish to offer you information."

"Yes?"

"Fern is located in the northwest corner of room three-twenty-two, level seventeen, sector five. Her life signs are stable and in the human norm for a person in stressful circumstances. There are eleven people in her immediate area."

A map rose to the desktop screen, along with eleven indicators. The eleven who'd conspired to murder Moungala had Fern.

And had nothing to lose.

Sweat beaded the back of Kelse's neck, slid over his skin and he had to regulate his rough breathing again. "Thank you, Ship. What else?"

"We have studied all the data of all Our systems during the time We were shut—"

"Unconscious," Kelse said.

"Yes. Unconscious. The previous Captain, Kiet Moungala, liked to walk Our halls unseen."

"I was unaware that Kiet had a Flair for invisibility."

"He did not. He had a cape made from light-bending fabric. Such information is in the files, and those who made the garments have since died. The cloak has a hood and gloves."

"An invisibility cape."

"Yes."

"Where is it?"

"We sense it in the secret drawer in the bed."

"Right." By the time he went to the bed, there was a slight vertical protrusion at the head. A drawer no more than fifteen centimeters deep. Reaching in, he found a package.

A ping came from the command console and Chloe's face showed up, along with Randolph's.

"We've found Fern."

"I know," Kelse said.

"Randolph, the guard, and I will meet you in the short corridor just south of three-twenty-two. It's usually clear."

"Chloe—" But her line went dead, and when Kelse called her back, he got her cache.

"We are on private red alert," the Ship said, "and accessing Our files."

Kelse grunted. He didn't know what the Ship meant, or what it could do. Maybe he'd been told, but it was too long ago.

Too many unknowns and too many untrained people on his side. Chloe hadn't fought in who knew how long. With placation in mind, he said, "Ship, see what you can find on the circumstances regarding Moungala's and the three security officers' death."

"Yes, Captain. We have been reviewing current events."

"Fine." Five minutes later he was dressed in the stupid but useful cloak and slipping along the least used corridors—as monitored by the Ship and whispered in his ear insert.

His heart was thumping hard, his palms sweating, and he kept images of past victims he'd seen and known from impinging on his brain.

Finally he was there.

The corridor was completely empty except for the two men who guarded the door, and Kelse certainly had surprise on his side. They wouldn't see their disablement coming.

They didn't. He took each out with one blow, then pulled thin flex restraints from his tactical belt and secured their hands behind their backs. He dragged them to the corridor where Chloe and Randolph should be, but they hadn't yet arrived.

Kelse didn't like the cloak. Terrible to fight in. Only good to spy with.

He returned to the door and slowly opened it a crack. The room was eight meters long and four wide. Big enough that no one was near the door. No one was watching. But there were too many for Kelse to take down by himself, either personally or with a blazer. He'd need at least two more decent fighters.

First he had to check Fern. He was incapable of leaving without seeing whether she was hurt.

She was still in the corner like the Ship had told him, sitting on the floor, her head on her knees. She wore her armor and didn't appear hurt.

He could hear only his own heart pounding. His breath stopped, held, then he managed to force it out. They'd been in worse situations. He could count on her if he knew whether she was in fighting trim.

A motion to his right caught his attention. To his complete surprise, Dirk, the tech, and the guards were looking at a star chart that showed the wormhole. Dirk was serious. Crazy, but serious. He believed what he'd convinced himself to believe. The wormhole led to civilized space.

Kelse used his lightest tread, aware of the slight sway of the cape's fabric, moving toward Fern. When he was within a couple of meters, she lifted her head enough that he saw her eyes over her knees, staring straight at him.

Love smashed through him. He could not lose her.

Live or die together.

Thirteen

Fern stared at him. Maybe she could see him.

Of course she couldn't.

But he could feel her. If he stopped and *felt* instead of acting with mind and body. If he accessed his heart and the golden bond throbbing between them that he'd been ignoring. Yes, he could feel her, the reassurance . . . the love.

And maybe he could tell how hurt she was. He opened himself completely. The rush of fear and love and need was sucked from him into her. Jetted like a cut artery, as if all he was, all he'd ever felt for her, went straight to her.

She didn't rock back, didn't move, didn't seem fazed by all he felt. He figured that if he'd been on the receiving end of such a surge, he'd have crumbled.

His woman was strong, and lately he hadn't acknowledged that in his marriage. Tried to keep all his worries from her. Hide himself.

But she was alive and he'd do better.

Now he studied her, the easy flow of emotions from her to him. Reassurance. He almost snorted. Yeah, he'd needed that. Love. Nope, couldn't live without that, either. Need and desire and yearning. He hoped she always felt that for him.

But there was a sluggishness in her, a touch of gray black that he didn't understand. She lifted her head and angled it, and he saw an angry red mark on her neck. She'd been drugged. He moved closer.

BLAZER came to his mind. Telepathy! He stiffened, noted that the cape didn't sway with any movement. Good.

His wife wanted a weapon. Of course she would.

HOW ARE YOU? he asked.

She rolled her head back and forth on her knees. Not one hundred percent then.

GOOD ENOUGH. She curved her spine in a stretch and lifted her torso vertebra by vertebra, stretched her legs out one by one and rotated her feet.

He didn't know if she was healthy enough. Didn't think so. *LOVE YOU!*

Her smile was faint.

Sinking in increments to a crouch, he reached for his small ankle blazer and pushed it to her. Their fingers brushed, and the relief, the yearning for more of her touch shot through him.

But she was looking down, huddling as if beaten—an image she wanted her captors to see.

Anger sizzled his blood and hazed his vision. He wanted to kill.

The curve of her fingers over his boot toe, barely a touch and not skin to skin. *OUR PEO-PLE!*

He didn't agree, these men had set themselves apart from their community, but he couldn't argue. And the edge of other anger, among the men, reached him. The tech wanted to steal an escape pod and launch it through the wormhole.

Dirk still wanted the Ship.

Kelse could use the disagreement, if he hurried, got reinforcements.

LOVE YOU, he sent to Fern.

WILL FIGHT, Fern returned.

He ghosted to the door, through it, leaving it ajar. The corridor was still empty.

The cape should remain secret. He stripped it and the gloves off, rolled them up, and placed them against the wall. They vanished. He marked the wall.

Randolph and Chloe and a guard, an older man, were waiting down the hall. Dirk's two men had disappeared. Chloe jerked a nod at him. "We have a brig. They're in it."

"I believe everyone remaining with Dirk was in the plot to kill Moungala."

Her eyes lit with anger and determination.

Randolph's jaw flexed. "I didn't know. I *wouldn't* know or see." Randolph stared at him with steady blue eyes, serious expression. There was a change in the lines of his face that showed he'd passed the boundary from youth to man. "I want to come. I'm not as strong as I will be, but I'm fast and I'm an excellent shot. I've been practicing with the guards." His shoulders squared. "This is my mess to clean up."

"It's Dirk's mess," Chloe bit off.

"I helped make it."

"We don't have time for this," Kelse said. A touch of fear had wisped through Fern. She'd sensed the argument winding down.

He glanced at the guard, an older man, who nodded and said, "Randolph will do."

"All right. Fern will be fighting, too. She's good, but will be slow. They drugged her." Fury spurted through him, ran along the network of his nerves. Energizing. He would not be stopped. "Try to keep them alive," he said as much to remind himself as the others.

Randolph's eyes widened, but he nodded. When the guard handed him another blazer, Randolph checked it competently, put it on wide and stun.

Chloe's mouth flattened, then she said, "If you hadn't stepped in and infused the crew with a sense of hope, a rededication to the mission, Dirk would have had all the power, all the luxuries the Ship could command. All the women he wanted. Simple motive for hating you, Kelse, basic greed. You took that away from him."

"I stole that from him, so he's—"

"Stolen Fern," Rudolph said.

Kelse briefed them on the men's placements. "Let's do this."

He went in, fast and low and streaming blazer fire. Two seconds and Fern was moving with him. Then they were too close and fighting hand to hand.

Dirk's men were good and they were fighting for their lives. Kelse's world narrowed to blows and kicks. It was over before his anger was purged.

He wheeled toward Dirk, who was running. The man rammed into Randolph, snatched his blazer. Dirk grinned at Kelse, that mad grin. He thumbed the blazer on high and shot, missed Kelse; Chloe screamed.

Randolph grabbed for the blazer, but Dirk was too fast again. He stuck the weapon under his own chin and fired into his brain.

The smell of blood and death rose.

"FatherDam!" yelled Randolph. He ran to his grandmother.

Fern was holding Chloe. Her eyes were glazed.

"No!" yelled Randolph.

"Don't crowd me," Fern snapped. "I've called for Healers. She'll be all right. She's tough." Fern looked at the guard and Randolph, said, "Pray."

They all did. The Healers ran through the door a minute later and took Chloe away, chanting spells.

Kelse prayed for her, and, holding his love, said words of thankfulness. Slowly they walked away from the room that Kelse never wanted to see again in his life. He stopped in the corridor to pick up the cloak and gloves, showed them to Fern.

Techs trotted past them, ready to take Dirk's body to the decomposer and clean up the mess in the room.

Kelse and Fern had barely reached their quarters when a large and booming voice announced: "This is the Ship, *Nuada's Sword*. I have accessed My files, reviewed them, and enhanced the images of the night Our former Captain was killed. Watch and listen."

They did. Kelse figured everyone's attention was glued to the action playing before them. First the killing of the security guards. Then Dirk was at Moungala's door, requesting to speak with him. He entered the Captain's quarters and killed the man with a poison dart, he tried to access the Captain's console. Failed, snarled, was called away to check on something new happening at the cryonics bay door.

Then the angle shifted, blurred, sharpened.

"These are the actions of the last hour," the Ship said.

Kelse saw himself rushing into the room to face the men who had killed Kiet. He watched the fight. "Your form is off," he said to Fern, glad to have her in his arms.

Ship explained everything, notified the crew of the status of Chloe Hernandez—good—and that the criminals were in the brig. It advised that the men be sterilized.

Snorting, Kelse released Fern and moved to the command console, interrupted the Ship, initiated his own vid. "We are pleased that the Ship's Autonomous Intelligence Module is working. However, the determination of the punishment of the remaining individuals who murdered the security officers and Captain Moungala will be determined by the crew."

He stopped a sigh. All he wanted now was to make love with Fern.

"My fellow travelers, I thank you for your support in this difficult time. Let us mourn for our lost ones and go on with our lives. Blessed be."

It wasn't a great speech, but it got the job done.

Fern watched him with violet, serious eyes, then said, "We need to talk. And this time we lay it all out."

Great. His gut clenched and heart plummeted. He checked the bond between them. It was open and still golden. Maybe he had a chance.

He rubbed a scar at his hairline, felt a red flush on his neck. "I am not coping well."

Fern couldn't believe the admission. She stared at him. "No. You're not coping well. You're coping *magnificently.*" She yanked his head down to kiss him, with her tongue running along his lips, then into his mouth to taste her man, then back out to nip his lower lip.

Setting both hands on his chest, she pushed him back. "You're coping magnificently in everything except relating to your wife."

He winced. Stepped back, glanced aside. "I know."

"Then don't do that."

"What?"

"Step back and glance aside. Kelse, haven't we been through enough together that you trust me?"

"Of course I trust you!"

"Really? When did you think you always had to be the strong one? Don't you get to be weak?"

He blinked, and she realized he'd never even considered the concept of leaning on her. He'd been in charge when they'd met, the leader of the NJNY psi underground. There had been plenty of physical danger and risk, but he knew how to cope with that—with everything in his environment.

Oh, she might have thrown him off balance in the beginning. But the man had psi-quick reflexes and had recovered rapidly. She hadn't been the first woman to fall in love with him. She'd only been the lucky one whom he had loved.

She'd always felt loved. She blinked away tears. "Let me put it this way, lover." She'd called him that in their first days, when they'd still been learning each other. She'd been too smug, thinking she'd known him. Who could ever know anyone? "Do you think I'm strong?"

"Hell, yes!" Now he stepped forward, placed his hands on her shoulders, and she liked the way they curved around. She'd never take his touch for granted again.

"Then why don't you let me help you, Kelse? Why don't you let me in and lean on me?"

"If I let go, I might break."

"And I'll be here to pick up the pieces. Let me help, darling."

Great shudders wracked his body. She drew him over to the bed and pulled him down. He lay stiff.

"We're all going to die," he said.

She stopped a gasp, swallowed.

"We'll crash," he said in a monotone. "We'll run out of fuel. No hope for us then. Terrible things will happen. People will go mad, will kill. Until someone takes mercy on us and gasses us."

Breathing through the thrumming fear in her temples, she forced her tone to be light. "Always considering the worst-case scenario."

"That's what I do."

She *couldn't* give in to the fear prickling along her skin. Shove it away. *They would live!* She insisted on hope, and with it, she could give it to him. For now. She poked him. "Relax. That's an order from your wife." She waited as he released the tension in his body, muscle by muscle, and rolled toward her.

She looked him in the face. "You aren't alone in this fear. But it makes it bearable if we share it and go on, together. I love you, Kelse, and I know you will give your last drop of strength to save me and the crew. That's enough."

"It can't be enough." His voice sounded raw.

"Yes, it is. You've spoken a lot about believing, and you have to do that, too." She drew in a breath. "I know that you mostly believe, but now you must believe with all you've got that all will go well."

"What if it doesn't? What if you die, horribly?"

"Thank you for that comment. We'll die together. Didn't we say so when we decided to marry?"

"Yes. But we lived with death every day, then," he said.

She moved closer, wrapped herself around him. Tucked herself against his fast-beating heart and spoke the truth. "We always live with death every day, even during peacetime. But you've never learned that, have you? I could fall and hit my head on a rock and that's it. So could you."

She heard a couple of puffing breaths from him. "You're more likely to, more clumsy than I am."

"Getting back to my regular Kelse."

"I'm not ever going to be the same after this," he said.

"Who could be?" she asked.

"I've changed."

"I have, too," she said. "I've found out that space is beautiful. That *when* we land, I will love that planet more than anything but you and our children and our people. I've learned to be stronger." She poked him.

"I've learned to be . . . stronger in a different way."

"Yes. We both have."

He sighed, rocked her. "We could burn up in the atmosphere, crash against a mountain, hit the planet and explode. I could die before you."

That was a real blow to her heart. She accepted the fear, moved through it. "I don't think I'd live long after that, Kelse. But if things go terribly wrong, we will cope. We will do the best we can to fix them."

"Yes."

"That's all we can do, all that anyone is allowed to expect of us."

He stretched, adjusting again to changes in his life. "If you say so."

"I do." She kissed his jaw, felt his body respond. For now, they could love. "We are tough and determined."

"Yes." He hauled her over him, up to kiss him again.

"And we never give up," she said.

"No."

Then they were too busy to speak.

A couple of hours later, Kelse stroked her body, over the curve of her hip. The loving after sex.

"Why don't we wake up our Pilot?" Kelse asked. His smile was one of those that showed he was giving her a treat. He was right.

"Yes. And Bella Larson will be Awake by morning. The crew will welcome her."

So they showered and dressed and walked openly to the cryonics bay, hand in hand. The people they passed nodded or smiled, and that was good.

But the alarm woke them at midnight with Ship saying, "Captain Ambroz is requesting a conference."

"Bad news?" Kelse asked.

There was a hissing noise, then the Ship said, "I did not want to wake you since you had mended your marital difficulties."

Kelse frowned.

There was a knock at the door.

"Randolph Ash, Chloe Hernandez, and the cat Peaches request entrance," Ship said.

Swearing, Kelse rolled from bed, taking Fern with him. He set her on her feet and grabbed his clothes. Chloe's voice came over the intercom. "We're waiting out here."

"We're dressing in here," Fern responded.

Despite the loving, Kelse had had nightmares. He wanted another shower. One with Fern. He wasn't going to get it.

Fern had dressed, made the bed and arranged chairs by the console, and made the wall ready for the projection of the other Captains. She didn't move with her usual briskness.

Kelse checked on their bond and found dread running through her. He kissed her. "We believe."

"Yes," she agreed, but he knew he was the strong one now.

Then Chloe and Randolph were in and sitting. Peaches wandered the room, and the screen showed Julianna Ambroz's immobile expression, Captain Hoku's impassive face.

"The planetary labs have crashed," Julianna announced quietly. "As lab one moved close to lab two, it tried to dock with it." The muscles of her face worked. "A default that all of us had forgotten about. The docking was unsuccessful and the orbits deteriorated. The labs fell. As they moved into the planet's atmosphere, the trajectory was too steep and too fast. They crashed." She grimaced. "Left quite a crater, too. We won't be getting any more information on the planet before we land. No planetside verification that the world will be good for us."

Fourteen

There was silence at Julianna's announcement. Kelse slipped his arm around Fern. Her body was quivering. Not enough to show, but he felt it. His own fear kept him stiff.

At least Julianna didn't do the *I told you sos*.

Hoku took a long, audible breath. His slanted eyebrows rose over melancholy eyes. "We are already committed."

Fern's fingers twined in Kelse's. As always, he appeared impassive, but his grip was hard.

They'd gambled and lost.

"We can't turn back. We don't have enough fuel," Chloe said.

Fern lifted her chin. "We'll have to proceed on the preliminary results. That's all we can do."

Randolph gritted his teeth. "We don't have fuel to do anything else."

Peaches sauntered over. *Gloom, gloom, gloom. You are humans with big brains. Use them.*

Kelse laughed, but blood had drained from his head. "We've gambled. I don't admit that we've lost."

He wouldn't admit that they'd lost until they breathed their last breath.

"The preliminary results that we based our decision on to

divert to planet six of the white star remain good. We can hope," Fern said.

"And pray," Hoku said.

The hours crawled for Fern over the next days. She felt a failure. But she forced herself to be as positive as Kelse, serving as examples for their people.

Neither of them slept well.

Kelse had begun to exercise the crew, section by section, as if they would need to be Colonists. Ship was giving classes in construction, farming, and several other subjects. It, too, seemed optimistic.

People continued to watch the planet as they came closer. Many played *Our Mission*.

Both Julianna Ambroz and Netra Sunaya Hoku had launched their own probes, particularly in the area where they were planning to land. One of Ambroz's crashed. The information received continued to be equivocal.

The Pilots in all three ships and *Nuada's Sword* itself practiced and coordinated approaches, orbital speeds, data—spoke in a language no one else understood.

Then, instead of the hours crawling, the minutes did. Fern thought she'd go mad, holding on to sanity by a thread. If they failed, a lot would be due to her. That was a burden.

Finally, as if the last grain of sand plinked from the top of an invisible hourglass to the bottom, it was time to land.

The nose bridge was no longer cut off from the rest of the Ship.

Kelse and Fern were in the main bridge that had also been unsealed. Both bridges were crewed, and the silver-gilt-haired Pilot, Bella Larson, sat in the command chair.

They all knew that the Ship itself would be integral to the landing process.

"Now leaving orbit," Bella said.

"Affirmative," said the Ship. "We are in good position to land on the peninsula We chose."

The Ship wanted to set down on some cliffs close to an ocean.

Kelse and Fern exchanged glances. He was not the one making the decision to use the explosive device if it appeared they'd all burn on the way down. Nor would he release any fatal gas if the planet was revealed to be unsafe.

He was not the kind of man who could do that, and they'd both realized it.

Larson held those triggers.

The planet enlarged before them, filling their screens with continents tinged a slight green, blue seas, the swirl of clouds in weather patterns.

"It's beautiful," Julianna said. All the Captains were audio linked. "A seeded planet of the Foremothers, like Earth was."

"Which means it might be compatible with Earth life," former Captain Umar said.

"That's the hope," Kelse said.

"Strap in and pray," Bella said. "We'll be down in under a half hour." Her mouth quirked. "Half a septhour."

"Septhour?"

"Planet's rotation makes sense to have seventy-minute hours," she said. "See that crater? That's where the labs crashed. We'll be landing a little to the south." She grinned. "And here we go!"

Gravs pressed against Fern, flattening her breasts, pulling her skin back on her face. Blackness threatened. She clamped her fingers around Kelse's. *I LOVE YOU!*

It took too long for Fern to wake. Others had, and were unhooking their harnesses. Kelse flung his off, stumbled to kneel in front of Fern to work her harness.

There were shouts. Screams of gladness and glee. Bella Larson was dancing, hips wiggling, arms pumping. "One crack, otherwise, *perfect, perfect, perfect landing,*" she sang.

Kelse knew *Lugh's Spear*'s hadn't gone as well. Hoku had lost people.

Julianna Ambroz, on another continent, hadn't.

It would be unbearable if Kelse had lost Fern.

But her chest rose and fell, she moaned, stirred. And love and gratitude weakened him so he fell on his butt at her feet. His eyes stung.

Peaches hopped over and licked his face. *FamMan not awake yet, either. You did good, Kelse. Fern did good. Not as good as Cats would have, but good.* He trotted away and Kelse just shook his stunned head.

"The planet outside . . . Celta . . . is fully acceptable for Earth-human life," Ship announced. "Atmospheric pressure has been equalized. Opening all landing bay doors."

"Wait!" Kelse ordered.

But it was too late.

Bella was there, boosting Kelse to his feet, freeing a conscious Fern from her restraints.

Kelse pulled his wife into his arms and kissed her. Her body was vital against his, their bond pulsed with joy. Hope flooded him and he tasted it in her mouth. Their hearts beat together and they held tight, tasting life.

There was a cough, another. A third. Then a loud cat yowl. *Come ON! I want out!* Peaches insisted.

Randolph said, "Kelse and Fern must go first."

Yes, that was Kelse's duty, take the first steps onto a new planet, see if it was all right. He broke the kiss, kept his arm around Fern's waist.

Her lips were red, her violet eyes bright and shiny. "I love you."

"I love you," he responded, blinked fast.

LET'S GO! yelled Peaches mentally.

His fingers met Fern's and their hands closed around each other. As he and Fern passed Bella, she bowed. Chloe did, too, and Randolph, holding Peaches.

The bridge doors opened and there were people in the hall, looking scared, holding belongings. They, too, rippled in bows as Kelse and Fern passed. Ship highlighted floor panels to the landing bay, though the crew had practiced disembarking.

Leaving the Ship after centuries of travel. Soon the rest of the sleepers, those who funded the journey and experts, would be Awakened. Soon the DNA banks would be opened and plants and animals would be introduced to this new land.

Soon.

But now he and Fern were before the last door to outside.

It, too, parted, and they stared at white-yellow sunshine angling into the huge bay.

They walked through the chamber and down the ramp to a large meadow of a green they'd never known, with summer flowers they'd never seen. On they went until his breath simply stopped.

He looked at her, unable to bear the loss of her touch even for an instant. He drew her into his arms. "We did it." His voice was shaky and he didn't care. "We are home. I love you."

"We are home, and I love you," Fern said.

He grabbed her and kissed her, and strange fragrances came to mix with her scent, and she was against him and life was fabulous.

Cheers filled the air.

Heart Story

To Brenna Lyons

Note: Arbusca/Blush appears in *Heart Dance* and here is her story, as requested.

Druida City, Planet Celta
406 Years After Earth Colonization
Spring

In twenty minutes she would be meeting her HeartMate, her fated love, for the first time. If Dri Paris was punctual. If he was early, he could walk through that door any moment now.

Arbusca Willow counted breaths to calm her excitement, slow her heart rate.

Twenty-five years since the links had been forged between herself and her HeartMate. She'd known that he had gone south, all the way to a different continent.

The bond between them had become threadlike. She'd suppressed it—if not the yearning for her HeartMate—so long.

In several hopeful moments over the last year, she'd given the bond gentle tugs. Last month he had contacted her. She'd felt him when he'd arrived in the city a few days ago.

Putting her hands in her opposite sleeves, she paced the private room in the social club. Everything must be *perfect*. He'd set the time. She'd arranged the location. This club catered to the highest of the household staffs of the most powerful nobles, which meant relatives of those lords and ladies. Arbusca herself was a housekeeper.

The FamCat yowled and sent a mental comment, *You are not listening to me.*

No, Arbusca hadn't been. The FamCat wasn't her Familiar, wasn't even her son's Fam. The cat was her daughter-in-law's, and the Fam had an agenda: Get Arbusca out of Willow Residence because she was too strict.

The old woman is dead. Finally, the cat said telepathically.

That got Arbusca's attention. Yes, her mother was dead more than a year.

Good riddance. Fairyfoot sniffed.

She stared at the cat. "Fairyfoot, you didn't know my mother."

Saw her long enough to know she was a mean GreatLady. Had all of you under her paw. Fairyfoot licked her own forepaw. *That's true?*

"Yes."

Tried to live forever. Lied. Killed. The cat snapped down her paw as if on a bug, looked at Arbusca slyly. *Maybe even killed your husband, years ago.*

Arbusca didn't think so. Her mother, GreatLady D'Willow, descendant of a FirstFamily Colonist, rich in psi magic, wealth, and power, had only intimidated Arbusca's long-late husband to death. As the lady had intimidated everyone until Arbusca's son had claimed the title.

She held up her hands. "That's past."

You deserve your own life and HeartMate, Fairyfoot said virtuously, repeating the oft-said phrase of Arbusca's son and daughter-in-law.

That was true, too. Arbusca longed for her HeartMate, and was nervous about meeting him. They hadn't connected in twenty-five years. Even then, they'd never met, but linked during hot, sexual dreams when their psi magic had been freed during vision quests.

"Tell me again why I brought you with me to this meeting?" Arbusca asked.

Fairyfoot lifted her nose. *You did not bring Me; I came by Myself.*

"That's right." Arbusca pointed a finger at the cat. "You're uninvited. Leave."

No, I must report to your son.

"You're just nosy."

The door opened.

Arbusca swooped down on Fairyfoot, avoided claws, and teleported the cat back to her room in Willow Residence. "You are *gone*!"

Her HeartMate walked into the room.

She straightened, hid her nervous hands in the folds of her long and heavy silkeen tunic. She was in the far corner of the room, not graciously by the table ready to pour cinnamon caff, as she'd planned. Dammit!

Dri Paris's gaze focused on her. The emotional connection between them seethed with feelings. "Who else was here?" he asked.

"No one of any importance," she said.

He was not the tall, lanky boy whom she'd seen from afar, but a solid man of broad shoulders and craggy face. Suddenly this venue seemed overcivilized as he brought the scent of the wilds into the place. Arbusca stilled to immobility.

He raised his brows. "No one?"

"Of any importance," she repeated.

He hesitated, then his hard gaze softened. As he strode toward her, little flutters of more than attraction—lust—stirred. She wasn't a young woman, but he wasn't a young man.

His lips curved and a quick thought *from him* impinged on her mind. *Both in our prime.*

Her shoulders relaxed, her hands unclenched enough so she curtsied to him. Deeply, as if to a GreatLord. Smoothly she moved to her place, near the caff set, ready to pour. Her hands were steady enough now.

He stopped and bowed, equally deeply. His left hand remained behind his back. Dri wore heavy leather boots and clean leather trous that were cut narrowly for a working man, both in black.

His matching sleeveless leather tunic also was workmanlike. His shirt underneath was a warm cream color of a soft weave; the material showed it wasn't a work shirt, and the sleeves had a faint blouse of fashion.

His smile was full as he stopped a little too close to her for anyone but a lover—or a HeartMate. "Well, if it isn't Blush Willow."

She'd forgotten that childhood name and, even as he said it, felt heat flowing up her neck, into her cheeks. So stupid. He made her feel like a teenager again, full of nervous anticipation.

"Now that's a pretty sight," he drawled, more than a hint of a southern continent accent in his voice. "Pretty blush on a pretty woman." He reached out and picked up her hand, bowed over it, and kissed the back. Tingles sizzled down her nerves, mixing with the flutters in her core.

He smelled of fire—his psi magical power, Flair—and man. Exciting.

"Greetyou, Dri Paris." Just saying his name made her tongue thick, sped up her blood. "It's a pleasure."

His thumb rubbed over her fingers. "So smooth." Gently, he released her fingers. Taking his other hand from behind his back, he revealed a large pink rose in full bloom. "A blush rose. Always reminded me of you, in my dreams."

Her cheeks were pinker than that now. She took the rose that had been stripped of thorns. It was plump and full, almost overblown. Like her. "Thank you." She fiddled with it, then caught herself. So she put the rose in the vase already sporting a daffodil, saying a small stayfresh spell.

Dri and she stared at each other.

His hair was ginger colored with a few strands of silver. Her own dark brown hair was streaked with gray. She hoped he thought it was due to genetics instead of being worn down by her mother's demands.

Weathered skin and a touch of lines were around his amber eyes. She fought time relentlessly and her skin was smoother, but she worked indoors.

"A hearth fire always reminded me of you," she said, sounding lame.

Smiling, he said, "And I thank you for that. I didn't know if you ever thought of me at all."

"I did. I thought of Dri Paris, whose study group met in the same park as mine . . . when we were teens. Later, I knew my HeartMate had fire magic. Though I didn't know he was you until your note last month in response to my telepathic call." She stopped and breathed deeply. "And I thought of my HeartMate." She'd wanted him so badly once. But it had been wrong for her to wish he'd come and take her away from her home when she hadn't had the courage to break away from her mother.

That idea led to emotions too deep. She wanted to concentrate on Dri, not the past.

She moved to her empty chair and hesitated until he seated her, then she gestured to the other chair. He sat, expression inscrutable.

With a quick smile, she said, "I like cinnamon caff, so I ordered that." She moved her cup close and poured. "Would you like some?"

His nostrils widened at the scent. He glanced at the floral china carafe, the delicate creamer and sweet holders. "Sure, a treat for me."

Arbusca took the second cup and poured as gracefully as she'd been taught, clamping her nerves tight so her hands wouldn't shake, mindful of her long, heavy sleeves.

When he took the cup, he made sure their fingers brushed. She got another little sensual jolt, but he didn't seem affected.

"I don't know how I've stayed away from you so long. Put you in the past." Dri shook his head.

"I don't know how I did, either. I'm glad the bond between us was never broken." She sipped and regretted the dim room. His face was too much in shadow. "I'm glad I . . . ah . . . sent questing tremors down our link."

"Yes."

The waiter entered. "Is everything all right, sir? Can I get you anything else?"

"Fine, thanks," Dri said.

"Madam?"

"I'd like a fire." A hearth fire.

"Certainly," the man said and walked to the fireplace, fumbled with the matches three times until the fire was lit. Arbusca's smile strained as she tried to think of something to say to Dri that wouldn't lead them directly into dangerous HeartMate territory.

After the fire caught, the waiter bowed himself out.

"You know," Dri said quietly, "either or both of us could have lit that fire from over here. We have the Flair for it."

"It's his job," she said. "You don't interfere with a server doing his or her job. It makes one nervous." She knew that all too well.

"Ah. Hah," Dri said. Then his shoulders relaxed and he drank. "Excellent caff. Good choice."

"Thank you." She inhaled, realized something herself, and let a smile hover around her lips. "Cinnamon reminds me of you, too."

He ran a calloused hand through his reddish hair. "Guess I understand where that comes from."

"I like your hair," she said.

"Beautiful Blush Willow," Dri murmured. He put his hand over hers. "Who'd have thought I was HeartMate to GreatMistrys Blush Willow, of the Colonist FirstFamilies?"

Now a tremor shivered through her at his touch . . . a touch she'd experienced in dreams . . . intimate dreams . . .

Dri's eyelids lowered, his smile grew satisfied, and his hand curled tighter around hers. Once more they stared at each other, and the only thing she heard was her pounding blood.

The waiter appeared again, coughed, breaking the moment. "Sweet or savory appetizers?" he asked.

Arbusca tried to slip her hand from Dri's. His fingers tightened, squeezed, then let her go. She sent a cool you-should-know-better-than-to-interrupt-an-intense-quiet-conversation look toward the waiter. He gulped, dipped his head, and left the room.

Taking his cup, Dri tilted it and drank it down. His smile had faded and his eyes had become wary. "You do that very well, the high-and-mighty-FirstFamily-lady thing. I had heard you became the chief of the household."

His tone as well as his words stung.

"I did not have the Flair to follow my mother as a GreatLady. My son holds the title and responsibilities."

"I meant that you run the household. You take care of the Family and Residence."

"I'm the housekeeper, yes."

Dri snorted, clinked his cup in his saucer, leaned forward with brows raised. "I'm betting that you hold the Family together. And you have plenty of Flair."

Arbusca drank her caff, forgetting she'd put a reheat spell on it, and burnt her tongue. She was rattled. Dammit! "Thank you for the compliment."

He made an abrupt, abortive gesture, grumbled, "FirstFamilies, can't do anything with 'em."

What he said might not have been incendiary, but his anger went beyond the moment, simmered hard and fast and flamed in the bond between them in ugly waves.

Carefully, Arbusca set her cup down, with no clink of porcelain touching porcelain. She breathed deeply through her nose, tried to dispel the effect of his ire beating against her, narrowed their link.

He scowled.

"What, precisely, do you mean by that?" she asked.

"I mean, most precisely, that maybe I made a mistake in searching you out. Seems to me that you have gone all arrogant. Great noble to lowly Commoner."

"What!

"You banish someone 'of no importance.'"

"That was a ca—"

"You expect me to seat you."

"Manners!"

"You treat the waiter like crap."

"I was helping the waiter learn his job. Such is required here. This is a social club for those who serve in NobleHouses. We train here and we hire from here. As for the 'no one of importance,' that was a nosy FamCat. I wasn't aware you wanted anyone to witness our meeting." She lowered her voice. "But that isn't the problem here, is it? The problem is that you have great anger toward me. Why?"

He sat, spine ramrod. His face appeared rougher as it set in harsh lines. "I wasn't quite sure who my HeartMate was during those Passage dreamquests we shared twenty-five years ago." His eyes went hotter as sexuality flickered in them along with anger. She flushed again but kept her gaze locked on his. This was a part of him that she didn't know, was cautious of. Most people hid their negative qualities at first meetings.

"And?" Anticipatory dread coated her stomach.

"I went to your mother, GreatLady D'Willow. She made it very plain, as *the* matchmaker of Celta, that someone like me, the second son of a minor NobleHouse, was *not* the HeartMate of her daughter."

Arbusca's throat tightened, but she forced words through it anyway. "You believed my mother when she said I wasn't your HeartMate."

His eyes dropped. He tapped a finger on his cup . . . and banked his anger. But now that had transferred to her. "You didn't believe her," she whispered. "You knew my mother lied."

He shifted, his lips thinned, but he met Arbusca's gaze straight. "Even in the entryway to her office, I could tell you were in the Residence. I sensed my HeartMate's energy."

Arbusca jerked back into the cushioned seat. Whatever color she'd had in her face must have drained. Her voice was an unattractive croak. "You didn't believe my mother when she said I wasn't your HeartMate, but you never communicated with me. You never asked—"

His laugh was short, humorless. "Your mother, the FirstFamily GreatLady D'Willow, made it very clear that she would ruin me and my Family, maybe worse, if I contacted you."

Arbusca yanked her hands back into her lap, clenching her fists. She couldn't look at him. Her lips were cold. "You didn't contact me. You didn't fight for me. Didn't care enough. I am your HeartMate."

"We were twenty-one," he said.

"That's past legal age!"

"It's still damn young, and I couldn't fight a woman of her power—riches and Flair psi magic and status."

"You didn't care enough," she repeated numbly.

"And you didn't wait for me," he snapped. "You let her chivy you into marriage with the man she wanted. Kept you under her thumb, didn't she? Forced you to send your boy to the country 'cause she was afraid how powerful he was and he'd depose her. As he did, last year."

All painfully true. "You weren't the only one who was threatened." Her son's health had been at risk. She couldn't speak. If she moved, tears would fill her eyes and fall. She refused to let Dri see them.

"Blush?" he said.

She held herself tightly.

"I'm done." He threw the pink napkin onto the table. Without a glance, he strode from the room.

She breathed steadily, forced the tears back, took a softleaf tissue from her deep sleeve pocket and dabbed at her eyes, blew her nose. How quickly everything went so wrong!

They were both so angry at each other and she hadn't even known.

After one last long, shivery breath, she finished sipping her drink. She reached for his napkin and gritted her teeth at the residue of his intense emotions, then folded it in a manner indicating that it should be cleaned minimally, folded her own the same way. When she thought her knees could support her, she stood. Though there weren't any caff stains or crumbs, she said a Word to ensure the tablecloth and table beneath were clean, and arranged the caff set so that it would be easy for the waiter to clear.

She didn't glance at the rose Dri had given her. Let others appreciate it. She was done. All her hopes had disintegrated. The past was too difficult to overcome.

Another Word cleansed her hands, and she adjusted her long sleeves so they hung properly. More fool she to have dressed up for this meeting in a long tunic-robe, full trous gathered at the ankle, pretty shoes.

She fingered the ring she wore on a necklace under her gown.

She hadn't been brave enough to wear it on her finger openly. And she'd waited for Dri to mention it.

He'd left the pattered circlet of gold with her mother all those years ago, but Arbusca hadn't known of it until last year. More guilt welled. She'd flashed into fiery rage and almost killed her tyrannical mother when the ring was found. Arbusca had sworn a Vow of Honor never to speak of that.

Stepping from the room, she lowered her eyelids to slide her scrutiny discreetly around, then let her shoulders relax. The club was dim and quiet . . . and one she belonged to but didn't often frequent. Since it was a weeknight, there weren't many people. No one seemed to have sensed any oddness about Dri or her.

She saw the waiter and he bowed. "Thank you for your service." She smiled. "You're coming along well."

"I made mistakes," he grumbled.

"We all do."

The majordomo's stand was near the entry door and teleportation pad. She stopped to have the caff and a good tip put on her account and found Dri had paid the bill for both the room and caff. At that, some of her anger rubbed away. He was honorable at least—maybe more. They were HeartMates, after all, still enough in tune that they had a good link—enough to hurt each other badly.

She saw a footman holding the door open for her and decided a short walk in the spring evening would be better than teleporting home. Where her whole Family waited to quiz her.

She walked through the door, turned left toward CityCenter, and ran straight into Dri's broad chest. Her ankle twisted, sending sharp pain up her leg. She gritted her teeth. He grabbed her upper arms. "Steady there."

Arbusca pressed her lips together to stop hot words. Her ankle *hurt* and here he was seeing her at a disadvantage again.

She wasn't an irritable person; why could being in his company distress her so? Because they were meant to be together. But they'd lost their chance.

As soon as she was back on balance, he dropped his arm and

stuck his hands back into his trous pockets. Had he regretted his words like she had hers and waited for her?

Is she going to do it, is she, is she, huh? The mental voice was accompanied by a small yip. Arbusca looked down to see a scruffy dog of an unfortunate butterscotch color. He was sitting, scratching his ear with his back leg, tongue lolling cheerfully from his mouth.

She kept her face smooth. "You have a Familiar Companion, a Fam?"

He has a dog who loves him. Yes, he does! The dog hopped to his paws, shook himself, which sent dusty hair flying, and smiled up at her. *I am Mel. I am his G'Uncle's FamDog. But I love Dri, too!*

"Of course you do."

You're going to help us, yes? Yes! We need a housekeeping expert.

She stiffened and slowly turned her head to Dri. He was scowling, his hands in his pockets had fisted, and she thought that his color had risen, though it was hard to tell in the twilight. Certainly, he radiated annoyance.

"You need a housekeeping expert." She put her hands in her opposite sleeves as her throat clogged and ached with hurt. She wanted to clear it, but wouldn't. So that was the true reason he'd seen her.

"It's not like that, Blush," he said, opened his mouth, shook his head. "I have few words."

"You had plenty before."

The dog yipped again. A fly flew by and he snapped at it, caught it, swallowed, and grinned. His whole body wagged with his tail. *We need good spells that work, and good housekeeping! We don't know spells and we need them.*

"I see," she said, even though she didn't.

"No. Ya don't," Dri said, and pulled his hands from his pockets.

"Pray tell me, then, what I don't understand."

The muscles of his jaw bunched.

A heavy, wheezing exhalation escaped the dog; he stared up at Dri with wild eyes. *She is not happy! You said she would be cheerful and happy! You said all would go well!* He sniffed at her trous and the hem of her embroidered tunic. *You made her angry!*

"That's right," Arbusca said.

FIX IT! The dog's mental projection was enough to make a few passersby stop and smile. Mel barked at Dri. *You said we were lonely and we needed help and she would come and be your HeartMate and help and we would not be sad anymore and things would get better for your G'Uncle and we would have all we need. FIX IT.*

Dri winced, met Arbusca's stare, hunched a shoulder. "I'm better at tearing down than fixing or restoring." He angled his chin. "I'm the best demolition expert on two continents, but fixing . . ." His big, rough hands spread wide.

Mel moaned and flopped on Blush's feet.

Arbusca settled enough to feel the links between them all—one had snapped between her and the dog, too. Dri was distressed, with an underlying loneliness he'd covered with the anger she'd triggered. Depths of emotions she hadn't sensed or touched.

Both of them were hurting.

"Blush is the one who fixes, who keeps a Family going, aren't you?" Again there was the lilt of the southern continent in his voice. Tenderness, understanding swept from him to her. Somehow he knew she'd kept her Family whole when her mother had done her worst by them, descended into obsession. Arbusca had protected her Family and her son until he could claim the title.

The connection between herself and Dri had been there all along. He was a strong man. Had she drawn on his strength through the bond? She didn't know, and the realization that she might have left her shaken.

Dri studied Blush, his Blush, finally within reach. Of his calloused and coarse hands. She'd gone pale and swayed a little, and he didn't like that but didn't dare touch her or he'd carry her away.

So many years had passed since he'd buckled under the pressure her mother had dumped on him and he'd gotten out of Druida

City, leaving only a ring behind that he was sure her mother had thrown out the next moment.

Had too many years passed for them? No. He wouldn't let that happen. He needed Blush too much, and not just her damn housekeeping skills. She was a woman who made a Family, whether it was one man and his G'Uncle and FamDog, or all those who comprised a FirstFamilies GreatHouse.

Her son couldn't need her as much as Dri did. He'd done his research; T'Willow had found his HeartMate and wed her. The man was a matchmaker; surely he wouldn't deny his mother her own HeartMate—who was Dri.

Dri was going to keep Blush.

Mel was on Blush's feet, trying to prevent her from walking away. The dog obviously wasn't used to a person teleporting. It would take little psi power, Flair, for her to teleport away from them.

Dri had to prevent that. Since Blush hadn't flinched when the dog collapsed on her polished shoes, and his hair clung to her elegant clothes, Dri figured he had another chance after the first he'd botched. Even though she didn't carry the rose he'd brought her. That hurt. He'd screwed up good.

Keeping his eyes on hers, he tried a smile, thought it turned lopsided. "I had great hopes when I left to meet you." He shrugged. "Guy hopes . . . that I could sweep you off your feet, that you'd come home with me. That you'd live with me forever."

Her eyes went wide in a stare, her mouth opened a little. Lovely. She shook her head, and he hoped it was simple disbelief.

"I'd give you both moons if I could," he said.

She blinked rapidly. "Where did this come from?"

He touched his chest, feeling really stupid. Mel thumped his tail in encouragement. "From my heart." Dri swallowed. "From my dreams and wishes."

Blush's mouth closed and lips firmed and she narrowed her eyes. "You said nothing like that when we met."

His turn to wince. "I messed up. I told you I was good with demolition, didn't I?" Another lopsided smile. It didn't seem to affect her the way he wanted, soften her. She was wary. Who could have guessed that he was the optimist of the two of them? But then he hadn't spent years living with her mother.

He offered his hands, palms up, for Blush to clasp. "We had hard words between us. Maybe we needed to get them out, and get them out first."

She looked at his hands. He thought a flash of yearning showed in her eyes. "You can't think that a few simple words after we revealed all this old ire between us has cleared everything up, can you?" Her beautiful breasts rose and fell with deep breaths.

"I know that we need to learn each other more. Spend the day with me tomorrow."

Her brows raised. "Doing the housekeeping spells?"

"Doing whatever you want, walking through the city, going to an art gallery or the theater or a concert. Plenty of things to do in Druida. Or we can head down to Maroon Beach. Anything."

Mel whined and she glanced at him. "You seem to have problems with your G'Uncle?"

He ran his fingers through his hair. "I'd like to say no, that I could handle this all on my own. But I'm out of my depth here."

"What's the issue?"

He didn't like that she was all business, so he took her hand and curved it inside his arm, linking elbows. Then he began walking toward the nearest park. There were sparkly lights in the trees. That would be romantic.

Or would be if Mel didn't pant with his tongue hanging out of his mouth. Dri gestured to the dog to move to his side.

"The problem is that my great uncle, G'Uncle—on my mother's side—is not living . . . well." Dri whooshed out a breath. "I didn't realize how he, and his home, had deteriorated, and there's no one else on that side of the family to take care of him. He's my responsibility."

"Caretaker," Blush said in an odd little voice. But he knew what she meant and squeezed her arm. "Yes, you've been one all your life and valued by your Family. Not me; I'm coming late to this job and I don't think it's one I've an aptitude for. I like to clear problems out of the way and get on with life."

"Um-hmm."

Now her mind and emotions, even her body, had gone opaque to him, just as if she'd been any other woman and not his Heart-Mate, a fated lover and partner.

"Our planet, Celta, has not been easy on us. Low birthrates, sterility. Families die out all the time," she said.

"Yeah, and he's the last of the cadet branch of the Conyzas."

"Your Family, the Parises, won't take him in?"

"Nope. He and my grandfather argued before my brother and I were born. Dad says he stole a Family heirloom, though he doesn't know what it was, only that the offense was great and he won't have the old thief in the house."

"And your G'Uncle says?"

"That my grandmother, his sister, loaned him something of the Parises' for as long as he wanted and he still wants it."

"I hear doubt in your voice," Blush said.

"I think he still has it but won't admit he . . . uh . . . misplaced it."

Mel snorted beside Dri.

"And you'd like me to try and find it with housekeeping spells?"

Dri couldn't suppress his flinch. "Yes." He sucked in the spring air and the scent of her, and he didn't want to burden her with his problems. He hesitated, then decided to reveal all. Get everything out, so they could deal with it. "He's my responsibility. My grandmother left G'Uncle Bonar an inheritance that my grandfather and father have blocked until they get the item back."

Blush turned to him; they were in the park now, near a low tree dripping with blossoms of sweet scent that tickled his nose.

"What else?" Blush asked.

He couldn't help it. She was there, and his HeartMate, and her manner had softened just enough. He reached out and pulled her close and kissed her.

They fit. She was soft and womanly against him, and he was aware that he'd led a hard life that had toughened his skin and muscles. Her lips were sweeter than any other woman's, any imagining, any recollection of their dream loving so long ago.

Through their link, he felt a quiet yearning. Long-suppressed need in both of them flashed.

She broke the kiss before passion fogged his brain. Then she stepped back, her cheeks flushed pinker than ever. He ached for her, and his arms ached with emptiness. But if he followed up now, he could make another mistake. She was already turning away.

A flash of inspiration sparked, and he sank into his psi power and *visualized* the rose he'd given her, the vase she'd placed it in. He calculated all spatial dimensions, held out his hand palm up, and *pulled* . . . and the rose appeared. Closing his fingers gently around it, he bowed, and offered it. "Please spend tomorrow with me, Blush."

"How did you do that?" Her eyes were wide. "You weren't in the club more than a few minutes."

The time had seemed a lot longer to him. "I'm a demolition expert. I know building space, can figure coordinates well enough to summon a rose."

Her glance had turned admiring and his chest puffed with pride. She stroked a petal around the rose and said, "I know where everything is in T'Willow Residence and can translocate items there but nowhere else."

"That's part of my Flair," he said.

"Yes."

"And I want you to have the rose. Please," he persisted, "be with me tomorrow."

She glanced down at Mel, who was sitting beside Dri. The dog gazed up at her and said mentally, *We need you.*

That softened her more. Leave it to a dog. Mel even whined a little and pawed her shoe. Dri thought he was overdoing it until Blush said, "All right."

"Maroon Beach?" he asked.

She shook her head, her cheeks less pink than the rose now. "I'll help you—and Mel—with your G'Uncle."

"I'm disappointed."

That made her chuckle richly, and he smiled in relief, added, "It's true. Something more romantic would be better."

Mel coughed.

"Perhaps." She glanced around and her color deepened again. "But a first kiss in a spring evening is romantic enough."

"For now," he said. Before he could take her hand again, she'd teleported away from him.

Wanting to savor the moment, he went to the nearest bench and let night fall around him. He breathed in relief. He'd managed to save the situation.

At home, Arbusca's son was discreetly hovering in the entry hall, along with a few other kinswomen who worked with her to keep the Residence and Family running. Since others of the Family had found their HeartMates or loves in the last year, Arbusca had a template to follow. She smiled at her son. "I'm tired and ready for bed."

He frowned. "It didn't go well, then."

The FamCat Fairyfoot, sitting beside the other FamCat, a male, sniffed. *I smell dog. If a dog was involved, of course there were problems.*

The other cat chimed in, *Dogs always cause problems.*

Arbusca couldn't deny it this time.

"Dri Paris has a Fam Companion?" Her son sounded relieved.

Dogs are not discriminating, his own FamCat warned.

"He's loved by a Fam," she said, twirling her rose.

Her son cocked an eyebrow at the cats, but said, "That's a good sign, as is the rose."

Again she felt blood heat her face.

Arbusca smiled, knowing she looked a little flustered. "A blush rose. When I was young, my nickname was Blush."

Some of her cousins murmured approval.

"It suits you," her son said, but she felt his scrutiny, so she continued through the entryway. She stopped at the end of the room and the door to the corridor that led to the stairs. She gazed at her son, tall and strong and powerful in psi magic and wealth and his own self-confidence.

She recalled the anger that had been between them when he'd returned to this Residence. He'd been banished to a lesser family estate his whole life as a threat to her mother. Their anger had taken months to work out.

Would Dri stay in the city for months? Or would he give up on her again? She was surprised to feel the stab of disappointment at the thought. How easy it was to fall in love.

While she was considering this, her son walked up and kissed her on the cheek. "Sleep well, Mother. If he's a match for you, he's extraordinary indeed."

"He is angry at me, as you were angry."

"Don't worry about that. Does he resent your marriage and your having me?"

She stilled to study the bond between herself and Dri—again surprising, she felt more than tender thoughts of her, more than attraction, enough to make her blush, but she sensed nothing her son had hinted at. "No, mostly the past is the past for him. The reasons we did not come together is sore for him."

"A demolition expert would live more in the present, focus on the future." One last kiss from her son. "Sweet dreams, Mother. Even a disastrous first meeting is nothing to worry about in the scheme of HeartMate love."

"Thus speaks the matchmaker."

"That's right," he agreed.

She hesitated, then said, "I'll be spending tomorrow with Dri."

"Good."

She nodded and returned to her floral-patterned rooms. Usually she found them soothing, but now they seemed fussy.

Dri walked to the public teleportation pad, whistling, with Mel grumping doggy noises. Dri didn't look forward to going back to his small, spartan room in his G'Uncle's house, especially since he had a suite in his father's home. But G'Uncle Bonar couldn't be left alone when Dri had the option of caring for him.

The best way Dri knew to overcome anger was through physical activity, sweating through a tricky fire demolition, practicing his fighting skills . . . or . . . sex. He and Blush could release their anger, move from anger to loving and maybe even the lifetime HeartBond with some good sex—making love.

But Dri sure couldn't make the kind of slow, sweet love with

Blush that he wanted in the tiny room that contained a one-person bedsponge. Not tonight.

Not physically, anyway. But there were dreams . . . they'd connected in dreams first; that should work again.

When he got to his G'Uncle's house, he tended the old and querulous man, made sure he was fed and clean and tucked in equally clean linens on his bedsponge. Mel lay on the floor and thumped a tail in gratitude as Dri extinguished the spell-lights.

Darkness and quiet settled over the Residence and Arbusca lay awake, considering each tiny detail of the evening. She wasn't foolish enough to believe that their anger at each other was gone, but was hopeful that eventually they could forgive each other and become true HeartMates.

She felt the feathery brushes of fingertips on her cheeks. A soft kiss. When she checked, the link between her and Dri was wide open—both mental and emotional. *No!* she sent him telepathically.

Trust me. Anger is fire, but so is passion, and I bet we have more passion between us than anger. Enough to burn away all old hurts.

She wanted to believe him, and her body was readying as if for a lover, recalling those sexual dreams from long ago. *Perhaps,* she answered. *But I would prefer any passion to be truly physical.*

She'd surprised him. And challenged him, she thought, and, of course, aroused him. His thoughts lost clarity in their link, and the connection became more emotional. He wanted her. Not just sexual passion was revealed in that wanting, but affection, the seedlings of love. Whether she admitted it or not, they *had* had a bond between them for many years.

When will you let me make love to you? His mental voice was tumultuous.

When we are ready.

She heard his groan clearly.

Sweet dreams, she sent.

That isn't gonna happen.

The idea he was suffering as much as she pleased her and she knew he sensed that.

Something we have in common—our yen for each other. That never faded, he said.

No. Good night.

That won't happen, either, but I'm gonna love seeing you in the morning.

She narrowed the link between them until she was sure he felt little from her, then she went to the waterfall room and stood under a cold shower.

Arbusca heard from Dri the next morning after breakfast and before she had time to get antsy. She exited the Residence just as he drove up in a glider, and as far as she could tell, none of her Family was watching except the FamCats. They were enough.

She'd dressed in sturdy gray work trous that were only slightly bloused and cuffed at the ankle, and a matching tunic that fell just below her knees and had side slits for easy movement. Her sleeves were still large enough for pockets, but shouldn't get in the way for any spellwork and actually boosted the spells when doing sweeping gestures.

Dri hopped from the glider and held the door up for her. His eyes crinkled with his whole-face smile. She received an extra thrill straight to her center when their gazes met.

Once again their link was open and their past ire with each other was overwhelmed by their hopes for the future. With their individual confidence in themselves and that they could build a future together, just because they were willing to work hard to do so.

He didn't talk, and neither did she, but let emotions flow through their bond along with fleeting thoughts and impressions. He found her beautiful and sexy. No man had ever been so attractive to her.

They drew up in front of a stone cottage, and Dri opened his door and vaulted out, hurrying around to hand Blush from the glider. He was relieved that things were going well today. She'd mindspoken with him last night, been willing to overlook how he'd messed things up. She'd only hummed with pleasure at the spring breeze and the fragrance of flowers as they drove from Noble Country, where the estates of the greatest nobles were, including her home, to this modest area mostly inhabited by Commoners.

He'd been the one to judge yesterday, she hadn't. She waited as he lifted the door, gave him both her hands—sweet touch!—and let him "help" her from the glider that stood a meter off the ground on its stands.

She eyed the one-story house set on a lot that was big enough that G'Uncle Bonar's neighbors hadn't been aware of what was going on. "Nice," she said.

Dri knew that she'd change her opinion the moment she saw inside. He braced himself as he walked her up the path to the front door.

Mel, the FamDog, teleported from inside to the front stoop and shot toward them, tongue lolling. *She came, she came, she came!* He tripped over his own feet and rolled-skidded to a halt near Blush, licked her hand as she bent to rub his head. *She is WONDERFUL. YOU ARE WONDERFUL!* he panted.

Blush was grinning, too, forgetting her manners. Good. Dri took her apron from her loose grasp, flicked it out, and caught the scent of fresh herbs and Blush. His throat dried. He waited until she straightened, then whipped the long bib apron around her. He slipped his fingers along the tabs that connected behind her nape, and satisfaction welled inside him as she stilled, then trembled at his touch. She fumbled with the waist strings until he said the Word to tie them and brought her back to lean a few seconds against his body. Oh, yeah, so sweet. He nuzzled her neck and gloried in her against him until Mel yipped sharply.

"Ready," Arbusca said.

Dri was more ready for loving than for taking care of his G'Uncle Bonar. He linked hands as they walked to the front door. "I've spoken with my father. If we find and return the Paris Family heirloom, he'll release the inheritance."

Blush frowned. "You said your father doesn't know what the item is." She hesitated, then went on. "If after many years no one's missed the object, why is it important?"

Good question and one he'd asked his father. "It's supposedly a Family heirloom, and is definitely a bone of contention, the basis for an estrangement. I was told that the piece was unmistakably marked *Paris*."

"Hmm." She nodded. "We can find it."

He swung their clasped hands, feeling as giddy as a child. "We can do anything together." They'd reached the stoop, and he dropped her hand to grasp her around the waist and swing her up the three steps. She laughed and the world around them sharpened into a beauty that dazzled his senses, and at the center of that world was Blush.

They stood, once again lost in the moment and each other. Her eyes were a little dreamy, her cheeks as pink as the rose he'd given her. She needed more smiles and roses in her life. He'd make sure she'd have them.

Mel hopped around them. *Let's go. Let's go.*

The last thing Dri wanted was to go inside. He wished to spend a carefree day with his HeartMate; was that too much to ask?

The FamDog whined pitifully.

Dri bit a sigh short. G'Uncle Bonar had no one but him. He said a phrase to drop the security spellshields, then stopped Blush's hand before she thumbed the door latch as misgivings swarmed inside him. "Wait. Maybe we shouldn't do this. No, we should definitely not do this. Especially not you. Just recommend a good housekeeping service and I'll—"

Her back straightened. "You think I can't handle whatever lies behind that door?"

"You can handle anything. You shouldn't *have* to deal with G'Uncle Bonar and—"

"He's your Family."

"Yes, and my responsibility, not yours," he said.

"You want *me* to be Family." That sounded tentative from her.

"You're my HeartMate; I want you to be my wife, to Heart-Bond with me during loving so we're so tied together so intimately that one can't survive a year without the other." His voice came out harsher than he liked. "That's the consequence of a Heart-Bond, and one I'm willing to make. But it's a heavy decision."

She lifted her chin in a stubborn manner that he thought he'd come to know well. "The FirstFamilies promote HeartMate marriages—they are more solid, more fertile. Such bonds lead to better Families. I've seen many people make such a decision, including my son. I wish for a more fulfilling life, want a partner linked to me emotionally, spiritually. My mother had no fated love, no HeartMate. If she had, perhaps my Family would not have suffered as we did."

HeartMates usually resonated with each other, characters matching. Dri shuddered inwardly at the idea of her mother marrying someone else just as cruel, the two heading a great NobleHouse. But wouldn't conflicting selfishness prevent that? He didn't know and it didn't damn matter.

Blush was pressing on, "Didn't you just say that we could do anything together? Do you doubt now?"

"But you shouldn't have to deal with this."

Her eyes narrowed. "Are you afraid of me going in there?"

Heat crawled up his neck. "Maybe."

"You've been living here. Is there any rotting food?"

"No."

"Dead animals?"

"Not that I know of."

When I find them, I chase and eat the mice, Mel added.

Blush winced, stared at Dri. "No dead-mouse smell?"

He considered it. Plenty of odd smells, but not that one. "No dead-mouse smell."

"Let's go." She put her hand on the door latch.

He covered it with his own. "Last chance for a trip to Maroon Beach."

She gave him a steely look. "I am not a coward."

Not resisting the temptation of her pursed lips, he stole a quick kiss. "Never," he said, though he felt self-condemnation from her through their link.

Putting his finger under her chin to pull her gaze back to him after it had slid away, he said quietly, "This isn't the time to speak of the past, but you haven't been a coward."

She shook her head. "I have been, and more than once, and

deep down you're angry with me." A false twitch-of-the-lips smile. "I can still feel that, and feel my anger with you, too."

Let's GO! Mel whined.

The latch clicked and she pushed open the door. She stood just within the threshold, in the two-meter-square spot that Dri had cleared, staring at the towering stacks of *stuff*, appearing appalled. Pressing her hand above her breasts, she whispered. "A hoarder."

All his defensiveness rose, maybe some of that lingering anger she'd tweaked. "There are more of them out there than you who live in intelligent Residences are aware of."

Blush gave him that greater-noble-to-lesser look. After a quick clench of his jaw, he spit more words out. "You FirstFamilies and great nobles have castles and plenty of storage space."

"No one in Druida City need live like this. Our ancestors constructed plenty of buildings for a multitude of descendants who did not materialize. There are many good, solid, empty places."

He forced his temper down, regretting his words. He was supposed to be old enough to learn from his mistakes. He raised his brows, infused a note of humor in his voice. "Be glad he chose a cottage. Otherwise he'd have filled a mansion."

She relaxed, but her gaze continued to scan the piles and the narrow walkway between them. "I suppose you're right." She shook her head. "It's a sickness."

He resisted running his hands through his hair. "I can't find the damn heirloom and haven't wanted to clean the place out in case I missed it."

"Unsurprising," she said.

I can't sniff it out, Mel said. *Everything smells like Bonar.*

Setting her hands on her hips, she turned in place, surveying the stacks, many of the *same* thing, like folded trous and tunics, towers of papyrus, even tottering old-fashioned books.

"Well, this should take a couple of days."

"What! It would take me months."

Again that greater-noble-to-lesser look, but this time he caught the glint in her eye, the faint quiver around her lips. "Yes. It would. But it will take *me* no more than two days. I'm that good."

"I bow to you." He did. And knocked over one of the framed pieces of art.

"Light!" Blush ordered, and a large spell-light flickered into existence.

Dri grimaced at how much worse the place looked. He'd been careful to leave it dim. "I've only been here a couple of days. I've concentrated on G'Uncle Bonar and his bedroom."

She ignored his weak words as she picked up a large work. "This is wonderful." It was a summer meadow, full of flowers and grasses. In the foreground the plants were graceful, detailed botanical studies. All the paintings were signed by Bonar.

"This should be hanging in a gallery." She handed Dri the picture, went over to others leaning against a wall, and flipped through them. "All of these are lovely. I can get them in a gallery."

Dri grunted. "Good luck to you on convincing G'Uncle Bonar." Dri knocked his knuckles against a small free space of the stone wall. "It's been like me beating my head against this, trying to get him to part with one. He won't do it. 'Art isn't for money; creation must be for its own sake only, otherwise art is tainted.'"

They shared a disbelieving look. Then, Blush shook her head and placed the piece carefully with the others. She dusted her hands, lifted her nose, sniffed. Frowned again. "There's some odor I can't quite place . . ."

Lots of good smells. Mel inhaled lustily.

Mel, FamDog? Dri, boy? The mental call was quavery, but Dri knew Blush had heard it.

Here, Dri answered his G'Uncle.

"Where is he?" Blush asked.

Dri stretched his arms out. "This is the mainspace and dining room. It runs the full width of the house."

Blush's eyes widened. There were no paths other than straight ahead.

Mel? A weaker call from Bonar.

The dog vanished, teleporting.

Dri continued, "There are openings leading to a kitchen on the right and a waterfall room on the left, then G'Uncle's straight back to the right, with his own waterfall room; guest room to the left—mine. No heirlooms of importance in my room."

Mel barked.

"Still think only a couple of days?"

Blush's lips firmed, then she said, "Two. Full days using a lot of powerful spells, but two."

"You're incredible." He kissed her again, withdrew reluctantly. He still wanted to learn Blush through play instead of work.

She said a Word and her trous tucked against her lovely legs so she could walk through the stacks. He appreciated the view.

Arbusca stopped at the small bulb of space at the end of the path. Weak light from a window or two off the back wall of the house filtered through the piles. There was a slightly more open space around the old man's bedroom entrance.

Dri stepped beside her, swung open the door, and she glimpsed a thin, bony man with pale skin and sweat-damp, straw-colored hair before the smell hit her. A strange, musty smell. Clamping her lips shut, refusing to breathe, she yanked Dri from the threshold, back into the small space, knocked over piles.

Stay! she ordered Mel.

"What?" Dri asked.

Breathe shallowly. No wonder your G'Uncle is ill. There's marwol mold in there.

Dri stepped back, stared at the door in horror. The mold was insidious, fatal.

How often have you been in there?

He clasped her arms. *Get out, get out now!*

She wrenched away. *No. A few hours won't hurt, and I don't think you've been much affected. I would have known.* Her nose twitched. Not much smell of marwol on him, just clean man.

But we need to get Bonar to a HealingHall. And, fire mage, you need to incinerate everything in there to cleanse it. She closed her eyes, tilted her head, sent her senses, her own psi magic Flair, questing for the smell-taste-emanation of the mold. On a soft breath, she said, "There's very little outside of that room. It likes to layer thickly in one place before spreading. I think we've caught it in time." She opened her eyes, found Dri was pale. "Whatever is in the rest of the house came from your clothing or Mel."

"Mel!" Dri lunged for the door.

"Wait!" She seized his tunic. "Animals aren't affected by marwol mold."

"You're sure?"

She raised her eyebrows. "I haven't ever had to deal with marwol personally, but I am an expert and sure. Use fire just short of burning the stone. I trust you can do that?"

"I can do it," he said tightly. "The door will go, but I can keep the fire at the threshold."

There were a couple of beats of silence.

"We have to get G'Uncle out of there," Dri said, seemed to brace himself.

She said, "I'll grab him, teleport with him to Primary Healing-Hall. They'll care for him, and check me. You can come for an examination after you fire the room."

Distress showed in Dri's eyes: love for his G'Uncle, caring for her?

"His favorite paintings are in there."

Arbusca thought of the beautiful renderings of flowers and herbs, the summer meadow she'd have enjoyed on her own walls. "I'm sorry, but that can't be helped. Nothing in there can be cleaned sufficiently to prevent the mold, and the mold is deadly. Fire's the only way."

Dri's expression hardened until she saw the tough mage ready to handle a demolition project. His amber gaze, darker now, met hers. "And if the Paris Family heirloom is in that room?"

"Then it will be gone," Arbusca said, accepting how that would affect them, too. Bonar Conyza was Dri's responsibility and she already knew enough of the man to understand that he wouldn't shirk his duty. Even if it meant living with a demanding elder for the rest of his life. She'd had enough of that with her mother and now she was facing it again. The notion made her want to weep, but fate had spun things out of her control.

"Throw open the door on three. I'll take your G'Uncle and

Mel. When you see we're gone, shut the door—don't slam it." She took a breath, continued. "And then practice your Flair talent. Incinerate everything in there."

He nodded, then said, "One minute."

"What?"

"Link with me mentally and show me how to recognize the marwol spores." He glanced around. "If there aren't that many and they're susceptible to heat, I can clear them from the house."

"Good idea." She reached out and his fingers were there, twining with hers. Their connection was open enough that they probably didn't need touch, but she wanted the physical bond, liked the cradling of her hands in his calloused ones, the intimacy.

Once again she opened her senses, quested with her Flair to locate and identify a small cluster of spores that appeared greenish black to her. *Showed* them to him and waited as he fumbled to recognize them with his own Flair.

He grunted, and in the next instant the spores heated to red, shriveled, and vanished. She noted a slight scent of his sweat and the heat of a summer's day with the sun burning down on earth.

"Well done," she said.

His brows lowered and she realized that trying to be casual had made her use a tone she would have with a new person training under her.

"Thank you." He let a breath out through his nose. His jaw flexed.

Following instinct, she kissed his chin. "We're both old enough to be set in our ways and too touchy. I *do* appreciate your Flair and skill, Dri."

"I'd rather show you other skills." His leer was exaggerated and belied the anxiety in his eyes.

Why are you out there? called the FamDog.

Tightening his grip on Blush's hand, Dri directed his telepathic reply to only her and Mel. *Can you teleport to the animal Healer?*

An excited yip. *I get to go there? Yes!*

Then I want you to go there when Blush comes in for Bonar.

She will be taking him to a HealingHall, and we want to make sure you are fine, too.

He barked. *What is wrong!*

Blush said, *There's a bad mold in that room, one that hurts people but not dogs. Still, you need to tell the animal Healer that you've been exposed to marwol. You should keep away from other humans there and NOT shake yourself at all.*

Oh. The funny smell is mold?

Yes. I will be in on three. Dri will stay here to kill all the mold.

Will FamMan be all right?

Those at Primary HealingHall will examine him—and Dri and me.

On three! Mel said.

Wait, Blush said. She stepped close to Dri and her arms slipped around his neck. Every thought in his head disappeared when her soft body leaned against his—and her mouth on his was amazingly hungry. He grabbed her, held her close.

ONE! Mel shouted mentally with a roar that shook them apart.

"Blush," Dri panted.

TWO! Mel continued.

Their eyes connected. She'd kissed him. Why? Because this was the most dangerous thing she'd done? Nothing like his job.

THREE!

Blush jerked, pushed the door open, and rushed to the old man. He squawked as she grabbed him, then they were gone.

Mel gave Dri a big-eyed look, then vanished. Dri pulled the door shut slowly, trying to minimize the escape of mold spores.

He stood outside the old man's door, anger at himself blasting through him. Why hadn't he taken his G'Uncle to a HealingHall despite the man's ranting at Healers? Despite Dri's father and older brother assuring Dri that Bonar just suffered from old age? Dri hadn't been in Druida a full week, but surely he should have been more concerned with Bonar's needs instead of his own. Dri had failed.

But he wouldn't fail at destroying the mold inside Bonar's

bedroom and waterfall room beyond. Nor would Dri fail at caring for Bonar—or Blush. He'd never fail Blush again.

Setting his palms against the door, he sent his Flair psi power into his G'Uncle's space until Dri was certain of the exact dimensions down to the tint on the stone walls. Everything inside would burn. The door, hardened wood, would burn, too. He set a shield in the space where the door was.

It would be a challenge to turn the contents of the rooms to ashes, sear the stone enough to rid it of mold and spores yet not damage the structure. But he could do it.

The use of his Flair talent and release of such fire energy could be used to scourge himself of some anger, too.

Sinking into his balance, he focused all his psi power for fire into the chambers . . . and heated the air, molecule by molecule until fire flashed and ate all. The bedroom appeared behind the shield where the door had been and he lowered the temperature of the air incrementally until it was normal. Before he dropped the shield, he tested for mold inside. Nothing.

If the Paris Family object had been in the chambers, it was gone forever, and Dri and Blush were stuck with Bonar Conyza. Would Blush accept that?

Dri strode into the room and opened the windows to the spring breeze, made sure the air whisked around the waterfall room, too. Then he studied the threshold, translocated an old door he'd seen in storage on his father's estate, and installed it. Good enough for now.

It took only a few more moments to fry the small motes of spores in the rest of the house. He did a thorough job, though he was impatient to get back to Bonar, and Blush.

But as soon as he arrived at the HealingHall—by glider since it didn't take as much energy as teleporting—Blush put the whole matter of his grumpy G'Uncle Bonar in Dri's hands to return to the cottage and supervise an inspection.

Dri saw his G'Uncle examined, Healed, and admitted overnight for observation before Dri returned to find Blush hard at work.

The door to the cottage was open and she stood with a young

priestess half their age. Dri watched as a stack of nicely folded clothes, appearing new—tunics, trous, shirts—was translocated from the house to the front sidewalk. The pile was as high as Blush's chin. She placed her hands atop the clothes, murmured a few Words, and drifts of dust fell, sinking to the ground or whisked away by the small breeze.

"Nothing here but clothes and they're now cleansed," Blush said with satisfaction.

The priestess raised her hands, palm out. "I agree. Nothing resonates of strong history or emotions as it would if a Family heirloom was involved." She pulled a pad and a writestick from her sleeve pocket. Her lips moved as she counted the items. "The temple will give you the proceeds from our sale, less our percentage."

"Thank you," Blush said.

The clothes pile disappeared—translocated to the priestess's temple—and another stack, nearly identical except for the colors, settled onto the sidewalk.

Dri strode forward. "You're sure you didn't get rid of the Paris item?"

The priestess jolted; Blush turned and stared at him. "Yes, I am, and Priestess Bursa of Buckthorn Temple is skilled in antique resonance, and has concurred with all my decisions."

"All?" How much had they cleared? He stalked past them into the front room of the cottage and was surprised and disappointed. For a moment he'd dreaded and hoped that a great deal of the house had been cleared. Instead about three layers on the left had been cleaned out . . . where a huge old breakfront cabinet stood.

Blush joined him. "As you can see, we've been careful." She stared at him in pointed silence. "And we're going on the assumption that your Paris Family item was not in Bonar's bedroom."

She was mad at him for questioning her expertise.

"Let's get this thing gone." He studied the cabinet.

Her brows went up. "I thought that you—or Bonar—would want to keep it."

The wood was stained, had warped doors, even sat crooked. "Why would we want the thing?"

Blush waved at the cabinet. "It's a good, solid piece with charm and only has minor problems."

"Looks like it's ready for splinters to me." Then he smiled, flipped out his hands, made the sound of fire. "I can make it go whoosh!"

"You want it or not?" she asked.

"We'll move it." He stared at the space, the light, the proportions. He took her hand, enjoying the jolt of desire, and walked from the room into the sunshine. There he took deep breaths. Squeezing her hand, he said, "The cottage already seems better. Did you do something?"

She shrugged. "A few minor housekeeping spells."

"Like?"

"A light dust suction spell that couldn't harm anything." She frowned at the stack of clothes still on the sidewalk. "An air-freshening spell. It will be better when we reach the walls and can open the windows." She led him to a level place in the front yard. "We can translocate the cabinet here." With a glance, she brought the younger woman to them. "Link hands and visualize the breakfront."

They did and a connection formed between the three of them. Dri had the best image of the cabinet and the spatial dimensions. Mentally he sent the women his image and they refined theirs to match his. He counted down, "On three. One, Arbusca. Two, Willow girl. *Three!*"

He put some Flair magic energy into moving the thing. Discovered that the priestess might be good at item verification, but Blush had been doing all the heavy lifting. Before his short grunt escaped his mouth, the cabinet was in the yard.

Blush dropped his hands, stepped to the piece, and put her palms on it, said a short chant, and the breakfront turned into a whole and gleaming piece of fine furniture.

Dri's gasp matched the priestess's.

Blush leaned against the sturdy cabinet, no color in her cheeks.

"You're doing too much." He reached for her, but she levered herself up.

"I know my limits," she said, a little breathless.

"Your limits helping me are *not* the limits your mother demanded."

He took her hands and clamped his fingers tighter when she tried to pull them away, then he sent her some strength and energy.

Blush sighed, leaned against him. When her cheeks pinkened, she stood straight again.

The priestess put her hands in her opposite sleeves and her face took on that fake serene expression that counselors use when giving advice. "You two must deal with your anger before it explodes."

"We're working on it," Dri said.

"Consider releasing such combustion in the bedroom," the priestess said.

Dri liked her a lot more. "My idea exactly."

"We've only known each other two days!" Blush sounded shocked, but not quite as much as he thought she should.

The priestess's eyes widened. "I never would have guessed that. You work together so well. Your link is strong and far more open than most people who've just met."

Dri caught Blush's hands in his own. "We've been HeartMates for a long time, if not together."

Mouth turning down, the priestess said, "There's still anger. I can contact a superior who will craft a forgiveness ceremony for you."

Blush drew her hands away. "Let's just get this job done." She turned and walked back into the house.

Dri said, "Thanks for the offer, maybe later."

Though Dri tried to pace himself and the others, they were all exhausted by the time MidAfternoonBell rang and one side of the front room was clear. Blush wasn't admitting she was weary, and it certainly didn't show on her the way it did in the clothes that stuck to his body with sweat or the priestess's damp face.

Soon the priestess left and he and Blush lay under a few budding birches in the front grassyard.

"How did you think you could clear something like this out in two days?" he asked.

She sat straight. "I can do it."

"You could do it if you had the staff you're used to, but not by yourself."

Her lips compressed, then she nodded. "It's not the staff, it's the other resources. I'm used to more energy being invested in a house, and the help of an intelligent Residence." There was a catch in her voice.

"You don't have to impress me, Blush. You already have my greatest admiration. You don't have to keep proving yourself."

She looked startled.

"I sure don't want to have to prove myself to you every day." He took a big breath. "And since we're on this topic, maybe we ought to talk about that anger thing again."

Arbusca stared at him. It had been an emotional day and she'd nearly worn herself out on his and his G'Uncle's behalf—and had shoved the anger issue out of her head. She didn't want to consider the matter. "You think this can be resolved by talking?"

His grin was fast. "Nah, I think *you* think that. Me, I'd rather get rid of the anger in bed."

She choked.

"I figure it could take lots of time—in bed—to work through our anger." He smiled that lopsided smile that reached inside her and feathered against all her deepest dreams of love.

"We've got to overcome these old negative feelings to move on. Redeem ourselves in each other's eyes," he said.

She was shocked at his language. It sounded too feminine. "Who have you been speaking to?"

He grimaced. "I recalled some time I spent with a counselor years ago." Then he sent her a hopeful look. "But *I* think that if we just spend time together, we'll know each other better and the negative feelings will fade."

"Especially if we spend time together in bed."

"Exactly!" He winked. "I'm ready to give it my all."

She refrained from looking down at his trous. "I'm sure you are."

"Yes. Are you following me?"

"I'm understanding you clearly, but I won't be following you . . . to your bedroom or anywhere else."

"Not ready to talk or love, eh?"

"It's been a demanding day."

His expression shifted and he rose from the ground smoothly. "I don't want to be demanding, Blush. I figure you've had enough of that in your life." He was standing very close, his aura impinging on hers, serious now. "I liked the kiss you gave me earlier."

He leaned forward and brushed her lips with his own, his eyes wide and looking into hers. All of her warmed. Blushed. He was right. With him she was Blush Willow.

Then he stepped back. "Tomorrow, Blush." He grinned. "Another day of learning each other."

She nodded, and with the last of her energy, she teleported home to her own waterfall room, quivering with need.

His small bedroom was sterile, and the smell of fire haunted his dreams. Fire and destruction was his business, but occasionally the odor shot him back into the past and the worst moment of his life.

"My daughter is not your HeartMate," the heavy old woman with calculating eyes and mean smile that showed sharp teeth repeated for the third time.

He knew she lied. And maybe she knew he knew and that pleased her even more.

"My HeartMate is in this Residence," he said, his voice not as strong as it should have been for the man he thought he was at twenty-one. But the previous and following moments stripped him of any pride, any belief that he was a man.

"You would do well to forget that. Forever." The woman leaned forward. "You are close to your father and brother, aren't you? That stupid G'Uncle of yours?"

He sat in wretched silence. Almost too petrified to answer as image after image of what a powerful woman like she could do—ruin them. Kill them and get away with it.

Then she nodded and settled back into the comfortchair built for her, still smiling. She flicked her fingers at him. "Go. And don't return."

He'd taken the ring that he'd had made for Blush from his pocket and put it on a small, fancy table. The ring gleamed as if it held all the hope he'd felt. Gone now.

He'd left, gone all the way to the southern continent, where he tried to prove to himself and everyone else he met that he was a man, and strove to forget he had a HeartMate.

She dreamt of a bad moment . . . one of a chain of memories— nightmares—that crept into her sleep and stole her peace.

Her mother surged into the room, beautifully dressed in an embroidered gown that would have fed a Downwind slum family for a year. She was smiling in a way that made Arbusca straighten to perfect immobility and shiver inside.

"Arbusca, I've concluded negotiations with the Fumitory Family. You'll wed the younger son in three months."

Despite herself, Arbusca reeled back, had to set her hand on a paneled wall. The younger Fumitory was a weak man. He'd live here, in the Willow Residence, under Arbusca's mother's rule. "No!" she cried.

Her mother slapped her hard.

"I have a HeartMate," Arbusca whispered.

D'Willow snorted. "He's gone. Why would he care to claim such a puny thing as you? Your only value is to me."

Arbusca knew that was wrong, but the slap had not been the first to pummel self-doubt into her.

Her mother's smile widened. "Gone far out of Druida City into the wilds, and you don't have the guts to follow? If you're lucky, you'll give me a female heir for the title. We'll sign the marriage contract this afternoon after luncheon. Go ensure that the food will be good."

Arbusca jolted from sleep to find the gray light of predawn seeping into the window. Her arms were clamped around a soft pillow and her nightgown stuck to her from fear-sweat. She wished with all her heart that her dreams would have been shared erotic ones with Dri. She panted and shoved the pillow away, rose, and stripped linens from the bedsponge and placed them in the cleanser, remade the bed.

But the dream could have been worse. She could have experienced that time when she'd found Dri's ring and realized what her mother had done. That time when she'd nearly killed her mother . . . and the consequences of that action.

In actuality, her marriage had been bland, and Parv Fumitory had given Arbusca the blessing of her life, her son. Who now slept with his own HeartMate in the opposite wing.

With dawn came a new day. One she could spend again with Dri. "Blush," she whispered, trying out the name of her girlhood, feeling that young again. "I'm Blush Willow." Plumping the pillows, she smiled. "And someday I'll be Blush Paris." In the waterfall room, she washed away the lingering failure that coated her, as she had for years.

A few minutes later she checked the nicely rope-sized link between herself and Dri. He was awake.

Blush? It's not quite dawn.

I'm surprised you're up, she said.

Damn dreams. I don't suppose you'd like a little mental sexual stimulation?

No.

Didn't think so, he said. *I can wait. Barely. But I will, until you're ready.*

Warmth filled her. *Thank you. Why don't you contact the HealingHall and see if your G'Uncle can be moved?*

It's not even dawn, Dri repeated.

Don't often work in the dark?

Demolishing something? Nope, not likely if I want to make sure nothing is around to be harmed. He sighed. *We'll do it your way. No bedsponge or anything else in Bonar's bedroom though.*

You leave the furnishing to me. I deduced his tastes.

You're a wonder. We can sell some paintings to pay for the furnishings.

She hesitated.

You sell them! We don't need any Willow castoffs.

Does your Family have any old furniture in storage? she asked.

My father wouldn't give Bonar a stick.

All right. I'll get some good, solid furniture from the Clovers. She had plenty of money; she'd buy the summer meadow. It was worth a bedroom set. *Set some paintings aside for me to take to the Enlii Art Gallery.*

She sensed Dri whistle.

Best gallery in the city. Bonar won't like it, but he's well enough that I can be tough with him. He won't thank you, but I will.

You're welcome. She was smug with the satisfaction of helping. *I'll meet you later.*

Yeah, later, lovely Blush.

The whole conversation gave her flushes and chills. She'd dreamt of a bad time and sensed he had, too. Their sleep wouldn't be good—the erotic dreams wouldn't come; they couldn't HeartBond during loving—until they'd settled the issues between them.

By the time she teleported to Bonar's house, the furniture had already arrived, along with the old man, Mel, and Dri. They were in the bedroom. Bonar, his linens, and his nightrobe appeared clean, even though his blond hair stuck out.

"So my prodigal nephy has returned." An old-man snort bounced off the walls. With a curled lip, Bonar looked down at Mel. "And my FamDog."

Mel smiled ingratiatingly, stood on his hind paws, and licked Bonar's hand. *You are much your old self. Much!*

The elder scrubbed the dog's head a little too hard, then shot a sneering gaze at Blush. "So you're the gal who's HeartMate to my boy."

"That's right," she replied. She couldn't help it, a couple of watercolors on the wall—floral bouquet studies—were crooked, and she straightened them.

"Keep your fingers off my work!" Bonar said.

"You have a wonderful talent," she said.

"Good enough," he grunted. "You're daughter of that vicious bitch, Saille D'Willow."

Blush turned around slowly, answered even more carefully as she met the man's gleeful eyes. "You may keep my mother out of any conversation. I will have respect from you." She stared at him until he shifted, dropped his glare.

"You got it," he mumbled. "Knew your MotherDam, your mother's mother; now *she* was a good woman. Maybe you take after her."

"Perhaps I do."

"But your mother didn't treat my boy right, and neither did you. She threatened him and you let her do it. You didn't fight for him. You didn't break away from her. Showed no spine until your own boy came back."

"I beg your pardon—"

"You should."

"G'Uncle!" Dri protested.

"Dri, don't you tell me you don't think the same thing," Bonar shot out, complete with spittle.

Mel growled.

"Dri and you aren't the only ones who were disappointed in this whole matter," Blush said.

"Humph. Looks like you're mad at my boy, too. Both of you angry. That's what comes of not claiming your HeartMate when you find him." He glanced at Dri. "Or when you find her. Despite everything. Couple of twits. Get out of my sight." He pulled the covers up to his chin.

"Blush came to help, and you try to alienate her so she won't stay," Dri said.

"Oh, got me all figured out, do you, boy?" Bonar still didn't look at them. "I don't have the thing."

Blush met Dri's eyes. "The what?"

"The whatever the Paris Family wants," Bonar said slyly.

"Who could ever tell?" Blush said with a sniff like one of the cats would make. "All this worthless stuff." She waited for an answer that didn't come.

Dri held the door open for her. The stiff slant of his shoulders showed the old man had stirred up Dri's anger.

Hers had revived, too.

"He riled us up deliberately," Dri said.

"Yes."

Dri hunkered into his balance, his jaw flexed. "So what are we going to do about it? The longer we hold this anger between us, the more it can poison us. And the more people can manipulate us."

"My prime manipulator is dead," Blush said, then thought of the cat Fairyfoot, who'd said some pointed words that morning. She let out a breath. "But the ire affects our dreams, too."

"Yeah." Dri met Blush's eyes directly. "I have a deep anger that your mother threatened me and my Family, that she intimidated me." He sucked in a breath. "And that by the time I got the balls to confront her and claim you, you'd married. You didn't wait for me."

She set her own shoulders and said, "I have deep anger that you didn't come to me, fight for me." Her eyes sparked. "Perhaps I wouldn't have had the courage to tie my fate to yours, but we'll never know. You didn't ask me."

He rocked back and forth, heel, toe, heel. "Yeah, we'll never know." Jerking his head in a nod, he said, "At least we've acknowledged our feelings." Glancing around, he said, "What are we going to do about the mess of this house and finding the heirloom?"

Blush jutted her chin. "I had an idea about that."

"You're the expert."

His admission wore away only a little of the pain of the previous words—his and her own.

"There is a sieve spell. If we phrase the parameters right, we might find the Paris antique." From her sleeve pocket, she drew out a papyrus with the spell she'd crafted that morning.

"What's the catch?" he asked, looking at it.

"It takes a lot of Flair energy, more than I have."

His gaze was steady.

"More than both of us have, if we tried to work together now. If we mend our quarrel enough . . ." Her voice failed her. His amber eyes were clear but showing once-liquid depths that had hardened until she thought they would snag her and trap her forever, a fate she was beginning to yearn for. "So I could tap into your energy and Flair and strength. If we bond more so we work together better . . ."

"You aren't talking about going to bed and loving, are you?"

"Not. Yet."

"All right." He tucked the papyrus into his pocket, reached out and took her hand, pulled on it. She resisted until he said, "There's a sacred grove in the back grassyard."

A frisson of wariness swept through her. Was she truly ready to join with him deeply? But she followed Dri from the house and into the fresh air laden with the scent of spring to a lovely circle of birch trees.

After a moment to settle, he put her left hand squarely over his heart, snared her gaze. "Feel me."

He opened the bond between them completely, so all that he was, proud and shamed, tender and lusty, was revealed to her. She closed her eyes at the feel of his old anger and disgrace and guilt and regret. "Oh."

"Know me." There was a moment of silence as emotions cycled between them. "Forgive me?" He stood there, patient under her hand, the thump of his heart rising with a beat of anxiety that pulsed in the wide link between them.

She drew in a breath, steadied by *him*, his nearness, his openness, his very character that resonated to her, through her, and back to him. But not enough. She reached for his hand and it was there, between her own. She pressed it against her breasts, over her own heart, opened all herself—mentally, emotionally, spiritually—to him as she'd never done to anyone since her son had been tiny.

A noise caught in her throat as the bond between them grew, brightened to dazzling intensity. "Know me," she said, though she could barely speak, felt the pulse of him shimmer to her, through her, cycle to him along with the cramped secrets she'd balled and stuffed into corners of her being. Her own yearning for him and failure to act. Her regrets for so much in her life.

Such as the action she'd taken last year when she'd discovered her mother had kept Dri's ring from her. How fury had filled her and she'd reached for a blazer, shot.

Blush heard Dri's rough gasp. She'd made a Vow of Honor to never speak of the events, but Dri was sharing her memories.

Her shot had not reached her mother, but the woman had died soon after, as a consequence of Blush's actions. She'd have to live with that knowledge for the rest of her life. And the knowledge that she'd been relieved when her mother had died.

Know me. Even her mental whisper was shaky. Again she felt the huge wash of relief at her mother's death, and the kernel of glee that she still lived and her son had triumphed. All the petty and great flaws of her being.

Enough! he said mentally. *My Blush is human and errs. As I do.*

She opened her eyes to find his gaze still fixed on her, remembered his words, and repeated them. "Know me. Forgive me?"

He matched his deep breathing to hers, and their hearts tuned, and she understood that the next part should be said together, and said mentally and physically by both at the same time.

"I forgive you. *I forgive you.*"

Knowing him, revealing herself to him, she could do no less.

A *clang* sounded in her mind, as if the iron tower of shields she'd erected around herself fell. She shuddered at the heat of his touch on her, too sensitized. He dropped his hand and narrowed their connection, and she sighed as the near-pain vanished.

"You have my ring!"

She pulled it from under her tunic, removed it from the chain, and slid it on her finger. "I've worn it ever since."

He swallowed hard, looked away. "Thank you."

She smiled at him and it was full and free and whole, felt no lingering resentment. She was sure he'd annoy her in the future, perhaps even move her to sputtering anger, but that would be based on new conflicts and not old. "We're starting clean and clear."

"Yes," he said, one side of his mouth lifting. "Though I think we should be safe and use the sex technique, too."

She laughed. "And I forgave myself."

He waved his hand. “I let those old mistakes that young man made go.”

Arm in arm, they walked back to the house. He stopped on the stoop. “One last thing I need to know.”

She endeavored to stay relaxed. “Yes?”

“Would your mother have really destroyed my Family if I’d persuaded you to run away with me?”

She thought of her mother, who had been at the height of her power, full of hubris but marginally less cruel then than when her health had deteriorated. Thought of herself then, trained to be the person who pampered her mother the most. “Yes.”

“Ah. I did the right thing.” He slid a glance to her.

“Yes. And if she’d caught us, she’d have killed you and my life would have been worse.” She turned toward him. “I value and respect the man you are today, Dri. I can’t regret the circumstances that made you who you are.”

“But do you regret the actions you took?”

She smiled and it held no taint of bitterness, only the freedom of understanding. “No, because if I had followed you, I would not have had my son, and he is precious to me.”

“As he should be. I look forward to meeting him.”

Boy! came the irascible mental shout from Bonar.

Blush strode over the threshold. “We need to get that man sorted out.” She rose. “Along with every other thing in his house.”

“Let’s do it,” Dri said. “G’Uncle,” he shouted toward the bedroom. “Be with you in a few minutes. Practice patience.”

Dri walked with her to the gleaming space in the front room, joined hands, and linked; the connection between them pulsed with strength, with trust, with respect. Plenty of energy to do the spell. As she felt the wash of positive emotions between them, her inner sight showed a golden rope—the HeartBond, ready to tie them together once they made it to bed. Soon.

As they chanted the spell together, their energy matched and flowed from them to form a sphere. Blush guided the visualization so it filled the house, ready to slowly descend, searching for the one *Paris* object.

“Ready?” she asked.

"Let's draw it down," Dri said.

To Blush's surprise, she provided more of the strength and Dri had the control to gradually sift the Flair through the cottage lower and lower until it vanished into the ground. Her knees gave out and she sagged against him. Wrapping her arms around him, she knew she loved him, knew she didn't want to live apart from him.

He held her close, stroking her hair.

When she found her breath, she said, "Did it work?"

"Extend your senses," he said.

Blush did. Mel's sniffing and snorting at the lingering scent of herbs quieted, and she felt a small swirl of Paris-essence somewhere in the room. But Dri was already pulling her to the far wall.

When they reached it, he carefully picked up a gleaming sword.

"Is that it?" Blush asked.

Glancing at the etching on the blade, he said, "It's a treasure all right, the sword awarded to GraceHouse Conyza. Bonar will be glad to see it again." A corner of Dri's mouth lifted. "Enough that he'll be mollified when we find the Paris heirloom." Dri set the sword aside, and Blush saw a panel in the wall, hidden for ages. When he pressed inward on the wood, a hidey-hole was revealed.

She waited, breathless, as Dri muttered a Word and a spell-light glowed on. They looked inside the cache and saw the dark wood frame of an art piece no more than thirty centimeters.

He withdrew the object. It was a framed Certificate of Testing and Nobility and Name, granted to GraceHouse Paris Quadrifolia by the NobleCouncils of Celta, and dated two centuries previous. A beautiful rendition of the plant took up most of the sheet, along with its common name. She inhaled, heard Dri do the same. He touched the glass of the piece with reverent fingers, then lifted his eyes to hers, and she thought she saw everything in his gaze, his Family's past, their own lives, their future.

"'Herb True-Love,'" he murmured. "Paris Quadrifolia. True-Love."

She laughed and pulled her hands away to fling herself into his arms. "It fits, herb True-Love. You *are* true love, my true love."

Joy filled her, the deep knowledge that all their days would be filled with love, tomorrow and forever.

"And you are mine, Blush, Arbusca Willow, ever were and ever will be. My HeartMate, my true love. Will you marry me and HeartBond with me?"

"Yes, my true love, my HeartMate."

Heart and Soul

For all my critique buddies, but especially Carla and
Alice, who read this work and made it better.

Note: Tinne Holly's and Genista Furze Holly's story is told as a subplot in several books. *Heart Duel*, *Heart Choice*, *Heart Quest*, *Heart Dance*, and the beginning of *Heart Fate*. I hope you enjoy Genista's growth, her new life, and her new love.

One

Gael City, Celta
407 Years After Colonization
Morning Before Halloween

Time to become a different person—or at least continue to become the person she wanted to be, leaving the past behind. Someday she'd be able to integrate her past persona and her new life, but it wouldn't be today. With the autumn came memories for Genista Furze.

But finally her life was in her own hands. And these last days of the year had her thinking the next year would be better. For the first time in two years.

The antique clock bonged thirty-five minutes before WorkBell, and she drew on her cape to leave for her job—the only job she'd ever held in her life.

She glanced around the mainspace in her small house in Gael City. She had been right to move here, away from the capital. Here she wasn't Genista Furze, one of the highest—and most notorious—ladies of the land. Here she was Nista Gorse, a woman who lived simply and worked in a clockmaker's shop.

It was unexpectedly freeing. She was not the disdained youngest daughter of a great noble, not the first divorced woman of the highest rank. As she adjusted her cloak and dispelled the security shield on her house, her hands brushed over her stomach and she flinched. Taking a calming breath, she set aside, as she did every day, the grief that she'd miscarried her baby. Two years ago this week. The end of the year would always be difficult for her. That the grief was fading was the real reason she had hope for the future.

One last glance at her room had her smile curving. Yes, this was a place she'd made for herself. Oh, she'd had money—gilt—personal property, and gifts and used them well, but her rooms were decorated and arranged exactly as she wanted. They were essentially *female*, something a man might even feel uncomfortable in, and she didn't care about that at all. Most men had loved her and abandoned her—except her ex-husband, who would have held on far past the time love had withered and turned into dislike between them.

She opened the door and the wind tugged at her cape, her bloused trous under her long tunic. Chill with autumn's touch. As she turned and closed the door latch, reset the spellshield, she caught a glimpse of her neighbor. Cardus Parryl stood beyond the low hedge that separated their front yards, raking leaves.

He was always in his front garden when she left for work and came home, no matter what the time. She'd *tried* to avoid him, to no avail.

There was something about him that lit caution within her. Maybe it was the way he carried himself that showed he was a warrior. Lady and Lord knew that having lived with the premiere fighting family of Celta, Genista knew how such men moved. She'd even had lessons herself.

Cardus had a noticeable limp and must be an ex-merchant or city guard, but she'd never seen him in colored livery. Since he had no visible employment and didn't appear to be wealthy, she figured he had a pension. He'd moved in no more than an eightday after she'd bought her own home.

"Greetyou, GentleMistrys Gorse, Happy Halloween eve."

"Happy Halloween eve."

At first she'd ignored Cardus but eventually believed that not returning his quiet greetings was churlish. They'd progressed to short conversations of a few sentences, and she'd begun to anticipate seeing him. Not that she would admit to any attraction, any tingles. She didn't want to be involved with a fighter, she knew them all too well. Strong, with definite ideas of what a person should or should not do . . . and there would be a continual reminder of the babe she'd lost with her fighter husband, Tinne Holly.

Cardus met her eyes, and she admired his coloring that suited the autumn so well—green eyes and russet hair, a hint of ruddiness in his face from the wind. He wore brown straight-legged trous and narrow-sleeved shirt, and a heavy leather tunic of a caramel color. Yes, he was the image of fall, and she was all too aware that she looked like the wrong season—blond hair and blue eyes.

"Pretty day, but windy." She smiled.

He glanced around at the leaves that he'd been futilely raking and shook his head. "I shouldn't have even bothered. Should have stayed on my porch reading my book on Earth."

A chuckle escaped, surprising her. She *was* becoming more lighthearted, somewhat like the girl she'd been. "Raking is good exercise," she said, though he didn't need it. He was lean and muscular, with broad shoulders. He didn't seem the type to read when activity could be done.

"It is that." He narrowed his eyes to the north, where distant mountains loomed that sent the wind. "I don't think there will be rain or snow tomorrow for the rituals and celebrations." Leaning on the rake, he asked, "Do you go to any?"

A month before she'd have considered that spying and impertinent, but they were making their way gently with commonplace conversation, meeting of gazes. He put absolutely no pressure on her, and she liked that. She appreciated that if he found her attractive—and most men did—he didn't let it show. He treated her with respect, courteously, and so she wasn't quite sure whether he really knew who she was or not. Certainly she'd had quite a reputation in the capital, especially before she'd married.

She liked being respected for herself, not her rank.

"Do you go to any parties?" he repeated.

Almost she tossed her head like the old Genista would have, careless, challenging, but she just shook it instead. "No, no balls, no parties, not even a special ritual."

He inclined his head. "You should socialize more, lady; it would do you good to be with people. We all need others in our lives."

Genista hesitated. That was the first personal comment he'd ever made to her. From the wariness in his eyes, the impassivity of his expression, she thought he expected her to snap at him . . . or go back to ignoring him.

"Do you go to any parties or special rituals?" She turned the question back to him.

He grimaced, splayed his fingers, and gave the side of his left thigh a hard rub. "Old wound makes dancing difficult, and I'm not much for parties." His eyelids lowered, but she still felt his gaze. "I hear there's some good rituals, indoors at several temples, even RoundDome Temple."

It wasn't quite an invitation. She didn't know if he meant it to be or was just stating a fact. The wind flattened her cloak against her, shot cold fingers through the gaps. Again she smiled but shook her head. "Even with the chill, I'd prefer the outdoors."

His lashes raised, revealing an intense and brilliant emerald gaze. "Plenty of people will attend Halloween and Samhain rituals in the sacred grove across from RoundDome Temple." He paused. "You should not be alone."

That was a little too personal for her. She lifted a hand to him in farewell and hurried down her front stepping-stones to the low iron-spiked gate. Once again she murmured a chant to lower another spellshield, went through the gate, and hurried out. But a few steps later, she glanced back at Cardus. He was watching her and frowning. The wind whipped, but the rake didn't wobble in his hand. He held it . . . like it could be used as a weapon.

Is Nista back in the workshop? I need to ask her about my mantel clock." The man's mellow voice floated through the open door between the workshop and the store, slithering down Genista's spine.

A few years ago, she'd have accepted the compliments that customer paid her as her due, and would have flirted with him. Before her marriage, she'd have had no qualms about bedding him.

She was older and wiser and, to her surprise, a whole lot more discriminating than she had been before her marriage to and divorce from Tinne Holly.

Divorce. The huge scandal of being the first to divorce at the highest noble level. Which was less important than the fact that she'd hurt a good man. But the pain of staying in the relationship was more than the severing of their marriage.

"Nista!" GentleMistrys Faverel's voice was sharp. She didn't like having an attractive woman in her business. It didn't matter that Genista was completely uninterested in the woman's husband. Well, in everything other than his skill with mechanical-Flaired works.

Genista set down the spell-coated gear she'd been working on—ancient clocks were a specialty of the shop—and strode into the store, wiping slightly oily fingers on her bib apron. She wore the gray apron to show she was all business. So far it had impressed no one.

As soon as the lean man with handsome features, curly black hair, and bright blue eyes saw her, he smiled. Genista returned his smile, but her heart—and other bits of her anatomy—were unmoved. No fluttering, no warmth. Years ago that wouldn't have mattered.

Tinne had been so good for her. She sent a mental blessing his way—and to his HeartMate, the woman she'd never met but who had hurt Genista just by her existence.

Flicking her fingers behind her apron to banish the past, Genista walked up to the counter. "Yes, GentleSir Asant?"

He leaned an elbow on the wide wooden counter and pushed the mantel timer toward her with a self-deprecating smile. "It seems to have stopped again."

This was the third time the clock had been in the shop in the last month.

"I'll look," Genista said, as she had twice before. She hadn't worked on this timer; Master Faverel had. And she never questioned his competency. If there was something wrong, Asant's environment was causing it.

GentleMistrys Faverel scowled at them both. Genista turned the clock around and tapped on the back; the wood panel fell into her hands and she checked the works. Everything appeared fine, the small mechanical parts all present, all having the proper amount of Flair magic . . . except . . . She glanced up at Asant. "Did you put this timer anywhere near a no-time storage unit?"

"But timer clocks and no-times are not mutually exclusive," he said.

GentleMistrys Faverel bumped Genista with her well-padded hip and answered him. "A timer and a no-time food storage unit work fine together *now*, have for the last century. But I know *you*, GentleSir Asant, love antiques."

"Yes, I do." He sent a crooked smile at Genista. "Or, at least, I have a lot of them. Trying to get my inheritance in shape after my cuz's death." His lips turned down.

Taking the timer in both hands, Genista said, "Let me put a stronger spell on the works . . . but be advised that it might affect the no-time, and if I had to choose between a functioning no-time and a clock—"

"A no-time is more important," GentleMistrys Faverel ended for Genista, motioning her back to the workroom.

"You know we *do* handle no-time refurbishment, reconstruction, and servicing here, too," GentleMistrys Faverel offered. "For anything prior to the last twenty years. Now, the spell reset will cost you fifty gilt."

Genista set the timer down on her table. The workroom was still empty. GentleSir Faverel had slipped out the rear door for his usual MidAfternoonBell caff break at the shop next door. She glanced at her wrist timer, a nice large unit that a working woman would wear, nothing like the twenty or so delicately jeweled ones she had in her cottage safe. She had a weakness for timers, which is why she was here.

"Nista!" Another shout from GentleMistrys Faverel had Genista wincing. Using the Flair she could command, the psi magic of a woman born of a long line of people with great magical powers, she sent a tiny but potent spell to coat the tech parts and form a slight shield that would spring into place as soon as she replaced the back.

"Nista!"

"Coming!" She picked up the timer, said a small housekeeping spell to remove any fingerprints and polish the glass of the face.

Asant straightened from a desultory conversation with GentleMistrys Faverel, whose smile was strained since there were two more people in the shop whom she wanted to wait on.

Genista tapped on the clock back and said, "Here."

The man took the timepiece, stroked the fine wood, smiled at Genista. Lowering his voice, he said, "New Year's, Samhain, is midnight tomorrow night. Will the shop close early on Halloween?"

Genista blinked. "I don't know." She shrugged. "This is my first year with the Faverels." She'd left Druida City immediately after her divorce, taken a few weeks to settle herself here in Gael City, applied for a job when she'd seen the sign in the Faverels' shopwindow, and renamed herself Nista Gorse.

GentleMistrys Faverel was helping her other customers. Business was picking up as people shopped for last-minute Samhain gifts.

The rear door slammed. GentleSir Faverel had returned from his caff break. The faint scent of cocoa from the mug he'd brought back for Genista wafted to her nose. *Now* she felt warmth. Comfort. From the thought of a cup of cocoa caff with white mousse topping and cocoa sprinkles. Her smile was genuine. "I have work."

Asant began to say something but she was focused on her treat and left.

GentleSir Faverel was tying on his own apron and looked up as she bustled in. "Customers in the front?"

"Yes. Three. Asant brought his mantel clock back in. I think he set it on a no-time."

"He has an antique no-time. That'd stop it, all right." Faverel handed her the mug.

She inhaled deeply. "Really lovely, thank you."

"'Welcome. Glad you're here with us, good help." His thin gray brows lowered. "You don't seem to understand that. You need to believe in yourself."

Genista's mouth fell open, then she swallowed, not knowing what to say. The man had touched her deepest fears. She shivered at his insight, unwilling to confront it.

But he was just slurping his caff and looking around the room. "We're caught up on all the minor projects."

Faverel walked past her to the front showroom, and she heard his gruff voice as he spoke to his wife and customers. He didn't care to interact with the public. Questions were asked and he replied briefly.

He came back holding a tiny china bedside timer all gold and white with a painted face, shaking his head. "This won't take five minutes," he said. "Regular five-month maintenance."

"Um-hmm," Genista said, sipping her luscious drink and leaning against her worktable.

Voices rose in the shop and penetrated the workroom. "Mille Thelypod claimed thieves stole a gold box."

Mistrys Faverel snorted. "Mille Thelypod always says that when she has to sneak out of her house and sell something. Why, we bought one of her Family clocks ourselves." Another loud sniff. "She didn't report this new 'theft' to the guardsmen or tell the newssheets, did she?"

"No-oo," the other gossip replied.

"There you go, then," Mistrys Faverel ended decidedly.

"Is that true about you buying Mille's clock?" Genista asked Faverel idly.

He grunted, flicked the back of the timer with a finger, and the tiny door popped off. "Yes. But I wish my lady hadn't said so. You should be out there in the shop. An attractive girl like you would draw in more folk, sell better than my lady."

Genista choked on her drink, spewed a little down her apron. "No."

Brows lifted, Faverel continued mildly, "I don't take you for an introvert like me."

She pulled a softleaf from one of her apron pockets and wiped her mouth, scrubbed at her bib. No use for it, she'd have to take it home and put it in the cleanser tonight. "I like working with timers . . . and clocks. I don't like selling much."

"Ah." He hummed a spell, said the Words to set the clock to the official time as determined by the Guildhall in Druida City, and polished the piece as he took it back into the shop.

When he returned, he appeared a little flushed, and Genista figured that the wet smacking noise she'd heard was his wife kissing him. An unusual public display of affection for them, but the woman had been doing that more often now that Genista worked with them full-time.

Faverel stopped in a shaft of light as if he wanted the autumn sun to warm his bones. He rubbed his hands together. "Speaking of no-times, we haven't worked on them together."

He was a good man and an excellent teacher. He didn't ask outright if she knew how to fix no-times. She'd been a dilettante with mechanical-Flair objects in her former life. "I don't know how to repair no-time food storage units," she said.

He nodded, went to the safe, and pulled out three slips of paper. "These are proprietary spells that the Thymes have developed and sold to others—creators and producers of no-times, and for people like us to service. These three handle the items we typically receive."

Genista scrutinized the elegant scrawls of spell formulas, in three different hands. She didn't know *how* such Flair technology stopped time, but she could inscribe the patterns and apply certain twists of Flair to power them, if she learned the original spells.

Faverel was going to tell her. Excitement sent blood to her cheeks. "You'll teach me?"

He nodded. "You have good manual dexterity, nice penmanship." He smiled and his face wrinkled into a dozen folds. "And the Flair, eh, that isn't too difficult. You should be able to master one spell by the end of the day."

Genista grinned and rubbed her hands, just like he was doing. This was better than caff.

When WorkEndBell was sounded by a multitude of timers and clocks in the store, Genista was glad to push away from her bench.

She'd practiced one spell formula for septhours until she'd gotten it right. Her brain felt heavy and dull with effort.

"Excellent job," Faverel said, his smile creasing his face. "There's a good reason to take older people as journeymen students."

A little shock sizzled through her, clearing some of the exhaustion from her mind. "Am I a journeywoman?"

He raised a brow. The man could do that, raise just one brow. It made her feel like a child, not a woman of twenty-six.

"I'm teaching you my craft. You're learning well. Want to formalize it?"

Genista hesitated. Formalize meant contracts and contracts usually demanded real names. On the other hand, she'd like to earn a certificate. A piece of papyrus that showed her worth, that she'd grown as a person.

The last formal piece of papyrus she'd signed was her divorce, and she still wasn't sure whether that showed she had grown or just wearied of hurting. "GentleMistrys Faverel might not care for it."

He shrugged off his wife's opinion like most men did. "May or may not. Might be if you have a solid status as journeywoman instead of just an employee, might soothe her." He shrugged again, opened his hands. "Might not." Then he actually winked. "Having you around has made her more interested in me, and I like that fine. Think about becoming my student." He opened a drawer in his worktable and handed her a document with sections he'd already filled out, then swaggered to the front of the shop.

Genista put away the shop tools, hesitating as she fingered one. If she became a journeywoman, she'd need her own tools. She would have a career. She would *be* someone that she'd *made* herself.

Not the ignored third daughter of GreatLord Furze. A girl who'd craved attention and found that men would give it to her.

She rolled up her soiled apron and tucked it into her bag, carefully placed the journeywoman form on top.

She could have teleported home, but the Faverels didn't have a teleportation zone. She didn't need one to leave, of course, but the lack of one indicated that they—and the people they knew—didn't teleport often, if at all.

Genista teleported, but not to and from work. Like the rest of her Flair, her teleportation skills had become stronger now that she practiced them more often.

And she liked walking from her job to her cottage on a pleasant fall day. She had plenty to ponder.

Evening was falling and the workday was done for her, but the store would stay open for another septhour. She lingered in the back room. If she entered the front area, she might interrupt a bit more of the public displays of affection—or there might be customers the Faverels would want her to serve.

Just before she was forced to go into the shop to say good-bye, GentleMistrys Faverel came back to stare at her, arms crossed over her modest bosom. "Taking off?"

Two

"That's right," Genista replied to her employer's question. If she was a journeywoman in timer service, would she have to work the counter? Or would she always stay in the back room? She'd check the duties on GentleSir Faverel's form.

"Harrumph," GentleMistrys Faverel snorted. "We've decided to close early tomorrow on Halloween—MidAfternoonBell. In case any of us want to participate in rituals, or celebrate Samhain early."

"Thank you for telling me," Genista said.

A sniff and a wave of the woman's hand. "Be off with you. And I want you in tomorrow thirty-five minutes early to make up for the time off."

Genista suppressed a sigh. "Yes."

"Yes, *mistrys*," the woman corrected.

Squashing rebellious thoughts, Genista said, "Yes, mistrys."

Two minutes later she was walking home. She enjoyed the scent of turning leaves and stopped now and then to watch an orange or red or gold leaf separate itself from the tree and drift down—symbolizing the end of the year and looking toward the future.

Neither she nor her ex-husband had been ones to watch serenely instead of acting. She didn't know if he had changed now that he'd found and claimed his HeartMate, but for Genista, becoming a contemplative person was a hard, ongoing process. And she knew and accepted that there was no HeartMate for her.

She sighed and scuffed her shoes through the dry leaves, breaking them. They cackled like old women. Plenty of old women and nobles who'd talked about her in Druida City. She'd be shunned if she ever went back there.

A man's voice lifted in one of the back grassyards of the houses she passed, and she flinched a bit as it reminded her of Asant. No, she wouldn't be taking him as a lover. Too bad he couldn't be her friend, but a man like that, one aware of his own attractiveness and self-worth, didn't settle for a friendship when he wanted an intimate relationship.

Maybe she did need to build friendships again, come out of this self-imposed isolation. A woman called out to Genista from her front porch and waved. With a smile, Genista waved back and revised her thoughts. She wasn't as isolated as she thought.

At the corner of the block where her little house stood, she stopped to really *look* at it. It was a bungalow with a small porch just big enough for a rocking chair and tiny table. Her home was tinted a cheerful creamy yellow with light teal trim. Her spirits lifted just to look at it. Hers. Her very own.

Not a noble, intelligent Residence that housed a FirstFamily like the ones of her birth Family and in-laws. She had wanted that, once, status and stability. Or stability and status. But had gradually discovered that her soul needed other things.

Her spine and shoulders straightened. She was constructing a good life. And she'd spent too much time thinking about the past and not the future. She would do better.

A sound of clipping came from the front yard beyond hers. Cardus Parryl was out. Again. He was always there.

He'd tinted his home the same light teal of her trim and trimmed it in the same soft yellow cream of her house. He was irritating that way. That unobtrusive way.

The cottages were alike, set no more than four meters apart. In the front, she had a low iron-spiked fence and gate. Cardus had low wooden ones. On the boundary they shared, the front half of her house was hedge. The rear half of her property was surrounded by a high iron fence with a gate to the park she backed up against.

Genista thought the houses might have the same layout inside, and she'd watched with reluctant envy as he'd built a porch all along the front, with lovely small columns and a nice overhang. And made a swing to put on the porch. And sat in that swing during the summer months to greet her as she'd arrived home.

As she drew closer, she saw him use flashing silver, wickedly sharp shears to cut the top of the yew hedge between their houses. Her teeth gritted. She'd liked the summer spearing of ragged growth. Now the hedge was down to waist high on him, again.

She lowered the spellshield and went through her gate.

"Greetyou, GentleMistrys Gorse," he said.

His voice was slightly rough, deep and dark, sending quivers of awareness along her skin, slipping into her blood. Thrills that were becoming harder to ignore.

Maybe she was cautious because he affected her.

"Turned out warmer than I thought. A lovely day, isn't it, GentleMistrys?" he prompted, shifting his weight slightly.

Genista wasn't fooled. He could be over that hedge in an instant. She was glad she had good spellshields.

At that moment the sun lit his hair, and it looked like a torch of red and orange. His body was outlined in a golden aura. Since she stopped to stare, she decided she had to answer. And considering the day she'd had and the journeywoman document in her bag, it *had* been a lovely day.

"Greetyou, GentleSir Parryl, you're right," she said.

Clouds hid the sun, and the man dimmed from larger-than-life to her quietly intense neighbor again. It was just that his coloring was so vivid. "Have a good evening."

A great sneeze came from him and she paused, threw, "Lady and Lord Bless You," over her shoulder, and caught a blank look of surprise on his face.

He rubbed his nose. "You smell different."

That halted her in her tracks. No one had ever said anything uncomplimentary about her scent since she'd given up mud puddles in the stable as a child. She turned toward him. "I am sure I didn't hear you correctly."

Snap. The clippers sheared a good length of the hedge. Cardus's cheeks had flushed, but now his shoulders squared.

"And that sounds like a Druidan upper-class accent to me, too," he commented.

Her stomach clutched. She'd tried so hard to fall into the slower, more slurred casual speech of Gael City and it had deserted her. "Good evening," she said and turned away.

"I meant to say that you have a scent of unusual spellworking to you," Cardus offered.

So his comment had been simple curiosity on his part. Nothing had changed between them. Good. As she entered her home and quietly closed the door behind her, she admitted she was attracted to him.

Slightly. Very slightly attracted.

She set the journeywoman form on her delicately burled desk, then went to the bathing room that she'd had remodeled and drew a bath, throwing in a handful of herbs.

Asant was so much more handsome and smooth and left her completely unmoved. Cardus Parryl was intriguing. She liked his looks, his muscular body, irregular features—and the tug of desire she felt.

He was dangerous.

Stup! Fool! Cardus's hands hurt as he tightened his grip on the clippers, slashing more height off the hedge. How brilliant he'd been to insult Genista Furze. Open his mouth for more than impersonal comments, and see what came out.

She wouldn't look at him again, would lapse into brief replies once more.

When the hedge was done, he was sweating in the cool autumn evening air. Easy enough to hop over if he needed to. He'd been given a spell charm to enter her property . . . and had vowed not to use it unless she was in danger.

He wiped his forehead with his sleeve, cleaned off the clippers, and stowed them in the shed in his back grassyard. The houses bordered a park in the rear. He peered into the dusk but saw no indication of the stray dog he'd been feeding. He suspected the animal had enough intelligence and Flair magic to become a true telepathic animal companion. Whether or not it did, dogs were rare and should be prized. He wanted it out of the coming winter.

As he'd wanted Genista Furze to notice him for months.

Well, she'd noticed him all right. Commenting on her scent. Something a sophisticated city man wouldn't do, though Cardus had noticed her personal fragrance the first time they'd met.

His leg throbbed and he closed himself into his tool shed, used the extra energy that anger at himself gave him to teleport straight into his waterfall room. Before he could shuck his clothes, the scrybowl in his bedroom sounded a hard thumping-beat tune. Cardus sighed.

Limping into the bedroom, he sank onto the bedsponge set on a platform. The scrybowl water swirled green and silver. He circled his finger around the rim of the bowl and said, "Here." The image projected, forming in droplets that hung above the bowl.

"Greetyou, Cardus," said the oldest Holly—Tab, G'Uncle to Genista's ex-husband, Tinne.

"Greetyou," Cardus replied.

"How is Genista?" Tab Holly asked.

Cardus hesitated. He believed the Hollys had only Genista's welfare in mind; if he didn't, he'd never have accepted the job of keeping an eye out for her.

"This week would have been rough," Tab continued. "She lost her babe in the womb two years ago."

Just the thought of Genista experiencing such pain tightened Cardus's throat. He stretched out his leg, kneaded it. "She was . . . subdued." He thought she'd wept for two nights straight, and had said nothing to her except commonplaces. But he wouldn't reveal such personal grief to the Hollys.

"She went to work?" Tab asked.

"Yes. She seems content in her job."

Tab shook his head. "I never would have believed she would

take a lowly position." Another shake of his shaggy head, then a charming smile. "But she is maturing. Good girl."

"Yes, she is."

"No threats?" asked Tab, as he always did.

"None I've observed."

"Good." Tab's pale gray gaze met Cardus's as he asked the next usual question. "No men in her life?"

"None I've observed."

And, as usual, Tab frowned. "Celibacy is not good for a person."

Cardus agreed. He'd had no sex since he'd first met Genista. Not that his celibate life would change soon.

"I worry about her. *We* worry about her," Tab said.

That was a new statement. "You do? And Tinne? He is HeartBound to another."

"All the bonds between her and Tinne have been severed—mental and emotional. None of us are connected with her anymore."

Which was why they'd hired Cardus.

Tab sighed. "Tinne is very happy in his HeartMate marriage."

Cardus and Tab shared a glance; neither of them hid their envy. They both knew the other had no HeartMate in this lifetime.

"Good that Tinne's happy." Cardus let the rough-edged lie rumble from his throat.

"Would Genista welcome New Year's gifts from us Hollys?"

Cardus considered the question, nearly closed his eyes to recall the *feel* of Genista's aura. After a hanging moment of silence, he said, "I don't believe so."

"Right," Tab said, then went on with the regular questioning. "She lives within her means? Has no need of more gilt?"

"She lives well." Cardus kept his expression mild. Another thing to ache about. He'd never have the gilt to match Genista.

"Let me know if she has any problems," Tab said, winding down the report.

"I will."

"Merry meet," Tab offered the standard noble sign-off.

"And merry part," Cardus said.

"And merry meet again. Have a good Halloween and Samhain. I'll call in a few days."

Never on a strict schedule, the Hollys were canny. A fleeting smile came and went on Tab's old face. "Scry you next year. Happy New Year."

"And to you," Cardus replied, didn't let out a breath until the man had cut the scryspell.

Yipping came at his back door and he went out to feed the dog. He might not get the woman soon, but it looked like he might have a Fam Companion. As he'd told Genista, it wasn't good to be so alone.

He yearned for her.

Genista was distracted enough by thoughts of Cardus Parryl that she automatically answered the scrybowl flickering a greenish white. "Here."

Asant's face showed in the bowl, and her own smile froze on her face.

He kissed his fingertips at her, a Gael City courtesy that was meant to simulate bending over and kissing her hand. But being on the receiving end of the gesture felt too intimate, and she didn't like it.

"I begged for your scry image from the Faverels, and the GentleMistrys gave it to me." Asant smiled with charm, and Genista kept the irritation at Mistrys Faverel from showing.

"Oh?" The word was a little unenthusiastic, but Genista didn't care. A flash of some dark emotion showed in Asant's gaze and she blinked, then wondered if she'd imagined it.

His smile brightened. "I have tokens to *the* Halloween and Samhain rituals—at RoundDome Temple. I would like to invite you."

She should be flattered, and the man was obviously interested in her. "I don't—"

"Please, lady, come with me." His voice was soft, lilting. "You are too lovely to keep yourself a hermit."

Since that was the third time she'd heard the sentiment that day, and Genista now paid attention to signs from the Lady and Lord, she nodded. "Very well."

"Thank you. The gathering is at NightBell, a septhour before the ritual. I have a glider, shall I pick you up?"

"Thank you, but I must do a small ritual here in my own home. I'll meet you at RoundDome Temple fifteen minutes before the gathering time."

He sighed, put a hand over his heart, then kissed his fingers at her again. "If you must."

She pushed more sincerity into her smile. "Yes."

"I will meet you there, though I warn you that I may need to drop by the shop tomorrow to see you before then."

"Ah." To her surprise, Genista felt her cheeks coloring, something that hadn't happened since she was a teen. She was woefully out of practice in flirting.

"Beautiful color. Farewell." Another smile and the scry faded.

As soon as the scrybowl water turned clear, Genista found her shoulders sinking back into relaxation mode. It was a true pity that she felt no pull toward the man.

A short bark sounded and jogged her from her musing. She glanced at her timer and realized she was late in feeding the stray dog who'd been coming around the last three evenings. She hurried into the kitchen and to the no-time food storage unit that kept food at the exact temperature as when it was placed in there. She'd made meals for the dog from her own food; tonight was bite-sized clucker meat.

The dish was warm, the food itself steaming, good-enough smelling to make her nose twitch and mouth water, ready for her own meal. Genista dropped all spellshields on her property, opened the back door, and to the sound of the chimes attached to the latch, she strode through her grassyard to her gate and into the park.

And saw Cardus petting the dog as it gobbled up food. From the smell of *that*, the dog was getting furrabeast steak.

She lowered her hand holding the plate.

Cardus looked up and his white and even teeth gleamed in a smile that was better than any she'd seen—or given—the whole day.

"Ah, we've both been duped by a clever hound." Cardus nodded at her plate.

Genista chuckled and she walked easily toward the dog, stared down at him. "His ribs are much less prominent than I recall. Maybe we aren't the only two feeding him. And I'm not sure he needs my clucker."

I do! the dog shouted mentally.

Genista met Cardus's glance.

"Who are you a Familiar Companion to, dog?" asked Cardus, a note of disappointment in his voice.

I am Fam to no one. After one last slurping lick, the dog covered the ground to Genista in two leaps, nudged her hand with enough force that the plate tilted, then fell.

"Dog! Mind your manners," Cardus snapped.

The dog ignored him, nosing out and gulping down the clucker.

"Did you hear me, dog? If you don't treat the lady well, you will lose both of us who feed you. Apologize." Hard command.

Genista knew better than to contradict Cardus, though she thought he was being too harsh with a needy animal.

But the dog raised his head, swiped his muzzle with his tongue, and sat on his haunches. Then he lifted one paw and held it toward Genista as if to shake. She was utterly charmed and stepped toward him, took his paw, and squeezed it slightly. "Forgiven."

"Good Fam," Cardus said, and he was there, scrubbing the dog's head between his tattered ears.

The dog's muzzle opened in a grin, then he got to his feet and began rooting around for bits of clucker that he'd missed.

She bent down to scoop up the plate, and as she straightened, she saw Cardus's glinting gaze had been focused on her derriere. Warmth unfurled within her, rippled through her blood. For the first time in months, she felt utterly female.

All too often she'd accepted male admiration and the feelings it engendered in her as the basis for self-respect. Even when she'd married Tinne, she knew he asked for her hand because he found her sexy, and he'd wanted some land that her father had. Soon after they'd wed, she'd understood that Tinne had also wanted to divert the attention of his parents from his older brother to Tinne and herself. None of that had mattered. She'd built a marriage, loved Tinne, tried to forget that she was only a wife and not a HeartMate—that he had a HeartMate.

Then, with her miscarriage, all changed. She couldn't get beyond the grief, wouldn't let Tinne help her, didn't turn to him. She'd blamed his parents and the curse they'd brought down on their Family for her loss.

"Past and done and *gone*!" she whispered, flicking her fingers to send thoughts away. "Now and future and *dawn*!" Live in the present, concentrate on the future.

"Lady?" murmured Cardus.

And she was back in the moment, thoughts of the past dissipated. She glanced at Cardus and realized that the evening light had faded and it was near dark. "Nothing," she answered.

He inclined his head, accepting, though she knew from experience that he had keen hearing, and thought he would have made out the words.

The dog munched a few bites, then projected mentally, *I can be a Fam.* The animal looked at Cardus, then her, from under bushy brows. *I can be a Fam to both of you.*

As a child, Genista would have flung herself at the dog and wrapped her arms around him, claiming him for her own, needing his love. Wanting something of her own that her sisters would not take from her, and would envy.

In the last couple of years, since she'd miscarried her babe, she'd have stepped back and let Cardus bond with the dog.

But tonight, with the scent of autumn in the cool air, the ticking of the minutes down to Samhain and the new year, she found that she didn't want to give up the dog. Straightening her spine and lifting her chin, she stared at Cardus.

One side of his mouth kicked up. He shifted until he was solidly on his balance, an easy fighter's stance. "Well, lady, shall we share the dog?"

"So you aren't going to cede the dog to me?"

Cardus grinned. "No."

An urge to tease came over her. She canted a hip. "What if I use my female wiles on you?" She nearly didn't believe what she was saying; flirting had been easy and natural once, but she'd hadn't had any urge to do so with a man for so long.

Three

Please. Do. Use your feminine wiles on me," Cardus said.

Her heart was beating fast. "I'm rusty at flirting."

He shook his head. "No, you aren't."

Every instant she stood looking at him, feeling his regard, she tingled more, got warmer.

The dog belched, ambled over, and swiped his nose against Cardus's hand, then came to her and did the same. His nose was cold. The warm day was chilling into a nippy night, but her blood was still heated.

I will stay with you two, the dog said. He trotted over to Genista's iron-spiked fence. The dog wasn't quite skinny enough to squeeze through the bars, but he could put his muzzle through and sniff lustily.

She didn't particularly care for the tall fence, and it hadn't been there when she'd purchased the house but had appeared around her property during the week before she'd moved in. She'd figured that the Hollys had had it erected but had never asked. Her ex-husband's Family would still consider her someone to protect, though she'd severed all ties—contractual, physical, mental, and emotional—with them. She'd disliked living behind bars so much that she'd removed the high fence from the front portion of her land.

This yard has no place for me during the hard winter, the dog said. He rambled to Cardus's back gate, a short wooden picket fence in honey-colored wood. With an uneven stride, Cardus caught up with the dog and opened the gate. The dog hummed with pleasure as he loped to a shed, then lifted his leg to urinate. *This is perfect.*

Of course he would think so, now that he'd marked it.

"You have a name, dog?" Cardus asked.

I am Whin Thistle.

Genista stilled. Whin was another name for gorse, for furze, her own name. How did the dog know? Cardus was frowning.

A warm breeze fluttered around her, and when it was gone, she was cold. Time to go back inside, have her own dinner. She turned toward her yard and began walking but looked over her shoulder at Cardus and the dog and stumbled.

Immediately Cardus was next to her, steadying her. Moving faster than she'd thought with that damaged leg of his. Reminding her that he was a fighter.

She didn't want to get involved with another fighter. She knew them all too well—aggressive, always sure they were right.

But he smelled good, like autumn. The thought that he smelled like how she'd always believed the Autumn Lord god to smell wisped in the back of her mind. Virile, a hint of sweat, of musk, of autumn leaves. Yes, she'd secretly always preferred the aspect of the Autumn Lord best. Something she'd hidden from herself and the Hollys—those silver-gilt-headed men whose Family ruled in the heat of summer.

Cardus offered his arm. "Can I walk you back to the door, lady?"

"It's not that far." She glanced to her home, saw that there wasn't a glimmer of light from the windows. They were far enough from his place to see the full back of his house. His windows showed bright yellow rectangles, shining comfort.

"It's dark and the park is public, open to anyone. And as you discovered, the ground is rough. Allow me."

"I know that tone. If I don't take your arm, you will walk with me anyway."

"That's right. But I am pleased to accompany you."

It sounded as if he meant it. Her brows drew down. "You may as well call me Nista." But she put her hand on his arm.

He inclined his torso. "Honored, Nista. I asked you to call me Cardus months ago."

And, oddly enough, she'd been thinking of him that way, by his first name. She blinked. She couldn't recall when she'd changed from calling him Parryl in her mind to Cardus. "I'm not that much of a lady," she said.

"Doubt that."

As they walked closer, her curiosity stirred and she found her gaze going to what she could see through his windows. Instead of the fancily carved spice and dried-food shelves that lined the walls of her small back room, the man had locked and spellshielded weapon cabinets. One each for swords, knives, and blazers.

She withdrew her hand from his arm, but he caught her fingers in a warm and calloused grip. "Look beyond my tools, lady, down the hall."

Scowling, she glanced at his impassive face—yes, his face showed nothing, but his eyes moved as if he was scanning the night for any danger.

She realized with a jolt that he was shielding her from any threat from the park. He'd put himself in harm's way to protect her. Just because she was an acquaintance, a woman he respected, not because of her rank or wealth.

At that moment she tipped from reluctant attraction to acute interest in the man. So she did as he'd asked, looked past the weapons to the hallway leading toward the front of his house. The wood on the floor gleamed a polished red brown, the walls were a soft cream with a hint of warm yellow. She could just make out a large, comfortable, and shabby burgundy furrabeast leather chair in his mainspace, manly but still welcoming for a woman.

After another glance to see that he was still focused on any threat, she strove to peer into the shadows of his bedroom, beyond the open hall door. The angle was such that she saw a shade of teal, close to the tint she'd painted her house. She could relax in that bedroom . . . or do more energetic things than relax.

Heat welled, gathering in her center. Focused on her newly admitted attraction to Cardus, the lovely trickles of desire that had been absent for so long, Genista forgot about the steppingstone tilted a few centimeters up and caught her foot. This time she fell into Cardus and felt the tensile strength of his lean muscles.

Again he steadied her. She stopped. "I didn't do that on purpose."

"Of course you didn't," he replied matter-of-factly, as if he believed it.

She stopped and he stopped with her. "I was a very sexual person earlier in my life," she said.

He laughed. "You still are."

"I've stumbled deliberately against men in the past. I had a lot of lovers."

"And that should bother me, why? Feel free to stumble against me anytime."

She felt foolish that she hadn't really noticed. "You're attracted to me."

"Of course."

The cheerful sizzles of lust inside her dimmed. He was straightforward as always, but it hurt that he only thought of her appearance.

"You're a fascinating woman. You could have any man you wanted, yet you live alone."

"I like living alone."

"Which is intriguing in itself. Your beauty and charm ensures that you could marry however high you wished—"

"I would never marry just for status." And she hadn't. For sex, to get out of T'Furze Residence, to be loved.

Cardus continued, "You don't need to marry for rank, but you could. But what is fascinating is that you work hard at your job."

Her chin went up. "I love my job."

"And that's fascinating, too." His arm had gone around her waist and now he urged her forward. "It's not a very interesting job."

"You don't know so much," she said, and used his word. "My job is fascinating."

Shaking his head, he said, "Most wouldn't think so."

They'd reached the step to the back stoop of her house, and his grip changed from her waist—drawing away slowly, and the tingles were back—to cup her elbow as she took the step. So she did, and to her surprise, he followed her up.

He leaned close, and again she became aware of the fragrance of his skin, the heating of her own blood, the pleasure of the rush of desire and anticipation of his kiss.

Closer, closer. His lips slid across hers, and there was a melting inside her as feelings long clenched in frozen stasis began to thaw.

She thought he smoothed her hair with the lightest of touches but didn't know for sure. Then he stepped back and she became aware of her rushing breath, that she'd closed her eyes.

Sweet, sweet stirrings of arousal.

An instant later he was back and strong arms were around her and she was pulled against a hard body and it felt *wonderful*.

He was a fighter, but he was not like Tinne. Cardus had shorter muscles, a bulkier build, wasn't as tall as Tinne. Was perfect in height for her.

Their centers met, and she closed her eyes in bliss that one crucial muscle of his was like steel. Her mind whirled. He *was* attracted to her.

"Nista." Her name escaped his mouth on a sigh. He lifted his soft lips from hers, kissing her down her neck.

He wanted *her*, Nista Gorse, not the notorious and wealthy Genista Furze! He respected *her*.

Fiery lust bloomed in her. She wanted him inside her and she arched against him. His hands came up to frame her face, and he pulled away.

A breath shuddered from her and she opened her eyes to see his skin taut on his face.

"Be very sure what you want, Nista Gorse, because I won't go back to being neighborly once we love."

Love! It was just lusty sex.

Wasn't it?

Her mind spun, trying to define concepts. She'd known love with only one man, and it had hurt, hurt, hurt.

She'd known sex with many and it had meant little.

She'd been celibate since her divorce, had no sex drive.

"What do you want?" he pressed.

There were words that had once come easily to her lips, but not now. She panted, tears of confusion pressed against the backs of her eyes, and she wouldn't let them fall. "I don't know."

He gave a short nod. Stepped off the stoop and flinched as if his bad leg had jarred. "Open the door to your bower, lady, and go in."

She fumbled with the latch, pushed open the door. Her chimes sounded a welcome. Light poured from the house in yellow comfort—from the spellglobes that had come on automatically in the mainspace at the front, the tiny ones lining the hall, to a bright one that floated in the back room.

Cardus made a choked noise. She glanced at him, but he was staring inside.

Voice strained, he said, "That holo painting looks like a student of GrandLord T'Apple." It was by the master himself, but Genista suddenly realized that her home didn't match the new persona she'd cultivated. She hesitated. "Yes. I like his work."

"Beautiful rooms," he said in still strangled tones. "Nice colors. Like shades of a ripe peach."

"Thank you." Genista smiled at Cardus. He seemed stupefied. She didn't think her little house should garner such a reaction. It was true, she kept the windows spell-tinted for privacy, so he couldn't have seen inside before, but her tastes were simple.

Cardus was shaking his head, expression stern. "Must you have such valuables displayed?"

She stared at him, shrugged. "Simple furnishings."

"Simple *antique* furniture, Chinju rugs, objets d'art that belong in a museum. Cave of the Dark Goddess, you have a fortune here."

Glaring, she said, "I have excellent spellshields."

"You should have that high iron fence around the front, too."

"Thank you for your advice."

"Dammit." His fingers speared through his hair. He bowed. "My apologies." Then he continued in a stiff tone. "I shouldn't have commented upon your personal belongings."

A retort was on her lips when she saw his gaze shoot once more into her home. Yearning was in his eyes, as if he saw something he'd always wanted but could never have. Her irritation faded.

And she realized that all flirting aside, he had looked at her that way more than once. She knew he wanted her, and just for herself. If she'd been ready, they'd be in her bedroom right now.

Was he craning to see her bedroom? Yes. And it was dark. And he wasn't hiding that he wanted to know more about her.

"Why stop commenting now," she said lightly. "You've said something about my fragrance—"

He winced.

"—my personality, and now my belongings."

"Again, I apologize." He jerked straight as a guardsman, bowed with the utmost formality.

She couldn't help it, she offered her hand. His gaze, which had been focused somewhere other than her face, lifted and met hers. Stepping forward, slowly raising his hand to take her fingers, he bowed over them. He dropped his head and his gaze—unheard of for a warrior, not to gauge the eyes and to present the vulnerable neck.

His hand cradled hers as if it was more precious than her treasures. With the utmost respect. As if she was truly fascinating.

His lips pressed to the back of her hand and he inhaled, once again drinking in her scent. He gave her a real kiss. Delightful sensation rolled through her.

Then he lowered her fingers, let them go, took a stride back. When he looked up at her again, he didn't mask his desire, and everything within her pulsed hot.

"Go inside. So I can see you're safe."

Her head was a little dizzy. He was the most dangerous person she'd met since she'd moved away from Druida City. A man who'd made her feel, a man who could threaten her new life, her heart.

"Blessed be," she whispered.

He inclined his head. "Blessed be." He hesitated, his stormy gaze meeting her own. "I don't have a woman, or a wife, or a HeartMate. I want you to know that." His next breath was audible. "The Lord and Lady keep you."

She bent and kissed his lips, stepped inside her back room, and closed the door, watched from the windows as he seemed to shake himself from a daze—from another simple kiss? He used Flair to jump over the high iron fence and whistled for the dog.

Then both man and FamDog were in his house and she was standing, alone and watching, behind shielded windows.

Cardus strode through his back door, holding it open for Whin. He tried not to compare his house to Genista's, where he longed to be.

The deep red furrabeast chairs he'd been so proud of now looked shabby. He'd purchased them secondhand after he'd received the most gilt he'd ever had in his life as a deposit from the Hollys to watch over Genista.

When she'd opened her back door, he'd barely believed his eyes. The house might be small and unassuming from the outside, but inside it was a treasure box full of luxurious items only a First-Family Noblewoman could afford. Of course Cardus hadn't known how much gilt Genista had, but it was obvious just from a glimpse of one rug that she would never be poor.

Bitterness coated his tongue as he realized that if the Hollys had provided a guard—himself—for her, they most definitely would ensure that she had plenty of gilt. Tab had said so, but Cardus had never seen a display of FirstFamily wealth until now. Staggering.

The woman lived far beyond Cardus's idea of luxury. What was he thinking, that he could ever have her?

He'd loved the light of the house, the colors. It was warm, welcoming. He wanted to be invited in.

Just like he wanted in Genista.

Whin stopped near the galley kitchen. *I could eat again.* His tail wagged.

Cardus hadn't had his dinner at all. The steak he'd prepared for himself and cut the fat and bone from for Whin was still waiting, steaming with white tuber in the no-time.

"I have another meaty bone." He'd gotten a couple when he'd decided to feed the dog. "But my food is furrabeast steak and I want to eat it in peace. You've already had your portion. No begging."

Whin's gaze slid to Cardus. *I don't beg.*

Cardus didn't bother to contradict the lie, just bent and took out a warm bone. A droplet of juice hit the floor behind a string of Whin's drool. Cardus handed the dog the bone and said a floor-cleansing spell.

After taking his meal from the no-time along with a tube of ale, Cardus went to a small area off the mainspace that held a single wooden table of pure oak. He'd bought it with a chair. After some weeks of speaking with Genista, in a fit of optimism, he'd purchased another chair.

They didn't match.

He knew enough to have a corkstone on the table so the heat of his flexiplate wouldn't ruin the wood, and his setting of good silver—an indulgence—waited at his place.

Automatically he ate, thinking of Genista. He wanted her more each day, loved seeing the changes in her as she discovered her strengths. Thinking of how he'd insulted her *again*, he winced.

If the steak is bad, I could eat it, Whin said.

Cardus's thoughts shot off toward his new companion. He had no doubt that somewhere during his time as a stray, Whin had dined on rotten meat.

First things first. First the Fam. Cardus had successfully lured him into his home. Maybe he could also get Genista. For a while there, when he'd forgotten everything but the woman in his arms and kissed her, he'd felt her response and figured they'd be lovers.

He'd forgotten his job, that he wasn't who he seemed to be to her. That he'd known all along who she was and she didn't know that. She didn't know *him*, either.

Whin woofed and Cardus realized that, once again, his train of thought had focused on Genista. Not his job, not his new Fam, but the woman he longed for.

Staring down at the dog, he asked, "You have any vermin?"

No!

Still eating his tuber, Cardus scanned the dog. Whin was beige and brown and didn't look too dirty. His brown eyes were bright and clear, his ears ragged but straight.

"Why don't you have vermin? Where do you come from, anyway?"

The FamDog whined, took his bone, and backed up to the hallway, where he could run—or teleport—away. He glanced at Cardus, then away.

There is a patch of BaneAll near City Salvage; I roll in it to prevent vermin.

"Good job," Cardus said.

Was born and grew in the south, near the Plano Straight. Was given to a merchant to be a watchdog for merchant trips. I like to run and sniff and hunt. I am not a good watchdog. Not like you.

Yes, Cardus was a damn good guard. And he keenly observed anything that affected Genista. He rubbed the back of his neck. Logic said that he wasn't in her class, never had been and never would be. But all his instincts said that she was the woman for him. More, he was the man for her.

As far as he could tell, no one had ever appreciated Genista just for herself.

Yes, her face and her body were fabulous. She had enough charisma and sex appeal to stun any man into incoherence. But during the days since they'd met, he'd looked beyond her physical attributes to the hurt woman striving to build a new life. A strong woman who hadn't let society's rules dictate her life.

She had known her husband had a HeartMate, had known her marriage with Tinne Holly was broken. By all the customs of the highest nobles, she should have continued to endure her husband until they produced children, then simply moved to a separate suite, a separate estate. She could have taken lovers; her husband would have had his HeartMate.

But her husband wouldn't have been free to offer marriage to his HeartMate.

Genista had taken a strong and honorable path. She had suffered through the long, arduous seven tests of divorce, then had broken with her husband.

Cardus admired her more than he could say, more than he had said.

Of course she hadn't been supremely unselfish. The life she'd lived had hurt her, so she'd changed her life so it wouldn't be so painful. And accepted the price of a scandalous reputation.

Given them all a new start.

Including him.

Four

After being wounded on a merchant trip, Cardus had been given thanks, a small pension—enough for him to eke by—and a slap on the back from the man he'd guarded. He'd known then that there were plenty of other guards, young and adventurous, who would be hired before him.

He'd had no idea what he was going to do, vaguely thought he'd apply to be a Gael City guardsman, but didn't care too much for the regimentation. Then an old friend had recommended him to the Hollys as a very discreet guard. Cardus had signed on to unobtrusively watch over Genista, and gotten a huge down payment and a nice monthly salary.

And his heart entangled with her.

Brooding again. He pulled his gaze back to the dog, who had sprawled in the small hallway, blocking it, gnawing on his bone.

"Let's get you clean, Whin."

The dog cringed, rolled over on his back.

"It's not going to be that bad."

Whin moaned.

"Let me put it like this, FamDog. I can cleanse you or Genista can do it."

One of Whin's eyes opened, rolled. *Saw her house. Very clean. Very fussy.*

Cardus didn't think so, but he wasn't a large dog who could inadvertently destroy something.

With a huge sigh, Whin rolled to his feet, his head drooping.

"Into the waterfall room." Cardus gestured.

Whin trudged inside.

Cardus closed the door behind them, eyed Whin. "I've done a lot of dry cleansings. You happy with that?"

Whin's head came up, he yipped, his tongue lolled. *Yes!*

Several minutes later, Whin was clean and Cardus stepped into the waterfall himself, scrubbed, massaged his thigh under the hot water. Each time he saw Genista, he wanted her a little more, his feelings for her deepened. His protectiveness rose.

She was a strong woman, but he didn't want her hurt again.

The hot water was fine on his thigh, but not on that part of him that needed her body. He ordered the waterfall to cold.

When he went to bed—his bedsponge was on a platform now for his bad leg—Whin welcomed him with a thumping tail.

Cardus rubbed his head.

Very good night, Whin said, settling into the bedsponge.

A year ago, Cardus would have been thrilled that he'd bonded with a rare Familiar Companion. Now, all he could think of was scheming on how he might win Genista.

The Autumn Lord strode through Genista's dreams, dazzling and dangerous. His eyes were intent, knowing. His smile promised sensual wonders. He held out a hand and she just stood, bespelled by his offer. The trees around them were glorious color: gold and red and orange, the grass yet green, green. As leaves drifted through the air, they released scent.

Fragrance that sparked desires in her body, made her ache. Made her sweat.

He stood there, not moving, with his hand still out, and she wondered how long he would wait.

Until winter.

She didn't want to lose him, to lose whatever precious gifts he could bring her . . . lead her to. So she took his hand—warm, callused fingers of a farmer, and a warrior—but she trusted him more than she trusted herself.

Until they reached the edge of a rocky cliff and stepping-stones that crossed a deep chasm. The stones were wide, the gaps between them moderate. She could make it. She'd never feared falling.

She took the first step and the chasm disappeared and the stones became tufts of solid ground in a swamp. The safe spots appeared smaller, the distance between them huge. Now fear invaded.

"Come with me. Trust me," he said.

"I am not good enough. I will fail you."

"You can't." His fingers encompassed hers, full of strength and assurance. He reminded her of someone else. And if you couldn't trust the Lord, who could you trust?

"Where's your Lady?"

He smiled and she knew she'd follow him anywhere. "I'm holding her hand."

Then the swamp was past them, and they were back into a grove of trees of beautiful autumn colors, green grass, summer flowers still in bloom. A bower indeed.

And the man limped and they fell to the sweet-smelling grasses dotted with blossoms. His hands roamed over her, and she knew he wasn't a lover she'd had before. His touch was intent, intense, caressing her with a sureness that aroused until fire lived within her, ready to engulf and set her soaring like the greatest flame in the highest bonfire.

His mouth was on hers, his legs tangled with hers, his sex meeting hers, and they plunged together and were wild and tender, then spent.

She rose just before dawn. She didn't recall anything about her dreams except that they were exceptional. Since she had to be at the shop early, she took a waterfall, dressed, and ate more quickly than usual.

From her bedroom window, she could see lights on in Cardus's home—the kitchen and the mainspace where there was a small area for dining. A twinge of envy went through her as she thought of Cardus having Whin with him.

A change, even since yesterday. She wanted company, wanted to share her home, at least with a Fam Companion.

Though as she ate alone, she could picture Cardus across the table from her, which seemed fairly intimate. As if the changes inside herself were progressing more rapidly than she'd realized. An image from her childhood came to her mind of ice on a pond on a warm spring day. How it had melted, shifted, broken, absorbed into calm waters that reflected the blue sky.

Today was Halloween, tonight that holiday would be acknowledged, and at midnight Samhain would be celebrated and the year would turn new. Time for change, and if she wouldn't force change on herself, she wouldn't delay it, either.

She went out to pick up her newssheet, and her heart bumped as she saw Cardus just within his gate, reading his own. Whin stood next to him with a large bone in his mouth.

"Anything interesting?" she asked.

"Thieves broke into GrandLord Quinoa's summer home and stole some jewelry and paintings."

He looked up at her and his glance was cool, not the warmth she was expecting. Her disappointment was deep—and unreasonable. They'd only shared a steamy kiss after all. And he was a man, kisses meant little to them. And he was a warrior, so crime would be of paramount importance.

"How much jewelry do you have in there?" He jerked a nod to her house.

Irritation rose. "Some. Things I like to wear." She angled her wrist so the rising sun caught the crystal of one of the antique watches she'd restored. "My collection of wrist timers."

He eyed her house. "You should have left the high iron fence up at the sides and in the front."

"I don't want to live behind bars."

He grunted, looked down at the newssheet, and his mouth flattened even more. When he glanced back up at her, his eyes were more than cool—glacial. "The gossip column says that GentleSir Asant will be taking an elusive beauty, one Nista Gorse, to the

Halloween and Samhain rituals officiated by the high priestess and priest at RoundDome Temple. Is that true?"

Genista was stunned. She shouldn't rate any mention in the newssheets here. She'd been careful not to do so. "What? You read the gossip columns?"

Cardus shook the papyrus at her. "Is it true?"

"No." She rubbed her temples, this was not how she'd expected their next meeting to go. "Yes. I suppose. He had tickets and people have been pushing me to get out more, and it's New Year's . . . and many people will be at that ritual so it's not like I'll be really with him . . ."

His gaze bored into her. "Yes or no?" he asked softly.

Her lips tightened. "I said I'd meet him at the RoundDome Temple and take one of his tickets for the rituals."

"He's not picking you up here?" Cardus's gaze flicked toward her, the gate, the front door.

She drew herself up. "I was planning on having a personal ritual here." She swept a hand around. "In my back grassyard, before I leave for the public rituals." Lifting her chin, she continued, "I had hoped to invite"—she paused, heavily—"at least, Whin."

Whin gave a half yip around his bone. *I will come to ritual. I am good. I have watched some.* His whole back end wagged.

Genista bestowed a smile on him. "Thank you." Then she let her smile cool as she sent it to Cardus. She scooped up her newssheet. "Are you going to have a personal New Year's ceremony here?" She stared directly into his eyes, knowing her own would be hot blue to his green ice chips. Who would win?

Second by second his expression eased. He inclined his head in a small nod, kept his gaze on hers. "Yes, I will be having a ritual here." He paused. "I might . . . like . . . a Lady to celebrate with me, opposite my Lord."

A breath filtered out of her.

Dog claws scraped the sidewalk as Whin raced back and forth. *Better, better, best! I will be here for party tonight! Gifts at New Year's!*

Now Cardus was smiling. Down at the dog, unfortunately, and why should Genista care? "Yes."

A Fam gets a collar from his FamPeople. Even a very new Fam, if he has been good. Whin slid a look at Genista.

"That's right," she said, ignoring the pang as she thought of the Holly Fams she'd known.

"I can get him a collar from both of us today," Cardus said.

She stopped herself from offering gilt and insulting him.

I have been good. Whin whipped his tail even faster. Sidled over to the hedge—the much lower hedge—and tried to put his front paws on it. He yelped as he hit her spellshields, dropped his bone.

Genista said a couplet and let down a section of the shield. "Come here and I will bespell you so you can always enter."

Whin picked up his bone, cleared the hedge in one leap, brushed against her legs, front and back. "Sit!"

He did.

She set her hands on his head, visualized the spellshields and the aura color that Whin would need to get through. The FamDog shivered under her fingers and dropped his bone again, hard on her toes, but stayed still.

"Done," Genista said, then murmured another spell to make her feet stop stinging.

Whin tilted his head and looked over his back. *I am pretty and silver.* He picked up his bone, leapt over the hedge again, and pranced back to Cardus.

Again disappointment speared Genista. "You don't want to come in?" she asked the dog but didn't stoop to offer him a bribe of food.

Whin waved his tail a bit more apologetically. *Fussy.*

Genista didn't believe that. She drew herself up but didn't contradict him.

Meeting her eyes again, Cardus said, "Have you dog-proofed your house yet?"

She hadn't even thought of it, and now was distracted from the man to all her pretty possessions. Which weren't nearly as important as the man . . . or the dog.

"No."

Another nod, but Cardus's face had gone back to inscrutable. "You have time before you must leave for work."

"Yes." She hurried back in, realizing she hadn't put on slippers and her feet were frigid.

Once inside, she slapped the newssheet on the table open to the society column. "Mysterious and elusive beauty, Nista Gorse." Dammit! Luckily they had no pic of her to print, and she'd better add a rippling layer of illusion to her face so her image couldn't be captured well by any kind of mechanical Flair. How irritating. She muttered, "Mysterious and elusive . . ." That piece had to be submitted by Asant himself. Naturally he hadn't included that she was a lowly tech.

Genista flinched to think what *Mistrys* Faverel would have to say to her, and thought of lines she could use as she puttered around the house, putting delicate objects beyond Whin's flapping tail or leaping paw reach.

Inside his own stark mainspace, Cardus took the newssheet in his hands and ripped it again and again. That didn't take much hand strength since the papyrus was constructed to disintegrate after a day or two, and it relieved most of his feelings. Genista would be going out with another man.

Whin growled and Cardus looked at him. The dog sent telepathically, *I do NOT need shredded papyrus. I do NOT pee in the house.* Another growl. *Or shit, either. I didn't last night and won't. I am a good FamDog.*

"Oh. Ah." Cardus chuckled. "Of course you don't."

But the dog still looked offended.

"I'll have a gift for you tonight."

A Fam collar!

"Yes, for the moment, but eventually Genista and I should buy a collar for you together." Nice idea. He liked it a lot.

Not the first thing they'd do together. That was celebrating Samhain tonight. Her Lady to his Lord.

Considering Whin, he said, "You said you weren't much of a watchdog, eh?"

Whin dropped his head and his bone but rolled his eyes up to look at Cardus. *Watching is no fun. Hunting is fun.*

"Understand that. But the thefts concern me." There was no better target for a gang than Genista Furze and her FirstFamily wealth. "I'll visit the local guardhouse today." He'd checked in with the guardsmen, both the main guardhouse and his local station, when he'd moved in, of course. Told them he was on bodyguard duty for a person living incognito.

That hadn't leaked so he knew those guards could be trusted. Perhaps now he'd have to reveal Genista's identity, but he hoped not. Having *the* most famous beauty of Celta living in a small bungalow and working in a clock repair shop was just too juicy not to share.

"Want to come with me, Whin?"

Whin looked mournfully at Genista's house. *FamWoman did not ask me to come to work with her.*

"Pretty sure that her employers wouldn't welcome a FamDog . . . at least not today. We might work up to it. Sitting in the back of a shop all day doesn't sound like fun, either."

No.

"Finish off that bone, and I'll get you another treat while we're out this morning."

We go to guardhouse first?

"After we see Genista off for work."

You in front every morning.

That sounded like Whin had watched before approaching them.

"I'm the good watchdog, remember?"

Yes. I will go bury bone. The dog trotted to the back door and used the pattern Cardus had given him to open the door and drop the spellshields. Which of their yards would have a hole?

Strolling into the corner of the mainspace he'd fitted as an office, Cardus studied the map of Gael City. His and Genista's homes were indicated as well as the Faverels' shop and the route Genista usually took, along with all the guardhouses. He examined the main sacred grove of the city just across the street from RoundDome Temple. Genista would probably teleport there. He hoped she wouldn't allow Asant to bring her back.

Cardus had to plan. If she teleported to RoundDome Temple,

he could follow, but teleporting took a great deal of Flair, and Cardus could teleport only twice—at the most, three times—in a day. Depleting his energy was not good strategy.

He could use the Holly name and arrange to be included in the celebrants at RoundDome Temple, but he didn't want Genista to see him. He decided to join the mass circle in the sacred grove and watch for her to exit the temple after the ritual inside was done, then follow her home.

Sooner or later he would have to tell her that he'd been hired as a bodyguard for her, but their association was still so new and tentative and growing that he wanted it to be later. When she was more attached to him, so she'd listen instead of just shut him out of her life. After he knew she would let him protect her full-time and he could tell the Hollys he was finished with the job.

He didn't know what she'd do if she found out now. Perhaps something that would keep him from safeguarding her.

And he didn't want another man taking care of her. Though he had no indication that Asant had any interest in Genista other than sexual.

Or more than sexual. How often had she met him? She wouldn't have gone out with a perfect stranger, so she must have met him at work.

The front door opened and Whin ambled in, saw the papyrus on the dining room table, and yanked it down with his teeth, brought it over to drop on Cardus's feet.

He picked it up, wadded it, and jammed it into the deconstructor.

Staccato pings came from the timing alarm he'd set last night so he'd be in the front yard to see Genista leave early for her employment.

He wanted to tail her, as he'd done when she'd first gotten the job—to and from the Faverels' shop—but there was no way she wouldn't notice.

And he didn't want to annoy her further.

Or show her his own annoyance.

He *had* told her to become more sociable. Truly believed that she was a more outgoing person than she'd shown herself to be in the months here. But he hadn't meant for her to go out with another man.

Even though she'd emphasized that she was attending a public ritual, one with the top hundred and twenty people in Gael City, there was no getting around the fact that she was meeting another man there. Another man was providing her with a ticket.

I understand now! Whin said. *You don't like that another male is sniffing FamWoman.*

Five

Cardus winced but couldn't deny the FamDog's observation. "No. I don't like her spending time with another man."

But WE will be HERE with FamWoman tonight for blessing and gifts. Being petted.

There was that. Though Genista would be seen with Asant in public by all the most important people, would hold his hand during the rituals, having a private ceremony here was better.

Better, but he wished it had been exclusive. He saw a shred of newssheet he'd missed, ripped it again, and stuffed it in the deconstructor.

Being PETTED! Whin shouted.

Yes, intimacy. Heat licked through Cardus, settled, as it so often had, in his groin.

Time to go out front, Whin prompted.

"Yes."

He stepped out and grabbed his recent prop, the rake, desultorily dragged it the length of his front yard from the stoop to his gate.

Genista exited her home, set the house spellshields, and stepped deliberately on the stones she'd set that just matched her stride.

She glanced at him from the corners of her eyes, appearing

gently vulnerable, and any harsh feelings he had for her evaporated like the rime of frost on autumn leaves.

Cardus went out of his gate, crossed to hers, and was there when she let down that spellshield. He opened her low front iron gate and bowed her out.

"Thank you," she said.

He held out a hand, and she hesitated, then put her fingers in his. He kissed them, reluctantly let them go. "Have a good day." He paused. "I thought I'd start the ritual just before sunset."

She smiled and the air around him seemed to warm. "I'll be home by then."

He shut the gate behind her and watched as she raised the spellshields. She was good about that, keeping her house and property shielded; maybe he was being too critical. No. He was a good guard and wanted her safe. He'd just mind his comments to her.

"Merry meet," he said the beginning farewell sequence.

"And merry part."

"And merry meet again, this evening, Nista." He tried to put a caress in his tones, and as she glanced at him with flushed surprise, he figured she'd heard it.

Whin barked for attention.

Genista petted him. "I'll see you later, too."

Whin licked her hand and she laughed. With a last wave, she headed up the street.

I want you to follow her to work, Cardus sent privately to the dog. *That's almost like hunting.*

I can hunt and explore on the way back?

Yes. Try not to attract her attention.

Mistrys Faverel was sour with an undertone of excitement when Genista walked through the back door of the shop.

Master Faverel winked and said, "Greetyou, my beautiful and elusive employee."

"Greetyou. Will we be working on more no-time spells today?"

"Humph." Mistrys Faverel crossed her arms and tapped her

toe, then flung out an arm toward the front of the shop. "You're working sales this morning. With me."

"I'd rather—"

"I'd rather you keep your hands off my husband."

"I never!"

"Brassi, that's enough." Master Faverel slipped an arm around his wife's waist and kissed her cheek. "I told you that I asked Nista to become my journeywoman. If she agrees, she will be working with me, and not much in the shop . . . unless you and she talk about hours. But I love you, not her. I will always love you. Try to think of her as a Son'sDaughter. I do."

Mistrys Faverel's eyes widened; she shot Genista a comprehensive glance from head to toe, then looked back at her husband. "You do?"

"Yes."

"Very well," Mistrys Faverel said, stepping from the embrace and turning to walk into the shop, swishing her hips. "But I need her today. For the curiosity seekers who've seen the newssheet and know she works here. And for shoppers who haven't purchased their New Year's gifts yet. It's one of our busiest days of the year, and we are closing early."

"Because for the first time in years we are attending the ritual at dusk with your family, like you've always wanted," Master Faverel soothed, turning his head to give Genista a wink.

"Come along, Nista," Mistrys Faverel said.

With lagging steps, Genista followed.

As soon as she entered the front, Genista saw that there was a short line outside the shop. Mistrys Faverel bustled to the door and opened it, beaming as customers surged in.

The day was busy, and Genista's smile stayed on her face but became tight. At least it felt like that under the blurring illusion that coated her head like paint. All the regular women clients had dropped by to scrutinize her and gossip with Mistrys Faverel.

Plenty of people had come in for last-minute gifts, and despite his words the night before, Asant wasn't one of them, and she was relieved.

Genista hadn't had any problem recognizing the local newssheet reps and putting on a bland and dull manner that deflected interest. By the time MidAfternoonBell rang and Mistrys Faverel shut the door on the last customer, the older woman was flushed with triumph. She'd been clever in winnowing gilt from each and every person. "We have done the best business ever!"

She actually smiled with sincerity at Genista. "You really should work the counter more often."

"Thank you, but it isn't as interesting as working on clocks and no-times."

Mistrys Faverel rolled her eyes. "You and my husband say that." She sniffed, tapped Genista on the shoulder of her apron. "You can take that off now and go home. You look a little tired." She frowned, tilted her head. "And not as pretty as usual."

The energy it had cost to keep the illusion spell going had worn on Genista. She just nodded, untied and slipped from her apron, and put it in her satchel.

"Have a good evening and Happy New Year," Mistrys Faverel said by rote, turning to get her own pursenal and leave.

"Happy New Year," Genista croaked.

While his wife was out of the workroom, Master Faverel handed Genista a small box, reddening. "New Year's gift."

He hadn't slipped her a bonus of gilt. That was good. Genista opened the box and saw a delicate wrist timer from a century ago. "Thank you!" She hugged him.

The tips of his ears reddened. He flapped his arms. "Go on, put it in your bag. You'll notice it's an Agave piece. Beautiful but needs constant tinkering to work."

"Thanks!"

"'Welcome."

She drew her gift for him from her tunic pocket. It was wrapped in a ribbon and easy to see what it was by the shape. She handed it to him.

"A clock key!" he said.

"I think it has the correct spell and shape to fix that cabinet corner clock."

He clutched it to his skinny chest, face creasing into a grin. "Really?"

"Yes. I found it in a stuff shop." She'd used discreet blackmail on her middle sister to have her scour the shops of Druida City for a key of that particular shape.

"Let's see." He headed toward the clock in the dim corner, key gleaming.

His wife caught him by his apron strings. "Time to go if we're going to prepare for the ritual tonight with a *shared waterfall*." She snatched the key from her husband's hand and slipped it into a pursenal that was an awful shade of green. "Good-*bye*, Nista."

Genista put her hands in her opposite sleeves—they were just big enough to do that—and bowed to the couple. "Merry meet," she said formally, using the old greeting of nobles to each other.

Master Faverel bowed. "And merry part."

"And merry meet again, Happy New Year!" This time she meant it.

She left and they followed her out. She scanned the street and found no one lingering who might be interested in her so she dropped the skim of illusion on her features. She only hoped the first ritual tonight gave her enough energy to replenish her Flair and her spirit, since she'd have to go disguised to the public ritual, too.

She walked in the afternoon sunlight. The autumn days were short and soon it would be twilight.

Cardus was in his yard, moving his hands in a spell to stuff dead leaves in a large cloth sack, looking like the Autumn Lord himself conducting a ritual: hair aflame again, broad shoulders accented by his leather tunic, shirt sleeves billowing in the wind.

Gorgeous.

His front yard showed only an occasional yellow or orange dab.

Her front yard appeared suspiciously clean, as if he'd drawn the leaves from it to his.

His appreciative smile warmed her, and instinctually her walk slowed, her hips rolled more. She wet her lips and wished she hadn't as the cool wind dried them.

Letting down the spellshield, she opened and walked through her gate, closed it, and raised the property spellshield again. Then she strolled over to the hedge. "Greetyou, Cardus."

Like this morning, she had initiated the conversation first. His gaze grew tender, and when he replied, his voice was lower, with that lilt in it that a man used only with his special woman. "Greetyou, Nista. You're lovely this afternoon. Did the day go well?"

"Well enough, thank you." She stretched. "I'm glad it's over."

"Anticipating the ritual?"

"Our private ritual, yes." She glanced around, didn't see Whin. "Did you get Whin's collar?"

Cardus dipped a hand in his trous pocket and pulled out a sturdy woven collar in red and pale blue with male and female symbols near the clasp. There were a couple of unfaceted gems representing him and her.

"Excellent," she said. "I had to rush during my short lunch break to get him a gift." And one for Cardus. She'd had to teleport a couple of times, also draining her energy.

He held the collar out over the hedge. "Take the gift and imbue it with some of your energy."

She opened her spellshields to do so. Her fingers brushed his palm as she picked it up. From under her lashes, she saw his fingers curl over his palm as if cherishing her touch, and her heart twinged. She *liked* this man who was attracted to her but didn't push her. Different from every other fighter she'd known.

But now she formed an image of the large and loving Whin, closed her eyes, and drew her Flair to coat the collar, sink into it. Fill it with loving, and she murmured a safety spell.

When she finished, she caught Cardus's raised eyebrows.

"What?" she asked.

"Whin can take care of himself."

She lifted her own brows. "I think you would agree that everyone should have a safety spell, whether or not they can take care of themselves."

"Why do you say that?"

"It's obvious you're a fighter."

He shrugged, leaned forward over the hedge, his gaze intent. "We'll need to talk. Someday."

She noticed the odd tone in his voice. "When we know each other better?"

His lips compressed into a serious line. "That's right. When you know me better."

Her eyes narrowed. "Are you hiding things from me?"

His mouth curved slightly, his emerald gaze stayed steady on hers. "Many things. I have my secrets."

She had plenty of her own that she was reluctant to share, though he'd never struck her as a man interested in status or wealth. She handed back the collar. "Why don't you go wrap this."

He stepped back, bowed. "Yes, my lady."

She winced. "I didn't mean to be demanding."

He smiled, his teeth even and white. "I like a demanding woman."

In bed, she figured.

"And you're right," Cardus said. "Whin will like it better if it is an obvious gift."

"I need to prepare for the ritual," she said, and thinking of safety, she needed to check that the artisan from whom she'd purchased Cardus's gift had translocated it properly to the spot she'd given him—her back porch.

"A moment," Cardus said.

"What?"

"Could you drop the shields between our houses so I might remove a portion of the fence and set up a mutual ritual space on our boundaries?"

She stared. "You can do that?" He had more Flair than was obvious.

"Yes."

She thought about it, liked the idea. "All right." She whispered the Words that banished the spell.

Cardus stepped back to the hedge, leaned over, and kissed her briefly on the lips. "See you later, my lady."

The kiss sent streamers of desire to her sex. "Later," she said, her voice husky, and she didn't know if she meant sex or not.

* * *

When he saw the light in her waterfall room blink out, he took that as a cue to leave his house and go to the space he'd made between their two homes to celebrate Halloween and Samhain.

Taking a large box that contained ritual items, he shut his back door and spellshielded it. The ritual would take place in the back-yards, and he intended that after the ceremony they would spend the time before she had to leave for the public celebration in her home.

Glancing around, he saw no sign of Whin, and he decided to test his mental connection with the FamDog. *Whin?* he called telepathically.

Only by straining his ears could he hear a distant bark, carried to him by the wind more than anything else.

I come! the FamDog shouted strongly in Cardus's mind.

We begin within a half septhour, Cardus replied as he strode to where he'd positioned a large marble altar that he'd moved from the ritual room of his home. Turning in a circle, he gauged the space and nodded in satisfaction. He'd removed a large section of her fence that separated their yards. It looked good.

From the box, he drew out a small wooden fold-up altar he'd had for years, set it down, and smoothed a black cloth over it. This one would honor the dead, the marble altar was to honor the Lord and Lady. Then he placed a rough carved statue of a family—parents and child—on the altar. It represented his father, mother, and older brother who'd died long ago when a sickness had swept through their small town one winter. He hadn't been with them but working in the stables on a noble's estate. This was an old grief that only shadowed his heart during holidays—especially this one.

He also set down a silver wheel, flat, symbolizing all the holi-days of the year, and the Wheel of Stars that souls cycled upon until they were incarnated.

On the marble altar, he placed a candlestick, the base of which was an image of the Lord. He also arranged his chalice, blunt rit-ual knife, a bowl of irregular salt crystals, and the small jug of wine. Drawing a little curled piece of papyrus from his trous pocket, he put it on the altar next to where Genista's chalice would go. On the paper, he'd written what he wanted to vanish from his life: unrequited attraction and loneliness.

In the best possible worlds, Genista would return his love. He'd work to make that so. If she didn't—he'd move on. No more of the old daily torture of seeing her and wanting her and not having her.

No more of the new torture of knowing she was with another man.

He put the gifts he'd gotten her and Whin at the bottom of the altar. Then Cardus turned and, with narrowed eyes, made sure the placement of the rope he'd laid in a large circle was even. It appeared fine, and so did the four spell-lights at each compass point for the elemental guardians. He took the box and set it near the shed, outside what would be the sacred circle.

All was ready.

He heard rapid claw clicks on the sidewalk in front, the quick breathing of a large animal, then Whin bounded into his backyard, skidded to a halt with a comical expression on his face.

You opened the fence.

"It's the only way to protect both our properties with one ritual."

Dropping his gifts, two slobbered-on rolls of cloth, at Cardus's feet, the dog panted. *I like.*

"It's not secure, so the fence will go back up as soon as the ritual is done."

At that moment Genista's back door opened with a tinkle of wind chimes she'd tied to the inside door latch. She stepped onto her stoop. She was dressed in a pale beige robe that probably cost as much as he would have made guarding four caravan trips.

Cardus's insides lurched as he studied her. Her blond hair was long and loose, her face and body were perfect. She looked like a goddess. His mind buzzed; his body throbbed with need.

He wanted her, all of her, who she was now—and he thought they could help each other. He had no illusions that he was without problems, but he firmly believed that they complemented each other.

He steadied his breathing and his pulse. This shared ritual should give them a common bond—he was ready to be vulnerable to her and to the Lady and Lord.

Six

Genista blinked as she exited her back door. Cardus had removed a large section of the fencing between their backyards and placed the altars across the property lines. It appeared a little odd, and she noted that the section of fence was propped against his southern boundary. He stood, waiting, his face impassive, watching her—to see if she'd object?

Something about the space, the flow of energy on this special evening, had her remaining on the stoop and closing her eyes . . . and feeling the last hint of summer warmth in a breeze, then the air stilled and thrummed with the promise of a new year.

A saying good-bye to the last, and a welcome to the new.

Cardus's energy was vital and masculine and pulled to all the feminine in her. She became aware of the soft, heavy robe she wore, her only garment. She recalled the kiss the night before, his lust that had sent heat through her body. The small and quiet moments they had shared.

Then another bounding energy swept toward her.

I am here! Whin projected. *And I have gifts!*

She laughed and her eyes opened and her cheeks flushed when she saw that Cardus still watched her. The FamDog sat beside him, two bundles of cloth before him tied with a string. Intriguing.

She moved toward them, carrying a basket containing items for the altars and food to honor the Lady and Lord.

Cardus wore leathers—good furrabeast that might have been harvested at this time years ago—honoring the animals that fed and clothed him.

Walking slowly, she watched the sun set with red and pink and orange at the horizon. Twilight blue gave way to deep black in the sky, and the full twinmoons soared high and bright and silver. Stars twinkled like diamond spangles.

The altar for the dead was small; he'd put a silver wheel there to represent acquaintances lost in the past. The object would serve for both of them. Her steps hesitated as she saw the weathered sculpture of a family of three, and she knew that it was his family. She'd never asked, but now she knew he was the sole survivor of a small family.

Her Family was large for the nobility, and no unexpected or tragic deaths had touched it.

She had only one remembrance marker for the altar, and it ripped the scar in her wide open. When she reached the wooden altar, she placed the small white stone image of a curled, sexless baby on the black cloth. Her womb felt empty and cold, and her cheeks colder still as tears ran down her face and chilled in the evening air.

Standing, head bowed, she wept as she'd wept the last two years when she'd done this, as she anticipated she'd always weep in the future.

Then warmth surrounded her. Cardus was close behind, then his body was touching, then his arms wrapped around her and drew her to him.

"I'm sorry for your loss," he said in a low, rough voice, and she knew it wasn't just a platitude; he meant it. Immediately after she'd lost her baby, there had been more pity than she could bear. Her pride had made her futilely grasp for outward status to set people at a distance.

"I've heard that nothing is as devastating as the loss of a child, and I wish you hadn't had to experience that," he continued, rocking her gently in his arms.

They stayed together until she pulled a softleaf from her sleeve and wiped her eyes, blew her nose. When he turned her to face him, his expression was sympathetic and tender.

He said, "We have lost, yet we go on. The old year is passing, the new year rushing toward us. We bring memory tokens of our loss, food for our Lady and Lord and our dead, a scrip of that inside us we wish burnt away." His voice was vibrant as he said the first words of the ceremony.

Reluctantly she drew away from him and stepped toward the altar. From her basket she withdrew her cauldron, her goblet, a statue of the Lady, and a rose quartz candlestick. She put a small shell bowl on the altar and poured fragrant herbal water into it. Last, she stacked oat and apple cakes that she'd made a couple of days ago.

Cardus set her candlestick on one side of his Lord candlestick and her Lady figurine on the other. Though they were of different materials, they all seemed to match, and a small smile curved her lips.

He caught her gaze. "They look well together."

"Yes." His Lord candlestick was leafy and green and taller than her voluptuous Lady.

Hesitantly she placed her rolled-up papyrus next to the cauldron and next to his. She wanted to vanquish grief and regret.

Whin stood and sniffed at the altar, sneezed. His tongue swiped out and caught a cake, and he crunched it, bits falling from his muzzle.

Instead of scolding the dog, Cardus flung back his head and laughed. Genista laughed, too. Cardus caught her fingers and lifted them to his lips, brushed a kiss on her fingertips, nodded to the small cairn of stones marking the north elemental point. "Shall we cast the circle?"

"Yes."

Hand in hand they crossed to the north and continued to each compass point, calling the Elemental energies to guard the circle and contribute to it. As they chanted the circle closed, the atmosphere was imbued with power. Inside the circle became a mystical, sacred space where they were linked to the Lady and Lord, where psi Flair could affect their lives. Every moment she was aware of Cardus's hand holding hers, of the energy they called cycling between them, closely connecting them.

Her breath and Cardus's whispered out at the same time. She turned back toward the altar and tripped over Whin.

Cardus steadied her and they both looked down at the Fam-Dog.

Genista cleared her throat as she spoke to their companion. "It's unusual for Fams to be part of such a small circle."

Whin looked aside, whined a bit. *Never been with people in circle. Like the feeling. Stay?*

"Of course you can stay," Genista said, just as Cardus said, "Sure."

Standing and wagging his tail, Whin lolled his tongue in a doggie smile. *Thanks.* He did a long stretch, popping joints. *Feels very good.*

Dog following, they walked to the altar. Cardus looked down at her and said softly, "I accept the godhood of the Lord within myself." She grew hotter at the sound of his low voice, with *more.* He lit his candle, took her hands again, and she experienced the jolt of attraction that melded into a bond between them.

His gaze caught hers and heat radiated from their hands throughout her body. "I cherish the Lady within you."

She breathed unsteadily, felt a sifting of feminine power shiver through her, from the earth, the moons, the stars, settling into her blood. "I accept the goddesshood of the Lady within myself." Her voice sounded rich and sultry to her own ears, and a flush tinted Cardus's cheeks. She squeezed his hands. "I cherish the Lord within you." Then she lit her candle and they sang the Blessing Chant, welcoming the power of the deities into their circle.

They took turns with the rest of the general ritual, singing songs that had been passed down through their culture for centuries. Genista felt both herself, and *Other*, and that Other was so much more than she, wise and knowing that this was a reverence for the dead . . . but underneath it all, joyous. That Other *knew* the mysteries of life and death.

And for a brief while, Genista sensed such knowledge and was comforted, her heavy grief was gone. She moved slowly, deliberately, and when she glanced at Cardus, there was Another below his skin, occasionally looking out of his eyes, a man of wisdom and wildness. Warrior. Lover.

He grasped her hands once more, and they seemed even harder with calluses. His voice was richer, deeper.

"We honor the dead," he said. "Those who have passed to the Wheel of Stars."

"We honor the dead," she repeated. "Those who have passed to the Wheel of Stars." She was so mesmerized by the flicker of candlelight in Cardus's gaze, the feel of the soft and warm breeze swirling around her, that she didn't look to her token. True surcease.

Cardus said,

And we celebrate Samhain, the new year,
As the twinmoons cycle,
As the seasons change and
Life itself cycles,
We honor the dead and the past
And embrace life and the future.

He reached out to his piece of papyrus and flicked it into the cauldron, where it flamed and vanished in smoke. She did the same.

Then they reached for each other's hands. She knew the next words, the old words, but felt them shiny with newness:

By the arcs and cycles of the twinmoons
By the dance of the sun through the sky and the seasons
By the circle of life and the circle of stars
I will live, love, die, and live again.
Always loving.
I will live, meet, remember, embrace love and life again.

It felt like a promise to this man.

Whin howled and that enriched the ceremony, enriched the

night. Then she looked at the FamDog and said the words again with Cardus.

They held his large goblet between them. He drank first, then she. She fed him an oak cake and he did the same. They allowed Whin to dip his tongue into the wine, eat another cake.

In a daze, Genista thanked the deities, felt the Other rise away, and opened the circle with Cardus.

Cold air rushed in and the stars themselves seemed to frost.

"Nothing like a private ritual of two," Cardus said, and his voice sounded rusty, as if his vocal cords had strained.

Genista found that she was leaning against him, his arm around her waist, and she didn't want to move, but jealousy flickered through her. She had never shared such an experience—had either been part of a large circle or solitary. "You've done this before."

His eyes were dark and soft, his arm tightened. "No. Never just two. Only heard about it." Then he closed his lashes and shook his head. "Never felt like that."

Whin barked. *They were beautiful. You are beautiful.*

Genista shivered, wanted to hold Cardus tight, celebrate intimately. And was that a thought from the old, needy Genista? She didn't know, but she stepped away and inserted a prosaic note into the conversation. "We'd best clean up. It's a good thing that the public ritual is a couple of septhours away." Unsteadily she walked to the altars. She was cold; her emotions were raw.

Moving slowly, she snuffed the flames of her candle and cauldron, bespelled the cauldron so it was safe for her basket. Reached out to the altar of the dead and slipped the stone signifying her miscarried child gently into the basket. Grief was still there, but muted, and she thought it had finally lost its sharp and gnawing teeth.

Cardus moved faster than she. By the time she'd walked to her stoop, opened the door, and set her basket inside, both altars were gone and the section of fence was back in place, surrounded by spellshields better than ever.

He and Whin were on her side of the fence, along with the gifts. She'd placed hers in the circle, too, but had hidden them with a spell and was thankful that they hadn't noticed.

Whin slurped his tongue around his muzzle. *Good food and gifts now!* He sat, head cocked in the direction of her house, tail wagging. Cardus kept himself still, as if unsure whether she would invite them into her home, but she shoved the door wide. "Go on in."

Cardus frowned.

"I'll set the spellshields behind us," she added. "I have a separate no-time food storage for ritual foods, and stocked it for Samhain meal—including furrabeast steak."

Whin had already passed her to shoot inside the house.

Come, FamMan, open the no-time for me! he called.

Cardus stopped near her. "You're sure of this?"

She wanted to kiss him, but didn't, swept a gesture to the open door. "Welcome to my home and my feast."

"*Our* feast." He lifted a jug she hadn't noticed. "I have wine."

He entered. She raised her property spellshields, then ran and picked up her gifts, now imbued with more Flair from being inside the circle, and trotted back. The staff she'd bought Cardus was difficult to disguise, but she hurried past the two in the tiny kitchen to her mainspace and rolled the staff close to the hearth stone, which shadowed the length of wood. With a wave of her hand, she lit the fireplace, and flames crackled noisily.

A few minutes later the feast was already demolished. Rituals always burnt energy. Genista took the empty plates away and Cardus helped put them in the cleanser.

Gifts now! Whin sat mouth open, droplets of drool falling toward one of Genista's thick rugs. She was glad she'd taken some time to dog-proof her house. The drool gave a little hiss as it vanished before it hit the fibers.

Instead of sitting in one of the large chairs, Cardus lowered himself to the floor with his back against a twoseat. During and after the ritual, he'd moved well, but that seemed to be wearing off. He was favoring his bad leg again.

Genista settled on the floor, too, next to the fireplace and opposite Cardus. Not that she was that far from him, only a couple of meters. Her house wasn't big.

Whin sat in the middle of the space and nosed his gift toward her. She wasn't sure how he'd gotten someone to wrap the thing, but whoever did it didn't do a very good job. She unrolled the cloth to see a filthy, battered pocket watch with a broken chain. Frowning, she picked it up, held it.

Panting loudly, the dog leaned on her. *You like?*

She stared into his eyes, shook her head. Cardus scowled at her, made a cutting gesture. She ignored him. "This is wonderful. It's very, very old. I think it might have been brought on one of the starships by a Colonist. Where did you find it?"

Whin's whole body wriggled. *On a trail to Gael City. South.*

"Lately the path of the Colonists who left the lost starship *Lugh's Spear* to go to Druida has been found," Cardus said. He nodded at the watch. "It's reasonable Whin unearthed the timer."

"Yes," Genista said. Slowly turning it over in her hands, she paid little attention to the dirt that fell from it and the grime that got under her fingernails. She stroked it with a soft touch, tried a Word to get it open, failed. Setting it carefully on a table, she lunged onto her knees and toward Whin and wrapped her arms around him. "Wonderful, fabulous gift," she said into his fur. "Thank you."

A long lick dampened her face. *You are welcome.*

"Good job," Cardus said.

When she let go of the dog, she found herself close to Cardus. He opened his arm closest to the fire in invitation. Without thought, she scooted to him, let his arm drape around her shoulders. Glancing up, she saw his face had eased into tenderness, his green eyes held . . . affection? At least affection. And as her heart thumped hard in her chest, she knew she was falling in love with him. All this time, his quiet and steady presence next door had comforted her at a level she hadn't recognized. He was solid. He didn't have a HeartMate and she didn't, either. No woman had ever come to visit him . . . and she thought she'd have felt female energy if one had been there when Genista was at work.

He had never offered her compliments, never shown overt interest in having sex with her—unlike most of the men in her past. Hadn't swept her off her feet, tried to get her into bed without any thought or consideration on her part. He made her feel special, like a woman worth knowing instead of just bedding.

His complete acceptance of her as she was had soothed her. Yes, she was ready to move to the next step in a relationship with him. She hoped he was as interested in her. Sucking in a breath, but refusing to be cowardly, Genista pulled the staff out from near the hearth stone and pushed it to Cardus. Her cheeks felt hot. "Here."

Cardus stared at Genista, glanced at her gift. Something in the energy flowing between them had changed. He wanted to close his eyes and feel the bond that had expanded between them during the ritual, but he didn't want to alert her to how much he wanted such a bond, a thick golden bond of love.

So he plucked the bright green bow from the top of the gray felt sheath, pushed the cloth carefully down. His breath stopped with a harsh sound as he saw the polished wood with spiral painting of the seasons circling upward, the bare branches of winter, the buds of green and hints of the pastel blooms of spring, full-bodied leaves of shades of summer green, the blaze of orange and red and gold of autumn at the top of the staff. He withdrew his arm from Genista, used both hands on the staff to rise. The wood was smooth under his grip, yet he felt spells—defensive and offensive—that made it more than a walking staff, made it a weapon. Several places on the staff were bound with different metals: copper, bronze, iron, glisten. And near the top and bottom were a line of spell runes.

He had a few quarterstaffs as weapons in his back porch, but nothing like this. He didn't even know there *were* such things. Had no idea where one might purchase them.

She was ducking her head, her cheeks pink. "The Autumn Lord's staff."

He couldn't prevent the same question she'd asked of Whin. "Where did you get this?"

A shoulder shrug from her. He was making her uncomfortable and he regretted that. "Never mind."

"An artist and weapons master," she said.

She would know weapons masters. She'd been part of the Holly fighting Family. Now he felt more than her wealth standing between them; her past rose like a shadow.

"Here in Gael City?" Lord and Lady, he prayed she hadn't obtained it from the FirstFamily GreatLord T'Ash. Then Cardus would have to give it back as too valuable, and he didn't think he could let the thing go. He wanted it secondary only to Genista herself.

"Yes, of course." She was staring into the fire.

He'd been a stup. Leaning down, he kissed the top of her head. "It's wonderful. Another fabulous gift." Letting his palms slide along the length of it, he sat again, set the staff aside, and leaned over to kiss Genista's averted cheek. "It's wonderful," he repeated. "I couldn't give it up if I tried. Thank you."

She turned back to him, but that wasn't enough. He opened his legs, lifted her, and settled her in the space between his thighs, so she could relax against him. So they were body to body.

Sweet.

Whin coughed, looked expectantly at them.

Seven

Cardus reached to where he'd put a package wrapped in thin softleaves, plunked it down in front of the dog.

Whee! the FamDog said and shredded the wrapping to reveal his present.

A COLLAR GIFT from my FamMan and FamWoman! Whin grabbed it in his teeth, hopped to his feet, and raced around the house, then came back and sat before them. *Thank you, thank you, thank you!*

Genista moved against Cardus, looking up at him with such approval that his chest instinctively swelled at pleasing his lady. "The fastening will break free if you get in trouble," Cardus said.

There are JEWELS!

He'd spent more than he should have but was well rewarded by the pulse of love coming from Whin, and Genista's smile.

"Yes, a large garnet cabochon bead that represents me and a sunstone for Nista." Cardus fastened the collar around Whin's neck, checked to make sure it was comfortable.

"Looks lovely," Genista said.

Whin pranced out of the mainspace and back.

"I have a gift for you, too, Whin," Genista said. Holding out her palm, she translocated a tiny square in a tissue softleaf, then placed it on the floor before their Fam.

With one claw, Whin ripped it open. He angled his head to see the golden tag with marks on it. *I can't read.*

Leaning forward, Genista clipped the tag on Whin's collar. "It's a chit for The Fam Place." She put her hands on each side of Whin's large muzzle and looked him in his eyes, fingers stroking. "The tag has your name and ours and is recorded in The Fam Place's records. You are allowed two meals a day and a place to sleep indoors for the rest of your life. Whatever happens to us, if you ever want to leave us, you will be cared for."

Whin whined and she let him loose. He licked her face, then pushed her back against Cardus. He swallowed hard. Warmth that he had them both, woman to love and FamDog, unfurled within him.

I love you both.

"I love you, too, Whin," Genista said.

Cardus rubbed the dog's head. "So do I." He kissed Genista's temple. "That was a very generous thing to do."

"I didn't want Whin to ever be afraid of going hungry or needing a warm place to sleep again."

I'm not, Whin said. Turning, he pawed the smaller roll of cloth and shoved it toward Cardus. *Yours,* Whin said. *From me.*

"Thank you." Smiling, Cardus untied the dirty ribbon to see a leather thong with a battered bead in the form of the Lord as Cernunnos, the antler-horned god, on the front and *Blessings of the Lord* written on the back.

It says I love you, *a cat told me,* Whin said proudly.

Genista choked. Cardus thumped her on the back. As far as Cardus knew, no Fam Companion could read. He replied to Whin, "I can see that. It's a great gift. Thanks again." He slipped it over his head.

You're welcome. Then the dog settled himself across Cardus's ankles. Whin thumped his tail. He craned his head up to look at Cardus. *One more gift.*

"That's right," Cardus replied. He couldn't begin to match the expense of the gifts that Genista had given them, but he *could* match the thought that had gone into them, the feelings he had for both of them. He'd actually purchased Genista's present a couple of months before, hoping that they'd be at a point to exchange New Year's gifts.

He drew it out from under the twoseat, where he'd put it before they'd eaten. The gaily wrapped box was orange and red, brown and black, Samhain's colors. The ribbon was twine and decorated with real acorns.

Her bottom wiggled against his groin as she moved in excitement to open her gift, and he almost regretted spooning with her. Carefully she untied the ribbon, slipped the acorns off, and held them in her hand, covered them with her fingers. Then she tilted her head and once again her smile seemed to light up the room for him. "These are viable seeds! I could plant them and have a Celtan oak!"

"An added bonus," he said, sending a blessing to the saleswoman who'd decorated his gift for him. His arms were still loosely around Genista, so he jutted his chin to point. "Open it up. I'm impatient."

She turned to look at him. "No, you aren't. You're extremely patient."

His blood pulsed quicker. He hoped she was recognizing how he valued her. He was yearning to love her but would not push.

She pulled apart the pretty papyrus and sitting, gleaming against the autumn colors, was a brass box.

"It's a music box," he said. He *was* impatient, he hadn't waited for her to open the lid.

"How lovely." But she was looking at him instead of his gift, and the dearness of the moment had him smiling slowly. She blinked, stroked the box, but still didn't open it.

"It's broken," he said. "You'll need to work on it to fix it."

She brought it to her chest. "Wonderful!" Then she stretched up and kissed him, her soft, lush lips pressing against his own, and he had to suppress a groan. She didn't withdraw so he opened his mouth to slip his tongue along her lips. She hummed and smiled, then gazed up at him. "Thank you."

He had to clear his throat before he could answer. "You're welcome."

Setting her hand on the papyrus, she translocated it somewhere out of view. Saving it for another time, and that notion pleased him.

She scooted back against him, stilled as she felt his hardness. He said nothing. For a few seconds, she was tense, but then she leaned back against him and held up the box so he could see when she opened it. He felt her interest switch from himself to the puzzle she held in her hands. "This will be fun to fix! Thank you again." She stretched to put the box on a table.

"You're welcome."

Gift giving is done. We are a family now, Whin said.

Genista jerked and Cardus smoothed his hands down his arms. "Only as much of a family as you want. Relax."

Whin crawled over and lay across their laps, his head pillowed on Cardus's thigh. With a soft sigh, he fell asleep.

For a while there was silence. Genista relaxed against Cardus and all was perfect in his world. He got hard and aching but didn't address the issue of his body, and she didn't, either.

Finally wind chimes rippled through the air. Sighing, Genista said, "That's my alarm to get ready for the public rituals in Round-Dome Temple. I'll need to take another shower, and change into a different ritual robe, something . . . lesser." Her voice lowered. "This one is special for me now."

Whin groaned and opened an eye. *MUST go?*

She pushed at the dog until he rolled onto the rug. Then she rose from in front of the fire. The smile she aimed at Cardus and Whin was ironic. "Yes, I must go."

Irritation flooded Cardus at the thought of her spending time with another man, but he masked it as he stood. He ignored the pain of his stiffened leg. Then he bowed over her hand, kissed it, looked into her eyes. "I don't want you to go, but a promise is a promise," he said.

"Yes." Her lips and cheeks were pink, her eyes gleaming with interest. With attraction. For him! He cherished that notion and couldn't prevent the yearning words from leaving his heart, his mouth.

"Will you promise to celebrate Yule with me? Only me?" It wasn't fair, this promise. Who knew what would happen between them before Yule? But he'd been waiting and wanting her for nearly a year and knew that he would always want her and was tired of waiting.

Her eyes shadowed.

He lifted her hand to his heart. "Please, Nista?"

She nodded slowly. "Very well."

Relief sifted from him. "You don't break your word."

She bit her lip and looked away. "I try not to. I have known sorrow because of broken oaths." She met his eyes again. "Including my own. I don't intend to do so again."

"Thank you."

Whin yipped.

"And I'll spend it with you, too," she said.

Yes!

"Come along, Whin. Enjoy the rituals, Nista. Sharing the private one between us meant more than I can say." Cardus summoned his most polished bow. When he straightened he saw her mouth was soft.

He couldn't resist. He took a stride to her, swept her into his arms, and pressed his mouth to hers, opened her lips with his tongue, probed, and tasted. Fabulous. Fascinating. Just like every other thing about her.

She shuddered and her body was rubbing against his, sex to sex, and his mind was about to explode and remove all restraint.

He couldn't take her the way he wanted. The way her body might demand he love her.

He knew who she was, and though that didn't matter to him, it would matter to her. That he protected her not solely due to his own need, but because he was paid, would annoy her.

Tearing himself away, centimeter by centimeter, his brain buzzing with red lust, he said, "Not yet. No loving until we know each other better."

She stared at him, eyes wide. "I can't believe a man would say that."

Cardus took another step back, tried to steady his ragged breathing. "Which is why we need to know each other better. I mean it."

Shaking her head, she smiled. "I can see that you do." She gestured in a shooing fashion. "I must prepare for RoundDome Temple."

His hands fisted. He didn't want to ask, but couldn't help himself. "Will you enjoy being with Asant?"

Her eyelids lowered. "He's a very handsome man, but I don't find him attractive. Not like I do you."

His control almost unraveled. He had to look aside from the temptation of her. "Come on, Whin."

Maybe I would like to go to a big ceremony. Show off my collar that I am Fam.

"I don't think they allow Fams. Nothing was said about them, anyway," Genista said.

Whin gasped. *What kind of party is that!*

A crack of laughter escaped Cardus. "Not much of one, obviously." He nodded in Genista's direction. "Later. Lower the spellshields for us."

By the time he'd reached her back door, the shields were down. He left without another word and blessed the cool of the night in chilling his lust. Whin accompanied him.

The moment they exited her back gate into the park, her shields sprang up again.

Whin began to bolt through the park.

Wait! Cardus called to the FamDog telepathically—his and Genista's Fam Companion, a wonder.

The dog skidded. *What?*

The public ritual in Gael City sacred grove, across from RoundDome Temple, is sure to have Fam animals. You could show your collar there.

Whin's tongue lolled. *Really?* He pointed his muzzle toward Genista's house. *You are being watchdog again?*

Still, Cardus agreed.

I do not like to watch, but I like to party and take my place in ritual circle. I will go with you and stay until bored.

"Thank you," Cardus said. "We'll leave after she does, and see if we can trail her." Even in this quiet area, there were people outside, walking to neighbors', to sacred groves and temples. They should be able to merge in the flow.

Let's sit on porch in front, where it is warmer, Whin said. The dog must have spent nights sleeping on the porch.

"Fine."

You watch, I'll nap, Whin said, a note of arrogant pride shading into his telepathy that hadn't been there before.

"We're family," Cardus said softly.

Not letting either of you go, Whin announced.

That comforted Cardus. "Good."

Genista hopped the last public carrier going to RoundDome Temple before they closed down the line. Everyone was in a cheerful mood that lifted her spirits from the resentment that she'd promised to meet Asant. The public ritual might be large and joyful with many participants, but nothing could have more meaning than her celebration with Cardus.

She'd used cosmetics and spell enhancements to make her appearance different, her eyes sunken a bit with shadows, her nose wider, her lips smaller. Enough that no one would ever associate her with Genista Furze of the FirstFamilies, even if they had such a thought.

Warm from the press of people on the public carrier, she pushed her cloak behind her shoulders as she hopped from the vehicle, following and followed by a lot of other people.

There the crowd diverged into two streams, most heading toward the sacred grove in the round park, a dribble toward RoundDome Temple.

Genista was well within the grassyard of the temple before she saw Asant standing near a beautiful ash tree.

He came forward with a warm smile that didn't reach his flat blue eyes, so different from Cardus. She shouldn't be comparing Asant and Cardus, but it was inescapable. Though Cardus's smiles were infrequent, he meant them. Genista thought the opposite was true with Asant. As for eyes . . . she found so much emotion in Cardus's eyes, and Asant kept his eyes expressionless.

How long had Cardus shown appreciation of her in his eyes?

From the first minute they'd met on the walk between their two homes, Genista realized. She'd seen it bloom there, reluctantly. And every day since when their gazes had clashed or connected. That appreciation—of a man for a woman that turned into a friend for a friend . . . a lover for the beloved—had sunk into her, readied her for Cardus and the changes in their relationship.

Asant, with all his surface handsomeness, couldn't match that.

She should return home, spend time with the males she liked, Whin and Cardus, not mill around with a hundred other people she didn't know, hadn't wanted to know.

But a promise was a promise. And despite everything, she did need to be less hermitlike. It would be all too tempting to accept Whin and Cardus as her family and need no one else. That wasn't healthy for any of them. She'd soak in the atmosphere of goodwill, of celebration, the energy of the crowd and blessings, be glad she was among folk and not alone and brooding.

Asant offered both his hands and she took them, summoning real sincerity. It wasn't his fault that she preferred Cardus, and they'd formed a bond. This was the last invitation that she'd accept from the man.

"Greetyou, GentleSir Asant."

"Call me Amule. You look lovely." His glance flicked over her and she sensed he was disappointed. Unlike the gown she'd worn for the private ritual, which was from her former wardrobe and cost about five years of her wages from the Faverels, she'd purchased this one for a spring ceremony earlier in the year. It hadn't been tailored for her and was loose and of middle-class quality, an uninspired cut in a pretty shade of pale green. At the time, she'd thought she'd attend a rite at a local temple just to get out, but in the end had done the ritual in her own home.

"Thank you, Amule."

He bowed. He was wearing black, as many were, but with no shine of leather or iron. He had a small hood cowled around his neck, perhaps to be pulled up over his face as a mask, too. A small black satchel was snug on his shoulder.

He pulled her arm through his and they took their place in the line winding its way to the door of RoundDome Temple. Laughter rose around them and Genista saw many people in costume, a tradition that had died out in the noble circles of Druida City. It looked fun—and she'd been wrong, an occasional Fam entered the temple with a human companion. Maybe next year . . .

Then she felt guilty at wishing she was with someone else and forced her attention back to Amule Asant. Glancing at him, she said softly, "Do you have a token for your lost cuz?" She hadn't brought the stone she'd used for her miscarried son, but a standard dark blue stone that many would use in a public ritual.

Asant's lips twisted wryly and he slanted her a look. "Actually, my cuz is alive, but has mind problems and is in a private hospital. He gave me a small estate just before his troubles overtook him. I'm trying to keep up the place the way he would want it . . . just in case . . ." He swallowed hard.

"That's so sad." She squeezed his arm.

"So, no, I don't have token for him."

"I'm sure you have a prayer for him and a slip that his affliction be taken from him to offer on the Samhain altar," she said. She had another piece of papyrus, on it was written *doubting my self-worth.* That was a problem she'd had all of her life, had put on the Samhain altar often, had worked on and still not accomplished.

"Of course I have something for T'Anise." His voice sounded flat, then he jerked under her hand, stared at her.

She smiled at him, knew she'd heard the name of his cuz before but couldn't place it.

Then they were at the door and snaked with the mass of people through the entry hall. They passed through the corridor that encircled the temple and into the main sacred space. It was decorated in brown and black and orange and red and yellow, autumn's colors.

They followed the couple before them along the circle inscribed in the floor and ended up in the northeast quadrant. The doors closed a couple of minutes later and the main priestess and priest in the city entered, dressed in costume as the Autumn Lord and Lady, leaves in their hair. There was a great shout.

The Halloween ritual was upbeat and fun and ended with a spiral dance. Genista didn't even mind the fact that she was hand in hand with Asant and a stranger. Asant's energy was high and mischievous, adding to the general atmosphere in the temple.

As they wound back to their original places, Genista found herself laughing with all the rest, and it was a good release. The flatsweets passed out at the end of the ceremony were excellent.

Then the circle was opened for a social interval before the Samhain ritual that would begin at midnight. The noise level increased as people milled around, talking with their friends. Genista was polite, but neither she nor Asant were considered interesting. She sighed with relief as she understood that Asant had overestimated his—and her—popularity. She kept on the edges of the crowd until she'd studied everyone to see if there was anyone who knew her, and found no familiar face.

Asant excused himself to get cool cider—which Genista didn't want—and she happily hovered on the edge of a large group. He came back and gave her a cup, then took off again. Which gave her time to think. There was something off about Asant. He'd been distracted. She'd had a lot of experience with men who wanted to display her on their arms before her marriage, and Asant wasn't the like others she'd known. Granted, she wasn't at her prime, and had altered her image, but she was still a beautiful woman and he wasn't showing her off.

The cheerful lightness of the Halloween dance had faded. A low dread of going through another Samhain ceremony with another good-bye to her dead baby pitched nausea through her.

As the bell rang the three-minute warning before the beginning of the ritual, Genista decided that she would leave. The closest door was near the eastern compass point of the room. Looking up to the crystal dome, she saw bright twinmoons and stars. The tree branches were still, so there must not be much wind. Walking would be good, with streets well lit and people around. Exercise would get her blood moving again, and she'd be on her way home to Whin and Cardus.

Fingers wrapped around her elbow, and Asant tugged her back toward the circle that was forming.

Eight

"Please excuse my long absence." Asant made a face. "My cuz's legal advocate nabbed me and wanted to talk business. I couldn't refuse." With her, he slid into a couple-sized gap near the western exit. He dropped his satchel, then bent over her hand, lifted it to his lips. "I'm sorry I've left you. Please say you forgive me."

"Of course." The crowd was quieting and Genista forced herself to settle, too. Contemplation, meditation, this ceremony would have time for that and she would work on her patience. Once again her thoughts winged off to Cardus. As a fighter, he'd be a man of action, but he'd been very patient with her. His wound and the healing of it would have taught him patience. He struck her as a man aware and accepting of himself. Another thing he could help her with.

"Ach!" Asant clicked his tongue, stooped to dig through his satchel at his feet. Mouth turning down, he looked at her. "I don't have my papyrus slip—slips," he said. "I added a line or two, a wish." He winked. "I'll be right back."

"I'll come—" Genista started, but he was already crossing the room to the corridor, stepping through the door.

Large double doors on the north side of the temple opened and the priestess and priest entered, moved through the circle of people to the altar in the center of the chamber. Once there, the priest lifted his hands. "A vote, my friends. Who wishes to open the dome?"

Genista added her voice to the roar.

The priestess smiled and said, "And who wishes to raise a weathershield?"

There was a much smaller assent.

"Very well, we will be opening the dome and *not* raising a weathershield. This will delay our ritual a few minutes. Please stay in your places."

But some of the more scantily clad people had stepped from the circle. Genista hesitated. She had her cloak and would be warm enough, and the atmosphere of the room was beginning to charge again with excitement and Flair and power . . . the magic of Samhain and the new year.

Yet she was restless. She hadn't been with so many people for two years, and several of them were now watching her . . . people Asant had whispered to. Could he have winnowed out her secret? If so, he hadn't acted any different to her, and that was a mark in his favor. She winced at the thought that she had a column book with tics in it for Asant. And he wasn't here.

The spell-lights in the room dimmed, then went out. A sliding noise attracted her attention, and she caught her breath with others around her as she watched the petals of the dome slip open and down into the building. There was a slight scuffle beside her as Asant joined her, but she didn't look away. Clouds draped over a twinmoon, edging the orb in silver; stars were so bright she thought she could touch one. The scent of smoke and incense from hundreds of cauldrons used in private rituals wafted into the room, along with the fragrance of incense, making her smile.

"Welcome to Samhain Celebration, friends!" shouted the priest and the priestess.

"Welcome!" Genista shouted back, finally caught up in the moment. She turned to smile at Asant and saw a man she'd been introduced to earlier, a city councilman.

"Your companion seems to have left you, more fool he," the man said.

"He'll be returning shortly," Genista said but frowned. How long had Asant been gone?

The councilman dipped his head. "Perhaps, but until then, may I keep you company? Here, we're at the very beginning of the circle, a few steps over"—with a charming smile and apologies, he exchanged places with another couple—"and now we are at the end of the circle when it will close. Give him a little more time." He grinned. "Though I think I'll make him stand on my other side as a penalty for his delay." The councilman nudged Asant's bag along the floor, and it gaped wide to show an antique white-handled knife to use during the ritual.

With a low whistle, the man shook his head. "Very nice piece."

"Yes." And Genista was reassured. Of course Asant wouldn't leave his belongings.

The priestess and priest began the opening prayer, and Genista followed the responses, but once again her pleasure evaporated and an uncomfortable tension lodged between her shoulders.

The first elemental guardian was called and the sacred circle began to be cast and closed. Genista shivered and drew her cloak around her. This was all very odd. Though the city councilman who now stood in Asant's place was taller and handsomer, dressed richly and ready to flirt, with that appreciation of her looks in his eyes that she understood, he wasn't the man who'd gotten her the ticket for the ritual.

He wasn't Cardus, her Autumn Lord.

There was the distant cry of a child and Genista shivered again. She'd already celebrated Samhain . . . then danced Halloween away. The new year was upon her and she wanted to start it, now. Where she most wanted to be. At home, with Whin and Cardus.

The priestess was coming toward her, wand ready, closing the circle. She was two steps away, then one. Just before she reached her, Genista stepped back and out of the circle, with an apologetic smile to the councilman. The priestess hesitated but continued, closing the circle and leading a song.

Genista moved quickly into the shadows, saw the western door more easily than the others, and slipped into the empty corridor.

No sign of Asant. She shrugged. She didn't know what game he'd been playing, but it was over, and she wouldn't be caught by any of his words in the future.

Soon she was outside, listening to shouting coming from the public ritual in the sacred grove. They were further along in their simpler ritual than inside the temple, nearly done. Which meant the public carriers would be running soon . . . and the streets would be clogged with people singing and dancing their way home.

She smiled at the thought, but she wanted quiet. So she began to hurry toward her house.

A piercing whistle caught her attention. "Lady, hey, lady! Blessings upon you! Will you be our New Year's 'favor for a stranger'?" a young man called out from a heavily loaded passing glider. It was an old generational vehicle, and there was an empty throne-like seat in the second row in the back.

"Where you going?" a girl shouted, giggling.

"Oakview Lane and Danu," Genista called.

"Nice neighborhood, nice ride!" said another youngster dressed in a fool's costume. "We'll drop you there."

"Sure!"

Two boys came on either side of her. "We have to get on and off while moving; the beast doesn't like to stop."

She laughed and let them help her on, though the glider had slowed to barely a walk. She sat in the throne, and someone started a Samhain song, and she joined in with the caterwauling. The "beast" picked up speed, and only a few minutes later, she was dropped off at her corner with hearty well wishes. Twenty seconds later they were gone, leaving heavy quiet in their wake.

Her neighborhood was silent. Most of those on the block were older people who would have celebrated the ritual at dusk in their homes or a local temple. They'd been in bed when midnight rolled around and the clock ticked from year 407 to 408.

Odd noises attracted her attention as she walked down the street, from the opposite direction than she came from work. Loud, rough male voices, an occasional tinkle or jingle.

Her breath quickened, sounded harsh in the quiet air.

Where was Cardus? He was always in his front yard when she came home. Always.

A loud crash echoed through the street. She hurried, saw that her front door was open, light streamed out.

Everything fell into place with blinding clarity, all the clues she'd been too naive, too comfortable to see.

She was being robbed.

She ran past Cardus's house, zoomed through the open front gate of her property. No spellshields were up. She said the couplet to ensure complete protection and nothing happened. She searched for Cardus. His windows were dark.

He wasn't home! Shock rolled through her nerves. *Every* time she'd arrived or left her home since he'd moved next door, Cardus had been in the front yard.

Now, when she needed him the most, he wasn't.

Steel slipped along her spine, through her bones. Iron pounded through her blood along with determination. *She* could do this, handle the thieves.

Stealthily she rounded the corner of her house along the hedged side next to Cardus's home. She was close to the back when Asant grabbed her, jolting her. "What are you doing here!" she cried.

He sneered. "You should have stayed in the ritual circle, not come back. Too bad for you."

"What—"

His elbow clamped around her neck, cutting her voice off. "To steal all your pretty things, Genista Furze. You have fortune enough in your house for all four of us."

She'd been right. Thieves.

"Yes, enough gilt for forty, not just us four." He gloated. "I was to woo you and get you away, you stup fliggering flitch. Then there's my partner, and a third guy who can get through any spellshield, and the last who knows where to sell your very valuable items." His hand ran down her body and she shuddered.

Think! Think and make an opening to escape, then *act*! As she'd been taught.

She snorted.

He loosened his hold; she sensed his energy now, excited and malicious. "You have something to say, flitch?"

"You didn't do your job, did you?" She put all the contempt she'd ever felt in her tone. "Wonder what your cohorts will think about your failure, and now, you're adding the crime of assaulting a FirstFamilies Noblewoman."

He yanked at her like she wanted and she went with his movement, throwing her weight against him, falling . . . and as she fell, her body twisted as it had twisted hundreds of times in practice, and she broke his grip, rolled away and to her feet.

"Weapon!" she snapped, holding out her hand. The sword leaning in her closet slapped into her palm and her fingers curved around the rough hilt.

He'd rolled, too, slower. Leapt to his feet, whipped out a long dagger, lunged toward her. She skewered him, followed as he fell, thrust her sword through his upper chest, sinking the blade into the ground.

He made an awful noise and Genista echoed it, her stomach lurching. She'd never put sword in flesh before.

She panted, her palms were damp. She looked at Asant. Her mouth twisted in a way she knew was ugly, but she didn't care.

The back door to her house was thrown open and she heard voices. More than one. More than *two*! Asant had actually told the truth.

Laughter, snide remarks. She didn't know where the closest guardhouse was, couldn't teleport there. A mental scan of local teleportation pads showed all were in use. She couldn't 'port to anywhere she knew! She nearly bit her tongue as her teeth clamped down in frustration. She should have visited the nearest damn guard station. She didn't even know the scry image. Too late now.

She couldn't even teleport to the Faverels' shop; she had no idea what it looked like at this time of night at this time of year, no mental visualization.

No lights in Cardus's house.

She had no real connection to him to mentally call him, did she?

Cardus Parryl! Need you. Home! Her mental cry seemed to echo hollowly.

She calculated how many thieves she might be able to stop. Perhaps one more. If they weren't fighters. She'd had training but never been in a fight for real. She'd never managed to defeat any of the Hollys, not even when they were distracted, unless they were fighting handicapped. But they were the premiere fighters of Celta.

Face it, she was out of shape and unprepared.

But the home *she'd* fashioned was invaded, her things being touched and taken. Defiled.

Mean laughter that slivered along her nerves came from her house. Asant was quiet on the ground beside her. She couldn't even hear his breathing, though his chest pumped raggedly.

Maybe she couldn't reach Cardus, but she might be able to contact Whin . . . and Whin could call Cardus.

Whin. Thieves. Here. Home! She sent images of the house, the back door open and spilling light, the back iron gate open, all spellshields down.

Asant groaned.

"Be STILL!" She hissed a Word that quieted him. He stopped twitching. His pale, sweating face showed an open mouth, lips forming words that didn't come.

She decided against removing the sword from Asant. Moving as quietly as she could, she picked up his dagger, weighed it in her hand. Her lip lifted as she stared at him. "Badly balanced weapon for throwing."

His breath whistled out of his nose and mouth.

"I'll take care of you in a bit," she said. She'd meant that she'd summon a Healer, but his eyes went wide and rolled back in his head.

Not the stuff that heroes were made of, not even much of a villain.

She crept along the side of her house, deep in the shadows. Stood and peeked around the corner.

"Anyone see Asant?" called a man.

"Lazy fligger," came a light, Druida City upper-class accent. "We get him in and do all the work."

A deeper laugh, another noble accent. "That's right, brother mine, but we'll get the best."

An awful *cra-ack* of something splintering came; the first noble said, "These timers are top of the pyramid!"

"Hey, we should split those—" the first man protested.

Cardus's house lit up and a shrieking siren bit the air.

Yells from her house. "Get the loot stashed by the back gate!"

"Nista!" Cardus yelled. He leapt over the fence from his back grassyard, rushed toward the three men running from her back door toward the open gate to the park. Cardus's blazer sliced over the group; grunts of pain came along with vicious swearing.

"Nista, are you all right!" yelled Cardus.

"Yes!"

"Stay there!"

"I've tripped over a fliggering dog bone," the first thief yelled.

Another bolt of blazer blue. One man was down and Cardus was running to her, letting the other two escape. They were black shapes staggering into the night, obviously injured enough that they couldn't teleport. A low, fast body streaked after them. *What's this? Fun! Prey! Hunting, and I'm missing it!* Whin mind-shouted as he zoomed after them.

As he ran, Cardus pulled a personal scry sphere from his pocket, shouted, "'Tention Gael Guardhouse four! Thieves, Twelve Oakview Lane!" He stuck the perscry back in a pocket and continued to sweep the area, blazer ready.

To Genista's surprise she saw bulky shadows pop into existence under the street globe—two guardsmen. They took one look at her open front door and headed in, blazers in hand.

Then Cardus was there and crowding her against the side of her house, keeping his body in front of her, his blazer in one hand, a dagger in the other.

"They're all gone," Genista said. "There were four. Asant said so."

"Asant!"

She wriggled an arm out from behind him and gestured to her left, where the man lay, sword sticking out of him.

Cardus laughed shortly. "Good job, Nista."

"Thank you."

She was shivering, feeling waves of cold, then heat. Reaction.

"All clear," one of the guardsmen shouted from the back.

The other shouted, "Cardus Parryl, are you here?"

"Yes."

"And the lady?"

"Here and unharmed," Genista managed with what she thought was a nicely cool tone. "We need a Healer," Genista said.

"Already called. He'll be teleporting to my location," the guard nearest to Genista said. She thought the other one was by Asant's fallen partner.

"There's a teleportation pad inside," Genista said.

"Even better." Her back door opened and closed.

"There's some jewels out here," said the first.

Cardus stepped aside, placed his fingers on the small of her back, urged her toward her back grassyard.

"We must take care of Asant and the other man first," Genista said.

Cardus grunted. They walked to where a guardsman was putting DepressFlair wristbands on the thief near the back gate. The intruder had brown hair and dark eyes, was average.

"I don't recognize him," Genista said, then wondered why she thought she would, just because Asant had targeted her.

They were joined by a Healer, who knelt by the man. "Blazer burn across his back."

"Mine," Cardus said.

"Not too bad, I'll teleport him—"

"I think Asant is worse off," Genista said.

The Healer blinked at her. "Yes, m'lady." Glancing at the other officer, he said, "The Captain of the guards will be coming shortly, as soon as the ritual in RoundDome Temple is done."

Genista blinked. Had events happened so rapidly then? She supposed they must have, but it hardly seemed possible.

"I'll teleport this guy in," said the first guard, and the two vanished.

Wild yipping came to her mind. *I got one. I got one!* Whin

shrieked mentally. *He 'ported us to the airship place but I hung on. Then* I *'ported us to City Salvage.*

Cardus relayed the news to the other guard, who scried it in with a suppressed grin. "Someone will pick up the thief at City Salvage. Thank your FamDog."

The guards thank you, Whin, Cardus sent, and Genista heard him clearly. The three of them now had a strong enough bond to mentally communicate. That pleased her.

Whin said, *Only one got away. I heard him say many nasty words.* The dog barked in glee, and she heard the echo of it telepathically. *He is running, running, running.*

Cardus made a disgusted noise.

"My other patient?" prompted the Healer.

Cardus's lip curled. "This way." His hand slipped down to hold hers, and she was glad of it.

Asant was still lying quietly under her sword, though he seemed conscious and his breathing was noisy.

"Cave of the Dark Goddess!" the Healer said.

Cardus strode over to the sword. "Say when for me to pull it out."

The Healer shook his head. "Nasty."

"You don't want to cross the lady," Cardus said mordantly.

Nine

Both the guard and the Healer gaped at Genista.

"You! You were the one who stabbed Asant?" the Healer asked.

She drew herself up, lifted her chin. "I've been trained."

"Of course you would be," said the guard. He looked at Cardus. "I will have your blazer to check the discharges, GentleSir Parryl."

With an easy, practiced motion, Cardus drew it, flipped it, and handed it to the guardsman. "Yes. Two blasts. I think both hit—and on the two who escaped, also." His voice held repressed anger.

The guardsman stared at the long dagger strapped to Cardus's thigh that didn't have the blazer holster. "You use that?"

"Nope." Cardus raised his fists, some of his knuckles were skinned.

"You'll have to take my sword?" Genista asked.

"For a short time. It will be returned to you or GentleSir Parryl tonight," the guard said.

"I need to get this guy to the HealingHall." The Healer once again knelt.

"His name is Amule Asant. Will he be all right?" Genista

thought Asant's gaze moved toward her, but she wasn't interested in getting any closer to him.

"Sure," the Healer said. "Fixed up in a septhour, though the damage to his muscle is considerable. Missed the lungs and heart though."

"That's good," Genista said, swallowing. Must have been pure luck.

Putting his hands on Asant's shoulders, the Healer glanced up at Cardus. "On three, remove the blade and I'll teleport with Asant to the HealingHall."

"Right," Cardus said.

"One, stup thief caught, two, Asant hurt, *three*!"

Cardus removed the sword swiftly and the Healer teleported away with Asant, but not before Genista heard another terrible moan. She stepped over to the wall of her house and leaned against it.

She'd let her training lapse, and now she thought that wasn't a good idea. The main fighting and fencing salon in the city was owned by the Hollys, of course, her ex-husband's Family. But there would be others. She'd look into them in the next week—another way to mold herself into the person she wished to become.

Cardus had given the sword to the guardsman, who had translocated it somewhere—to the guard station or laboratory. Again, Genista was ignorant, but in this, she didn't care to know.

Cardus put his arm around her waist. He wasn't wearing a cloak, but heat radiated from him, and she leaned into him.

"You're not hurt, are you?" she asked.

"No."

The guard turned to them, expression grim. "We'd better look at those jewels now."

"Dammit, they must have gotten away with valuables!" Cardus said.

She shrugged. "They're only property." She looked up into Cardus's dear face, into those intense emerald eyes, kissed him, then wrapped her arms around him and shuddered against him, murmuring into the curve of his strong neck. "You weren't hurt. I wasn't hurt." She loved how his arms came around her, how she could lean a little against him and he'd know that she might not be strong in this moment, but she'd want to stand tall on her own two feet in a bit. He respected the woman she was forging. And this night had shaped her more. She was pleased with how she handled herself.

She said, "You were wonderful. Thank the Lord and Lady you came and knew the yard." Steadied her voice and forced a lightness into it. "It pays to have a warrior as a neighbor, after all."

But his mouth was flat and he was shaking his head. They walked over to where gems sparkled in the bright star and twinmoonslight. Cardus snapped a Word that flashed three spellglobes into existence over their heads.

The cracking sound had been her spellshielded and locked jewelry box, an antique she'd purchased when she'd received her first annual NobleGilt from the councils for fulfilling her duties—in that instance, hostessing a gathering with ambassadors from the other continents of Chinju and Brittany with the FirstFamilies Heads of Households when she was seventeen.

Tears rose, stinging. She'd loved that box, and now it was shards of wood, too shattered to be restored. The pretty painted pastoral scenes were disjointed, in pieces, making no sense.

Something glittered and she stooped to see better beyond the blur in her eyes. There was the first wrist timer she'd ever received—from her parents after her First Passage dreamquest at seven—a simple crystal face and furrabeast leather band dyed the gold of Furze blossoms.

Tightness eased in her chest as her trembling fingers found others in the grass and dead leaves—all more bejeweled. The couple her parents had given her for Second and Third Passage, an antique one she'd bought broken and fixed herself. A couple Tinne had given her, one for their first anniversary, and their second . . .

Missing were the three most expensive—the exquisite delicate platinum, yellow diamond, and emerald watch Tinne had given her upon the announcement of their pregnancy; the red gold, gold, glisten metal, and diamond one the Holly Family had given her at the same time.

Thank the Lord and Lady they were gone! She'd been unable to insult the Hollys by returning or selling those.

The final piece stolen was an "anonymous" gift that had been delivered here after her divorce—a very gaudy gem-encrusted timer that had the sensations of the Hollys all over it. An item she could sell if she somehow ran through the fortune of her marriage settlement, or the gilt coming to her from her own Family, or her own annual NobleGilt salary.

If she hadn't been so exhausted and wretched when she'd received it, *she'd* have been insulted. Her parents had drummed thrift into every child of the Family. She had never been profligate.

"I think what was in this box is the only jewelry that the thieves got away with," Cardus said, rejoining her. She'd been absently aware of the cold breeze flowing along her side when he left to check out her house, now he blocked the wind again with his warmth as she rose. "The safe is open but other jewelry cases are still there."

His face was grim, his lips tight when she looked at him. "Your collection of wrist timers?"

She nodded. He'd commented on one or two of the plain ones that she wore during their conversations, and she'd told him she collected.

"How many of them did the thieves get?"

"Three."

"Three!"

"Out of twenty-five." Discreetly she stretched. Her muscles, unaccustomed to the workout, were cooling and stiffening.

Cardus swore, looked away, muttering something about failing, said, "How much were they worth?"

She shrugged. "They weren't that precious."

Another hard stare from him. "Lady, I am sure my idea of precious and yours vastly differ."

She wasn't sure of that. He'd value the most personally meaningful more than outwardly expensive. She put her hand on his arm. "You can't believe that you had any failure in this matter."

"Yes, I can."

"What's the value?" the guardsman pressed.

Genista didn't want to announce outside that Asant's *four fortunes* was near enough to correct. "Can I take these inside and reset the spells?"

A new guard joined them. He had a higher rank embroidered on his cuffs and chest. "Yes." He glanced at Cardus, cleared his throat. "We checked on the spellshields a coupla days back. Good shields."

"Yes." Her own words were clipped.

The younger guard said, "The guy we caught said they had a man that spellshields couldn't stop—'cept a sentient Residence, he said."

"Ah-hmm," Cardus said in a tone that demanded action.

"We'll figure this all out," the higher-ranking guardsman said. With a couplet, he'd gathered all the pieces of her lovely box and the rest of the timepieces. Genista couldn't help it, the rush of adrenaline had crashed and the tears she'd been swallowing dribbled down her cheeks.

All three of the men looked uncomfortable.

She fished a softleaf from her cloak's inner pocket and took care of her eyes and nose. Then, for the first time, she heard the short buzz announcing that someone was teleporting to her pad.

The lower-ranking guardsman straightened his tunic. "That'll be the Captain."

Genista hurried into the house and the mainspace. A tall, athletic woman nodded to her. The Captain was wearing a tunic trous suit of dark blue, not ritual robes.

When she saw Genista, her eyes widened. "Merry meet, GreatMistrys Furze," the Captain said, bowing low.

"How did you—"

She gestured to Cardus. "Your bodyguard kept us apprised."

Genista's stomach lurched. "Bodyguard," she said faintly.

"Yes, notified us as soon as he moved in, though he only told us your incognito name."

Cardus's expression was impassive, his eyes impenetrable.

Her heart squeezed. She didn't really know him. At all.

A draft of air whooshed through from the open back door. "Can you close the door, please?" she choked out to the guards.

Cardus was right behind her, solid and motionless and silent. All the confidence that he'd liked her for herself shattered, blew away in the cold autumn night like frozen motes of dust.

She forced herself to think through the painful shock, moved numb lips. "Please sit down . . ." She managed a smile, gestured to the kitchen. "Or help yourself to the drinks no-time. I'd like a minute to change."

"Of course," the Captain said, though one of her guardsmen frowned.

The Captain raised a brow at him. "You think a FirstFamilies daughter to be anything less than honorable? One vouched for by Cardus Parryl and the Hollys?"

"No, sir," the guard said.

Genista smiled brilliantly. "Thank you." She swept a blind look at the other two guardsmen. "Thank all of you, for coming so quickly and being so helpful." Raising a palm, she said, "I swear, I won't be longer than five minutes." She glanced in Cardus's direction but barely saw him. "Can I have a quick moment of your time?"

"Of course."

She felt as if there was one large, raw, and throbbing nerve inside her. Lied to. He'd never known her, never liked her for herself.

Blinking back more useless tears, she fled to her small bedroom, grabbed another softleaf, and swiped at her face, flung the cloth in the cleanser and fumbled at the clasp of her cloak.

"Bodyguard, Hollys," she muttered.

Cardus stood at attention at the threshold of her room. His expression bleak. "That's right. I work for the Hollys."

"So you knew who I was all the time."

"Yes."

She tried a smile but it twisted on her lips. The closet doors were open. She turned away, hiding her face. She knew all the salacious rumors and hurtful truths that attached to her name—a woman who had sex with many men before her marriage, a woman who divorced her husband.

Nothing her new and cherished and ordinary life could overcome. She sucked in a breath of air, and it seemed to ice her windpipe all the way down to her belly. She realized her window was open.

"You're cold. Let me close that window." He passed her and she moved into the closet. Her damn cloak clasp *wouldn't* open.

The window slid shut. "Let me help you with that," he said, coming too close.

She ripped the cloth of the cloak, flung it on the floor. "Thank you. I don't need any more help from you." She winced as she realized how that sounded coming from her tight throat. "I'm sorry for the harshness. It's been a—disillusioning—night. I do appreciate your help in stopping the thieves."

He made a rough noise, said, "I knew you would hate me once you discovered I was placed here by the Hollys." A note of melancholy laced through his quiet tone.

Genista frowned, turned to look at him. He was pale, his hair contrasting red and dark with his skin. She'd never seen him pale. He was braced as if for a blow.

"Why didn't you tell me?" Then she answered her own question. "No, the Hollys asked you not to."

"They left that decision up to me." He was brutally honest. "But they believed you would not be easy to guard if you knew who I was."

"I wouldn't have stayed."

"GreatMistrys?" One of the guards was at the door.

"I'll be right there." She smiled falsely at Cardus. "You and I are finished." She narrowed the bond she had welcomed to a filament.

He jerked a nod. "We will talk." He stepped back and motioned for the guard to precede him back to the mainspace, shutting the door.

Genista didn't allow herself to sag in relief. Now she was running late and she, Genista Furze, was the representative of the highest class to the Gael City guards. So she did what needed to be done, namely a whirlwind spell. The spell cleansed and scoured her, yanked her hair into fancy braids, and dressed her in a simple, elegant damask tunic of blue that matched her eyes, and bloused trous cuffed at the ankles.

Glancing in the mirror, she saw her cosmetics were perfect, definitely not showing the bruised, hollow-eyed person that she felt like.

Despite the Captain's deference, and the support that seemed to flow from Cardus through the minuscule bond that hurt with its existence, the time with the guards was trying. She gave her birth name, of course, Genista Furze, and described the three missing wrist timers, glad she wasn't going to be the one to report to T'Ash, the great blacksmith/jeweler and one scary man, that pieces of his work were missing.

Her sword was returned to her, cleaned, and she propped it against the arm of her chair.

Finally, finally, they were done questioning her and Cardus. She'd gone over every instant she'd spent with Asant three times and asked the guards not to bother Master and Mistrys Faverel until the morning.

And she was left alone with Cardus. She didn't look at him. Hadn't met his gaze directly the whole time.

He came over and sat on the plush ottoman in front of her chair. Their knees bumped. Just hours ago she would have enjoyed the touch . . . his touch, the attraction tugging between them. Now she didn't.

"I love you," he said. "And I love you for being Nista Gorse . . . and Genista Furze, who is creating her own life." He jerked his head impatiently around the room and its treasures. "I don't care about this gilt, except that it makes me itchy. I have enough to keep you." His lip curled. "Without any gilt from the Hollys."

"You lied to me."

He laughed shortly. "From the moment we met, I didn't know what to say to you." He ran his hand through his hair. "I didn't mean to fall in love with you, but it was inevitable. Then I only knew I didn't want you to leave me." His nostrils flared. "I was planning to tell you when we knew each other better. As for the Hollys—I resigned earlier tonight."

"I don't know what to think," she said tonelessly.

"Then consider what you feel, Nista-Genista, what flows between us."

"Hurt."

"I'm sorry."

She shook her head, rose. "And I'm tired and confused."

His manner was still open, making her think that he was as vulnerable as she. That the attraction between them was real.

He stood, too, and their bodies brushed, and she was reminded how well they might have meshed, and she wanted to lean into him again.

Taking her hands, he said, "I respect you more than I can say. But I can say that I love you again."

She met his steady gaze; his eyes were dark like pools in a mystic forest, and actually seemed wounded.

"If I hurt you, I've hurt myself, too." He answered her thoughts.

"I'm going to bed now," she said. She didn't know if she would sleep, or what dreams might come. All she knew was that she was tired of the new year already.

With a yip, Whin appeared on the teleportation pad. His eyes still gleamed from the chase. *Greetyou, FamMan, greetyou, FamWoman!*

This time Genista's smile was real. "Greetyou, Whin."

I am a hero!

"Of course you are."

And FamMan is a hero, too!

Her gaze touched Cardus. "Yes, he is."

And you! You caught Bad Man. Whin pranced around. *We all caught Bad Men. We are all heroes!*

Yes.

But Whin had sensed the atmosphere. He sat, frowned. *You are sad.*

"The thief who got away took some of Genista's pretty things," Cardus said.

Whin touched a paw to his collar. *Bad Men!*

"Yes." She walked away from them, stood in the doorway. "Good night."

Sad and angry at FamMan, Whin said. He came over and leaned against her legs.

"Yes. He was paid to watch me." That was the best she could come up with for the dog, and it didn't explain much.

He is a watchdog, Whin agreed. *Watched you all the time.*

"That I did," Cardus said.

In the park we watched you go into the temple but not come out!

That explained why Cardus wasn't here when she'd gotten home—what felt like a betrayal at the time, but was so much less than now.

We watched you and caught Bad Men and are heroes.

That was the end result. She put her hand to her head. "I can't think."

"I love you," Cardus said softly.

I love you, too.

Cardus went to the front door and Whin followed him. "Raise your spellshields after we're gone. One minute."

"Yes," she said.

Then the house was quiet, though it seemed as if all the voices and talk yet buzzed in the air around her.

And there was still a tiny bond between herself and Cardus. She could break it. But she'd been abandoned by men, broken other bonds, had them broken. Not tonight, the first morning of the new year.

She fell on top of her bed and whirled down into sleep. What would tomorrow bring?

Ten

Bundled up in a thick robe against the cold morning, Genista sat in her rocking chair on her small front porch, sipping her creamy caff and watching the pastel streaks of dawn against a gray sky fade as the sun rose. In a few minutes the sun would be blue white and the sky a deep blue.

She'd gotten her newssheet, noted that her robbery was the first story, and rolled it back up, went back to her chair to contemplate the tracery of black branches against the lightening sky. Her identity had been revealed.

She wasn't quite sure how she felt about that. One thing she knew, her job was safe. Master Faverel might be intimidated at first by her being a FirstFamily daughter, but he was a practical man and they shared a love of clocks. Mistrys Faverel, of course, would be thrilled at the cachet that having Genista Furze as a journeywoman would bestow upon her shop and business. So that was not a problem.

But mostly Genista felt hollow. The surge of adrenaline and the triumph of capturing thieves had long since faded, and she was left with the aching disappointment that she'd just been a job for Cardus.

Somehow, when she wasn't paying attention, she had let the attraction to him grow into more . . . almost love.

A man walked down the street, and the shape of him caught her attention, as did the roll of his seafaring but silent walk. She squinted. Surely that was Tab Holly? The uncle of the current Lord T'Holly. Tab was her ex-husband Tinne's G'Uncle. She set her cup down on the table, and it sloshed over her fingers, bringing a quick burn. She wiped her hand on her blanket as she disentangled herself and rose.

Of course someone, probably the guards, had called her own parents and they had let the Hollys handle the situation, as usual. Tab had always treated her well, from the first moment she set foot in T'Holly Residence as a bride. Cared for her as if she'd been a daughter.

When she looked up, he stood almost hesitantly at the hedge separating her house from Cardus's.

"You don't need to pretend, Tab," Genista called. "I know that GentleSir Parryl works for you Hollys." She folded up the blanket and put it on the chair. She was cold in her quilted robe over her thin nightgown, but didn't care. Getting rid of him wouldn't take long. They didn't have much to talk about.

She picked up her warm mug and cradled it in her hands, and a movement from Cardus's porch caught her eye. Her neighbor stood, too. How long had he been out there watching? Brooding like she was? Or just doing his job?

Cardus said, "You've been through a lot, Genista. You don't need to talk to him. Or even see him. And I resigned as of the last minute of last night." Cardus's voice was rough, and as intense as always.

Genista gave an elaborate shrug, but didn't answer, just walked toward her small iron gate and murmured the chant that would drop the spellshields.

Cardus vaulted over the hedge, landed slightly unbalanced on his bad leg, and winced. No throb of caring went through her at that. She was over him. Good.

But he moved fast and was at her side as she walked along the stepping-stones, though he wasn't touching her, wasn't as near as he had been the last week.

The sun rose fully, then, illuminating all the lines in Tab's leathery face. His expression was grim, his eyes sad.

He wasn't there to comment about the events the night before.

Fear snatched at her with greedy, ripping skeletal fingers. She clutched her mug with one hand, the other fluttered to her throat. "What's wrong? Is it Tinne? His HeartMate?" If one of the pair died, as HeartMates, the other would follow within the year.

"They're fine. No deaths," Tab said gently, opening the gate and walking in without a sound. "I have some news about last night, but that can wait." He cleared his throat. A really bad omen; Tab was rarely at a loss for words. "We thought I should be the one to tell ya."

Cardus's shoulder brushed hers; his foot was against hers, almost like he was there to support and brace her.

"Tinne and Lahsin are expecting a baby."

Genista opened her mouth, but all the words were gone from her mind as hideous pain gouged her. She didn't love Tinne anymore. She *didn't*. But his HeartMate was giving him a child to replace the one Genista and he had lost. A child of a HeartMate bond, conceived in love that she could never have matched.

Her fingers went nerveless and her mug crashed to the ground.

A hole opened inside her and sucked her in. The blackness of her deepest fear: She was not good enough.

Never good enough.

Not good enough to be a daughter who was praised and cherished instead of ignored. Not good enough to be wed by a man who wanted anything but sex and land and other things instead of her.

Not good enough to give the man she loved a child.

Never good enough to be loved for herself.

She swayed in a cold, cold wind full of dead and brittle leaves cackling around her. So much pain. She could endure it. She'd survived. She was good at *that*.

Rough fur pushed under the fingers of her left hand. Shouts pummeled her ears? Someone trying to draw her back? No. But a surging wave of feeling demanded she return to harsh reality.

Well, she would. She'd clawed her way out of the grief of the loss of a child. She'd endured seven horrible tests to get a divorce and break the brittle chains of a love that had died, a failed marriage. She'd established a new life, become a new person.

Maybe others might never think she was good enough—good enough to be a beloved daughter instead of a third afterthought and drain on attention. Or good enough to marry because she was pretty and sexy and had something they wanted.

But *she* knew she was good enough to carve and claim a space in this world for herself. She'd lived by herself, found and kept a fine job, was learning excellent skills.

She *was* good enough as Nista Gorse or Genista Furze to do what she wanted to do. To build a career, to find a man who would love her for herself. To have more babies—the Furzes were the most prolific of the FirstFamilies. She could have a child. She could even have a child or three without a husband, if she wanted.

This was a new year, with new possibilities. This was the year she'd *become*.

If she wanted to have a man, like Cardus, she would make sure she got him.

He said he loved her, for herself.

Did she want him?

Maybe.

Of course she was hurt that he hadn't told her the truth right off, but if he had, she wouldn't have stayed. Would have left this house in anger, never found her job, never crafted her new life.

And she believed what he said, that he'd reluctantly come to love her. Hadn't she done the same?

She also believed her own instincts, the bond that they'd made between them, and with Whin.

She was good enough to work and get what she wanted. So she drew the pieces of her new self together and mended them with will and determination and let the tumultuous yells around her pull her out of the hole within her. The hole she filled and banished forever.

Cardus was fighting Tab Holly. Whin leaned against her side, panting, watching.

She blinked against the bright sun of the autumn day. *Cardus was fighting Tab Holly.* Now and then G'Uncle Tab could whip Tinne, or Holm, or the best fighter in the world, T'Holly himself.

Genista blinked again, drew in a shaky breath of crisp fall air. She hadn't been in her pit for long, a couple of minutes maybe.

"I will find them and kill them." Cardus thrashed against the older man's hold.

He couldn't be talking about Tinne and his HeartMate! Of course he wasn't.

But at the thought, Genista realized she'd never acknowledged Tinne's HeartMate by name, even in her own mind—Lahsin Rosemary Holly. And no stab went through her as Genista thought of Lahsin. Genista was finally over that pain.

Tab was swaying, holding a struggling Cardus. "They're just two punks who escaped. They'll turn up later. Men don't change their thieving natures," Tab said, in a tone that Genista knew meant he was a hairsbreadth from wiping the floor with Cardus, the sidewalk, whatever.

"Stop it!" She ran to Cardus and tugged at his biceps. "Stop it."

His eyes were wild, and she thought he might be seeing the world through a red haze.

"Stop it!" she repeated.

Tab let go and stepped back. Cardus wheeled but caught his balance as Genista helped steady him.

"Nista? Genista?" Cardus shook his head as if ridding himself of fury. He settled under her hands, took her fingers in his own. Then he glanced at Tab, who was standing like a large statue, arms across his chest, watching them with a piercing gaze.

"What happened?" Genista straightened her spine and settled into her own balance, something Tab had taught her. He nodded approval.

High color was fading from Cardus's cheeks. The dark forest green of his eyes was changing to emerald as he held her hands and met her gaze. "Asant and his partner are still in custody, but the other thief that was caught got away last night."

The one I caught, growled Whin.

"They haven't been able to locate him, and didn't have him long enough to discover who he was."

Whin whipped his tail. *Stup guards.*

Tab stared down at the dog. "I can't fault ya for thinkin' that. But let's not say it aloud." He looked back at Genista. "Asant blamed an older cuz for starting him on the road to thieving, someone who was the head of the gang and working in Druida. Someone who has already been sentenced for theft and put in a house for the mind-broken. Another of Asant's kinsmen has been banished."

Genista frowned. "This ties into that case last summer?"

"Always plenty'a thieves around," Tab said. "Asant said two men, not related to him, were in on the plan, too. Said they were brothers." Tab shrugged shoulders thick with muscle. "Even said they were minor nobility. Who can believe him?"

Cardus scowled, slipped an arm around Genista's waist. The scent of Cardus's perspiration and the man came to her; the heat of his body warmed her.

"I told the guards two had Druidan City noble accents," Genista said. "And that they were brothers."

"No one can say that all Noblemen are honorable," Cardus said.

"That's right," Tab agreed. "Just like no one can say that Commoners ain't without honor." Tab's smile was sly. "You going to hold on to that girl there, Cardus?"

"You Hollys can't have her. She's no longer part of your Family."

"No, but we wanna make sure she's always well." He beamed at Genista. "She was my G'Niece, T'Holly's and D'Holly's daughter, Holm's sister. We mind what's ours."

Genista swallowed. "I don't have any ties to you Hollys anymore."

Tab waved a large hand. "Don't mean we don't care for you. Still want to see you happy."

Genista wondered how much guilt bit at Tinne's parents, realized that she *was* carrying a burden that tied her to the Hollys. "Please tell T'Holly and D'Holly that I forgive them for breaking their Vows of Honor and bringing such a curse down on their Family." It was true, the bitterness toward them was gone. The scarred slash of grief on her heart for her lost baby would always be there, but she no longer had to blame anyone.

Tab nodded. "Good job, lass. Better for you." He stretched his arms, linking his hands and cracking his knuckles. "You willing to fight for her, boy?"

Cardus dropped his arm from her. His eyes lit. He loosened his limbs. "Yeah."

She knew those stances, too. Hadn't spent three years in a household of male fighters without learning which challenges were real and which were posturing.

"No," she said, moved closer to Cardus, and took his arm again. He didn't pull away.

"You want him, girl?" Tab asked.

"Yes," she replied without thought, but admitting the huge feeling in her for Cardus. Quiet, intense Cardus, her Autumn Lord.

Tab shifted and stared at Cardus. "What makes you think you're worthy of her?"

Cardus flinched, stood tall. "I'm not. She's the most beautiful, fascinating, strongest woman in the world." He hesitated. Genista felt his gaze on her and looked up. He seemed to search her face, took her hand, and locked his fingers with hers.

He didn't want to let her go, she realized. For some reason *he* didn't believe he was good enough for her. The concept was a little dizzying. He stepped so he could steady her, set his arm around her waist with a gesture that meant he'd keep her always, wouldn't let her go. Wouldn't let her fall.

Or if she fell and needed help up, he would be there.

As he might need help right now.

"But I want her," he said, as she said, "I want him."

"I love her." Cardus flashed one of his amazing smiles at Tab. "And she can *fight*. You should see her with a sword."

Tab laughed, and pleasure and pride flooded Genista. She said, "I was good enough to capture Asant."

"You skewered him."

"Ya look good together. Good job, both'a ya." Tab bowed with all the flourish that a properly brought up son of a NobleHouse of the last century could offer. Genista felt heat in her cheeks.

He nodded at them. "You'll do, and do well together." Though his smile was wide, his eyes held a shadow. "People don't have to be HeartMates to have a great love."

"No," Cardus said, his arm around her waist tightening to near pain.

"No," Genista whispered.

"Don't be strangers. The Hollys'll welcome ya both." Tab rolled his shoulders, lifted a hand, and grinned. "Happy New Year!"

"Happy New Year!" Genista echoed with Cardus.

Tab teleported away.

"Bed," Cardus said, and cursed his stupid tongue once more as Genista stared at him, color painting her face. He thought he'd done well last night—well enough to tell her more than once that he loved her. Well enough that she had claimed him. In words. Before a FirstFamily man.

"I need you, need to know you're mine for sure," he said.

Her head was tilted. "And sex will do that."

"Yes." And, yes, he was losing his words just thinking about it.

She bumped him with her shoulder. "You're a man."

"*Your* man. Want you in my bed." He tugged her toward his house. Too slow. He scooped her up and used the lust wheeling inside him to jump over the fence.

Her arms came around him tight, and he liked that. Good first step.

"Where's Whin?" she asked.

"Gone hunting. Something." They were at his door and his mind was hazing and he could feel only her hands on him, her weight in his arms, the line of warmth of her body against him. "Shields down, door open."

He leapt through it with her when the door swung back. "Close and lock, shields up," he panted. Had to protect her. Newssheet reporters would come soon. Gossips. Who knew what else?

But loving first.

He nearly tossed her on his bed, atop the unmade linens of a restless night.

There she was, Genista Furze, on his bed. He stopped to stare at her loveliness.

Saw her surprised and amused expression.

Winced. "Too fast."

"Maybe." And her smile was all siren temptation.

He tried to find more words, heard echoes of emotions with words attached that he could use. "People don't have to be Heart-Mates to form a bond."

Her smile faded to musing tenderness, and he hoped that was a good sign.

"No," she said softly. "And I have a bond with you."

"Yes!"

And she was laughing. "Your words really have deserted you." She shook her head, whispered, "My Autumn Lord."

At her warm look, eyes full of desire, he felt like a god. "Clothes off!" he ordered roughly and stood nude before her, then flushed as he recalled the scars on his thigh.

"Beautiful." Her eyes had dilated. She liked what she saw, then. His mind was losing great chunks of sense, shearing away.

She sat and opened her heavy robe to show a nightgown so fine it must be silkeen. He could see the color of her skin beneath it, pale and pretty and flushed. Dark pink nipples. Ready for him.

He tried to speak but the trickle of words were gone.

"Clothes off!" she said, and her robe and nightgown fell away from her, and she leaned back on her elbows and let him look, and there was only her in the universe. The lady, the goddess, his Nista.

He lunged toward her and blessed his leg for giving way so he caught himself, and one thought swam through the wash of desire to his brain. Had to do this right.

So he lay beside her, staring up at her. No woman should ever be so beautiful. But she was, and if he wanted her to stay, he had to show her how much he loved her.

He lifted a shaking hand to her face. "Love your blue eyes." He trailed his fingers down her cheek. "Love your lips." He tested them, and she gave his finger a quick kiss, and he hauled her close. Now he was on his elbow, looking down at her.

"Gen. Nista. Genista. So lovely. Will you love with me?" He cupped a full breast, played with her nipple. She moaned and her eyes went blurry, and he feathered a touch down the curve of her waist and hip, over her thigh to the seat of her femininity.

She opened her legs for him, and once again he felt a hero, a god.

So he leaned over her and outlined her lips with his tongue, and the movement rubbed his shaft against her smooth skin, and his fingers felt her dewiness and he was lost.

He wanted to mate, to ride her hard.

Wrong.

So he flung himself back, panting.

"You go too slowly," she said.

And the next moment she was sliding atop him, taking him inside herself, and nothing mattered except the heat between them and he arched and plunged and let her ride him hard until they broke together.

He lay, destroyed, soft woman upon him, and he wrapped his arms around her to hold her to him forever. His eyes were closed and the inside lids painted with all the colors of fall, of New Year's, red and yellow and orange. Among them all he saw a thick bronze bond, a real mental, emotional link, connecting him to Genista.

Maybe that was enough.

Or maybe, now that he'd claimed her, and *believed* she would stay with him, he could find more words.

He actually had Genista in his house and in his bed. He opened his eyes to see her staring down at him. Her golden hair was tumbled, her eyes bluer than he'd ever seen. He remembered her clenching around him, so he'd managed to please, to pleasure her.

"I love you, will love you always, will never leave you," he said. He set his hands around her face and stared into her eyes to make sure she believed it. For some reason the woman didn't understand she was a treasure. *The* treasure of the world.

"Never leave?" she asked.

"Lady, you will never, ever get rid of me."

Genista studied his face. His eyes were green fire.

"I'm willing to take the ancient vows—Vows of Honor—to prove it," he said.

She thought her heart stopped; her breathing certainly did, and everything in her chest constricted. He would know how much she valued Vows of Honor. Broken Vows of Honor had cursed the Hollys.

"You don't need to." Her voice came out whispery and high.

He rolled her under him and he was hard and strong. He kissed her, his tongue penetrating her mouth and rubbing hers, withdrawing. When he lifted his head, his cheeks had a ruddy flush and his face his most intense expression. "We will *both* take the ancient marriage vows, Vows of Honor."

"Yes." She kissed his mouth, then had to look at him again. Her voice was strong and steady. "Yes."

His muscles eased, and she realized just how tense he'd been.

He glanced out the door and she followed his gaze. "We'll combine houses." His entire body flexed as if it was already at work. "I can do it."

"You do wonderful work. We'll have a fabulous, long front deck and porch. I think we should keep this as your den or the library. You aren't going to be a stup about my gilt?"

He hesitated, but replied, "No."

"Good." She smiled slowly. "Most of the gilt is in a trust for my children, anyway."

His hips arched and she enjoyed the rush of sensation.

"We'll have children," he promised roughly.

She knew that he couldn't be sure, they couldn't be sure of that, but accepted his word. Now she stroked his face. "My Autumn Lord."

"That again." He shook his head.

She kissed him on his lips, liked watching his skin color even more. "Auburn hair."

"It's red."

"It's a nice many-shaded head of hair, even some golden highlights. Leaves in the autumn." She tugged at a swatch, then continued ruthlessly, "Green eyes the color of leaves before they turn or ponds under the fall sky. And don't tell me you haven't heard that before." She grinned, expansive in her delight. She was home with him, would always be home and his greatest treasure, as he would always be hers. "When we go up to Druida to inform my Family of our marriage, I will get T'Apple to do your portrait as the Autumn Lord. I'm sure the idea would intrigue him."

Cardus squeezed the breath from her. "Only if you sit with me, or if *I* get a portrait of the Summer Queen."

"Done."

"You will work on our house, and maybe others." Oh, she had ambitions for him that didn't include fighting. "*I* will become a clockmaker. I am signing journeywoman papers."

He stroked her hair, slid his fingers through it, and the sensations from her scalp rippled through her whole body. A tender gesture that had feelings welling within. This time she didn't hide them, didn't think she'd ever hide them from him, let her vulnerability show.

"My Genista." He tugged her hair and she smiled. They would always be equal. "I've been reading about Earth lately and I know of old Earthan phrases."

"Yes?" She was interested, everything about him intrigued her.

"They did not have HeartMates," he said with an ease that seemed to take any sting from the word. It would only be a word for them, from now on.

"No?"

"No. That is a Celta phenomena."

She knew that but didn't mind hearing it from him. "So?"

His smile was slow and his expression so loving she knew her pulse would always race when he looked at her in such a way. She returned the love in her smile. He seemed caught in the moment, the quiet moment that they shared. An autumn moment of contemplation and gathering in to home.

Again he stroked her cheeks. "Summer Queen," he whispered.

She wouldn't always remain summerlike, but with him, she didn't fear growing old. "Beloved."

"Yes," he said, cleared his throat. "The Earthans didn't have HeartMates, but they had soul mates. That's what we are. Soul mates."

"Yes."

"Wishes do come true."

"Yes."

"Happy New Year," he murmured with another kiss.

"Happy New Year," she whispered back, pressed her body against his, smiled under his renewed kiss. "A year full of possibilities," she said.

"A lifetime full of love," he answered her with the truth.

She stroked his hard and still watchful face with her fingertips, feeling the slight coarseness where his beard grew. A strong man. A *real* man. Finally a man for her? "I want *you*."

"You have me. Always."

Noble Heart

One

DRUIDA CITY, CELTA
411 Years After Colonization
Winter

Walker Clover must have caught a fever, probably from his student, Nuin Ash. Mortifying that a seven-year-old boy could bring down a twenty-seven-year-old man.

His weathershield spell against the frigid cold heated until it pressed on him like a damp and searing cloth. He couldn't get enough air. Going home after work had never been a challenge.

Now it was. The street angled up, then down. Buildings warped. He had to get home. He couldn't just fall.

But he did. Even as his feet slid on ice and he hit the pavement stones, he heard curses of people he'd fallen against on the way down. Pain shot through him, his wrist, arm, knee, head. Then he knew.

He wouldn't make it home.

Heated darkness washed away his vision.

Home was beyond him. He hoped survival wasn't.

Nightmares claimed him.

* * *

He awoke, mouth dry, to see the strangely misshapen faces of his parents, then the FirstLevel Healer Lark Holly. An expensive Healer instead of one provided by AllClass HealingHall. How much was he costing his family?

His mother squeezed his hand, and he realized his fingers were twined with hers in a desperate grasp. He knew he was bruising her, but he couldn't let go.

He moaned and tears leaked from her big, big blue eyes and rolled down canyons in her cheeks.

"Passss. Grrr. Saaa. Stt!" his mother said. The nonsense syllables echoed around the room, seemed to fly up to the ceiling and paste themselves against it like the stars she'd painted against a night sky. His bedroom. He was in his own room, on his own bedsponge, and should be happier, more comfortable.

His entire body ached. His nerves throbbed as if shocks ran up and down them in an endless cycle. He felt as if a hot stone was wedged in his chest, making breathing difficult, crisping his throat so it dried shut. He blinked rapidly to try to focus on the Healer. "Wha—?" he rasped.

"Pass—igg," she said. Her voice was quiet but he still didn't understand.

"WHA—?" he shouted.

"Passage," his father boomed back, and Walker's ears rang with the sound. He knew the word, a dreamquest that tested a person's mind and emotions as it freed the psi power within him. But he didn't understand. He had minimal psi power, Flair, just enough to use the Flair technology in everyday objects. He was a Clover, a Commoner. None of them had more than medium Flair.

"You'll make it through," the Healer said. His mother put a tube of liquid to Walker's cracked lips, tipped it, and nasty drink flowed across his tongue and down his gullet. "Argh!"

"You'll make it," his father said.

Blackness swept over Walker before he could spit.

* * *

Every guilty feeling he'd ever had, every mistake—omission and commission—haunted him.

The climb up the steep mountain was everything. He didn't know why he climbed, only that it was vital.

He moved rocks—pebbles that shifted under his feet, twisting his ankles and bringing him to his knees. The rocks laughed at him with grinning faces. He moved boulders that he had to set his shoulder against and grunt to dislodge.

He thought he heard the piping childish voice of the boy he tutored, Nuin Ash. Crying. That hurt, too, yanking at his emotions. He wasn't able to help the boy.

Sweat rolled down Walker's body. With one last effort, he reached the top of the mountain, a dangerously small space. Wind buffeted him from all directions, whistling eerily as if with words just beyond his hearing. Stuck in the middle of the meter-square rocky summit was a sword. The sword had a golden handle with the hilt curving down on each side like wings of some creature, the rest of the beast curled around it. A huge red ruby heart was the pommel. Engraved in fancy letters on the blade was *Flair*, as if that was the sword's name. The weapon seemed to sing, too, and it bent in the wind, flexible. A great prize. Yearning filled him. He wanted it.

His chest worked like bellows to draw in air, puff it out in ice crystals. His mind spun. He reached for the hilt of the sword, and the minute his fingers closed around it, they were fused in searing cold. He cried out.

He couldn't let go of the handle, even if he wanted to. But he had to master the sword. The sword was a weapon, a tool. *He* used it. The sword did not use him. He controlled it.

The mountain, the wind, the sword. Deep in his bones, the back of his mind, he knew them for metaphors, images of something different. No time to think of that. The sword was leaching away his body heat, throwing it to the winds to scatter to the stars. If he didn't stop the drain, he would die.

Gritting his teeth in a grin-rictus, he wrapped his other hand around the rest of the hilt, and pulled. Yanked. Swore and set his feet and screamed and jerked.

The sword came free and he toppled off the mountain, falling, falling.

He knew he could use the sword to save himself, but not how. As he swung it through the air, the sword cut swaths of the scenery and it peeled away. Illusion!

He wasn't falling.

No. He was on solid ground. He would *not* fall, hit, break. Firm land was beneath his feet. He wasn't in a mountain range, scaling the highest peak. He was in the courtyard of his home, Clover Compound, practicing swordplay.

No, he didn't grip a sword, it was a quarterstaff.

His mouth relaxed. This he understood. He was a Commoner, knew more about staves than swords. Automatically, his hands shifted on the wood, twisted, thunked the bottom of the staff on the ground. And he was home and all was right around him.

The sun angled in, lighting the opposite wall of the west wing, painting it a deep golden. Leaves from the trees rustled and dropped their spring blossoms, and he smelled the scent of his favorite season, looked around him at his favorite place.

He was home and the staff was in his hands and he lifted it and twirled it smoothly, lightly, moving in a pattern he knew perfectly. At the end of the last figure, he thumped it on the ground again, held it in one hand while he bowed to an unseen opponent. Then the staff melted *into* him, his forever, his *Flair* found and mastered, and the courtyard whirled around him . . . and he woke once more.

A deep breath shuddered into his lungs. The air was warm from his bedroom fireplace, drying the sweat on his face. Logs fell with a muted *clunk*. Walker strove to lift the weight of his eyelids.

The window curtains were open and showing the bare branches of trees in the central courtyard of the Clover Compound and a cold, clear, late-winter morning.

"You're back," his father said.

"Thank the Lady and Lord!" cried his mother in a choked voice, putting a hand on his forehead. Her cheeks looked thinner, not as rosy. He slid his gaze to his father. Gray creases lined his forehead.

Ma. That's what he meant to say, he thought his lips formed the word, but only a raspy croak came from him.

His father slipped a strong arm behind Walker's shoulders, lifted him. His mother held a tube of water to his lips, tilted it so the sweet fresh liquid trickled down his throat. Water from the well in their own sacred family grove. Nothing could be better. He gulped.

Then his mother wiped his face, and the crust around his eyes vanished and his breathing steadied. "Wha' happened?" he asked. "Fever? Did Nuin Ash infect me with something?"

"Something like that. Nuin is going through his First Passage to free his Flair."

"He's seven." Walker vaguely recalled that he and the Ashes had been expecting Flair fugues.

His parents shared a gaze, then his father met his eyes. "His Passage triggered yours."

Walker's body went weak, he leaned heavily on his father, his neck felt wobbly. "Passage! I don't have enough psi magic for such a dreamquest to pummel me."

"Yes. You do," his mother said. "Ease him down, Nath. It's time we explain everything to Walker."

His father winced, then his face went into serious mode. He shifted Walker back to recline against stacked pillows. "Maybe we should wait. He's already had a bad shock. Shocks. When a guy undergoes three Passages at once, it takes a toll on a man."

"Now, Nath," his mother said. "We've put off telling him for years. Now."

A bad feeling coated Walker's gut. It wasn't often that his mother demanded her way, but when she did, there was no forestalling her. His stomach rumbled from emptiness and new acid.

His mother's face softened. "I'll go get him some clucker soup and bread."

Walker would rather have had furrabeast steak.

"You tell him, Nath," his mother said. "He should know." She narrowed her eyes. "And I'll be sending Pink in, like we discussed."

Why would Pink Clover, the head of the Clovers, be coming to talk to Walker? Swallowing bile, he shoved away resentment. He was being treated like a child—adults discussing heavy matters about him while he was sick, coming to decisions, with no input from him. But a thin and cold coat of perspiration slicked his body, and he didn't feel up to protesting.

His mother came over, put her hands around his face, and kissed him like he was Nuin Ash's age. Her blue eyes were bigger again behind tears. "You've always been my child, my boy, Walker."

Then she left.

He turned his neck, heard it crack as he looked at his father.

His father's jaw clenched. He glanced away from Walker's gaze, rolled his shoulders as if donning a heavy pack, ran both hands through his thick hair. It looked more silver than it had a week ago.

Silence buzzed in the room, a counterpoint to the crackle of the fire.

Walker shifted, too; the sweat had dried and itched. "What?"

His father reached over and took one of Walker's hands in both of his own. "You're my son, Walker, but you aren't Fen's."

"That makes no sense."

Clearing his throat, his father grimaced, said, "You're not Fen's biological child. Before Fen and I were married, I had an affair with a noble GraceMistrys. She's your biological mother."

"What?" Walker said blankly.

"You have noble blood in your veins, and your biological mother came from a strongly Flaired Family, so you've picked up her psi power, too."

At that moment the door opened and Uncle Pink came in carrying a tray with a big bowl of soup, which steamed clucker smell throughout the room, and a half loaf of dark bread. He was the Head of the Household, the large Commoner Clover clan.

"Boy's awake? Good."

"I've told him," Walker's father said heavily.

"Everything? That he's my heir? I'll be stepping down?" Pink asked.

"What?" This had to be a dream, a fever dream. Walker must have picked up a bug from the Ash children.

Pink beamed at him. "Three Passages at once! Your Flair has manifested, for sure. You'll be the strongest Flaired person in the family. *You'll* be Head of the Household."

"Nooo," Walker moaned as blood pounded like a hammer against his brain. He couldn't face that everything he knew about his mother, his whole past, was nothing like it seemed.

His place in the family he loved wasn't what he thought. His brothers and sisters not completely his blood. His mother not his mother!

Couldn't comprehend his father and mother lying to him for so many years. How could they love him, *she* love him, and not trust him with this knowledge?

Were Pink and his parents really expecting Walker to take responsibility for the whole family? He couldn't think of that, too much to comprehend. "Why . . ." But Walker couldn't finish his sentence, couldn't think.

"Why didn't we tell you? Because it didn't matter. Didn't seem as if you got any major Flair since you didn't show it, didn't go through Passages at seven or seventeen or twenty-one."

"Makes no sense," Walker grumbled.

"Stop whining," Pink said, putting the tray down on Walker's lap. "You've got Flair from your mother's—"

"Biological mother's," his father corrected.

"Yeah, yeah. Biological mother's Family, the Heliotropes," Pink said.

Walker tried to think of that Family, who the woman might be, but his wits were as scrambled as the streaks of egg in his favorite clucker soup. The older generation just kept yammering at him.

"But we Clovers have been getting stronger in psi Flair, too," Pink said. He clapped Walker on his shoulder, picked up a spoon, and jammed it in Walker's hand. Walker decided to eat. Maybe if his stomach was full he could think better.

"Everyone's been watching us for years to take that next step up the social ladder." Pink hooked his thumbs into his trous pockets under his round belly. "We've been associated with nobles for over a decade now. In the family we've been wondering who'd be goin' through testing to become the first lord or lady."

Walker choked. He reached for a softleaf and rubbed his mouth. "That should be one of cuz Trif's children."

"You, Walker," Pink said. "Your combined Passages were hard enough to free some major Flair power inside you."

"I don't feel any different."

"You are, though," his father said quietly. "We've talked to your former employer, T'Ash, about testing your Flair, to find the strength and type."

"I don't feel any different," Walker repeated, his voice hard. He chewed a small chunk of clucker.

"You will," Pink said.

Walker ripped off a piece of bread with his teeth, savored the earthy taste of dark Commoner bread. He'd had no ambition but to be the best man he could, the best teacher he could, and to fit into his family. His Commoner family who had little Flair.

Apparently he now had great Flair and that set him apart. Like his having a different mother than he'd thought set him apart. Now everything had changed.

Too damn much to be expected to cope with on an empty stomach. He stared at Pink. "You knew about my . . . biological . . . mother, too?"

"Yes," Pink replied.

"Just how many people know about this?"

"Since your Passage, everybody." Pink shrugged thick shoulders. "Before that, most of your father's and my generation and elders."

Finishing the food, Walker set aside the tray, rose from the bedsponge, uncaring of his nudity. He locked his knees as they threatened to give way. Weak. "What day is this?"

"You've been abed a full five days," his father said.

Walker waved a hand at them. "Later. We'll talk about this later." He needed time to process that the foundation of his life sifted away from under him, dumping him on his ass.

"We'll talk about it now," Pink said.

"No."

The door opened and his mother—the woman he'd thought was his mother—came in. "You're shouting. Everyone in the courtyard can hear you. Walker, you should get back in bed."

"No."

"Don't use that tone," his . . . mother . . . said. "Be courteous."

He stared at her, then at his father, then at Pink. "You all lied to me. All. Of. My. Life. Since when does that show respect for me?"

His mother made a strangled, hurt noise that stabbed at Walker, but he was awash with a maelstrom of anger and pain.

"Walker!" His father's face was red and furious. Nath swung an arm around his wife.

Pink scowled, too. "Not well done of you."

"I can say the same." Walker flicked open his hands, but his body was unruly and his arms jerked wide. "Outside this room everyone in the family is talking about me, knowing my circumstances earlier than I do myself. Speculating about who I am or am not." He didn't know who he was, either, and that had fear lacing through all the other churning emotions.

He was even older than he'd thought, than they'd told him. Must be. "You haven't shown me much courtesy."

"We are your elders and your parents," his father stated. "We raised you and loved you all your life. Your *mother* reared and loved you."

Walker meant to touch fingers to heart, but his hand thumped his chest. "That doesn't mean what I thought it did." He ignored the darkening expressions. So much was going on, nothing else could touch him. "I don't remember any other mother, woman." No one, except this one who looked at him from haunted eyes, but who had lied to him every day of his life.

Pink stared at him. "She gave you to us within a septhour after you were born, left to live on her Family's estate in the south. Her Family didn't want to raise you. Your father and Fen—we did."

Walker had thought he couldn't feel more. But he did. As if the knife in his guts twisted. "Who?" He grated the word from a dry throat.

"Latif Heliotrope."

Again, that meant nothing. He didn't even know what kind of Flair might be in that Family, what kind he might manifest. Because no one had bothered to tell him his true past, no one had prepared him, trusted him.

"Please, leave." His voice was slurring. He wanted to think. Or rest. Or escape into sleep.

"We need to talk this out," Pink ended grimly, lowered his heavy frame to Walker's bedsponge.

"No," Walker repeated. "Leave, please."

"You're too sick and upset," his moth—Fen said.

The men exchanged looks but didn't move.

Walker braced an arm against the wall to steady himself. "How do you expect me to be the head of the family if you don't show me respect?" Was he making sense? He thought so, but his mind was so churned up, his body quivering inside, he didn't know. Not that he wanted to be the head of the family, but *they* seemed to think it was important to talk about now. What he wanted to do was figure out his whole past.

He waited as seconds of silence ticked by. He didn't want them here, *needed* some place to be alone and safe. Anger and urgency poured through him. He took a step and dizziness grabbed him with swooping claws and everything went dark and his breath was sucked away as he *teleported* for the first time. He landed somewhere else with a thump, crashing into a wall.

Two

All Walker had wanted was to get away to someplace quiet. Maybe to think, but he wasn't sure he was up to thinking rationally.

He banged his head on wooden paneling, and they thunked, both head and wall, and he slid down onto a woven straw mat. He was in a childhood hidey-hole, still in the Clover Compound—row houses built around a block with an inner courtyard.

Curling over himself, wishing he weren't naked, he tried to ignore the fact that he'd *teleported*. The room was a small storage chamber on the short, southern end of the rectangle. This was the first room he'd "helped" finish as a youngster. He hadn't been more than four years old, and proud to learn the wall-glazing spell, do his hand-sized patch.

He rested his head on his knees, chest pushing in and out raggedly as he caught his breath from the exertion of instinctively teleporting. He remembered how Uncle Pink had taught him the glazing spell, his father had guided his hands, his mother had praised.

Even then they'd known he wasn't Fen's child, had pretended he was. Had treated him as if he were just the same as every other Clover child. Which wouldn't have mattered if they had continued to do that *now*. But the last week had changed his life, with his Passages and the dramatic increase in his Flair. And the revelation that the woman he'd thought was his mother wasn't. He had a whole set of genes from some woman he didn't know.

He'd just teleported by himself, with no instruction. That demonstrated true Flair. Though it was dangerous as hell, and he hoped never again to do it spontaneously under stress. He could have killed himself or others.

Yes, all was changed, and not in ways he could ever have anticipated. If he'd even imagined he'd had a chance at great Flair, noble Flair, he could have been more ready for the Passages that had buffeted him, and what his life might become.

His previous comfortable life had been ripped from him. His place in the family was gone, as was his job. He was now the Head of the Household, responsible for matters in which he'd had little interest.

Would Pink have handed over the reins of the family to Walker if he hadn't gone through Passages, developed his Flair? No.

But he'd seen the gleam of ambition in Pink's eyes, how his uncle had rubbed his hands when he'd spoken of a noble title. Not only would Walker be responsible for the entire clan, but now everyone would have huge expectations of him.

He felt the tugging of emotional bonds in the back of his mind: his father, moth—Fen, Pink. They were all worried about him. Something else he'd have to do—allay their fears.

A knock came at the door. Walker sensed that his brother—his *half brother*—Barton stood in the hall. Barton was a trainer at The Green Knight Fencing and Fighting Salon, and knew his status there, and in the family, and in the outside world. Barton was one of Fen's real children. Walker was adrift.

"Walker?" Barton called.

"Is my standard fifteen minutes of brooding time over?"

"Yeah," Barton said.

"Come in."

Barton opened the door and ordered, "Lights!"

Spell lamps lit.

"How did you know I was here?"

"Everyone heard the shouts when you disappeared, even some mental ones. And this is where you always come to brood."

Walker grunted.

Barton threw him a heavy bright green robe that had a sheen to the cloth. Walker caught it automatically. "What's this?"

"Your new lounging robe." The corners of Barton's mouth quirked up.

Walker stared at it, appalled. Saw the embroidery on the chest, four four-leaf clovers, in eye-watering yellow green, stems meeting, arranged in a crosslike pattern. "Clover Coat of Arms?"

"Uncle Pink commissioned it as soon as you finished your First Passage. He's very proud of the color and design." Barton coughed. A lot. Walker knew he wasn't coughing; he was laughing.

Then Barton straightened and leaned against the jamb, shook his head. "You look like you've been down to the Cave of the Dark Goddess and back."

"Feel like it, too." Walker scrubbed his face. Bristles rasped against his palms. He met his brother's—half brother's—hell, *brother's* eyes, the same blue as Fen's. "Is my bedroom empty yet?"

Barton stared past Walker. Walker's flesh pebbled.

"You know how Dad has been wanting you to move out of that room for a while?"

Walker gritted his teeth. He already knew what was coming. "They put me somewhere else."

"The new luxury suite on the west side of the compound."

"I don't like the west side."

"They're not going to move you to the main suite on the east side. Security isn't as good." Barton shrugged, hooked his thumbs in his belt. This time he met Walker's eyes. "They were wrong not to tell you about your birth mother."

"Doesn't change a damn thing," Walker said.

"Nope. But we—everyone in our generation, your brothers and sisters and all the cuzes—are angry, too."

"When did you find out?" Walker snapped.

Barton gave him a cool look. "Just a little before you did."

"Sorry." Walker grunted, rubbed his face again. Maybe that would stimulate his brain, too. "How are the elders now?" He'd rather not talk to them. He was shivering from cold and reaction, so he put the damn robe on.

"The elders are acting stupid, self-righteous, and guilty."

"The youngsters?"

Barton smiled. "Fascinated and excited. Can't wait 'til you become a noble lord."

Walker belted the robe. "Knowing Pink, he's already made an appointment for my Flair testing to ascertain how strong my Flair is, and what kind I have." The strength of Walker's Flair would determine how far the family would rise in social status. Whether they'd be the third tier of the nobles, Grace, or the second tier, Grand.

"Yeah," Barton said. Tapping his wrist timer, he continued, "You have about fifty minutes to clean up. You can use my rooms."

"Hell, I don't—" Walker stopped. Nothing would be accomplished by cursing or fighting.

"Don't know what you're doing? You know what my employers, the Hollys say," Barton reminded.

Walker had spent a few years training with them. "Same as T'Ash," Walker said, speaking of his own employer. Ex-employer. Hell. Nothing was the same. "If you don't know what you're doing, pretend you do until you figure it out."

"Right."

"I hope the family gives me some time to adjust."

Barton hooted with laughter. "Every living soul is in the courtyard waiting to see you off. Cuz Mitchella has a glider to take you, and is staying to prepare for the big party tonight. The whole Family has risen to the nobility. You're just the one with the title. We're all nobles now. Not just you."

"Glad to be of service," Walker mumbled. He groaned when he took a step.

With a shake of his head, Barton closed his hand around Walker's bicep, steadying him as he wobbled when they left the room and walked along the southern corridor and down a flight to Barton's rooms.

Once there, Barton pushed him toward his waterfall room. "Go soak your head under a waterfall."

"Thanks."

"Anytime."

Walker stood under a hot waterfall for a long time, and when he came out, Barton handed Walker his silkeen loincloth and best tunic and trous suit of beige raw silkeen. Walker eyed it, stared at Barton. "I'm going to T'Ash's for testing. The Ashes have seen me every workday for the last six years. Good clothes aren't going to impress them."

"The elders insisted. You're representing the Family now."

Walker's jaw worked. "I didn't ask for this."

Barton punched him on the shoulder, and Walker had to settle into his balance not to go down. "Too bad that life took a hard curve for you." Barton's smile flashed. "Glad it's you and not me. I like my life just fine. Here." Barton handed him a tube of green liquid. "Restorative. The Healer left it, guaranteed to perk you up physically and Flair-wise."

The drink didn't taste too bad. "Thanks for the clothes, too. Now can you get me out of here and to the glider without seeing anyone?"

"Mom and Dad are worried."

"Don't tell me you didn't talk to them during my waterfall."

Another shrug from Barton. "Sure."

Walker stared at his younger brother, spoke softly. "I can deal with testing, or I can talk to them about the past, or I can talk to Pink about the future. One option—one skirmish only—today. Particularly since I have to move to new quarters."

"You're angry."

"Damn right. I'm being forced down a path not of my choosing. That wasn't what we were told or taught as children. We were supposed to be able to choose our own goals."

Barton cleared his throat. "Everyone in the Family has always been strong on fulfilling potential."

"And I'm no longer just one of the Clover boys. Now I have Flair and my potential has suddenly gone up. I can fulfill Pink's ambitions for the Family. I understand that. But while the elders have had twenty-seven years to contemplate such an event, I've had about a septhour."

Crossing to a no-time food and drink storage unit, Barton opened it, sent a tube of ale sailing toward Walker. He caught it, squeezed open the top, hesitated.

"Healer said ale wouldn't hurt with the mixture," Barton said.

"Thanks."

"And I can get you to the glider without meeting the folks."

"Good."

"Probably easier on you to go to the Ashes than dealing with the rest of us."

"I don't know about that, but I'm not angry at any Ash."

Walker's former employer, GreatLord T'Ash of the FirstFamilies—people descended from the original Earth Colonists—met him at the front door of his Residence, with a wide grin on his face. He gave Walker a strong arm clasp. "I heard that my son triggered Passage in you. That you survived three in one night." He shook his head. "That's tough."

"How is Nuin?"

"Good." T'Ash smiled as he scanned Walker top to toe. "Better than you look."

"Thanks."

"'Welcome."

T'Ash's wife and HeartMate, Danith D'Ash, pushed by the GreatLord and hugged Walker. "Three Passages at once can be difficult." She stepped back, studying his face. "I was like you, without obvious Flair, and I suffered all Passages at once. If you need to talk with me, I'm here for you, Walker. Always."

The nape of Walker's neck heated. T'Ash scowled. "Thank you," Walker said in a tone that he hoped conveyed to her that he appreciated her offer but wouldn't take her up on it.

Since T'Ash's expression cleared and D'Ash's clouded, he thought he'd gotten his tone right.

She shook her head. "You could always do that."

"What?" Walker asked.

"Convey a load of meaning in a few words. Make T'Ash feel better but not insult me."

T'Ash frowned at her.

"Must be part of your Flair," D'Ash continued. "You could usually manage Nuin, the other children, and us, too." D'Ash nodded. "Yes, part of your Flair."

T'Ash stared at Walker.

Walker said, "I thought it was skills I developed." He cleared his throat. "Can we get on with the testing?"

"Yes, it's cold out here," Danith and T'Ash moved aside.

Walker entered and nodded to the butler, who was hovering—a man he'd worked with for six years. Then Walker strode into T'Ash's den. T'Ash caught up with him in a few long paces and Danith D'Ash rushed.

"We'll learn what Flair you have during your testing," T'Ash said. He shooed his HeartMate.

D'Ash didn't move. "Walker might like me to stay."

"Thank you, Danith, no," Walker said. "I am nervous enough as it is." He gave T'Ash a man-to-man look.

T'Ash said to Danith, "We'll tell you the outcome as soon as testing is done." He glanced at Walker. "I made a deal with her to keep her out of the way—unless you specifically asked her to stay."

"Good deal," Walker said, but now Danith was frowning. He bowed to her. "Thank you for the offer."

"You've always been one of my favorite people," she said.

"Later, Danith." T'Ash gave her a lusty kiss. Walker studied the den. Except for his original interview to be Nuin's tutor/wrangler, he hadn't ever been in the famous room that held the best Flair Testing Stones in the world.

The room itself was octagonal, with a lush carpet in the bold colors that the Ashes favored. The desk was huge and battered, with the most disgusting cat perch he'd ever seen next to it.

As if his thought had conjured up T'Ash's Fam, the cat swaggered through the cat door.

Greetyou, Walk, said Zanth.

"Greetyou, Zanth. I note you have a new emerald stud for your ear. Looks great."

Zanth always expected everyone to notice anything new with regard to his person, and if you didn't, it was the worse for you: a shredded shoe, a nice trous-rub—after Zanth had killed a sewer rat—that would ruin your clothes . . .

Thank you. With one bound Zanth landed on his perch. It didn't even wobble under the weight of the huge cat.

The Ashes broke apart and said their good-byes, something Walker had heard for years. A pang went through him that his time with this Family was lost. The job and life he'd loved had vanished forever, and not by his choice.

He ripped his glance from the couple and sat in the large chair with wide wooden arms.

Zanth folded his front paws under himself and watched Walker through squinty eyes, roughly purring. Each of his tattered ears had an emerald stud, and he wore his famous collar of emeralds.

Walker smiled at the cat slowly, knowing that he could tease Zanth without repercussions. Walker said, "It occurs to me that if I now have enough Flair to become a noble, Danith might give me a Fam."

Zanth stopped purring, opened his eyes.

T'Ash grunted as he went to a cabinet and unlocked it. "Probably get your pick of whoever is in the Fam adoption rooms." The GreatLord pulled out a large, ornate box about a meter long and three-quarters of a meter wide. Inside were T'Ash's Testing Stones; sweat dampened Walker's armpits. Thankfully his tunic had spells that absorbed and dissipated sweat. Worth every piece of gilt he'd paid for it.

Still aiming his glance at Zanth, Walker said, "I'm sure there are some very attractive cats in the adoption rooms." He cocked his head, kept his smile bland. "On the other hand, I haven't had a great deal of luck with cats. I may prefer a fox . . . or a dog. Something very loving."

Zanth hissed.

"Quiet, Zanth," T'Ash said absently as he set the box on the arms of Walker's chair, then removed the lid.

Walker's breath hitched in his throat. The Testing Stones were beautiful! Polished egglike rocks of every color, some with glinting sparkles, some dull. He glanced up and found T'Ash grinning.

"Always nice to impress someone I respect," the GreatLord said.

"Yes, I'm impressed, and thanks."

The GreatLord leaned against the front of his desk. He nodded to the stones. "If matters proceed as I expect, I'll be the first to offer you Clovers an alliance."

Walker jerked back as if slammed into his chair. He'd never considered that. Being part of the web of alliances between some of the most important people in the world.

"You will be the head of your Family, of course," T'Ash said, with the exact assumption that Pink must have anticipated. Of course any noble with great Flair would want to deal with someone also with Flair.

Ears ringing, Walker gathered his wits. He hadn't thought things through about alliances. The Clovers already had ties with the FirstFamilies since his cuz had married into them . . . but still, formal alliances of support were vital.

Nobles still settled some problems with feuds, which meant lives were at stake. The burden on his back got heavier and heavier. He drew in deep breaths. Binding ropes seemed to have wrapped around him, constricting his chest and lungs.

His becoming noble raised the status of his entire family—*Family* with a capital F. None of the Clovers had ever spoken of Family with a capital, as an organized community that was lasting until . . . well, forever, if Walker had anything to say about it. But once they became noble, they'd be a Family indeed.

"Walker?" T'Ash asked.

Walker realized the man's voice had been a rumbling smear of sound that he hadn't paid attention to. "Sorry. Didn't catch that."

"Yeah, it's a lot to consider," T'Ash said. "First I have a Flair strength measure. Hold out your hand."

Walker did, and T'Ash dropped a clear, glassy stone in Walker's hand. He closed his fingers, then stared as streaks of light shot through the cracks. His whole hand warmed and glowed from the stone.

"Good," T'Ash said. He held out his hand and Walker let the now-hot stone fall into the GreatLord's palm.

Once again T'Ash grunted. "Not as strong as any FirstFamily lord or lady, but strong enough to let you rise from Commoner, past GraceLord to GrandLord status. Welcome to the nobility, Walker Clover."

Walker sank against the chair. "That's it?" The words sounded easy, but his pulse was rapid. As if he were back climbing that mountain with a boulder on his back.

T'Ash appeared mildly insulted. "My stones are extremely accurate."

"Heard that."

"It's true. They don't make mistakes. *I* don't make mistakes."

A wheezing laugh came from Zanth at Walker's discomfort. He noticed the cat kneading his perch, really setting his claws into the tough material and giving it little rips. Maybe there were compensations for not working for the Ashes anymore. Walker wouldn't have to put up with Zanth's sense of humor.

"Now let's find the nature of your Flair. The way it manifests, is, of course, indicative of your personality, what you are naturally good at."

"Appreciate that," Walker said.

"That's what the stones are for. Run your forefinger along each stone starting at the white one in the top left of the box, row one, ending with Celtan Volcanic, the black, in the lower right corner. Got it?"

"Yes." Walker sucked in a good breath, then did as he was asked. T'Ash went to sit behind his desk. Now and then Walker felt a pull . . . or a repulsion, until he got to one that wasn't stone but metal—solid gold. It *clung* to his fingers.

"Hmm," said T'Ash, but surprise was in his eyes and his brows were up. "Very interesting. Please continue."

Walker wanted water. He wasn't going to say so. When T'Ash glanced down to make some notes on a piece of papyrus, Walker wiped his hands on his trous. Setting his shoulders, he lifted his right forefinger and began where he left off. Now he felt more than just mild tugging or dislike, occasionally sparks lit when he touched an egg, and he gritted his teeth and suffered the mild shock.

Here and there an egg seemed to drain strength and Flair from him. He began to use three fingertips, just to get through the procedure. Then his hand hit an egg, and once again his fingers curled over the stone, drew the egg from the box. It was warm. And wet. And pulsed as if he held a heart in his hand—which should have been sickening, but was comforting. Maybe because it matched his own heartbeat.

"What do you have there?" T'Ash asked.

Grimacing, Walker turned his hand over, but his fingers remained locked tight. So he angled his fist to see the top. The stone shot golden and red light into his eyes. He jolted and dropped it. After blinking away afterimages, he saw it floating over to T'Ash's desk, where the man lowered it to rock gently next to the golden one.

"Heart's bloodstone," T'Ash said. "First, gold—gift of easy speech and relating. Heart's bloodstone, dark red with flecks of gold, indicating people."

"What does it mean?" Walker asked.

Three

It means you're a born diplomat, will interact well with people." T'Ash frowned. "This is one of the few testing results that automatically indicates a person should be considered for the position of Captain of All Councils."

"No!"

"Don't want the job?" T'Ash asked. "I don't blame you. Councils are all like a congress of cats."

Walker felt his face hardening. "Twenty minutes ago I was a Commoner. You know damn well that none of the councils, let alone the FirstFamilies Council, would elect me as Captain."

"You'll have to work your way up, for sure. But by the time my generation is firmly established in our seats, I think we would prefer someone who we knew was good for the job. Like I said, there are prescribed qualities that we have determined would make good leaders." T'Ash flicked a gesture at the box of stones. "Yours is one of them."

"But not the best?"

Raising his brows, T'Ash said, "No."

"With the younger generations all becoming stronger in Flair—" Walker started.

"Including you," T'Ash interrupted.

Walker rolled an itch out of his shoulders, as if he had a target on his back. "Including me—there are undoubtedly people in the FirstFamilies or old noble class who will have equal or superior qualities to mine."

"Hmm," T'Ash said as he opened a drawer and got out a heavy piece of papyrus used for important documents. "That might be. But I think if some of my colleagues in the FirstFamilies Council had the choice between a young, powerfully Flaired person of high noble birth and a nicely Flaired ex-Commoner . . ."

"They'd choose the ex-Commoner," Walker said, "thinking I'll be easily intimidated."

"That's right, they'd choose you. Though they'd be wrong about the intimidation. They might think you'd be easier to work with, and in that, they'd probably be right."

"Huh," Walker said.

T'Ash placed his large blacksmith's hand on the papyrus and said, "Through the power invested in me as Celta's premier Flair tester, I certify by my Vow of Honor that the results shown below are the outcome of standard testing upon Walker Clover, using the best of my abilities and tools."

T'Ash studied the Certificate of Testing and Nobility, a corner of his mouth kicked up. "Diplomacy, people skills. Seems to me you might have done some subtle manipulation of our household while you were with us."

"No—" With the fierce blue gaze like a blazer on his, Walker coughed and amended his answer. "Not often."

T'Ash smiled, then tilted his head. Walker faintly sensed that the GreatLord was communicating telepathically with his wife on a private mental channel.

Walker froze at the discovery. He shouldn't be able to sense that—other than by watching a person's body language. Just how much was this new Flair of his going to impact his life?

T'Ash frowned and Walker knew that look. An obstacle had arisen to upset the smoothness of his day. And because Walker knew that expression, he relaxed. Of course he wouldn't be that sensitive to others. He'd worked in the Ash household for years, knew everyone very well.

"What's the problem?" he asked.

With a sharp look that faded as another smile took its place, T'Ash said, "That's what you always ask. What's the problem? How can I help?" T'Ash widened his hands. "Your personality showed up in your Flair and testing. Believe me, I've always been grateful for your help."

"Really?" Walker asked sardonically.

Laughing, T'Ash said, "Usually. I'm going to miss you handling Nuin. Without you he's been difficult."

"He's got a lot of his father in him."

T'Ash looked pleased.

"What's the problem?" Walker repeated.

"Ah . . ."

"Something to do with me, then."

"You Clovers are the most prolific Family on Celta."

Walker brushed that away. "Everyone knows that. Just tell me the bottom line, T'Ash."

To Walker's surprise, T'Ash opened the drawer again while chanting a short spell under his breath. As he brought out the papyrus, letters wrote themselves on the page, bold and black, finishing up when T'Ash passed the sheet to Walker.

"Alliance contract between T'Ash Family and Clover Family," Walker read. He glanced up. "I thought things like this were done with handshakes, words."

"They are."

"Between equals you mean, like you and Holm, the Hollys. Both of you FirstFamily GreatHouses."

"I didn't have an alliance with the Hollys for many years after my friendship with Holm," T'Ash snapped.

Walker didn't know that. He figured there was a huge amount of things he didn't know. He'd have to come up to speed fast and wasn't quite sure how he could do that.

"The contract is not for you and me." Again T'Ash's stare bored into Walker. He was used to that and didn't react. It occurred to him that his training in this household would stand him in good stead in the new and vicious pool into which he'd been thrown. There were a lot of people who ran after a harsh glance from T'Ash.

"I trust you." T'Ash leaned back in his chair. "Hell, everyone in my house trusts you, down to baby Dontea. None of us would doubt you or your word." T'Ash straightened. "This is for your Family and to be filed with the councils. Formal alliance with us—and through us, the Hollys, the Blackthorns, others"—another casual wave of his hand as he named some of the most powerful Families in the world—"would be good to have on file. Don't you agree?"

"Yes." Walker took a writestick from his pocket and signed, pushed the papyrus back to T'Ash and watched him sign the alliance contract. Then he translocated it somewhere, probably to the councils' clerk. "My Family isn't so stupid as to turn down an alliance with you."

"No. You may be the titular Head of Household for your Family as shown in the noble rolls, but you have elders."

"Oh, yeah. A lot of them."

"And you'll be figuring out your status with them, too."

Walker said nothing.

T'Ash nodded. "None of my business. But they might prefer to see a contract."

"Fine," Walker said. "Please send a copy to our cache."

"Done."

"But that's not what bothered you, so spill, T'Ash."

"Yeah, you're good at this," T'Ash said. He jerked his head toward the door. "The Clovers are prolific and an up-and-coming Family. You just happen to be the first of your clan who has Flair strong enough to be a noble. Others in your Family will follow. And I'm not the only one who wants alliances." He actually looked aside, flushed a bit. "We FirstFamiles, nobles, prize children."

Walker just stared. "Are you saying that there are others here with contracts?"

"Yeah. More." But T'Ash didn't say another word, just looked red and irritated.

"I'm not understanding, T'Ash; tell it all."

Throwing up his hands, T'Ash bellowed mentally and physically. "Danith!"

Zanth woke up from a doze, grumbled, then his ears perked up as if he listened to the mental conversations of his Family.

Now that T'Ash mentioned it, Walker directed his attention—his Flair—to outside the room. His Flair expanded, surprising him, and as it did, he became aware of everyone in the house. The Ashes themselves were easy, he knew them all well. Nuin, his seven-year-old charge, was fussing with his food. If Walker had been up in the student rooms, he'd have packed up Nuin for an outside excursion . . . The Ashes were easy to focus on, familiar, and so was the minimal staff.

There were five people in the Residence whom Walker didn't know. Yet. He'd soon be associating with many nobles. He felt like he was traversing a swamp full of pitfalls. That could kill him. Worse, could harm his Family for generations. He needed better instincts. Training at The Green Knight might hone those instincts. Sharper in physical fighting might make him sharper at meeting other threats.

Danith D'Ash opened the door. She was flushed and sent Walker an unusually inimical look. "Messing around with people I dislike instead of doing my work. 'Cause of *you*."

Walker donned a hurt expression. "And here I thought you liked me. Does this mean I don't get a Fam? None of this whole thing"—he swept out an arm—"was my idea. Has Nuin finished his Passage?"

"Yes, Nuin's fine. Looks to be a fire mage, like you thought." Danith tugged at her hair. "And his Passage set yours off, didn't it? Did I apologize? Sorry, and sorry I was short with you. Of course you get a Fam!"

"Residence," Walker addressed the intelligent house.

"Yes, Walker?" the Residence asked.

"Tell my replacement to take Nuin out to look at his father's forge. *No touching. No Flair touching.*"

"Yes, Walker."

"Also, send a glider to Clover Compound and request that my

cuzes Mona and Clypea, who have assisted D'Ash before, come here and help with hostessing and Fam care."

"Oh, thank you, Walker!" Danith sat on her husband's lap, closed her eyes. "I suppose we both can't stay in here for the rest of the day?"

"If you let me know what to expect, I can handle it for you," Walker said.

"You're too good," Danith said.

He pretended to be. The more he thought about The Green Knight, the more he knew a good fight would release some of his tension at all the changes in his life.

Danith said, "The NobleCouncil clerk is here, Monkshood. He's never liked me. Or T'Ash. We don't like him, either. He's been sniffing superciliously all over the papyrus that T'Ash has been translocating him. He has that big nasty manual of rules and stuff that new nobles have to memorize."

"Ah." Reading. That might be helpful.

"And wants to set up a time for your testing on it."

Walker smiled. "I've always been a quick study."

"He's a pain in the ass," T'Ash said but made no move to do anything but cuddle his wife.

"Residence," Walker said.

"Yes, Walker?"

"Have the butler and one of his helpers entertain the Ashes' guests until my cuzes arrive."

"They aren't guests. They weren't invited," Danith said darkly. Then she snorted. "*Entertain*, our butler can juggle." She opened her eyes and looked at T'Ash. "Think we should have him juggle for them all?"

T'Ash's smile was slow. "Irritate them all."

"Who else is here?" asked Walker, standing.

"D'Grove and her daughter Sedwy," T'Ash said. He looked straightly at Walker. "She 'ported in right after you, so she has plans for you. Since she was Captain of All Councils, she'd know what your testing results mean."

"I asked her why she came, and she just said a lot of

nothingness," Danith grumbled. "After your testing document was given to the clerk and he translocated it, reps from T'Reed and T'Furze showed up. They didn't say why, either."

"But you can guess?" asked Walker.

Danith made a face, elbowed her husband in his flat stomach. He didn't react.

"Ah, um." She flushed. "It's a matter of, um, genetics."

Walker stared at her. She started talking fast. "The last Commoner who was raised to the nobility and married into the FirstFamiles was me." A quick smile that was only nerves. "And what with the twins, T'Ash and I have had four children within eight years. Most FirstFamilies rarely have more than one or two children." Her gaze met Walker's, deflected. "How many children are usual per couple in your Family, Walker?"

"Six. Average."

"Well, you see, then," she said.

"I—" he started, then suddenly he did. "Genetics," he said flatly.

"Yes, you will be wooed." Danith nodded.

T'Ash grunted. "Our visitors might even have marriage contracts with them. Make sure you get a good deal."

Walker sat down again. His insides iced. When his voice emerged it was equally cold. "I won't consider such an idea."

"The FirstFamily nobles will pester, pester, *pester* you." Danith looked at him with big eyes. "They do that."

"The smart ones will have sent reps to Clover Compound to talk to your elders," T'Ash said.

Walker was sunk.

Zanth laughed until he fell off his perch.

*A few minutes later, Walker's female cuzes had arrived, and Dan*ith reluctantly exited the den to instruct them, then head to her own work. Walker had asked permission of the Ashes to check on the children—before dealing with the various other people who had arrived to see him.

He was walking through an upper gallery around the great hall when a whispered conversation came to his ears.

"We've waited for the Ashes and Walker Clover for nearly fifty-five minutes. I don't want to stay." The voice was feminine, impatient.

"I know you don't," said an older woman's voice. "But you will stay here and you will do as I say."

An intimate argument. That must make these two D'Grove and her daughter Sedwy. Intrigued, Walker went to the railing along the loft and looked over. The older woman was a commanding presence, tall and with a good figure. Her daughter Sedwy was about Walker's age. She had a combination of noble features that made her stunning—straight nose and full mouth, delicate but stubborn jaw, and high cheekbones. Her hair was golden brown and he could tell her eyes were light.

He liked the looks of her.

"No, I will not follow your orders indiscriminately," Sedwy said.

"Then you should continue building your anthropology career and leave Druida again, take the Chinju project."

Sedwy gasped. "You don't want me here?"

"Only if you will do something to bolster your reputation." There was a long-drawn sigh. "You *can't* have any objection to Walker Clover, or this little job I'm asking you to do."

"Of course I don't have any objections to Walker. He's probably an interesting man. But as for this *little job*, we both know what you want to happen and what motivates you."

"What motivates me is love for you. And I'm quite sure that Walker will need a liaison to the FirstFamilies, to nobles. Someone who will smooth the way for him. Someone intimately aware of our habits, *our* culture, and who can explain such and communicate well. There's no one better for that position than you, and I can defend that decision before the whole FirstFamilies Council."

"Mo-ther," the younger woman said in tones that had been used throughout time.

"Sed-wy, we *must* rehabilitate your reputation. You've only been back in Druida for a week and already the old scandal is talked of. This assignment will help you."

"And unlike other nobles, Walker Clover might not know of my reputation," Sedwy said with a touch of bitterness.

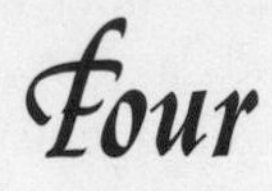

Walker racked his memory to recall any gossip about Sedwy. Nope, he knew nothing, couldn't remember any scandalous sexual affairs. More's the pity.

"Just think," D'Grove said. "As a liaison between Walker and the Clover Family and the rest of us, you will be able to observe the Clovers, might even be invited to Clover Compound."

Hesitation, then, "I won't be your spy," Sedwy continued.

Sure she would, Walker figured. She was already losing, and she knew it.

Walker liked her attitude. She wouldn't be smoothly humoring him. As for him, it would be interesting to fence with Sedwy Grove, whom her mother wanted to marry off to him and who was reluctant . . . but found him and his Family intriguing.

He'd learn all he could from her about the nobles, the Noble-Council, the FirstFamilies and their Council. That knowledge would serve him well in protecting his Family, climbing up the ladder of success until the Clovers were solidly noble.

He felt more in control.

He was a quick study.

But contemplating Sedwy, he might not be *that* quick in learning, might need a lot of tutoring. Impulsively, he strode to the stairs down to the oval hall, ran down them quietly until the last few steps. Then he made sure his footsteps echoed through the room.

The women turned his way. He moved forward to them. Sedwy was even more gorgeous up close than from afar. Her lush figure was staggering. What's more, her blue green eyes were heavy-lidded, adding sensuality to her appearance.

He stopped, pretending he wasn't struck still by her beauty, and bowed to the older woman, forced proper words to his tongue. "Merry meet, FirstFamily GrandLady D'Grove." He gave Sedwy a slightly lesser bow. "GrandMistrys Grove. I am Walker Clover."

"The Ashes informed you we were here?" D'Grove asked. Her gaze went to the half wall of the gallery above. Probably thinking that she and her daughter might have been overheard.

"Indeed," Walker said. "I believe they said that the GrandMistrys could help me with my recent status upgrade."

Sedwy's eyes had narrowed, also focusing on the gallery.

"And you do need help," D'Grove said bluntly. "Your bow was good, but not correct. It was the bow of a Commoner man to a FirstFamily lady who has been Captain of All Councils of Celta."

He'd learned that bow from the Hollys while he was training at The Green Knight. Knew it was elegant—more elegant than T'Ash's. Walker kept his face bland, raised a brow.

D'Grove gestured to Sedwy. She smiled at him and he strove to keep his expression impassive.

Sedwy said, "You are no longer a Commoner man, Walker Clover. You are a GrandLord. GrandLord Clover."

It was the first time someone had addressed him by his title, and the words prickled through him. Something he'd never wanted.

In a persuasive voice, D'Grove said, "The FirstFamilies Council thought that your inclusion in our ranks would be easier if you had a liaison. My daughter Sedwy has volunteered for the position. We would be pleased if you'd accept her advice while you get to know us."

A mouthful of mis-speech. "Thank you. I'm honored." Nodded to Sedwy. "Thank you."

"You're welcome." She'd flushed at her mother's fib.

"That's settled," D'Grove said. She smiled again, and it was interesting that her expression was more sincere than her words. Walker fumbled with his Flair to gauge her feelings—she *did* like him. Furthermore, she was glad that he found Sedwy attractive, was hopeful.

D'Grove wore the same sort of smile that Uncle Pink had when he'd closed a good bargain for the Family. "Congratulations," D'Grove said, "your official status will be determined after you take the Nobility Examination, but I'd imagine you'd be somewhere in the middle of that rank. Your Flair is stronger than some of the older GrandHouses who have been declining for centuries."

That thought just reminded him why they were here. So their Family wouldn't decline. The idea ground in his head like a screeching gear.

"Thank you for the correction."

Sedwy blinked as if surprised. "You don't sound as arrogant as a GrandLord."

"Or as a man who might someday be the Captain of All Councils of Celta," D'Grove said.

Sedwy gasped, and her mother patted her shoulder. D'Grove's sharp gaze stayed on Walker.

He managed an amused smile. "T'Ash told me that my Flair results might lead me that way."

"The potential is there," D'Grove said. "I'm sure your Family knows, too."

Walker kept the smile but lost the sincerity. "Everyone at Clover Compound is excited at our rise to the nobility. Big party tonight."

Curiosity flashed in Sedwy's gaze.

D'Grove narrowed her eyes. "I wonder when the newssheets will have the information."

"A reporter or two might even be waiting outside T'Ash's gates," D'Grove said.

He chuckled. "Well outside. T'Ash still has a formidable reputation."

D'Grove lifted her chin. "That doesn't always stop them."

Rolling a shoulder, he added, "None of the members of the newssheets Families have animal companions, which are pretty much regulated by D'Ash. Not many people want to alienate her, either."

D'Grove's own expression went flat. Sedwy's mobile face went still. A sore point for them, Fams. And he knew just how to change that.

He bowed again, this time an inclination of a torso that he'd been told could be used at any time during a conversation with nobles. "Why don't we go to the Fam adoption rooms and see who we can match with you?" He offered his best smile.

Both women's eyes opened wide.

"You can do that?" Sedwy said on a rush of breath.

Walker grinned. "I've been a member of this household for six years. T'Ash and I are allies." He raised his brows and glanced at Sedwy. "I believe it is common for other nobles to bestow gifts upon those newly ennobled?" Gifts, Walker hoped, that didn't include marriage contracts.

Sedwy nodded. "That's true."

He stepped between them, touched their elbows, and indicated the hallway that led through the house to D'Ash's office suite and the Fam adoption room.

The women's auras surrounded him, and he sensed their interest, their excitement. Sedwy's nearly fizzed.

Everyone wanted a telepathic animal companion. He did, too. The only one in his Family to have one was Trif Winterberry. She had a cat that nearly ruled Clover Compound. Though her husband had a fox, that Fam ruled a den outside the compound.

Walker opened the door to D'Ash's suite for the ladies, saw D'Ash herself there, sitting behind the reception desk. She nodded to them, said, "I have some veterinary appointments." She was the animal Healer of Celta. The only one, though it appeared as if one of her sons had inherited the Flair.

"Ah, D'Ash." He sent her his most charming smile. "You've known D'Grove for some years, and GrandMistrys Grove has been here for a while this morning. Long enough for you to be able to match her to a Fam, I'm sure." He gave a self-deprecating shrug. "And I've always wanted a Fam. Now that I'm a noble, and the Head of my Household, I think I'll need the companionship."

D'Ash softened as he knew she would. *Oh, very well,* came her voice in his mind.

Walker simply froze. He'd never heard clear telepathic words. The sensation might have had him running, if he could move, and if Danith didn't sound like the woman he'd interacted with daily for years. The hint of exasperation came through, sounding just as if she'd spoken aloud. He analyzed everything about the three words, decided the sensation wasn't any more intimate than if a friend had whispered to him.

Yet a shiver slipped down his spine. Before he moved, Danith was gesturing to a door on her right. "Ladies, please go into the Fam adoption room and meet the companions there." She smiled at him. "I need to talk to Walker of his own Fam."

Walker watched the women leave. More particularly, he watched the sway of Sedwy's hips.

He dimly sensed anticipation, but when he tried to deduce how many animals were currently in the room, he couldn't.

His Flair was for people, not Fams, a relief. In this area he was just as he'd always been, with no Flair to impinge on his previous experiences and turn them strangely intense.

As soon as the door had closed behind the Groves, D'Ash said, "Fams for both of them, Walker?"

"That's right."

D'Ash narrowed her eyes. "You're up to something, Walker Clover."

He smiled. "Sure."

D'Ash stared at him thoughtfully. "You're much more you, now, Walker."

"And that means?"

"Less subtle."

"I don't think the FirstFamilies appreciate subtle."

"Of course they do. And that's what you're going to do, aren't you? Have a bold, confident manner and be scrutinizing and maneuvering subtly all the while." She shook her head. "Better you than me."

"You don't have to maneuver. Your Family is set."

Danith leaned forward. "Your cuz, Mitchella, is my best friend. We would never let anything hurt you Clovers."

"Maybe not you or T'Ash, or Mitchella's husband, T'Blackthorn, or their children. But what of two, three generations from now? Whatever I do now, in these first years, will set the course for my Family."

Silence for a long minute.

"This is going to be tough on you, isn't it?" Danith asked.

Walker shrugged. "No choice."

"No, but I can make it better for you by giving you a Fam. And if you think Fams for the Groves will help you, they'll get animal companions. Let me think a bit." She was still. He knew that look, she was using her Flair. *She* could probably sense the Fams beyond the door, how they were interacting with the Groves.

This moment was nearly like a regular day. The wrenching pain that he'd never be back, doing what he loved, but instead becoming a noble lord, was so huge and black he strode blindly to a chair against the wall and sank into it.

A few deep breaths later, he had a handle on himself, even though he still felt as if he were alone on a raft that was thrashing through tumbling white water. Heading for rapids.

D'Ash made a humming noise. Smiling faintly, she stood, not seeming to notice Walker was unsteady. If he could maintain his facade before her and T'Ash, he could do it before any other noble.

"D'Grove will be easy. I have someone for Sedwy to bond with, but not in the adoption room. He's ready to leave his mother."

Walker cleared his throat. Danith chuckled. "The Fam I chose for you is a young fox who needed seasoning. He's with Winterberry's Fam, Vertic. He might be a little wild and will need a bit of socialization before—"

"Danith, I'm very good at socializing wild young ones." Walker stood, grounded again.

"Oh, that's right." She grinned. "My children are examples. I'll send Argut to you."

"A Clover name."

"Yes. He was meant to be yours all the time."

Walker bent and brushed her temple with a kiss. "Thank you."

"You're welcome. Now for Sedwy's Fam." Danith went down a short hallway, through an examination room, and into the non-public space. "My latest experiment in genetics."

Walker winced.

"I'm definitely increasing their Flair with every generation."

His steps lagged. He was sure that she wasn't poking his sore point on purpose.

"They only had minimal Flair when I first started the breeding program, but after several years of working with them, I've developed some very good, Flaired Fams." She opened another door, glanced up at the mask he kept over his expression.

"Uh-oh." Turning, she hugged him quickly. "*No one* has been experimenting with the Clovers, unless it's your Family yourselves."

His teeth set. Apparently, despite the flow of information between the Clovers and the Blackthorns and the Ashes, Danith hadn't heard that his mother wasn't his biological mother. "Danith," he asked softly. "Just what kind of creature are we talking about?"

"What? Oh." She shrugged. "Housefluffs. Hybrids of Celtan mocyns and Earthan rabbits. One of the few Earthan species that has done well on Celta, and proof that both planets were seeded with the same DNA aeons ago."

"Um-hmm," Walker said, stepping into a small room that was tinted beige and spotlessly clean, but nevertheless had holes in the far wall and floor, burrows angling down into the ground.

Burrows thankfully too narrow for a toddler, Walker knew from his first week's experience at the Ashes.

"Housefluffs have always been popular pets, but since I've boosted their Flair, they are in great demand. Not as destructive as rabbits and more easily trained and—"

"They're Fams, they're intelligent," Walker said.

"Yes." Danith lowered her voice. "Not as intelligent as cats or foxes or dogs, but sentient." She went over to a hole in the wall and cooed. Several housefluffs hopped out, thickly furred with large ears. "Here they are. Adorable."

He studied them. Most women would want one. For himself, he was glad he had an adventurous fox on the way.

"My Fam won't eat it, will he? Since Sedwy will be my liaison to all you scary nobles, explaining FirstFamily customs, I don't want to irritate her."

"Of course not," Danith said, then called, "Baby number four."

Ears lifting, eyes gleaming, a small brown housefluff hopped on top of her feet. Danith lifted the young fluff with long ears edged in cream, held him close to her body, and stared up at Walker. "Sedwy's going to explain customs to you?"

"That's right."

"Oh, good. Someone I can ask when I get confused. Even if T'Ash knows stuff, he never explains."

"Always glad to be of service."

"Take the housefluff. You know any good Grove names?"

Walker answered, "Not offhand. You know those FirstFamilies are weird. Never paid much attention."

"That's fibbing, Walker. You probably know every secret this household has and a lot about the Blackthorns." She tilted her head. "Know more about the Hollys than they'd care for, some about the Furzes. And you know the Hazels' and Vinni T'Vine's most private secret. All FirstFamilies."

"And you are all weird."

"Not me," she tapped her chest. "Commoner, like you."

"Just go on believing that."

She snorted and gave him the fluff. It was softer than anything he'd ever felt in his life. "I'll take care of D'Grove. A fox denning on her estate has been wanting her attention for some time. We'll have a little talk."

"See?" Walker said. "You can have a little talk with D'Grove as an equal."

Danith drew herself up to her full height. "In my professional capacity."

"Right." The Fam wriggled in his hands until it could fix both big brown eyes on him. *Greetyou,* it said in a tiny voice in Walker's head.

"Danith, you're sure this little one is right for GrandMistrys Grove?"

"I think she needs something young and vulnerable to take care of. Something innocent." She went to a table next to the wall, opened a drawer, and pulled out a square ventilated pouch with a long strap. "Carrying case." She handed it to him and took off to the door leading to the adoption room. He followed her through.

The three cats who had been encircling D'Grove left her, as did the two puppies tumbling over Sedwy's lap. The rest of the Fams who'd been sitting or lying, showing the best aspect of themselves, settled back down.

Danith said, "We'll have more people in this afternoon, Fams. I have at least six appointments." A rush of purring came from the cats as they curled back up on their perches. "D'Grove, will you come with me?"

The older woman who had been tolerating the cat stares appeared interested again. She stood and brushed hair from her elegant silkeen robe. With one last look at Sedwy, she said, "I'll see you later."

Walker said, "I hope Sedwy will come to our Family celebration tonight."

D'Grove relaxed enough to smile. "Good. Congratulations again."

"Merrily met," Walker said one of the noble farewells. His gaze sliding toward Sedwy, he tried another bow to D'Grove. This time slowly, careful of the animal he held. When Sedwy's fingers twitched, he knew it was enough and straightened faster, smiling.

"Merry meet again," D'Grove said. "Well done, GrandLord Clover and Sedwy." With a wave, she left the room after Danith.

He stroked the housefluff and it chuffed a pretty noise of contentment. Wearing his most mild expression, he looked at Sedwy.

"Very good," she said.

"I'm a quick study."

"I'd say so. Nice Fam," she said, and something in her tone made him think she didn't think it was appropriate for even an unarrogant new lord.

He said, "One of the most powerful FirstFamily GreatLords, the prophet, Vinni T'Vine, has a housefluff as a Fam." Granted, Vinni was eighteen, but that was a full Celtan adult.

She frowned. "I didn't recall that."

"It's true. And besides, this gentleman housefluff is not for me. He's yours." Walker smiled wickedly. "Danith informed me that my young fox is enjoying an adventure."

"Mine!"

Greetyou, FamWoman! This time the housefluff's mental stream was loud enough for Walker to hear the echo of his telepathic words to Sedwy.

Her mouth opened. Shifting the creature along his arm, Walker lifted one of Sedwy's hands to pet the Fam. "Oooh," she said. A few seconds later she was holding the small animal, bonding.

What is my name? asked the housefluff, his ears high.

"Lucor, your name is Lucor." She sounded choked, glanced at him. "Thank you. And thank you on behalf of my mother."

He nodded. "You're welcome." He guided her back into the main house.

In the grand hall, he met his cuzes, both accompanied by attentive men. Noblemen by their bloused sleeves and trous legs.

Mona grinned and waved at him with papyrus in her hand. "The Ashes have said we can go and are loaning us a glider. *We* have a couple of interesting offers, too." Her eyes swept down, then up as she glanced at the young Nobleman. Clypea's hand was tucked in the other man's arm.

Walker scowled. This is what he'd have to deal with, and he didn't even know who these guys were. Before he could say anything, Clypea pulled her gallant along with a bright smile tossed over her shoulder. "See you in a little while."

After a look at his face, Mona and her man followed quickly.

He took a step and Sedwy laid a hand on his arm. "What's wrong?"

"I don't want them hurt."

Sedwy stared up at the quiet man she'd just met. This fascinatingly complex person who had just risen from Commoner status to noble and brought his whole Family with him.

"Your cuzes are in a FirstFamilies glider on their way home where your elders will be waiting, right?"

Walker looked at her with gray green eyes like the ocean. He was about ten centimeters taller than she, a long, lean man without the bulk of muscle most Noblemen packed on. Still she felt his strength—of body, of Flair. Of character. Once she wouldn't have given him much time, wouldn't have appreciated his quiet manner.

She'd been so foolish. She shoved the thought away along with the stinging behind her eyes. She'd trusted the wrong people and that had ruined her reputation. She wouldn't let it ruin her life. And this man needed her knowledge and that was a balm.

"I don't know those men," Walker said.

"The Nobleman garbed in the bright yellow color that clashes with his hair is T'Reed's daughter's youngest son."

"T'Reed, the FirstFamily banker."

"Yes."

Walker stared at the short hallway leading to the front door. "My Uncle Pink will like that."

The one sentence alerted Sedwy to additional problems. On the home front with the Family, which were the worst kind. "We need to talk," she said.

Five

If we need to talk, we'd better do it here. Clover Compound is bound to be as active as a beehive." He glanced at the antique clock standing against the wall, grimaced. "I can maybe squeeze out another septhour and a half before they expect me. I want to know who the other guy was—the one who walked out with my cuz Clypea."

"That was the youngest Alder. That FirstFamily is very long-lived, but they tend to only have one child every generation. It's a concern."

"I'd imagine so." He frowned.

"Your unmarried Clover Family members will now be seen as good matches."

"Maybe not." He offered his hand and she took it. His palm and fingers felt different, didn't have the calluses she knew were from noble fighter training or Commoner work. Smooth but strong. A frisson of attraction fired along her nerves. They walked to a door at the right end of the oval, tucked under the curving stairway. The sitting room was small and cheery, decorated in floral chintz. Sunlight made the room golden, and she sighed. The last couple of days had been gray, the days shortening to Yule.

Warm! Sunny! Pretty! Want down! said Lucor.

Carefully she set the small housefluff down. He hopped to a patch of sunlight fading a thick Chinju rug. With innate manners, Walker led her to a large, thickly cushioned chair.

She wouldn't have to work much on that—except to teach him noble flourishes and rank.

He took the butterscotch leather wing chair that angled toward her, separated by a small table.

"I don't think marriages with us will be that popular. I'd bet both the Alders and Reeds are just checking us out. T'Reed might just want us to move our funds to his financial institution. The rest of the FirstFamilies will wait until we're really established.

"Maybe some lower GraceLords and GraceLadies will court us now, and we'll be more attractive to the upper-middle classes, wealthy merchants. But the oldest and highest Families will wait until . . . I'm not sure. The only ones who will woo us now are the risk-takers or those who have an extra son or daughter who is shady and has nothing to lose."

Sedwy's muscles stiffened into immobility. Her flush was hotly visible on her face; she felt it on her neck. How much did Walker know of her? His cuz Trif had suffered because of Sedwy, how much would he—and the other Clovers—blame her for that?

Walker glanced at her and his eyes widened. Color flagged his own cheeks. "I didn't mean you."

Her jaw was tight. "What do you know of me?"

He raised his brows, and she felt a wave of calm emanate from him, as if instinctively soothing her. Interesting, but not strong enough to banish the anxiety crashing inside her.

"I don't know much," he said mildly. His gaze locked with hers. "I promise what I want to know about you, I'll ask."

She sent him a slanted and disbelieving look.

His casual manner dropped from him. "My word is as good as any noble's."

As she stared into his eyes, she understood that she'd hurt him. That they'd hurt each other. Already. She took a deep breath in and let it out slowly. "Do you want to . . . associate with me?"

"Work with you, you mean?" He nodded shortly. "Yes. I'm not too proud to know that I need help." His gaze went past her to the snow covering the rolling lawn. "And not just in manners or studying for the noble test, or for insights on all the nobles." His direct look met hers again. His brows stayed down and his eyes got grayer, his gaze more intense. "I suppose I should tell you that I teleported impulsively this morning."

Sedwy choked. Her Fam hopped to her, indicating he wanted up. She lifted and petted Lucor. "That's not good." Walker must have been under a great deal of stress. Of course no man would admit that.

"No. Can you teach me to teleport?" His gaze wandered down her body. "I hear there's a lot of hands-on work in that." He smiled slowly. "My cuz Trif wooed her HeartMate that way."

Sedwy swallowed but kept her chin high, held out her hand. "I should be able to sense your Flair, whether it's strong enough to teleport."

He linked fingers with her, and she felt a connection flick open between them, a rush of sensation back and forth. "Plenty of Flair," she said, focusing on it for the first time. The quality of his psi power was different than she was accustomed to. Quiet, tensile strength. The flash of a sword came before her mind's eye, a rapier, flexible steel that would not break.

That image faded and was replaced by something Walker himself sent her—a solid quarterstaff. That's how he thought of his Flair, of himself.

He was wrong; the sword was appropriate. She hid the thought from him.

She let her "Yes" out on a sigh, repeated it. "Yes, you can teleport, and yes, it is best if you master that talent as soon as possible."

Walker's lips flexed in a grim line, then he said, "Because nobles will be expecting me to teleport. You and I will have to visit places so I can see them well enough to be able to teleport to them."

Sedwy tightened her grip on his hand. "Visualization is key, and the most important component of teleportation is the light. You must know what the light looks like in all seasons, all times of the day and night."

He smiled and stood and drew her up, too. Sedwy put Lucor in his transportation bag. Inside there was bedding and a little pouch he could open for food.

Walker said, "There are a very limited number of places for me to teleport, then." He waved at the room. "Here, T'Ash Residence, Clover Compound . . . the courtyard, and my *old* room." That sounded bitter—more difficult Family stuff, Sedwy believed.

He shrugged. "Banksia Park where I had grovestudy." Tucking her hand in his arm, he opened the door, leading her up the left-hand staircase. "The teleportation pad in the ballroom is rarely used and will be empty. Plenty of space to practice if we do short inside hops."

For an instant Sedwy recalled her mother teaching her to 'port soon after her First Passage. That had been an easy talent for her to master. Her mother had been so patient . . . then pleased and proud. A lovely memory.

Things hadn't been good between her and D'Grove since Sedwy's disastrous mistake seven years ago.

"The ballroom will be fine," she said.

And it was. The curved western wall was full of windows, the light excellent.

"Residence," Walker addressed the sentient house.

"Yes, Walker?"

"Lock this door and inform the household that Sedwy and I will be practicing teleportation in the room and no one must enter."

"Done, Walker." The floorboard creaked and Sedwy knew it was punctuation by the Residence.

"Yes, Residence?" Walker asked.

"May I say that I will miss you, also."

Pain flickered across Walker's face, but his voice was calm when he answered. "Thank you, Residence."

"You are very welcome. Always welcome within my walls, Walker."

Walker coughed, said, "Thank you." With a smooth motion, he pulled Sedwy into his embrace, wrapping his arms around her. Her pulse skittered, then throbbed fast. His muscles were tougher than she'd anticipated. She could feel his long, lean thighs, his chest, wider than her back. He was solid. He wasn't aroused. That was good, wasn't it?

"Very nice, GrandMistrys Sedwy Grove." His warm breath stirred her hair by her ear.

She cleared her throat, tried to relax against him. "Just a minute, I must put Lucor in a safe place."

He dropped his arms and the room seemed cold around her. Her Fam was sleeping. She set the bag carefully on a sofa.

Then she trod back to Walker, stood a little farther away from him than before, took his arms, and wrapped them loosely around her, put her own hands on his. "Study the light by the windows, visualize the room. How the shadows fall, the scent of the polish on the floor, the herbed housekeeping spells. Let me teleport us, first."

"Yes." His voice was husky. Inwardly she quivered.

"You've heard the countdown."

"Essentially three seconds."

"That's right." She tried to ignore him, scrutinized the width and color of the floorboards, stared at the light, judged the distance . . . "Ready?"

"Yes." He pulled her closer until their bodies brushed. His grip around her was tight but comfortable. She ignored the fact that she liked the feel of him, the scent of him, some essential spring greenness like grass.

"One, Clover man, two, Sedwy Grove, *three*!" She teleported them, landed exactly where she'd anticipated, close to the windows but with no chance of materializing in the glass or wall, which would be fatal to them and distressing to the Ashes.

Walker's arms had clamped her tight to his body, and she realized she'd been wrong, he was aroused. His breath whistled from him and he stepped away from her, stood staring at the windows and outside at the snow-covered estate. Then he looked at her. "We didn't just move through space." He waved a hand. "We were there, then here. A slight darkness, no sense of moving."

Sedwy nodded. "I gauged your height correctly, too. No arriving a few centimeters above the floor."

"Good job." His smile was wry. "When can I try?"

She kept her gaze on his. "That's what we're here for."

He cocked his chin. "You're a trusting soul, Sedwy."

That was an unexpected pain. She'd been far too trusting. "I trust the strength of your Flair and your knowledge of the room."

He nodded solemnly. "You can trust me."

She guessed her discomfort had shown or filtered through the connection building between them. She nodded in return.

Walker moved to the far end of the room, held out his hand to her. "Shall we try?"

Keeping a smile on her face and her step light, she crossed to him. "Sure."

Again he wrapped his arms around her, but this time she noted that the back of her body did not brush his. They stood in a long moment's silence until she glanced up at him, saw him examining the room as if he were memorizing the briefly glittering motes of dust. "Think of your five senses, how that end of the room smells—colder than this end and with a hint of outside frost against the windows, et cetera."

He chuckled. "Et cetera." His arms shifted slightly as he took a deep breath. "On three. One, Sedwy Grove, two, T'Ash ballroom, *three*!"

And they were there. Again his arms squeezed her tightly, this time as he picked her up and spun around. "I did it! I did it!"

"Congratulations." She smiled.

He dropped his arms. "Let me try something." His brows dipped, then he vanished. Sedwy froze. She shouldn't have allowed him to talk her into this. He was moving too fast. Odd, when she considered him such a calm man, that he could move fast enough to surprise her. She'd have thought he'd take his time about things.

And he was back, arriving at the proper teleportation pad in the corner of the room. He flipped the switch to show it was free. Picking up the rules fast.

"Wonderful. Truly wonderful." His eyes lit with pleasure, his smile showed a deep dimple crease in the left side of his face. She thought this was the first time she'd seen him unshadowed by events all day, and that was a pity.

So when he grabbed her hand and hustled her back toward the pad, she didn't drag her feet. Again he set the indicator showing the pad was in use, counted down quickly, and the next instant they were in the corner of a different room that held child-sized tables and desks, shelves, and play areas. Though the room had a curve and the wooden floors were remarkably unscarred, the chamber immediately brought back Sedwy's study days—being tutored in her own home, grovestudy outside during the clement months, and her apprenticeship. The scents were the same.

And though T'Ash Residence was relatively new, the master had rebuilt on the same grand scale of his Colonist forebears. The space was large, but one partitioned area holding a desk and cabinets was bare. Sedwy understood that was where Walker had kept his things.

He was addressing the Residence. "Thank you for locking the door to the children's study area, Residence."

"You are welcome, Walker. May I compliment you on your teleportation skills?"

Walker threw back his head and laughed as if carefree, then said, "You're accustomed to people teleporting in and out of your walls; you think I did a good job?"

Despite the fact that Sedwy had grown up with a Residence and considered them individuals, that was a question she never would have thought to ask. Walker surprising her again.

"Yes, Walker. No missteps," the Residence said.

"Thank you."

The door was flung open and a boy of about seven with scruffy black hair and T'Ash's olive skin shot through. "Walker, you're back!" He flung himself at Walker.

Walker picked him up and threw him in the air, caught him surely, and set him on his feet. "Good to see you, Nuin. Passage went well?"

"Oh, fabulously well." The boy flung out a hand and fire zapped from his fingers to whoosh into large flames in the fireplace.

"Excellent. A little flashy, though. You might want to practice control."

Nuin Ash scowled. "Father came to the forge and let me practice and practice. There was only one little accident, and Father moved fast."

The man entering the room winced. He appeared singed.

"Control, Nuin. Practice more. With your father," Walker said. T'Ash might let 'one little incident' occur, but not more than that. Walker bowed to the newcomer, equal to equal. "Greetyou, I'm Walker Clover." He offered his arm for clasping.

"Heath Honey," the man said, taking Walker's arm. "You're a strong man, Walker Clover."

Walker laughed again.

"He's a *cook*," Nuin said, not quite offensively.

"The better to understand fire," Walker said. "A cook will know heat in all its degrees."

Sedwy snorted at the pun, Heath laughed, and Nuin pouted until Walker explained it.

Walker said, "It's good of you to step in to help the Ashes."

"He was supposed to be your replacement, but he is not working out." Nuin had flung himself in a chair.

"Up, Nuin, now. And apologize." Walker's tone was iron.

Nuin rose, flushed red and not with anger. He bowed to Heath, equal to equal, which is what Walker was expecting, Sedwy thought. Then he gave a more subdued bow to Walker, and Sedwy noted that particular bow was from a student to a master.

"Heath, do you have any inclination to work with the Ash children?" Walker asked.

"No." The man smiled. "I'd rather cook."

Walker waved. "Go ahead. And take Nuin. He can be cook's apprentice this afternoon."

Nuin's mouth dropped open.

Walker said, "To learn the value of cooking, and perhaps the degrees of fire needed."

"Oh, yes!" Nuin said.

That sounded as if it were both punishment and treat.

"I'll check with my Family to see if there's anyone else who would want to take you and the twins on, Nuin."

"That would be fabulous," Nuin said. Again he flung himself at Walker. "I'm sorry you're gone."

"I'm sorry, too, but if we know anything about life it's that it is—"

"Constantly changing," Nuin ended. One last hug and he donned a quiet manner that appeared to be a copy of Walker's and joined Heath Honey. Heath nodded to the boy and followed him out of the open door.

At the last moment, Heath turned his head. "Thank you!"

Walker nodded, but his expression was no longer light. As soon as Heath closed the door, Sedwy saw his hands fist, his face fall into torment. "I *hate* this."

"I'm sorry," she said and felt helpless with worthless words.

He jerked his head in denial, sucked in a breath, walked stiffly over to the window, and stared out. "The change was so abrupt." His mouth twisted. "Just this morning I . . ." He tapped his fingers on the window. "No, it's been the past week, but that was taken up with Passage."

He met her gaze with a dark gray one of his own. "You know that my birth mother was a Heliotrope?"

"Yes."

"I didn't. Not until this morning." Walker's shoulders rolled as if he shifted new burdens.

Sedwy didn't think he could become accustomed to all his new responsibilities so soon. She put a hand on his arm. "Like the Residence, I think you're coping with the changes in your life very well."

"I agree," the Residence added.

Walker shrugged. "Too late now. No going back. Everything's altered." He looked out the window again. "I have a good idea of what Clover Sacred Grove would look like, and there's a small teleportation pad there, and it's not in use, but I don't want to risk it."

"I don't know that part of town at all," Sedwy admitted.

"Walker," said the Residence. "One of our gliders is in the front, waiting for you and GrandMistrys Grove."

"Thank you, Residence," Walker said. He offered his arm to Sedwy, with just the right deference, and she took it. When they left the room, the door shut quietly behind them and Walker's face went immobile, then he led her down hallways and flights of stairs and finally through the great hall and to the front door. They didn't speak, and she knew he was closing other doors—doors of the past behind him, bracing himself for the future.

Change and a future that she now understood he hadn't wanted.

She wondered how that was going to affect them . . . affect her.

Six

During the glider ride, Lucor roused from his nap and kept both amused. Sedwy was glad to see Walker smile again, especially since she extrapolated that his time with his Family might be difficult. Perhaps even more difficult than her meeting Trif Clover Winterberry again and apologizing. Again. She could never apologize enough to make up for what the people she'd thought of as her friends had done.

Several minutes later the Ash glider stopped in front of a solid line of houses on the right and a large park on the left. There were no side yards between the buildings and no doors facing the street, though window placement and roof lines varied, showing individual houses. Most were colorfully tinted. The door to the vehicle lifted, and Walker slid out and offered his arm to her.

I'm here! I'm here! The mental voice was loud and boisterous and male. A young red fox zoomed from the park to them, spun in a circle that had it blurring, then sat two centimeters from Walker's boots, panting and tongue lolling. *I am Argut, Fam to GrandLord Walker Clover, and I am HERE!*

Walker laughed. "Greetyou."

Argut lifted his paw. *Greetyou.*

Hunkering down, Walker stared into the dark brown eyes and

took his Fam's paw lightly in his fingers. The pads were smooth and warm. "Greetyou, Argut." Then he tried it mentally, *Greet-you, Ar-gut.*

Argut swiped his tongue over Walker's fingers and Walker laughed again. He stood and Argut did, too. The fox sniffed Lucor Fam's carrying case. *Who is in here?*

The flap opened and Lucor peeped out. *Eee! Eeek!* The squeal was mental as well as physical. Lucor disappeared fast.

Sniffing at the bag, Argut said, *I will not hurt you. You are no more than a mouthful, and not plump.*

Walker choked on laughter.

Sedwy lifted the pouch and angled it so that Lucor could creep out on her arm, settle in her palm, high above Argut, though Walker thought Argut could get that mouthful of housefluff if he really wanted.

Walker said, "Glad to see you, Argut."

The fox switched his gaze from the young housefluff to Walker, seemed to grin again. *Vertic fox who lives here and across in the park helped me teleport in jumps here. So I could meet my Fam-Man! Celebrate!*

"For sure," Walker said, kept his mouth smiling as it faded from his eyes. His Fam was better than he at both telepathy and teleporting.

It was a very hungry trip, Argut offered.

"Ah. Well, the Clover cooks have food in the no-time for Vertic—" And Argut was off, bushy tail waving. Walker sent mentally to his Fam, *Play when you wish.* Walker was rewarded by excited yipping.

Thank you, FamMan.

I might like him, said the tiny Lucor, nose wiggling. *I do not think he will eat me. None of the FamFoxes at Danith's ate me.*

"Nope, you're still here," Walker said.

"I'll protect you," Sedwy promised.

FamWoman is wonderful.

Sedwy's expression softened, and Walker wished the tenderness that she was aiming at Lucor was his own, that she caressed him the way she petted her Fam.

She was a very dangerous woman.

"Hey, Walker!" a man yelled, and Sedwy saw a guard in front of the large door.

A young man of about twenty, with a blazer at his side, waved as they walked toward him.

"Hey, Cago. This is GrandMistrys Sedwy Grove, who is a guest and my teacher and liaison to the nobles."

A quick, charming grin from Cago as he bowed to her. "Must be interesting to be the student instead of the teacher."

"Always," Walker replied.

Cago made a face, waved open the heavy double doors. "Go on in. It's crazy in there. Tell Barton I'm fine for another shift out here."

"Guard duty outside the doors?" Walker asked.

"From now on." Cago threw out his chest, grinning. "We're nobles now!"

"I heard that," Walker said.

Cago laughed.

Taking her hand, which had Cago's brows raising, they entered a wide, cold corridor built between and under the houses. There were doors to her right and left to each section, and open double doors to a courtyard at the end of the passageway.

"Doesn't seem too secure if the other doors are open," Sedwy murmured.

"No." Walker sighed. "We like to cultivate being an open and friendly family. We make and sell furniture, so that's been a priority."

A rush of loud sound, shouting voices all at once, hit them. "And we *are* an open and friendly family."

"Emphasis on the first initial, Walker. *F*amily."

"Yes."

They stopped at the end of the corridor. People colorfully garbed arranged huge tables, putting linens on them, plates and glasses, gleaming silverware. There was no snow in the block-long courtyard, and Sedwy glanced up to see the thin wavering air denoting a weathershield.

Walker followed her gaze. "It's an expensive spell but a priority for the family . . . for the *Family.* This is our main gathering place."

"So I see."

He tugged her hand, and they stepped into the courtyard that was actually warmer than the passageway had been. No wonder with all the people gathered . . . and moving.

He turned to shut the doors, and a middle-aged woman shrieked, "Not the doors. We need them open." She hurried to them, and from the way people parted, and Walker's body angled, Sedwy determined that the woman—the GrandMistrys—was the alpha female of the Clover culture.

"Aunt Pratty, security," Walker said.

She snorted. "All the children are here and they're wildly excited; you don't think they'd send out an alarm if they saw a stranger?"

Even as she spoke, a large clump of various-sized young people ran by. Sedwy had never seen so many together except at grovestudy. And they were all Clovers. Amazing.

"There is that," Walker said.

"Coming through!" shouted a man behind them.

Walker stepped closer to Sedwy and nudged her out of the walkway, into the courtyard, and to the side. Two large men, guiding equally large potted trees with an anti-grav spell, passed Walker and her and Pratty.

"In the northwest corner for a conversation area!" Pratty ordered.

Tall trees grew in the courtyard, branches bare in the weak winter sun and being decorated with low-Flair-and-tech fairy lights.

"Staggered greenery adds interest," Pratty said. "There'll be potted plants, too. We'll have a few noble visitors talking to our young *ladies* tonight." Her eyes narrowed at Sedwy. "Sorry, my manners! Have we met?"

Sedwy curtsied, lower than she should, but she would always be lower than this woman.

"This is GrandMistrys Sedwy Grove," Walker said. "She's to

help shape me into a Nobleman and be my liaison with the First-Families and higher noble class."

Pratty's smile faded and her face fell into harsher lines worn by worry and fear. Sedwy was all too aware that she indirectly carved those lines. "I'm sorry," she said.

The woman jerked from her reverie, waved an impatient hand. "Not your fault."

They both knew she was being gracious. Sedwy said, "I'd like to apologize to Trif again, too."

"Not necessary." Pratty nodded to them and took off diagonally across the courtyard to supervise the arranging of the trees.

Sedwy looked up at Walker. "It *is* necessary."

He nodded. There were questions in his eyes, but he said nothing, knew that they should not be speaking of private matters in the courtyard where people milled close and children had big, listening ears. Not that Sedwy's part in the whole Black Magic Death Cult had been hidden. His gaze slid around the ever-moving Clovers. "Ah, there she is." Linking Sedwy's arm in his own, he began walking to the right. Soon two people blocked their path. Walker resembled the older man. The woman had blue eyes and soft brown hair and features Sedwy had seen on a child or two, but not Walker.

"My parents," Walker said.

They relaxed a little, though their arms still wound around each other's waist. They moved easily like that, were obviously lovers and still loved. Sedwy's heart twinged.

Walker was continuing, "My mother, Fen Clover, and my father, Nath Clover." A hint of strain ran through his tone and the couple tensed again. The revelation of an unknown adoption was a tough situation all around. "This is my liaison with the nobles, Sedwy Grove."

Sedwy curtsied. Both older Clovers bowed.

"A pleasure," rumbled Nath.

"Welcome to Clover Compound," Fen Clover said, and Sedwy sensed a rush of embarrassment through Walker. Because he hadn't said those words?

"We need to speak with Trif," Walker said.

Nath cleared his throat. "A minute. We received your notice of nobility. Congratulations."

"Thanks."

"We knew you could do it! Wonderful Flair." Fen blinked rapidly and made a motion toward Walker, who withdrew a little. She swallowed and beamed a bright smile.

"Thank you, Mother," Walker said formally.

Sedwy thought he hadn't often called her *mother.*

Nath said, "We got your formal alliance with T'Ash and are very pleased. Two gallants arrived with other proposals." Now Nath smiled. "Pink is stacking up the contracts and proposals on his desk, not wanting to review them until tomorrow."

"Good news," Walker murmured, his shoulders lowering from high tension.

Fen lifted her chin. "Yes, this celebration must not be marred by business."

Sedwy slid her eyes toward Walker, met his gaze that had slipped toward her. They both knew Fen was naive in this.

"Trif," Walker prompted.

"Oh, yes." Fen scanned the courtyard, then her brows lowered, she glanced at her wrist timer. "Nap time for her."

"Oh," Walker said, looked down to where Sedwy realized her fingers squeezed his arm. A brief smile crossed his face. "She's very pregnant. We'll have a new Clover shortly."

"It would be lovely if it were a Yule baby," Fen said. Words that seemed to be standard. Her eyes searched Walker. He didn't meet her gaze.

"Why don't you show Sedwy around the compound," Nath said, too heartily.

"We'll eat dinner early," Fen said.

"We closed the furniture workshops as soon as your nobility was confirmed." Nath's chest expanded. "Though the store is still open, of course."

"Of course," Walker said.

"Pink's thinking of moving the location to something more upscale."

"Of course," Walker repeated. He looked at Sedwy, and his smile, while a faint curve of the lips, was sincere. "Come along, GrandMistrys. Let me show you how the Clovers live."

"That would be wonderful." She smiled at Walker's parents. "I'm an anthropologist by training." And she'd studied cultures since the murders. No more delving into the dark side of Flair.

"See you in a couple of septhours," Fen said, then switched her sad gaze to Sedwy. "The party will have food and wine, too, but dinner is always important."

"Yes, Mother. Father." Walker nodded, pressed Sedwy's hand against his side, and they moved away.

"Two septhours! To see the compound?"

Walker chuckled. He seemed unaware that his parents were still watching them. "Well, sure." His tone changed as if lecturing. "The Clover Compound comprises three large Celtan blocks. This is the main courtyard. We also have a smaller courtyard where the Family's sacred grove is located. Houses are continuing to be built along the other blocks as needed, but this area is complete . . ."

They strolled through the courtyard, and Walker named the row houses that belonged to each portion of the Family: Pink's, Mel's, Nath's . . . Trif Clover Winterberry and Ilex Winterberry's . . . Sedwy made note of that one. His explanations were clear. She saw the mainspaces of the Family, the gathering rooms, the guest wing. They stopped for chunks of homemade bread in the huge kitchen.

The rest of Walker's close Family made a point of hugging him, talking to him. Those his age gave him significant and supportive looks, and Sedwy deduced that they were standing with Walker against the elders in some issue.

Walker accepted their affection, returned it, but Sedwy caught him scrutinizing each of his two sisters and brothers. Each did have some feature bequeathed by Fen—the blue eyes, her smile, the way her ears were set. One of Walker's sisters held an infant and was married and living with her husband's family. Walker's other sister was about twenty and had a gleam in her eyes when she introduced a gallant who was there to celebrate with the Clovers. Since the young man had a matching gleam, and a possessive arm around her waist, Sedwy thought there would be a wedding before spring.

When they met Barton Clover, the closest in age to Walker, some of the tension in him drained away, and Sedwy was glad of it.

Barton moved like a fighter, and Sedwy learned he worked at The Green Knight, and some of the Clovers had trained there, including Walker. That explained the way Walker bowed and some of his mannerisms. Barton accompanied them as Walker pointed out the three doorways to the compound from the outside world.

It *was* a world in itself.

A world that was changing as she watched. The Family culture of the Clovers was different today than it had been yesterday. Now they were noble and they knew it.

The buzz of ambition rose through the members, infused the energy of the Clovers as a group.

Sedwy smiled. She highly approved of ambition.

Finally the early winter night was falling and the lights along the walls of the courtyard came on. The place was well decorated, and Walker decided the Family, especially the ladies, were getting a head start on Yule. Trees blinked shades of green and red, white and gold from the small lights in their branches. That spell was known by enough people that it was easy—and much of the Flair that had been used was simple, funded by the excitement of the Family. Now and again, Walker had felt a pull on his own Flair as Pratty or his mother used a greater spell—for cleaning the flagstones of the courtyards and polishing them, then making them non-skid. That had never happened before. As he considered it, he thought that the pull might usually go to the Flair infused in the compound during the quarterly rituals, but since he was better connected to the women, it had come to him. And he'd shared his Flair. It hadn't weakened him much, and his psi power seemed to refill as the Family swirled around him, emitting energy. Still, something to ask Sedwy about. He was making a mental list.

Walker and Sedwy were led to the head table, away from the third one in line where he usually sat. At least he wasn't seated at the top, but at Pink's right hand. As he filled his plate with feasting food—tender roast furrabeast, fat white tubers fluffy and herbed in their own skin, his favorite greens—he pondered whether he'd have to make a point that he was the Head of the Household. Reluctantly he decided he would. He didn't *want* to be the first noble of the Family. Didn't want to be the Head of the Household, didn't want to *run* the Household, but that was his job now.

Damned Cave of the Dark Goddess. Automatically, he turned the curse into an equally reluctant blessing. Bless the Lady and Lord for their abundance.

That he could well have done without.

Sedwy was holding her own in conversation, mostly with Walker's cuz Mitchella and her husband, FirstFamily GrandLord Straif T'Blackthorn, both of whom were in great spirits.

Though Sedwy often glanced at Trif, who looked pale and was picking at her food. Trif's guardsman husband was out on a case. Something between Sedwy and Trif, but Walker was patient enough to find out later.

After dinner, the tables were cleared by the teens—who could be trusted with the good china—while the children handled the linens. The tables were shoved near the walls of the courtyard. Everyone was full of food, but in about a septhour more snacks would be laid out. The wine that had been served with dinner would be replaced with the best in the Clovers' cellars for celebratory toasts.

He was far from accustomed to being the center of attention. In fact, he'd never been the center of attention. Barton had been the outstanding one, the one with the drive to prove himself with the Hollys. Walker supposed he'd become accustomed to the feeling, but he didn't like it.

Sedwy stayed close beside him, and he liked that very much. Trif had disappeared into her own house with her four-year-old son. After a dismayed glance, Sedwy had slipped her hand into his elbow as each person came up to congratulate him. He liked the hugs of the under-ten crowd the best, their artless questions—though he didn't have many answers for them.

Then a flushed Uncle Pink strode to the center of the courtyard and yelled for quiet.

Walker drew in a great breath beside her, and Sedwy followed his gaze to where the alpha of the clan, Pink Clover, stood in the middle of the courtyard, shouting for silence. After a couple more times, people stopped talking.

Pink strutted, thumbs in the top of his pants. "Nobles, us. Pretty good for a new Family that only came to being a century ago." He grabbed a wineglass and raised the glass. "To the Clovers! Descendants of the lowest maintenance tech on *Nuada's Sword*! Lady and Lord Bless Us!"

The inner courtyard roared.

Walker shouted beside her, drank off his wine. Sedwy did the same, eyed a wall to send her glass shattering.

Excited babble rose again and people pressed around her and Walker, all gesturing with empty glasses.

"They didn't throw their glasses against the walls," she murmured.

Walker angled his head away from an excited teen who was hopping around him, patting and congratulating him and asking if she could be apprenticed to D'Thyme. He put his hand on the youngster's shoulder, looked at Sedwy. "Break good crystal? Why?"

"To celebrate the moment, a drink to the moment that will never come again? The glass will never hold a drink so important again?"

The small group around them quieted and stared at her. The girl, who probably had her first taste of wine, clutched her glass to her small bosom.

"It was an Earthan custom," Sedwy explained weakly.

Walker put his arm around her shoulders, and she felt warm and accepted, part of the group once more. An individual in this mix of individuals who were melded into a Family.

"Always knew our ancestors were crazy," Pink said. Chuckling, he carefully placed his glass on the table beside them. "Who else would go on a starship away from their home instead of staying solidly on the planet?"

Another small shock trickled through Sedwy. She was descended from Earthans who had psi power and had scraped together every bit of gilt that they had to finance the journey to and colonization of a new world. And every born FirstFamily person she'd ever met held the belief that their ancestors had been brave and right. Her mouth fell open.

Walker's brows lifted in question.

"Was your ultimate Celtan ancestor really the lowest maintenance tech on *Nuada's Sword*?"

One side of Walker's mouth slanted up. "Don't know. To our Family, the past isn't as important as the future."

"It may make a difference to the nobles. We need to understand what slurs we might be fighting."

Snorting, Walker gestured widely with the hand not curved around Sedwy's shoulder. "Is that so? Our past will outweigh our fertility?"

Feeling defensive, something that hadn't happened in a long time, something that shouldn't happen to a true scholar, Sedwy's mouth pinched before she said, "You don't know as much about nobles as you think."

He squeezed her shoulders again, spoke quietly. "I never thought I did." His eyes grew thoughtful. "You think the GraceLords and -Ladies I passed in rank will hold my Flair against me."

Seven

Sedwy replied, "Many GraceLords and -Ladies have held their titles since the first century of colonization. Yes, I do. Though since you have a GraceMistrys as a mother, they won't target you as much as your Family."

His arm dropped away, and he inclined his head. "Then we will fashion a way to protect my Family."

"Spoken like every noble Head of Household I've ever met," she said.

He turned a brooding glance on the joyfully singing, dancing, and celebrating members of his Family spread out through the inner courtyard. "We are not equal in our Flair. Some of my cuzes can just work the Flair tech that everyone uses." He rolled his shoulders, nodded with his chin at a caged-off area with a locking door. "Teleportation pad. A few of us can teleport."

"Why the cage?" She squinted. "And is there a slippery-shield on it so it can't be climbed?"

"It's too dangerous. The children can't resist the temptation to jump on the teleportation pad. We put another play pad in an opposite corner." He pointed. "And we have one inside in the play area, but that still won't stop the odd child from hopping on an unsecured pad impulsively."

Her throat simply closed. "That could lead to death."

"Yes, at the worst."

Something in his tone told her there was more to the story.

"What?" she asked.

"That reminds me, twelve of us, personally and individually, owe Guardsman Ilex Winterberry a favor. The man is married to my cuz Trif. Guess you should know about those favors."

"Yes. I should know of any debts to nobles, and he's a close connection to the Hollys and a GrandSir in his own right. What reminded you of that?"

Walker winced. "We had an incident of children bouncing on the pad when the light showed it was open for teleportation."

Sedwy gasped a breath.

"Thus, the cage." He cleared his throat. "I'll get the names of the offenders. I don't recollect each one, though I do know the oldest is seventeen and the youngest is seven. You'd better draft a list of items that you need from me, Family history, et cetera."

"Your birth certificate is the first," Sedwy said absently.

Walker flinched beside her. Then he grabbed her hand and hustled her into the darkest area of the courtyard, a small space beside a large tree with a seat around it. The area was black with shadow.

"My birth certificate," he said heavily. "I've never seen it. Now I know why."

His stress built her own. "I'm sorry." She knew he needed to talk the hurt out some more, waited.

"I didn't know my birth mother was a noble, a GraceMistrys, until I was told after my Passages. This morning."

Sedwy leaned against him, and his arm came around her almost absently. Unlike most nobles he had plenty of sisters, and she'd already noticed that the Clovers were the kind of people who touched often.

But she was pretty sure already that she didn't want Walker Clover to think of her as a sister. Still, he needed to talk, and touch, and she could be supportive.

"I always thought I was the son of Nath and Fen Clover. Didn't know m'father had had an affair before he and Fen married.

Didn't know GraceMistrys Latif Heliotrope was my natural mother."

His words held an edge of inner bile that Sedwy knew all too well. Family hurting Family. She struggled to find words, but he continued raggedly. "Regarding the birth certificate, I don't even know when I was born. Different than when I was told, for sure. My Nameday is in the month of Oak."

"A good solid month."

His laugh was short. "Probably why they waited until then."

She cleared her throat, put a load of sympathy in her words. "You finished your Third Passage and learned this information this morning."

"Yes."

Her legs simply gave out and his arm stayed around her as she lowered to the seat around the tree. Then he let go and took the three paces to the edge of the shadow and back. After a couple of breaths of silence, she said, "I'm shocked."

"I'll point out that my Family, the Commoner Clovers"—again the edge of bitterness—"weren't the only ones who kept their mouths shut. I never heard a word from the Heliotropes."

"Not that." She reached up and brushed his hand with her own; his fingers clasped hers and she tugged. He sat beside her. She couldn't really see his face in the dark, but could feel his seething emotions. "You Clovers are a tough bunch."

"Yeah." He let out a breath in a sigh. His head turned to watch a group of youngsters stream by, shouting at the tops of their lungs. "I was like that," he said.

"What?"

"Just one of the Clover boys, same as everyone else my age. With brothers and sisters. Now I'm not, and I'll be treated differently, even by my brothers and sisters."

"This new information for you," Sedwy said evenly, "must have been difficult to bear."

He just pushed out a hard breath.

"Your Family disappointing you."

She saw the rise and fall of the dark line of his shoulders in a shrug. The darkness and his pain and the circumstances pulled words from her. "I've been on the other side."

"What?"

"I've been the cause of huge disappointment to my Family."

He echoed her. "*What!*"

She gazed straight into his face but couldn't see his eyes, could barely note his puzzled expression. "A few years ago I was involved in a great scandal."

"I don't recall that. When?"

"Four hundred and five, autumn. The Black Magic Death Cult." She laughed and it wasn't as casual as she wanted it. She still hadn't gotten over being betrayed by a good friend, of having such poor judgement as to trust people who deceived her. "I study culture. At the time I was fascinated by the dark side of Flair."

"You weren't part of the cult. All but one of them were caught and died, and the one who escaped was a man."

"That's right. But they used my knowledge to craft their filthy rituals."

Walker's intake of breath was harsh. "My cuz Trif was targeted, nearly died on their altar. That's why you want to apologize to her."

"Yes. Apologize again, I talked to her after the tragedies. She was very gracious." She'd been very young and in love and had bounced back from the terrible events more than Sedwy could imagine. More than Sedwy had. "My best friend almost killed Trif, and I didn't even know my friend was bad."

A few more heavy breaths from Walker. When he spoke again, he still sounded angry and upset. "They used you."

He was concerned about her? Everyone outside of her Family was concerned about what the circumstances looked like.

"Yes, they used me. I knew nothing of their terrible activities. But my reputation was besmirched all the same. Since then I've been studying small towns." Another humorless chuckle. "I've learned a lot, written and published my studies, am considered a scholar, but not respected by anyone other than a few colleagues."

She lifted her chin. "But I earn my NobleGilt salary from the councils. No one can deny that."

"In 405 I was just hired by the Ashes to tutor Nuin. It was a busy time and I didn't pay attention to much else—until Trif was rescued and all was well."

"Then you rallied around with your Family."

"Yes, of course, that's what Family does." His arm came around her shoulders and he squeezed, and she was aware of the warmth of his body. "Your mother has rallied around you."

The hard ball of tension within Sedwy loosened a bit and she found her lips curving. She hadn't thought she would smile about her mother's interfering ways. "She only has the two of us, my sister and me. The other Groves that work in the Residence aren't close to us. So Mother tends to hover." She added something she knew Walker would identify with. "She takes her responsibilities seriously." Sedwy patted her carrier where Lucor slept. He'd played and was tired.

Walker looked into the courtyard, where the Clovers were getting even louder. Some of the young men had set up a wrestling match. They were beautiful. All of them. Beautiful in their numbers.

When he spoke, he'd changed the subject, and Sedwy was disappointed. "I suppose I might hear something from the Heliotropes now," he said.

"I'm sure they were informed by the NobleCouncil clerk when the results of your Flair testing was filed."

He stiffened beside her.

"We'll talk about how to handle that, too." She sighed. "As for your own mother and father." She chose her words carefully. "I think you did well when we met them."

"Thank you."

"Sooner or later you'll have to speak to them, and without anger entering into it."

"I know. But it's going to be difficult. They lied to me my entire life."

"They only wanted you to be treated like one of the Clover boys."

Air-splitting shouts rose and bounced around the walled courtyard as the final wrestling match was won and a boy stood up, sporting a bloody nose.

"I was always just one of the Clover boys. Not the strongest, or the brightest, or the fastest. I was happy with my job at the Ashes and my life."

He was talking in past tense; no matter how great the shock, as she'd said, the Clovers were tough. He was already moving on. That was good.

Then his tone sharpened and he sat straighter, looked at her. "So, Sedwy Grove, you're going to be my liaison and teacher."

"So it seems."

"What do you say to staying here with us?"

"What?" She was jolted to more awareness of him, the scent of him, a hint of perspiration added to his fresh-grass fragrance; his lean strength. Despite what he said, she thought he was a very strong man emotionally, and flexible enough to survive the blows of the day.

His hand moved in a wide curve. "Stay here with us. Observe us Clovers. You can document how a Commoner family changes into noble."

"Are you serious?" A thrill went through her as she thought of staying with Walker, relief at avoiding her mother. Those were emotional reactions and he was trying to appeal to her scholarship. She set her mind to follow his, and what she'd considered earlier. These were unique circumstances. The Clovers would be changing, their interactions, their Family culture. Fascinating.

"Yes, I'm serious." He eyed her. "My cuz Mitchella D'Blackthorn keeps some clothes here. There are others about your size. You could get a nightgown or whatever."

He didn't even want her teleporting home? She gave that an instant's thought. He might be delaying her report to her mother. She'd like to put that off until tomorrow, too.

"Stay tonight and for breakfast. I'll arrange a guest room—suite—for you."

"I suppose I could get clothes and my work tools tomorrow."

Walker lifted her hand to his mouth, kissed her fingers, and she felt it all the way to her core, a nice steamy, melting sensation. It had been a long time . . .

"Stay, Sedwy."

She wanted to ask if he'd come to her door that night. Thought he might not, and felt ambivalent. Yes, there was attraction, but they'd just met. The man had just finished his Passages—notoriously emotionally difficult—and three at once. She shouldn't be considering that they might have a nice bout of sex tonight. "Yes," she said.

He nibbled her fingertips and it felt far too good, then he carefully placed her hand on her lap and stood. "Thank you." His shoulders squared against the darkness.

"Mona!" It was a low call backed by Flair to a person who might have only minimal psi power. Sedwy was impressed at Walker's control, and not surprised when one of the young women she'd met earlier glided up to them with a smile.

"Here, Walker," Mona said.

"Can you have the southwest corner guest suite prepared for GrandMistrys Grove?"

Mona's brows lifted and she turned her smile on Sedwy. "Sure. Good to have you stay here. Welcome to Clover Compound."

"Thank you."

Mona nodded, looked back to Walker, and winked. "You know, Walker, I didn't care too much for that Reed guy."

"Your choice, Mona."

Her smile widened into a grin. "Glad you're thinking that way. Uncle Pink liked him fine. Bu . . . ut—"

"Yes?" Walker said.

"Both the Reed guy and the Alder man came, and I do like Japon Alder."

"Didn't Alder accompany Clypea here today? What of her?"

Mona shrugged. "She's given it some thought and isn't interested in being a noble. She'd rather have an exciting career. She'll be talking to you about that." Once again Mona glanced at Sedwy. "Walker should be able to place us to study with higher people as apprentices and journeymen and journeywomen, shouldn't he?"

"That will depend on how hidebound the noble is, but we'll see if we can make that happen." Sedwy hoped she wasn't just reacting to the Clovers' optimism.

"Excellent." Mona kissed Walker's cheek. "Walker's a very good guy. He'll be a wonderful GrandLord." Mona strolled away but made good time to the southern door of the courtyard, gathering a couple of other girls on the way.

Walker winced.

Once again the noise level increased, and Sedwy glanced over to see a bunch of young men around a crate in the middle of the courtyard. One of them was FirstFamily GreatLord Vinni T'Vine, along with Antenn Moss-Blackthorn. Vinni caught her glance and sent her a smile, and she moved slightly behind Walker. Vinni T'Vine was a prophet, and she'd heard that when he looked at you, he could sometimes see your future. She didn't trust his smile.

Then there was a huge explosion and gasps. A rainbow of fireworks bloomed in the now-cold air. They'd dropped the weathershield and she hadn't noticed. She shook her head, blinking away bright after-blurs. More loud pops and she flinched.

"You don't like fireworks?" Walker asked.

"Not particularly," she said. Suddenly the long septhours of the day pressed on her and she wanted to be alone in the quiet.

"We'll go to your room." Again he linked arms with her.

"Thank you."

Sed-wy. Pret-ty Sedwy.

She glanced at Walker. A faint smile hovered on his lips. *Walker Clover, are you speaking telepathically to me?* She knew he was. Was glad that he continued to try something new, even this late in the day, even after all he'd experienced.

Pretty Sedwy. His mental voice was light, teasing.

Handsome Walker, she teased back.

No, just one of the Clo-ver boys.

He'd managed to establish a private connection with her, no fumbling, no several tries to get it right. Impressive. Perhaps that was an effect of coming into his Flair at an older age and all at once, but more likely it was a function of his Flair for people. He'd been in her company for a full afternoon and evening, was learning her, had been watching her as she had him.

Did she dare comment on what he'd just said, dare to push him a little more? *Special Walker,* she sent mentally.

No, just one of the Clover boys.

No, Walker, she contradicted him. *Your skin is a slightly lighter tone than most of the Clovers, your hair has a different tint of red than other brown-haired Clovers. Most of all, your ears are different.*

"My ears!" he said aloud.

She didn't switch, better he get accustomed to mindspeech. *If you have one noble feature, it is your ears. They are fine, delicate, set well against your head.*

He flushed, including those ears. "We are going to the southern wall. We've been buying the land around us, and the lower south block was once a street. We petitioned to close it since it wasn't used much. It's part of the three-block-by-three-block area we own. Eventually we will encompass both south park and north grove within our buildings." He flashed a not very sincere smile. "At least that's the last plans I heard."

She settled the strap of Lucor's case across her body. They went through the southwestern door of the courtyard, angled through the corridors until they came to a wall that had once been an outside wall, but was now the north wall of the new southern block.

"It's top-of-the-pyramid construction," Walker assured her. "And borders directly on the park now. Of course we've landscaped the park, too."

She slid a glance his way as they climbed the new, elegant stairs. Spell-lights came on as they passed. Then they were at a gleaming and polished cherry door. She wanted to set her hands on his face, comfort him. Once again she realized how easy it was to be in his company, how she'd felt completely natural with him. Because of his Flair, or his innate manner, or his solid character and kindness.

Nothing deeper than attraction and affection, of course.

Now he was staring at her, his eyes an intense green with hints of silver gray.

She hadn't noticed his lips but they were fine, too, and coming closer . . .

His mouth was on hers and she withdrew her arm from his to wrap her hands behind his neck. He was warm and she was colder than she thought. His muscles were hard, and she felt softer than she thought. His kiss was demanding and his tongue ravaging, and she didn't think at all.

Heat enveloped her, and a strong throbbing need pounded within her, radiating from her sex, shivering her nerves, exploding in her brain. Lord and Lady, he felt good!

Eight

Then he was gently setting her aside, and they gazed at each other. Sedwy was all too aware that if the door had been open, they'd have made it to bed, and sex.

"I don't do this," she gasped. Her words were a little high, her eyes felt wild, her hair tumbled. Had he put his hands in her hair?

Yes.

And clamped one on her butt. She wished it were there now.

"Of course you don't." His voice was so patently calm and his features so fierce with yearning that she was able to yank her own calm around her. If she looked at him from the corner of her eye, she believed she could see the sparking of his Flair.

"I don't sleep with women after a few hours of meeting, either."

"Of course you don't," she echoed, blinked to clear the red mist of sex from her vision, drew in a deep breath to settle herself, ignored the demands of her lusty body.

This time she followed her instincts and ran her fingers down the side of his cheek. She'd also noticed that his overall bone structure was finer than most of the Clover men. "You *are* special, Walker, and despite everything, you'll be fine."

He inclined his head, took another step back, lifted her hand to his lips. His bow was perfect. He actually kissed her fingers, and the ache wound tighter inside her. Sweet desire. Kind Walker.

"Thank you. With your help, I hope so."

He turned on his heel and strode away. She touched the door latch and the door opened into an airy, high-ceilinged room of a pale blue facing south. The curtains were filmy white, nearly transparent. Beautiful. Welcoming.

Humming with pleasure, she walked into the sitting room. A corner was set up like an office with an elegant small cherrywood desk and built-in cubbyholes against the wall for recording spheres and viz spheres.

The door to the bedroom was cracked open, and she peeked in to see the walls were a darker hue and one wall a deep blue. That matched the silkeen nightgown laid across the thick and puffy comforter of the bedsponge.

Fragrance swirled through the suite. The usual fresh Clover note mixed with a heavier spice. She liked it. Putting Lucor's carrier on a twoseat, she whirled with her arms out. The last few years had consisted of cramped attic rooms in inns in the small towns she'd been studying. When she'd returned to D'Grove Residence, her small, round tower room had been a brownish rose with sturdy dark brown plush chairs. Not to her taste.

This was. The furniture must come from Clover Fine Furniture, of course, and the decorating must have been done by Mitchella D'Blackthorn. Perfect.

She pushed open the bedroom door, and low, soothing flute music lilted from a player. Trif Clover Winterberry's music? As Sedwy undressed and drew on the nightgown, her eyelids lowered with sleep. She slipped under the covers with heaviness on her heart. She still must apologize to Trif.

Walker was special. Sedwy smiled as tingles sparked along her nerves. He wouldn't come to her tonight. But someday . . .

Walker thumped down the corridor, his footsteps louder than he wanted. The brief spurt of energy he'd gotten from lust wouldn't last long. If he knew his uncle Pink, and he did, the elder would be wanting a talk right now—a report of the day, and a hashing of all that might be important. Walker was a morning person. Pink was not.

It took only minutes to run down the stairs, through the door to the old southern block, through that, and into the courtyard. Walker stopped a couple of meters inside. The fireworks were over and the younger children had been packed off to bed. No one but Clovers remained. The Blackthorn contingent and Vinni T'Vine had left. Walker's cuz Trif Winterberry and her husband were in her house. Walker was sure that he'd be having individual conversations with all of them, but not now. Good. Breath filtered from his lungs, then he inhaled mindfully, keeping the breath steady.

He noted his Fam, Argut, and Vertic fox were sniffing the walls as if for mice.

"There's my boy!" Uncle Pink shouted. Lifted a glass of ale. "To Walker!"

"To Walker!" everyone left in the courtyard shouted.

"Already we have alliances proposed! Four other contracts to read, three marriage nibbles for Walker, and a couple for the girls. Good work, boy." Pink downed the last of his ale and thunked the thick glass on the table. Then he rubbed his hands.

Walker gestured to Barton in a way he'd seen Tab Holly, the owner of The Green Knight Fencing and Fighting Salon, do to his heir, Tinne Holly. Barton raised his brows, obviously also recognizing the motion, then came over and fell in to Walker's left and slightly behind him.

"Time to talk, Uncle," Walker said pleasantly, but caution flashed in Pink's eyes.

"Sure, my boy." He made to slap Walker on the back, and Walker stepped away, keeping his smile.

"You can't have it both ways, Uncle. Either I'm the Head of this Household or you are."

Pink's smile turned to a baring of teeth.

Walker said, "Let's go to my suite." The western suite that he didn't like. And which was probably decorated in the manner

Uncle Pink considered appropriate for Walker. Which wouldn't suit him.

He waited until Pink huffed and turned, marched to the door in the western wing and up the wide stairs.

On the third story, Pink regained his usual manner and nearly swaggered with pride to the door in the middle of the wing. He threw it open.

Walker saw a violent explosion of bright green. Barton made a muffled noise behind him, a laugh, Walker was sure. He ignored it and followed Pink through the door of the sitting room to the nearest table. It was a round one that would seat six and was covered in a patterned green and gold cloth with little golden bobble fringe along the bottom.

Barton coughed and Walker sent him a mild gaze. "Sit."

"Yes, boss."

Pink frowned. Slowly he pulled out a padded green chair that clashed with the table and sat.

Walker sat, too. He stared at Pink. "Now. Think on whether you want me to be the Head of the Household or if you want to keep that job."

Pink gnawed at his lip.

Leaning back in his chair, a decent piece of furniture even if it did look lousy, Walker said, "First I'll say that I have no interest in running Clover Fine Furniture or any other businesses. I won't be handling or investing our funds."

Pink's breath whooshed out.

"I don't know if you've looked at my testing results?" Walker asked.

"I got them."

"T'Ash says that over the long term, I might rise as high as Captain of All Councils."

Barton choked. Pink's mouth fell open and he gasped like a fish out of water. Which he was. Which they all were.

Walker said, "So we need to decide if we want that great of status. With big status can come big problems."

"Envy, feuds," Barton said.

"That's true," Walker said. "In any event, I consider my job now to be networking with nobles. So we must discuss exactly what you want from individual nobles, the NobleCouncil, the FirstFamilies."

"First you gotta take your place in the NobleCouncil," Barton pointed out.

"Yes, and I have rules and documents to study and another test." Walker saw the centimeters-high materials on the shelf of the green-painted cupboard and nodded to it.

Barton's eyes widened. "Better you than me."

"And Sedwy Grove is going to school me in noble manners and culture," Walker said.

"Ahh." Barton wiggled his brows.

"You don't want the businesses?" Pink asked.

"No."

Pink's mouth pursed. "I've got a coupla more ideas for businesses." He shifted as if the chair was too small for his weight, but his face knit. "And we have some funds that we could invest, if we could get good advice or invest in projects with, say, T'Hawthorn."

Barton gasped. "Nothing like shooting for the best investor on the planet."

Pink nodded. "Yep."

"So, boy, what do you want?" Pink stared at Walker.

"First, I want you to stop calling me *boy*. Then, I want you to let me choose my own rooms. That won't be this suite."

"This suite is the most secure," Barton snapped.

"That may be true." Walker gave him a cool smile. "But I don't like the west side of the compound. I never have, and I don't see why I should stay here. You'll have to adjust."

Both the men goggled at him.

Barton whistled. "Who'd you copy that manner from?"

Walker couldn't afford to answer or crack a smile at his brother. "I understand security needs and I'm willing to have rooms modified for a suite on the top floor of the new south block of the compound."

"The new south block doesn't have an outside entrance," Barton considered.

"We can put a door in the east end of the block," Walker said. "And I want cuz Mitchella to consult with me on how to decorate my rooms."

Pink winced. "Woman has expensive tastes."

"I'll be entertaining and meeting nobles in my suite," Walker said. "Perhaps even FirstFamily nobles or Heads of Households. They'll expect the best."

Sucking on his teeth, Pink nodded. "There is that. All right. The third-floor south-facing rooms are yours. We'll start work on any modifications tomorrow."

"Cuz Antenn Moss-Blackthorn can design it," Walker said.

Pink scowled. "He's young."

"He's good."

"All right, all right." Pink gave in. "As for the Head of Household. We'll think on it."

"Think on this," Barton said. "Nobles dealing with us will want to talk to the Head, no one else." He glanced at Walker. "Sedwy Grove told me that, if she didn't tell you, Pink."

"Of all the formal offers of alliance, how many needed only your signature?" Walker asked.

Pink's mouth tightened. "None. T'Ash's needed only *your* signature."

"Cave of the Dark Goddess," Barton swore and sat straight. Slowly he turned his head toward Walker. "A formal alliance with T'Ash."

"He offered alliance just after he translocated my testing document to the NobleCouncil clerk. Who was there in T'Ash Residence." Walker smiled coolly at his brother. Now Barton knew how Walker felt about life spinning from his control. "It's been an eventful day. And you're the new Family Head of Security, formally now, not just informally. Responsible for all one hundred and ninety-nine of us."

"Cave of the Dark Goddess," Barton repeated. Walker knew he wanted to express a rawer curse but was constrained by Pink. Barton rubbed his forehead with finger and thumb. "This is terrible."

"Wonderful!" Pink said.

Turning the look of a warrior general on Pink, Barton laid it out. "Allying with T'Ash means we're also in an alliance with whoever he is in alliance with, most notably the Hollys, the Blackthorns, the Willows."

With a nod and rubbing his hands, Pink said, "All the up-and-coming young generation of the FirstFamilies. Good connections."

Barton leaned forward. "Yes, but if one of those Families gets in a feud-duel, like the Hollys and Hawthorns did a few years ago, guess who will provide numbers for the fights. We will. We are now their most prolific allies." Barton swung to Walker. "Did you sign the alliance?"

"Yes."

"Fligger. Where's the papyrus?"

"My office," Pink said. "On the corner of my desk."

Walker knew the dimensions of that office and that desk, even in the light of a winter night approaching Yule. In his mind's eye, he brought up the recollection of the sight of the papyrus, the aged color of it, T'Ash's bold scrawl in brown ink. Walker remembered holding the document, the smoothness of the sheet, the weight. He *found* it in Pink's office, and with a bang and a whoosh, it appeared, flying through the air.

Barton snagged the papyrus, bent a sardonic look on Walker. "Need a little work on translocation, bro."

Walker smiled slowly. "Spent much of my time working closely with Sedwy on teleporting."

"Nice." Barton grinned, then skimmed the alliance. His next breath was a sigh of relief as he glanced back up at Walker. "T'Ash was looking out for you."

"He does that." Then Walker considered. "Or he will for a while until he thinks I've found my balance."

Barton grunted, tapped a finger on the papyrus. "The language is good for us. It *doesn't* say, 'the Clovers will provide one-fifth of their Family as fighters.' That's usual. In a Family of five that would mean one person. In a Family like ours, it means—"

"Forty," Pink said, turning pale. "Lord and Lady Bless Us." He breathed heavily through his nose.

Walker blinked at Barton. "I'm not sure how you know standard language, but we'll check all the contracts and strike any such wording. Better have the alliance state something like 'an equal amount of fighters to the largest contingent of one Family's fighters.'"

Nodding, Barton said, "That should work. This alliance states we would 'provide an equal amount of fighters as T'Ash.'"

"Hell," Pink said, rubbing his forehead. "It's going to take all of us to figure this stuff out."

"Looks like," Walker said.

Pink drummed his fingers on the table, staring out the window black with night and framed in quilted green with darker green clovers embroidered on the drapes. "That lady, Sedwy Grove, might have helped us with that?"

"Probably," Walker said.

"You did well in inviting her to stay," Pink said. He slid a glance to Walker. "You like her, right?"

"And that gets us to the next item on my agenda." Walker smiled.

Pink narrowed his eyes, shot a thick finger toward Walker. "You're a lot tougher and more savvy than I knew. Been hiding your light in a barrel."

Walker and Barton exchanged glances. Another ancient Earthan saying that made little sense.

Barton snorted. "You think he hasn't handled the Ash children, the Ashes, and the Ash Residence without picking up stuff?"

"And you think Barton hasn't worked with the Hollys in a fighting salon that caters to the best of the best without also learning a few things?" Walker asked.

Pink's big shoulders slumped, and he gave a great sigh and sagged, trying to look like a pitiful oldster. It didn't work.

Both Walker and Barton kept quiet until Pink gave in and spoke. "All right, what else do you want, bo—Walker?"

"Why did you marry Aunt Pratty, Pink?"

The tension of wariness straightened Pink's muscles. "This has a bearing on Family affairs?"

"That's right. Answer the question," Walker said. Barton began to hum under his breath, a really irritating habit.

"I love your aunt. Did when I married her, do now," Pink said.

Walker nodded. "That's right. And why did Uncle Mel marry Aunt Alli?"

"Because he loved her," Pink answered.

"Yes, and why did my father marry Fen?"

"Your mother," Pink said.

"Yes, my mother who raised me, not the woman who contributed her genes." Walker was willing to concede that point. But the room and the atmosphere seemed to pulse around him, and he knew he was coming to the end of his strength.

"Nath's affair with GraceMistrys Latif Heliotrope was a passing thing." Pink waved a large hand. "No question of marriage on either side, and Latif and her Family were up front about giving you to us from the minute she knew she was pregnant."

Barton grimaced, then his face went impassive. Walker felt a blow, but it was muffled. Too much had happened to him today. "That's not what I asked."

Pink reddened. "Nath met Fen a couple of weeks after his affair with Latif, fell in love with her." He glanced at Barton, Fen's son, who must be closer to Walker's age than they'd both thought. They stared at each other.

Pink said, "It was real awkward all around for a while."

"Until I was born," Walker said drily.

"Yeah," Pink said.

"Why do most Clovers marry?" Walker continued softly. He'd like to wrap this up fast, not take a long and winding trail, but he intended to get what he wanted, and to do that, his progress had to be step-by-step slow.

"For love, boy," Pink said. "Best thing for the Family."

"I'm glad you agree with me. Which means you will leave the choice of my bride to me."

"You haven't shown interest in any particular woman," Pink grumbled. "Easy enough to fall in love with a Noblewoman as a Commoner."

Walker's smile was sharp. "My father didn't."

Barton cleared his throat. Not looking at either of them, he said, "Holm Holly's HeartMate story is still told in The Green Knight."

Walker tried to grasp for the tale through the thick fog of weariness, couldn't.

"Holm Holly, the heir to the Hollys, had to go through some bad stuff, grow emotionally, before he could match his HeartMate. Unlike most couples, they didn't connect during their Passages to free their Flair."

"That's true." Pink nodded.

"Did you hook up with a HeartMate during your Passages, Walker?" Barton asked.

At the thought of the dreamquests, misty images swam through the fog in his mind, and Walker knew he couldn't go on. He stood. "I don't know." He gave his uncle the hardest look he was capable of. "I don't know how many marriage offers for me you'll get. But *I* will decide who I will marry, when, and why." Turning his back on a frowning Pink and a surprised Barton, he used the last of his strength to stride through the door to the bedroom. The room's colors were a pale green and white, which made him think his mother—Fen, *his mother*—had something to do with it. He fell on the bed facedown and passed out.

The night had gone and the room was bright with reflected light from the windows when Walker swam out of dark sleep and gasped awake. He wished he had real sunlight.

His Flair naturally expanded and fed information to his mind. He felt every life-beat in the compound. All of those who made furniture in the workshops and attended the business office of Clover Fine Furniture were gone, left for the day's work. Nor was Barton here. He had early hours today at The Green Knight.

Walker's cuz Mitchella D'Blackthorn, the decorator, was in the new south block on the third floor along with her adopted son, Antenn, Walker's father, Nath, and Uncle Pink. Argut was in the kitchen.

Everyone else who should be here was. Including Sedwy Grove.

It pleased Walker that he could sense her and that she was in his house. A shudder of awareness passed through him as he realized he was possessive of the woman, the compound, the Family. He'd changed, would continue to change. His Flair would change him. He didn't want to. Tough. No way out.

His mother, Fen, tapped quietly on his door. He knew without thinking that it was she . . . something he wouldn't have last week.

Would he really have rather grown up in the Clovers with everyone else knowing he was different, had a mother who wasn't with his father, had abandoned him?

No. He could deal with that easier now. It didn't hurt as much this morning as it had even last night.

He was gaining his balance. He might not be the Clover he thought he was, but his character—the man he was and wanted to be—hadn't changed much with the revelations.

He rose and slipped on some loose and shabby trous and a shirt with blotches of unidentifiable stains. Opening the door, he looked down on the woman he'd loved all his life, all his memory. "Good morning, Mom."

Nine

She flung herself into his arms, sobbing. "Oh, my boy. My wonderful Walker." Her arms clamped around him and she cried, making him supremely uncomfortable.

He rubbed her back. "Come on, Mom."

"I-I l-l-loved you f-from the m-minute they p-put you in m-my arms."

He winced. She'd probably been pregnant with Barton with all those nesting hormones. Best not to say that, and why should that hurt him? She loved him, she was weeping hard all over his chest and looked like hell, pale and with circles under her eyes. He thought how he might feel if his child went through three Passages at once—long days and nights. Would he stay with him or her? Absolutely.

And he hadn't been anything like stable the day before.

"I-I'm sor-ry we did-didn't t-tell you," she wailed. Grabbed his shirt.

He held her and rocked. She was littler than he, now, had been for quite a few years.

"Most, most of-f th-the time I f-forgot you weren't m-mine!"

Time to man up. "I am yours, in all the ways a son could be a mother's." He kissed the top of her springy hair, light brown that masked some silver. "I love you, Mom. Now can we quit this? I'd rather have your help designing my new suite. You know they're meeting about that *right now*."

One last, surprisingly hard, squeeze from her. She snuffled and pulled a softleaf from her sleeve, wiped her eyes and blew her nose, looked up at him. "You never did like your belongings changed when you weren't around, like at grovestudy or your job."

"No."

Sighing, she shook her head. "Of all my children, I think you're the most set in your ways."

Walker would argue that, but not now.

She blinked wet lashes, stared up at him. "Maybe it's the Heliotrope in you. What kind of people couldn't accept a child into their Family?"

That punched him in the gut. He supposed he'd have to think about stuff like that now, no matter how much he didn't want to. "Bunch of snobs," he said.

His mother lifted her chin, nodded. "We always thought so."

He cleared his throat. "Have they sent any note—"

"No." Her voice was hard. "No voice message, nothing in the compound cache box, no scry. They don't deserve you, never did in the past, and certainly won't in the future." Her eyes gleamed; she straightened with pride and glowing face. Uh-oh. Expectations were falling on him like shards of glass, piercing him. "Captain of All Councils! That means even the *FirstFamilies* Council."

Walker swallowed. "Far in the future, Mom." He patted her shoulder again.

She drilled his chest with her finger, face set. "You can do it, Walker, and you can start right now."

He suppressed a scowl. Cast his mind, his Flair, outward. "Sedwy Grove is up, and people are still moving around in the rooms that will be my suite. I need to change and get over there." He grabbed his mother's fingers, pressed and planted a kiss on them. "Go and make sure they aren't doing anything horrible, will you, Mom?"

"Yes, I will." She headed toward the door, paused, with a little frown line between her brows. "What of this Sedwy Grove, Walker? We've recalled who she is and—"

"She was used, Mom. She and D'Grove were very gracious yesterday. Sedwy will tutor me for my"—he coughed—"future job . . . future. I need someone to do that."

His mother nodded. "You're right." She ran an eye down him. "Take a quick waterfall, shave, and dress in something that doesn't need to go in the rag bin." She frowned. "Didn't I throw those into the deconstructor?"

He'd saved them. "Mo-om, Pink and the others could be screwing things up."

She waved a hand. "Not your cuz Mitchella."

"Pink can overcome her. Did you *look* in there?" He pointed to the sitting room.

She winced. "All right, I'm going. I'll make sure no firm decision is made without you."

"Thanks, love you, Mom."

Her eyes filled again. "I love you, Walker."

She left the room and he rubbed his face, shifted his shoulders under the new weight of expectations and responsibility, and headed to the waterfall room, hoping to take a little time to make sense of his life.

Sedwy rose and scried her mother, who was pleased that Sedwy had been invited to stay with the Clovers and would have someone pack a couple of bags for her. D'Grove's face showed disapproval only when her new fox Fam made remarks in the background unheard by Sedwy.

She felt great. The rooms remained beautiful and serene, pleasing. Her own Fam was sweet . . . innocent. She hadn't been in the presence of a being so young for a long time. It was refreshing. So far she hadn't hurt Lucor's feelings, hadn't inadvertently been too rough with it physically. No matter how people tried, thoughtless words or gestures happened daily.

Both she and her mother had hurt each other the day before, as

Sedwy and Walker had inadvertently blundered into each other's emotional messes.

But today was a new day. The sun was angling into her windows—she'd slept later than usual—bright and beautiful blue white. The park below showed snow melting.

She would do better by Walker today. He was so much more than she'd imagined.

She'd met his type before in small villages that she'd studied. A man who had quietly shaped his life just the way he'd wanted it—and had enough character that he served as a model for others. He might not want leadership, but he wouldn't back down from a fight, and he would do what he believed to be right.

The Clovers were an exceptional Family to have raised a man like that. And she could see him fitting into many of the noble circles—a man with a calm and composed manner would be underestimated by some but prized by most.

Pink had announced that the Clovers were already allied with T'Ash. Sedwy was pretty sure she knew that web of alliances . . . and she could see Walker fitting in with that group, too. Men who had a code of honor, and the training to face and accept the consequences of adhering to that code of honor.

He could very well become the Captain of All Councils in a few decades; she had no trouble visualizing him as that leader. Maybe because, again, she'd seen men like him as town mayors.

She smiled. Now it was her job to prepare him, a worthy goal. One that would refurbish her reputation again as her mother had planned—she'd be seen as helpful, contributing to society by teaching a new noble member its rules.

Help! Help! Help! FAMWOMAN.

Lucor! Panic zapped Sedwy and the next moment she was down in the courtyard of the Clover Compound, spontaneously teleporting to her Fam. Dangerous, very dangerous.

He cowered under the shadow of a cat.

The female cat wasn't large, but she was showing teeth.

Sedwy scooped up Lucor and scowled down at the small cat, then wrapped her arms around herself. Lucor was a pulsating warmth. "What's going on here?" she demanded.

The cat was odd, not cat colored, but swirls of pastel rainbow colors.

Was just playing. The tinted cat lifted her paw and licked it guilelessly. Sedwy didn't believe her for an instant.

"What's going on here!" Another woman, heavily pregnant, waddled from one of the houses. After a couple of eye blinks, Sedwy recognized Trif Clover Winterberry.

Was JUST playing! the cat insisted.

"You do not intimidate guests," Trif said in Tones of Doom that the cat paid no attention to. Now she was washing her ear and staring across the courtyard.

He doesn't smell like a guest and this is MY house.

A growl echoed from behind Sedwy. She froze. Every rainbow-colored hair on the cat's body raised.

This is MY house! said Argut the FamFox.

No! the cat hissed.

Argut snapped his teeth. *MY FamMan is Head of Household. That makes ME the number-one FAM.* Argut narrowed his eyes. *Vertic told me so. And he told me of you, cat-without-natural-color-of-your-own, Greyku cat. He told me that you are Clover-Winterberry, like Vertic fox is Winterberry-Clover. But* I *am ALL Clover. This is MY house.*

Trif placed a hand on the mound of her stomach, smiled at Sedwy. "Vertic has a point, Greyku. You aren't all Clover."

I am a CAT. I am the best FAM.

"You *are* my best Fam," Trif soothed.

I am THE CLOVER FAM, Argut insisted. He pointed his nose upward at Lucor in Sedwy's palms. *And Lucor is my friend.* Again he showed his teeth. *If you play with Lucor bad, I will play with you bad.*

"Cave of the Dark Goddess!" The gate of the teleportation cage clanged shut behind Walker. He was rubbing his temples. "All the *noise.*"

"Good morning, Walker," Trif said. She stretched a little and kissed his clean-shaven cheek.

He looked wonderful to Sedwy, dressed in fine raw silkeen trous and tunic of light brown. He took Trif's elbow. "Let's move this inside. The weathershield is good, but it's still cool out here. Have you had breakfast, cuz?" He nodded to Sedwy. "And good morning to you, Sedwy."

"I'm afraid we need to get this Fam status issue settled." Trif sighed.

"Ah."

I am your Fam, said Argut, rubbing against Walker's leg.

Walker scrubbed the fox's head with his knuckles. "Yes, you are."

And you are THE Clover. So I am THE Clover Fam.

No! Greyku arched her back and hissed again.

You are a Clover-Winterberry Fam, Argut said.

"*The* Clover-Winterberry Fam, *the FamCat,*" Trif added. Her mouth was straight but humor showed in her eyes.

This is MY house, insisted Greyku. Her fur had risen, showing a strange swirling pattern of darker colors on the shafts of her hair than on the pastel tips.

Walker rubbed his chin. "Now I think this is a question worthy of taking to Danith D'Ash. Why don't we ask her to breakfast?"

"It's more like brunch time, Walker," Trif said.

"Danith likes a midmorning tea break," Walker said.

Greyku sniffed loudly, proceeded across the courtyard to the door of Trif's house, tail up and undulating. *I am the Clover Compound FAMCAT.*

Trif tilted her head, looking at Walker. "Well done, cuz."

"Thank you." The corner of his mouth quirked. "The status of the Fams of the Ash household occasionally fluctuated—if Zanth was on a trip with T'Ash or Danith. I've had a little practice."

Sedwy found herself meeting Trif's gaze and that woman smiled. "How much more difficult is noble status to negotiate with respect to Fam status?" Trif asked Sedwy.

"Walker can grasp all the nuances," Sedwy agreed.

Walker snorted.

"What?" asked Trif.

"T'Ash said yesterday that the councils were like a congress of cats."

Trif laughed and Walker's arm encircled her waist protectively.

Cats are the worst Fams, Lucor said. He ruffled his fur. *Housefluffs are the best.*

Now Argut snorted much like his FamMan. *Foxes are the best Fams, little mouthful.*

"Housefluffs are the sweetest Fams," Sedwy said.

I am the Clover Compound housefluff. Lucor's whiskers twitched, tickling Sedwy.

"Cave of the Dark Goddess," Walker murmured. "Come on, Argut, the elders are messing around in our new suite."

Yes, we must make sure the rooms are good, Argut said and loped toward the southern door.

Sedwy accompanied Walker and Trif back to her house, and as Trif was closing the door, their glances met—and Sedwy felt a bond unroll between them: women who had Fams, women who were living in the Clover Compound—women who cared for Walker.

Women who had been used by the Black Magic Death Cult.

Sedwy's breath caught. That was what Trif believed, that Sedwy and she had both been harmed by the Black Magic Death Cult—Trif physically and Sedwy emotionally. More, Trif believed that she had Healed faster than Sedwy.

Heat flushed through her, but she couldn't deny the woman's insight, as much as she wanted to.

"Did you have breakfast yet, Sedwy?" asked Walker. His gaze was fixed on her face, and she realized that she was wearing only the blue nightgown.

It's been a hungry morning, Lucor said, copying Argut's words from the day before. *I wanted breakfast.*

"From now on, we'll make sure that you have food in your rooms," Walker said. He took her hand, and she realized her fingers were cool.

"Maybe you can stay mostly in my suite," Sedwy said. She held the Fam up to her face so she could look in his big eyes.

Lucor's fur fluffed a bit. *This is a very big place.*

"That's true," Walker said, pride infusing his tone.

Sedwy blinked. Whether Walker realized it or not, he *was* THE Clover.

* * *

For the next two weeks, Walker's schedule cycled through the same things every day. Talk to Pink and the Elders. Wearing.

Train at The Green Knight Fencing and Fighting Salon—physically and mentally challenging. That place was *the* informal venue to meet the highest nobles of the land. Also, the nobles there tended to be the most active in the councils. He'd also been invited to two new social clubs—one all male and one both genders. These, too, he could handle, though he was more comfortable with the all-male club, not that he would reveal that to Sedwy or his cuzes Mitchella and Trif, who'd all sponsored him. A lot of conversation and politics went on during those casual get-togethers.

As well as the Yule parties. He found more invitations to parties, musicales, theater outings, and balls than he cared to attend—as well as more formal clothes appearing in his closet. Luckily there were only one or two robes he'd refused to wear. He guessed that his mother, Mitchella, and Sedwy were advising Pink on the clothes.

Then there were a couple of rituals he'd been asked to attend in GreatCircle Temple—New Twinmoons and FirstQuarters, but he wasn't ready to meld his Flair with others'.

Mostly he studied the thick book and papyrus for the noble test, with pointers from Sedwy. Quiet time. Wonderful. Studying was something familiar, something he might have actually done in his former life. The den in his suite was now the most comfortable room in the compound for him. The walls were tinted a warm yellow with gold tones, the chairs were furrabeast leather of a bronze brown color, the rugs were thick and sturdy. They were made by a subcontractor of Clover Fine Furniture in the south, supervised by the branch there.

He loved the discussions he had with Sedwy about customs and traditions, FirstFamilies, Commoner, Clover. He learned more deeply about the history of the space travel—frightful—the founding and building of Druida—fabulous—and various unspoken secrets, such as First Grove, the hidden sanctuary that only admitted the desperate—fascinating.

Family dinners were great, the time where he felt more like his former self than any other. He didn't sit at the head of the table, but at his own seat . . . with Sedwy beside him. Good food and conversations and keeping in touch with those of the Family who *weren't* having problems. Lots of fun.

And teleporting with Sedwy. Thank the Lady and Lord he had teleportation lessons with Sedwy. He wasn't sure how he'd have managed all the other changes in his life without her. Everyone in the Family treated him differently.

Pink and his mother and his father—and, all right, Walker himself—were waiting to see if the Heliotropes, his birth mother's Family, were going to do anything. Walker wasn't sure what he wanted there, either. Acknowledgment? Welcome? He was ambivalent and disliked that he wondered about them at all. Of course they must have known that he'd been raised to the nobility by now; the newssheets had screamed headlines throughout the whole damn planet. And they'd have been officially notified.

Nothing.

So he concentrated on his new life.

The two weeks unrolled moment by engrossing moment for Sedwy. Walker was an excellent student, and mastered the written material regarding a GrandLord's responsibilities quickly.

As for the Clover Family, even as Walker's suite was built and decorated, so did the Family itself begin to change. Sedwy tried to document each modification.

The women of the household began dressing better, and some of the public rooms were redecorated to entertain visitors who might be interested in marrying into the Family. Time and again, Sedwy would see wide-eyed nobles touring the compound.

Barton Clover transformed from a security-conscious member of the Family to the actual Head of Security for a NobleHouse. He walked straighter; his gaze scanned the compound for any problems, particularly when outsiders were there. His eyes took on the gleam of ambition as he began singling out more youngsters for a household guard.

From overheard conversations, she thought the Family furniture business was booming.

There were more discussions that she was a part of—anything to do with the FirstFamilies, of course—alliance contracts, a couple of marriage proposals, an offer of financial investment or two. All her knowledge of the nobles was mined, and she consulted with her mother now and again for the Clovers.

Some topics were thrashed out loudly at dinner—the Coat of Arms, the noble colors. Walker had made the whole thing a competition, irritating Pink, with the colors and the motto voted on by the entire Family. He, Sedwy, Mitchella, Trif, and Ilex judged the Coat of Arms, which was a good three-leaf clover Celtic knot. The colors were dark green and silver, and the Family chose *We Make Our Own Luck* as the motto. Completely appropriate for the Family.

Walker was growing into his Flair. She could almost see his psi power increase daily. When he passed his test, he'd be informally admitted into the NobleCouncil. The council itself had recessed for Yule.

Walker was growing in stature, too. His manner was altering. He'd been a diffident man, downplaying his skills the day she'd met him. Now his gaze was straight and penetrating and his bearing that of a GrandLord. Mostly because of the way people treated him outside of the Residence. He hadn't been well known before, not as well known as Barton, who had met more people as a trainer at The Green Knight. The nobles' lack of personal knowledge of Walker worked in his favor. He could step in as a confident, strong GrandLord.

And the more she was in his presence, the more there seemed to be a connection forming between them. She liked how he looked, enjoyed watching him transform into a GrandLord. The heated desire was still there, a sweet yearning tension between them that neither of them had acted upon. Yet.

Now and then she caught him looking at her, and time and

again, he glanced up to catch her gaze on his hands, or shoulders, or chest. His muscles were firming deliciously as he trained with Barton.

The morning Walker had scheduled his test, he awoke heavy-eyed and with the laws of Celta throbbing in his brain. He didn't think he'd had much sleep. That wouldn't be a problem for the test . . . but for the reward. He smiled slowly as he drew on the sleeveless tunic—no answers hidden in overbloused material. He *ached* for his reward. Sedwy in his bed. Not, of course, that he'd told her.

He'd begun to think of his life in terms of goals and rewards. Three meetings with Pink and the Family elders and Walker allowed himself to take Sedwy to Trif's music room for a septhour and listen to good tunes. It didn't matter that he'd become a project for Trif, too. She'd been assigned to do a series of songs about the Clovers, and a processional march for his investiture as a noble in the NobleCouncil. When he was in Trif's house, he could relax, even when her young son was around. As long as he didn't bring Argut. The fox and Trif's cat still didn't get along.

After he'd finished drilling and a practice test on the first half of the manual, he'd allowed himself a day off with Argut and Sedwy. Walking the streets of Druida and showing her the several locations Clover Fine Furniture was contemplating for the new storefront. Lunch at a fancy restaurant and linking arms with her to watch Argut play with other foxes at a den on T'Ash's estate—where Lucor met up with some of his siblings in the adoption rooms and also played. Where Walker got a septhour to talk to Nuin and wrestle with the boy.

But today was the big goal, and the big reward.

Ten

The day of Walker's examination on Responsibilities of a Head of a GrandHouse, Laws, Rules, and Regulations Pertaining to the Nobility had arrived.

Sedwy felt more nervous than Walker seemed. They met at breakfast in the kitchen and he ate a meal prepared by his mother, drank mint tea, and joked with others who were there, eating before leaving for work. He'd set the test scandalously early at WorkBell.

The NobleCouncil and FirstFamilies Council began work at MidMorningBell. A lot of the negotiations and compromises were hammered out late at parties or social clubs the night before votes.

She wondered idly how much Walker would change the councils; she had no doubt that he would.

Of course Clerk Monkshood would administer the test, and Walker had asked T'Ash to witness on behalf of the FirstFamilies, something neither Monkshood nor she had anticipated. Monkshood usually invited a lord or lady of his choice from the FirstFamilies to monitor. Sedwy would be there to monitor, too. Both Walker and her mother had requested her. Walker for moral support, he said; her mother to make sure she got a full report that *she* could pass on as soon as the test was done.

So they congregated in Walker's new den—a chamber that Sedwy could see hosting a Captain of All Councils. The walls were a pale green and the furnishings had discreet touches of gold.

Walker sat at an imposing desk that had been created especially for him, a workshop table and chair had been brought in for T'Ash, which he smiled at and settled into after a few words of welcome. Sedwy sat at another small desk and chair with her own work—notes on the changes of the Clover Family from Commoner to noble.

Monkshood arrived just as the elegant mantel timer chimed WorkBell, appearing cool in manner but a little wild around the eyes. From Walker's smile as he rose and greeted the man, she thought the clerk had been brought to the main door of the compound and through the courtyard full of Clovers to Walker's suite. Sedwy curtsied to the clerk. He nodded brusquely, with the hint of a sneer that she ignored.

"Let's begin. Are you sure you are ready, GentleSir Clover?" Monkshood asked.

T'Ash looked away from a suede pocketed pouch that he'd unrolled on the table. "He's a GrandLord; are you questioning my testing results, Monkshood?"

"Of course not." Monkshood coughed. He looked back at Walker, who wasn't as intimidating. "I have scheduled the full day for your test, until MidEveningBell. Does that suit you?" He set out a stack of papyrus and a special writestick.

Walker nodded agreeably. "Fine."

"You know, Walker, you don't have to do this," T'Ash said. He wasn't even looking at them, but fingering an emerald. "You can have three FirstFamily lords or ladies quiz you on the laws . . . say Straif T'Blackthorn, Holm Holly senior, and me."

Monkshood snapped straight, glared at T'Ash.

"I'm fine with this, T'Ash, thank you for the offer," Walker said. He smiled slowly at Monkshood, and Sedwy's attention sharpened. She hadn't seen that deliberate smile from him, must be a tool.

And it was effective. Monkshood relaxed, slipped the cuff of his outrageously bloused sleeve back to check his wrist timer. "Why don't we go in five minutes, then?"

"Good for me," Walker said and settled into the comfortchair that conformed to him. That piece of furniture wasn't made by the Clovers, but was top of the pyramid, like everything else in the suite. Understated elegant quality.

A knock came at the door, and Sedwy opened it to Fen Clover, who glided in with a large tray with three carafes, several cups, and a plateful of baked goodies. "Snacks," she said brightly. "Cocoa, tea, and caff."

"I don't think—" Monkshood started.

But Walker's mother had poured out a large mug of black caff for T'Ash and set it on the worktable. The scent of the drink had Sedwy's mouth watering. Monkshood weakened and Sedwy saw his gaze fix on a flatsweet with cocoa chips. Fen lifted the plate and offered it to him. He took the treat. "Thank you. Cocoa would be wonderful."

"You told us you might be here all day," Fen said. "There will be plenty of snacks, and, of course, you'll join us for meals."

From the corner of her eye, Sedwy saw Walker's jaw tense. They'd had several practice tests and Walker had told Monkshood that he wouldn't be here longer than MidAfternoonBell, which was much longer than any of their prep sessions.

"Food here is always great," T'Ash said. There was a little zip of Flair as he applied a spell to the emerald. Then he stood and took most of the cocoa chip flatsweets.

Walker coughed.

Sedwy said, "Thank you, Fen." Sedwy picked up the cocoa carafe and poured herself some. Monkshood's nose twitched.

Zanth, T'Ash's Fam, and Walker's Fam, Argut, strolled in. Dust fell from their fur and vanished as the housekeeping spell acted on their dirt.

Walker raised his brows. "Welcome, Fams."

Monkshood shifted from foot to foot, then took the caff carafe and filled a mug to the brim, took the mug and another flatsweet to a large chair with soft cushions and a table nearby. Sedwy was glad to see that he used a coaster for the mug.

Zanth smiled ingratiatingly. *Me want cocoa!*

"I actually think that fish would be better for you, Zanth," Fen said. "We have some fresh in the kitchen."

Zanth slid his eyes toward Walker. *Me here for Walker.*

"I appreciate that, Zanth, but would hate for you to go hungry for me. Perhaps you'd like to eat first."

We had good wrestle, Argut said. *I am here for my FamMan, too. But I will nap before I eat.*

"Come along, Zanth, let's leave these folk to their noble business," Fen said.

Me noble, too, Zanth said.

"Of course you are," T'Ash said absently as he worked.

I will nap on your feet, said Argut. *I like the smell of your shoes.*

Walker bent to rub a hand down his Fam, then scratch his head. "Thank you." He glanced at Monkshood where he sat. "Tell me when to go." Walker arranged the test slightly, and picked up the writestick.

Fen left the tray on a low cupboard at the end of the room closest to T'Ash, then swept from the chamber, Zanth trotting behind her. The door closed softly after them.

"Go," Monkshood said, tapping his timer.

T'Ash drew a polishing cloth from his pouch.

Sedwy sat and watched Walker begin to answer steadily, brows knit.

As the minutes ticked by, Sedwy became aware that only Walker was involved in his work. T'Ash did a few things with jewelry pieces but didn't appear wholly occupied. She made desultory notes on papyrus with a writestick, not recorded spheres that she preferred, and kept track of Walker's emotions through the bond that had grown between them. He was confident, no hint of panic. That let her take a few good breaths.

Argut snored. Zanth didn't return; she sensed he was too busy being admired by Clovers.

And two septhours later, Walker finished checking his work and stood. "I'm done."

Monkshood jolted, and Sedwy realized he'd fallen into a doze.

T'Ash snorted. "Good." He stood and stretched, and his joints popped impressively. He stared at the mantel timer. "Should be able to get us some results by MidAfternoonBell." He smiled at Monkshood and it wasn't nice. "Who'll judge the essays?"

"My mother, D'Grove," Sedwy said, standing and moving to the middle of the room. She wanted to hug Walker. She felt his satisfaction. He thought he'd done well on the test; she was sure of it. "I'll tell her to teleport to the Guildhall."

"I had already requested T'Birch read the essays," Monkshood said.

"Huh. I can do it," T'Ash said. "Right now."

Monkshood grabbed the papyrus and stuffed it in a case. A page fluttered to the ground. T'Ash picked it up, perused it. "Really? I didn't know that about the line of succession. Seems obscure to me." Instead of handing the sheet to Monkshood, he passed it to Sedwy. She skimmed the questions and the brief essays that Walker wrote in response. She and Walker *had* covered the material thoroughly, but T'Ash was right, the questions were about the intricacies of the law instead of general knowledge. T'Ash's big forefinger tapped the item he'd commented on. Sedwy nodded, smiled at Walker. "That is correct."

"Huh," T'Ash said again. He went back to his table and tidied up. "I didn't know that about what degrees of cuzes can inherit, but I bet Straif does. Think I'll talk to him and Holm about it. Holm probably knows, too. Not that I have cuzes, but my grandchildren will."

Now he looked at his wrist timer, nodded to Monkshood and Sedwy. "Think your mother can finish judging the test by MidAfternoonBell?"

"Surely."

Monkshood said, "There are blocks of the examination of specific data questions that I will process."

"Ah-hmm," T'Ash mumbled.

"T'Ash, let the man get out of here and back to work," Walker said. Sedwy heard him mentally call, *Zanth!*

"All right. But I want those exam results by MidAfternoonBell." Another wide smile with teeth from T'Ash. "For my testing files." He winked at Walker. "And for Walker's employment file and my alliance files."

Walker's eyes had widened. Sedwy was certain that T'Ash had minimal files.

Me here, Zanth announced as the door swung open. He sniffed. *Food is gone.*

"That's right," Sedwy said, "and T'Ash is about to leave."

"Right," T'Ash said.

"Rrroow," Argut said and trotted from around the desk. *Greetyou, Zanth.*

"I'll be going, now, too." Monkshood cast a disapproving glance at the Fams. He nodded to T'Ash and Walker. "Good luck," he said grudgingly to Walker.

He should have said that before, but Walker bowed—*slightly* a bit more than Monkshood deserved. Not enough flattery to be obvious, not a deep enough bow for Monkshood to believe he didn't understand proper status. That would have reflected on Sedwy.

Now that she thought about it, how Walker scored on the examination could reflect on Sedwy. She glanced at the small desk and her project. Her work was more important to her career.

"Later, Monkshood," T'Ash said. Zanth had leapt onto his shoulder and they vanished.

"Thank you for your time," Walker said.

Monkshood nodded stiffly and teleported away.

Walker rolled his shoulders. "Should have given him another flatsweet or two to take with him." He took a stride to Sedwy, placed his hands around her waist, and spun her like she was a girl. "We did it! I damn well passed that test, Sedwy!"

He plunked her down on her feet, and she was breathless more from his touch than the spin. She kept her hands on his arms. "I'm sure you did."

One of his shoulders lifted and fell. "Oh, I might have missed a few questions." His eyes narrowed in calculation. "Maybe four or five. Nothing like the fifty percent that would have me taking the thing again."

He kissed her. It was a jubilant kiss, a press of his mouth on hers, and it had the bond between them expanding wide and fast, joy running back and forth between them. Of course they'd kissed before, not quite every day, but now his mouth nibbled at her lips, his tongue plunged inside her mouth, and she tasted him—mint and a touch of caff from his drink. His arms wrapped around her and brought them center to center, and she felt his erection.

Argut yipped. *Time to play.* The fox butted their legs. *You said we would have special play today after test done.*

Walker pulled away from her, looked down at the fox. "You're right." His arm slipped around her waist. "We can go to that new restaurant that caters to people with Fams."

Argut yipped again, ran around the room in a blurred circle.

Sedwy winced. "I think your mother and your aunt Pratty have prepared a special meal for you, Walker."

His expression clouded. His hands dropped from her, and she missed the connection, the warm touch of his palms, his fingers squeezing into her hips. "Oh. Of course," he said.

"There will probably be a party tonight, too."

"Yes," he said.

"What's wrong?" she asked, feeling the joy that had been emanating from him diminish.

Again his shoulders moved, as if he was adjusting burdens. He smiled lopsidedly. "Not much. Argut, we're postponing the meal, but we *will* take the afternoon off." Walker glanced at the small desk with her project.

"I didn't get much done," she said.

"I know. Too concentrated on me."

She raised her brows.

"What? You didn't expect me to feel that? Or how T'Ash was putting more ambient Flair in the atmosphere while he was stone polishing in case I might need to use it?"

Sedwy blinked. She hadn't realized that.

Walker tilted his head. "Monkshood's back in his office, where he's more comfortable."

Sedwy *felt* her eyes widen. "You can tell?"

Walker shrugged. "I have a . . . thread to him now that we

spent some septhours together. You and I have spent time in the Guildhall and I know the floor plan and where his office is. I knew he teleported to his office and now I can tell you that he is more comfortable." Walker smiled. "As anyone would be." Then his brows knit and Sedwy understood that he was about to communicate telepathically.

Mother and Aunt Pratty, can we return my den to regular?

"I heard that," Sedwy said.

"Good." He took her hand in his, swung it. "We did it!"

"Yes."

Then he kissed her fingers, glanced at Argut, who had collapsed, panting on the thick rug. "Let's go eat and give my cuzes time to move out T'Ash's worktable and the desk for Sedwy."

"I still don't know why you had three small desks built, and areas made in this room for them to be moved in and out."

He stared at her, shook his head with a quiet smile. "I've visited several FirstFamily Residences lately."

She still didn't know what he meant.

"Sedwy, where does your sister, D'GroveHeir, work?"

"In an office off my mother's ResidenceDen."

"I'd rather have my heirs work with me."

Her throat closed and stomach clutched. She should remember he was all about Family. Of course he'd want his heirs close.

"Most Residences have a major ResidenceDen and smaller adjacent offices for apprentices and journeymen or journeywomen. I didn't know that when I first set up this block, but this will do fine until a more formal den and offices are built. And, of course, the compound will take centuries to become an intelligent Residence. It's new."

An image of Walker and three small children looking like him had hit her, along with a great yearning that was . . . inappropriate. She hadn't thought of having children for a long time. Of course, when she'd first started her career, she'd planned to be married by now, and perhaps with a child, but after the wreck of her life, she'd had to concentrate on her career.

She blinked and cleared her throat, withdrew her fingers from his—had he noticed the leap in her pulse?—and slipped her arm in his own, just as a brief knock came on the door and it opened to show four Clovers ready to rearrange the furniture.

"Thanks, guys," Walker said.

"Won't take long," the burliest replied. He touched the worktable and initiated a built-in anti-grav spell. The table rose a few centimeters from the floor.

The youngest man, recently adult at seventeen, wiggled his shoulders as he smoothed a hand over the chair. "T'Ash actually worked here. I can feel it."

Walker's eyes narrowed. "Maybe you should be tested by him."

Flushing, the young man said, "I'm not like you, Walker. Mom's a Commoner, and I didn't have any Passages."

"But you have more than ordinary Flair," Sedwy said. "I feel it."

He flashed her a smile. "Maybe my kids will have really good Flair, and be tested."

"Maybe," Walker said, knuckled the youngster on the shoulder as they passed. "Think we're having an early lunch, come join us when you're done."

"All right. This won't take long," said the one in charge. All of the excess furniture brought in for Walker's examination was floating.

She and Walker left the room and walked down the wide hall with pale yellow-patterned silkeen on the walls. "Lovely place."

"Yes. It fits the image," Walker said.

"I hadn't heard of the office block."

"We're still discussing in which direction to expand," Walker said. Before they turned a corner, he glanced over his shoulder. The other men were moving in the opposite direction. They headed into the short western arm of the new block. Walker stopped in front of the door that would lead to the more populated part of the compound. He was frowning.

"Monkshood doesn't like me, and the numbers of my Family makes him nervous."

"Monkshood doesn't like many people."

"He's a GraceLord himself, right? His Family has been noble for centuries."

"Yes."

"So I've passed him. He won't be easy on the Clovers. We need to talk about this, Sedwy."

"Let me think on options." She leaned against him. "Time enough for problems tomorrow, let's celebrate today."

Walker's smile was slow and deliberate and made her heart thump hard. A smile she hadn't seen before, perhaps one just for her. The bond between them was wide and strong. She shouldn't allow it to be so wide or so strong, but it felt wonderful. His smile was that of a lover, and her body responded. Kisses would no longer be enough.

Eleven

Walker couldn't wait. Though the Clover women had made all his favorites for his meal, it wasn't what he was hungry for. He wanted Sedwy. Now.

He was pretty sure he could have her, if he could only find the right place. It had to have ambience. It had to be out of Clover Compound so that they wouldn't be interrupted. Some of the more Flaired members of his Family had learned to mindspeak with him, and didn't hesitate to shout to him telepathically if they wanted him. He needed to work on that. But not today.

And as much as he loved Argut, they had to ditch the fox. A real ditch might work.

As soon as they finished eating and he thanked his mother and others, he grasped Sedwy's hand. "Let's take a walk."

She stared at him. He grinned at her. "There's plenty of snow on the ground, but the temps are fine—and someone taught me how to make personal weathershields."

Her body eased, and he realized she hadn't loosened up since the exam.

"We deserve a day off," he said, squeezing her fingers. "Let's go."

"Bundle up," Fen said, then beamed at Sedwy. "The neighborhood is wonderful to walk around."

"And we own most of it," Walker said drily.

Sedwy laughed, pulled away. "Let me get my outdoor gear." Her lashes slipped down over her eyes, then swept back up. "There are various ways of arranging personal weathershields. Sometimes I like to leave my head out."

"Hats and scarves," stated Fen. "Flair for weathershields takes energy, and you don't want to run out and not be protected."

Walker glanced at the large plate that he had cleaned of food. "I don't think that will be a problem."

"You were stoking up after *spending* energy on the test," Fen said.

He couldn't win this argument with his mother, and besides, she was right in thinking he wanted to expend a lot of energy with Sedwy. "I'll meet you at the door in five minutes."

Smiling, Sedwy nodded. "I'll be there."

Walker went to the corner of the room and made sure no one was around, then teleported to his bedroom, using about as much energy as if he'd run flat out from the kitchen to his suite.

Once again he opened a closet door and saw none of his favorite coats. These were all long and sleek and made of expensive materials, probably had some spells woven into the fabric, too. Warmth, anti-wet, others. He fingered the cuff of a dark green one, pulled it out. It was definitely stylish. Narrowing his eyes, he thought his cuz Mitchella D'Blackthorn was responsible. And he'd bet that none of his older coats were anywhere he could find them.

More change.

There was a fast rap on his sitting room door, and Sedwy opened it. "Walker?"

"I'm ready," he said, pulling the coat on. It sure wasn't one he'd be wrestling with his cuzes in. Surely the women didn't throw *everything* away. He'd have to ask Barton. Barton was getting fashionably upgraded, too, and could be sneakier about finding out where their stuff went.

As always, when he saw Sedwy, his problems lightened. A very good feeling.

She was dressed as elegantly as he, in a black cloak with gold trim and a jaunty hat that covered her ears.

He stepped out into the corridor, drew her arm through his, murmured a spellword to lock and shield the door. Argut zoomed down the hall. *We are going out!*

"For sure," Walker said.

I like the snow, and I have been stuck IN.

"Thank you for staying with me so we could bond these last two weeks."

Argut glanced up with a smirky smile. *I love my FamMan.*

And I love you, Walker returned mentally. He didn't need to speak the words aloud to Argut, the bond between them was large, and the Fam could feel Walker's wash of love.

The bond with Sedwy was nice-sized, too. He was aware she liked that he was happy when he saw her.

Instead of going into the old southern block, he held the new door in the eastern wall open to the stairs so she could precede him, and Argut could roar past and down.

"They did a very good job putting in the staircase," Sedwy said, her free hand stroking the fancily carved rail set into the wall, though there were also anti-fall spells in the stairwell. No one wanted nobles visiting Walker hurt.

"When you continue to enclose large areas with houses, you learn the trade." He bent near her, let her hair scented with a fragrance that reminded him of a forest glade filter through him. "I'd like to show you something special of the Clovers." The tickle of his fingers on her palm was as much a signal of desire as the pulse of red yearning through their bond.

He was rewarded by the heightening of pink in her cheeks, a deepening of her blue green eyes to more blue. Which only fueled his aching. Her fingers clung to his.

Life was good.

Argut yipped and his claws scrabbled against the heated flagstones as he danced before the door. No pet entrance in the impressive three-meter-tall and two-meter-wide oak door.

Sedwy gestured the security away and they were out into a brilliant winter day. The snowy drifts of the park before them were trampled with the evidence of a large den of foxes.

Walker nodded to the guard at the door, then called the head of the fox den telepathically. *Vertic?*

I am here today, the fox replied.

Good, Argut needs some good exercise.

Of course, Vertic said. Argut had sped to the elder and was crouched and hopping before him, teasing him to play.

Vertic gave a quick bark and other foxes leapt from concealed ditches. Most of them looked Argut's size or a little larger. They rushed together and tumbled down a snowbank.

Vertic, Sedwy projected so Walker and all the foxes could hear her.

Yes, lady? the elder asked.

My mother has a female Fam who wants a mate.

Vertic's ears flicked. *Grove den?*

Yes.

With a dignified inclination of his head, Vertic replied, *I will tell my dog foxes.*

"Thank you." Sedwy bowed.

"Thank you." Walker bowed, too.

Vertic gave a fox-chortle in absent agreement and trotted off to supervise—or play himself.

The whole thing reminded Walker a lot of the Hollys and the melees at The Green Knight, though he wouldn't tell his brother Barton that.

"Come," he said, and tugged on Sedwy's hand to stroll north on the wide, cleaned Clover sidewalks.

There must have been something in his tone, in that one word, because he got a throb of heightened sexual desire from her. The air suddenly felt less cold and more crisp as his skin heated.

His voice dropped to an intimate whisper. "I don't think you've seen the inner portion of the Clover Sacred Grove." She'd celebrated the last two weeks of rituals with her own Family. He wondered if she'd accept an invitation to their huge and cheerful Yule ritual.

"No," she said, sounding breathless.

"It's in the north block we're enclosing. Centered in a small labyrinth." He chuckled. "We are generally an impatient Family, so my cuz Mitchella insisted."

"And she got her way?"

"She's a FirstFamily GrandLady and she paid for the construction and the spells."

"Ah."

Walker said, "I've heard walking a labyrinth with someone special is a . . . unique . . . experience." He'd heard that if the two were lovers, every pace wound desire tight. He was looking forward to that. Right now their bodies brushed with each step.

When they reached the middle of the block and the main door to the compound, Walker nodded to the guard. One guard today. After the formal results of the examination were announced, he'd be a GrandLord. No way back from that. He shoved the thought that had dampened his sexual urge aside, greeted the guard as they passed, and strove to recapture the moment.

Sedwy tickled his palm with her fingers.

That helped. He picked up his pace and then they were in the next area to be enclosed, the northern block that they'd been landscaping into a park and a sacred grove. In the middle of the wide block was a circle of trees. Like other high priorities for the Family, they'd paid a GrandLord to help them grow. Their branches were bare, but the underbrush the Clovers had also planted blocked any view, as did the outer circle of beautifully shaped pine and spruce. Some of those trees had been potted Yule trees for the Family.

There were grasses and flowers all along the first two meters of the park, then the labyrinth began, opening in the east. Walker was surprised to see that there was a path through the snow to the labyrinth. Obviously people had been using the meditation tool. A small, warm bloom unfurled inside him. He wasn't the only one anxious about the future. And he should have come here—and the sacred grove—before. On the other hand, he was glad he was sharing this first time after his Passages with Sedwy.

He wasn't quite sure the last time he'd used the labyrinth alone. He'd had no pressing problems or challenges in his life. So he was growing. He could have done without that.

They stepped into the pathway together, one large enough for two. The Clovers were a loving Family and built on the basic unit of a couple.

So they crossed through the snow to the beginning of the labyrinth path. In the high summer, this was short, green grass. Now the grass was brown and flattened—but a slight, earthy hum radiated through his feet, and he stopped, astonished. He could *feel* the Flair in the path . . . and as it rose through him, he knew what it was. It was one of the spells funded by the great Family rituals, where cheer and energy poured out from the Family to an intricate web of spells and Flair that kept the Clover Compound going. Walker wasn't sure how it worked. He glanced at Sedwy, whose eyes were sparkling and lips were open as if she tasted the magic. Her fingers clasped his strongly.

She was the most beautiful woman he'd ever seen. He cleared his throat. "Ready."

Her lashes lowered, covering any reaction showing in her eyes, but her cheeks had pinkened, and he didn't think it was because of the cold or the wispy breeze. He thought it was because of the pulsing bond between them.

"Yes." Her gaze traced the rounds of the path before it curved into the grove. "This is wonderful. Yes, I'm ready."

He found himself smiling, and they took the first step together, and their bodies continued to brush.

"The labyrinth was my mother's idea, she insisted. She and my father attended the first Great Labyrinth Fair a couple of years ago."

"You are an exuberant and outgoing people, so she wanted it as a tool for quiet spirituality?" Sedwy asked.

"No," Walker said. His steps matched Sedwy's. "We were growing as a Family. She wanted it for the community. A tool for each member to experience outside rituals. Any of us can come and walk the labyrinth—and meet anyone else." He smiled. "I've met my cuz Trif's husband and his Fam, Vertic fox. And a couple of youngsters who were set on the path as anger management." He frowned. "I'll have to be more aware of each individual now, so we can help them find their joyful profession. And how much Flair each might have, what type, so they can be taught." He lapsed into brooding thought, but that lasted only a few steps until Sedwy bumped him with her shoulder.

"Appreciate the day."

He stopped, so she did, too. "You're right." Standing tall, he stretched every limb except the hand that held hers. "Mindful meditation. Clear the brain. Lady and Lord knows it's stuffed full of too many Celtan rules and regulations and laws."

"They can be boring," she agreed. "But I'm sure you passed the test and you won't ever have to do that again."

"The heirs to the FirstFamilies don't have to take this exam." It was the most common complaint he'd heard when he'd asked around the small—the very small sampling, mostly Danith D'Ash—of people raised from Commoner to noble. There were protests on file.

"No," Sedwy said with the heavy sympathy that she'd used every time he'd mentioned it.

"The people who marry into the FirstFamilies don't have to take this exam." He'd pointed that out to his cuz Mitchella D'Blackthorn, who'd just fluffed her hair to tease him.

Sedwy said, "But most noble children are drilled on the material. That depends on their Family and their training. My sister was trained by Mother. And I'll bet you anything you want that Laev Hawthorn could quote those laws word by word and with punctuation."

"Um-hmm." His shoulders had tensed. He pushed aside the notion that Sedwy was more in line with his parents than with himself in her basic beliefs. She firmly believed in ambition and drive to fulfill that ambition. He would always have preferred to have lived a quiet life, part of a whole, doing what he liked and not going after some external goal of fame and power.

But they both believed in doing their duty.

As they walked in silence, the peace of the land—his land, Clover land—worked on him. He was a child of the city, they all were. But the elders had been canny in claiming the area. Celta had been built by the Colonists with their strange machines, a great city laid out and enclosed by a wall. But the Celtans hadn't thrived as much as their ancestors had anticipated, and land was available for people with an eye for growth and development.

Within a decade this labyrinth would be private, and the Clover Sacred Grove part of another courtyard. A special treasure.

He asked, "What of other small communities? How many of them have labyrinths?"

"Not many. The art colonies, Mona Island and Toono Town, of course. And Gael City has three."

"Have you studied that aspect?"

"Touched on it, perhaps, but it's an interesting idea."

"To be studied after The Rise of a Commoner Family to Noble Status."

She slid her head against his shoulder. "I can report on what occurred with you Clovers, but not extrapolate. Your Family is unique."

"Every Family is unique. Every *individual* is unique." And every individual should be allowed to follow their own dreams—whether they were ambitious or not.

"You certainly are," Sedwy said, and just those three words had him realizing that as they'd walked, their bodies had leaned toward each other. Every step was leading to making love. Suddenly his sex was as hard as a rock, his blood had pooled in his lower body, and that's what he wanted. No thought about how he and she were different, just how he and she would come together. Soon.

Lowering his eyelashes against the brightness of the sun, the white reflections of the snow, he drew air into his lungs. The scent of pine and fir and snow that meant Yule. The holiday was coming and he'd been too busy to enjoy the season.

The path turned inward, was flanked by trees, and they walked in the quiet, ever aware of the throbbing bond between them, the unspoken knowledge that their long desire for each other would soon be fulfilled. That the bond was so large should have concerned him. It didn't. Worldly ambition might be beyond his understanding; risking all for his heart wasn't.

He was linked to her and the Family, and, oddly, this land.

When they got past the evergreen trees and circled into the deciduous grove itself, and the large center of the labyrinth came into view, Sedwy gasped. "What is it?"

"Not one of those fancy pavilions you nobles have." Walker smiled as he looked at the white ovoid. "It's a bubble, a material construct and not a weathershield, though it has spells to keep it warm and cozy. We take it down during the nice part of the year and major holidays. This Yule, the whole Family might gather, even those in other cities might return home. So we'll invest in spells." He flexed his biceps. He *knew* that he might have to be the one doing the weathershield spell casting, that it could be hard work, work of the mind, but his body reacted anyway. "It's very nice inside."

Last time he'd been in it, there had been thick rugs and huge floor pillows like a casual ritual room, along with a small altar. "And it's private. Not many people come here during the workday."

Sedwy tilted her head. "I think I've heard of such shelters, but I've never seen one." As they drew closer, Walker noted that the flaps over the windows were rolled up on the inside. Like the bubble itself, the windows were oval. Though he liked the idea of making love in the sunlight, it would probably be a good idea if he closed them.

They continued the last few rounds of the labyrinth, but Walker didn't meditate. His blood flowed hot, his body remained hard, and all he could think about was how he'd make love with Sedwy.

Each breath he breathed in the fragrance of her, each step their bodies touched, hip or foot or shoulder. Their steps matched, and he knew when their heartbeats matched. Faster than normal for both of them.

Then they were there, and he touched the seam of the door flap and murmured the spellwords to unshield it, pump up the heat. "Open to the Clover Heart." The bubble had a simple recognition spell. Only Clovers could open the door. He lifted one side of the flap and stepped in and onto a small area of flagstones, heated enough to convert the snow on his boots to melted water. As soon as Sedwy was in, he sealed the door, let her look around for a few seconds before he turned to her.

"Will you love with me here? Now?" he asked. He'd tried to make the words romantic, hoped his husky tone was sexy. He'd had affairs before, of course, but none that were important. Making love with Sedwy was vital. His own emotions and the link between them confirmed that.

"Yes," she said. Since her reply came out on a quivering breath, he was reassured.

Twelve

His hands went to her face and framed it. "So lovely," he said. "So damn beautiful it makes my heart hurt."

He lowered his mouth to hers. Her eyes had dilated wide, and when she closed her eyes, he closed his. There was scent around him . . . of the last Family ritual of New Year's, Samhain. It had been a cold autumn. The spices of the new year mixed with the smell of Sedwy and were perfect. New relationship with a woman. Perfect.

They'd kissed before, but now he pressed his mouth harder against her lush lips, his tongue probed deeper, rubbed against hers until her flavor filled him, sinking into his blood pulsing with desire. This time he wouldn't have to stop. This time he could enjoy every slide of skin against skin, every touch, and know he would have all.

He'd caught some of her hair under his palms, and it was thick and silken. Then he wrapped his arms around her and pulled her body to his to feel her, sex to sex. Only to be thwarted by his thick coat and her cloak. He broke the kiss and raised his head. "Too many clothes." His tongue was thick. He was usually a good talker, but words were sliding out of his brain.

So he gulped air and stepped back and touched the Celtan

knot–design clasp at the throat of her cloak. He unlatched the pin, then had to steady himself so he could unbutton the fancy frogs. When enough of them were open, he widened the top so she could step out, and she did, gracefully. He watched every move of her body. All beautiful, all to be cherished in memory. The angle of her head, so, the gesture of her hand.

He hung the cloak on a rack and jerked his thumb down the tabs of his, opening it. He shrugged from it and threw it at the rack.

"Let me help," Sedwy said. "Clothes off!"

And they were naked and he couldn't pull air into his chest at all because she was everything he'd ever loved in a woman. Nice shoulders, full breasts slimming to her waist, rounded hips, and a slight curve to her stomach. He swallowed hard, aware that his cock was big and hard and more erect than he could remember since his teen years. "You look like the goddess."

She pinkened all over. It was wonderful. He particularly liked how her rosy nipples tightened.

"You look like the god," she said.

He shook his head, knew that wasn't true. He still felt lanky, though he was moving better and had added muscle with regular sparring. He was too lean for the depictions of the god. "No," he said. "I'm just Walker Clover."

"GrandLord Clover."

That meant nothing to his lust-fogged brain. All he recalled was that he had to go as slowly as possible so he'd impress her and she'd want to lay with him over and over. This couldn't be a one-shot deal. He closed the space between them, noted a nice, soft, fat pillow from the corner of his eye. Good.

His hands went to her breasts. No! He was supposed to take her by the hand, lead her to the rug and the pillow, sink down onto it. But he couldn't release her breasts. His thumbs rubbed the little peaks, and she arched to him and moaned, and all thought in his head vaporized.

He swung her up into his arms. *Now* he felt like a god, holding a woman. *This* woman. His woman. No, he wouldn't let her go easily.

"Walker," she whispered.

He bent his head and claimed her mouth again, lips redder than her nipples, swollen from their previous kiss. She opened her mouth and welcomed him in, and she was warm and slick and wet for his tongue, and he wasn't touching her marvelous breasts and he needed to. He took the four paces to the pillow and the rug, lowered her, followed her down. Her neck was cradled on one arm, and he brought up his other hand to weigh and cradle her breasts, treasure them with teasing caresses.

Not enough. He had to see those wonders up close, taste the tips. So he moved, and set his hands around her waist and lifted . . . She moved, too. Her legs twisted and her skin slid against his skin and his sex. Then she slipped right on top of him. Intimately. Sheathing him in her body.

He couldn't prevent the groan, and after it was out, had trouble drawing air in. She wiggled on him and that brought a gasp.

She laughed. "You look so surprised." Her tender expression was all he saw. She kissed him, nipped his lower lip.

He plunged and her head tilted back and whimpers of need shuddered from her.

Lust flashfired in his veins and the link between them, and he had to have her. His hands settled on her round hips and he squeezed. He was going high and taking her with him. He drove into her, and the hint of ecstasy trickled through him.

Her fingers curved over his shoulders, her nails biting into his back, and the little pain slid like the rarest liquor through his veins. Last thread of control broke and he surged, grabbed her hips and forced her to ride, to move the way he wanted, needed. To rotate and angle, and then she screamed, and low sounds came from his chest, but he didn't hear them break from his mouth because he was soaring through bright blue sky to the white blue sun. She was with him, a fiery phoenix, and she squeezed him, and then he was exploding and his pleasure went on forever, like sunlight over the land.

He hit ground again, and it was a jarring thud when he knew he loved her. Truly loved her. No woman before her existed in his memory, only the feel of her now, and the dark knowledge, thick as blood, that she could leave him and take his heart with her.

Then sound did thrum against his ears and he heard his own ragged panting . . . and her continuing little moans of completion. That was good. Almost reassuring him that she would stay.

The air in the bubble had heated until it was as warm as a summer's day. The scent of their sex wasn't as strong as the herbal freshening spell that had been released by their perspiration.

"You are one wonderful man, Walker Clover," she said.

"You are a goddess," he replied.

She laughed as he'd meant her to. She was all too human, he knew that, but she looked and felt like a goddess to him. Raising her head from where it rested on his shoulder, she said, "Very special man." Her voice was sleepy and that pleased him. He'd satisfied her; they'd tired each other. He hoped it wasn't just that she'd had a difficult time sleeping the night before, as he had.

He stroked her hair. "Let's stay here awhile." Out of the natural flow of the world, any pressures and expectations. Soon enough to take up those burdens when they left.

"Sounds wonderful," she said, then she shifted her head to look at him, and her eyelids raised slowly. Her eyes were a foggy turquoise, more blue than green. "You're an extraordinary lover, Walker."

"Just did what came naturally," he said.

She laughed again and it seemed to wake her a little. She rolled off him, and that was a loss. He pretended it didn't matter by stretching, heard a few joint pops and winced. That was romantic. What else could he do for her?

"We have some liqueurs in the no-time." He didn't care that they were for rituals and special occasions. *This* was a special occasion.

"Lovely," she said. Then sat. Her breasts swayed and his mouth dried, his body began to stir again.

"Someone's coming." Sedwy laughed.

Walker scowled. "Lady and Lord, it's a workday morning."

"I think that it's NoonBell."

"Hell."

Sedwy raised one of the window flaps with a spell couplet. "It's your cuz Trif and her husband, Ilex Winterberry. They look loving."

"She's nearly ready to give birth!" Walker was outraged. He should have had a lot more time with Sedwy.

She laughed again. "That may make intercourse out of the question, but otherwise . . ."

He raised his hands. "Don't need to know. And we don't need to meet them." And, damn, the inside of the bubble looked as if people had rolled around and had vigorous sex.

Sedwy lifted her arms and spun in a circle, chanting a short housekeeping spell. The rugs smoothed, pillows plumped, and nice floral fragrance banished the last scent of sex. Walker nearly growled. He wanted time with Sedwy. All her attention.

He grabbed their clothes, then stood behind her, clasping his arms around her more tightly than when they usually teleported. "On three," he said. Then he murmured in her ear. "I want you in my bed tonight, Sedwy."

He felt her heart bump under their twined arms. "Yes," she said.

"And every other night."

She swallowed. "Yes."

"Is anyone there!" called Trif. At the same time, Walker felt the brush of her husband's Flair.

"One, Sedwy Grove. Two, pretty woman. *Three*."

There was the brief sense of darkness, of motion, then they were on the small teleportation pad in the corner of his bedroom. He dropped his arms and turned Sedwy so he could kiss her again, a kiss of promise. "And I want you to attend Yule with us."

"Yes," she said.

Walker's scrybowl played the dignified notes that Trif had programmed on it. Walker glanced at the colors being projected from the water into the air. He didn't know those . . .

"It's the Guildhall!" Sedwy hurried from his arms. With a few Words, her clothes were on. Walker yanked on his tunic and trous. "Monkshood." She stood by the bowl and waved. "Come *on*!"

So much for his private time with Sedwy. It would always

be like this, he knew. Moments stolen from his life. The most precious moments. He wanted her, always. But would she stay with him? And who would she love, the GrandLord or Walker Clover?

That night Walker enjoyed the party much more. People didn't treat him any differently—or he was fitting into his new place in the Family—it wasn't as raucous as the one two weeks before, and he danced a lot with Sedwy. Then he took her to bed and they made love a couple of more times before they slept well in each other's arms.

They were resting after morning sex, and Sedwy studied him, appreciating the view. He lay loosely sprawled in the bed. He fit there. But she'd seen his small original room in his father and mother's house. He'd fit there, too. "You have no ambition," she said. That was the lack she'd felt in him.

He gave her a half smile, his eyes still sleepy. "I beg your pardon?" The words were casual.

"You have the potential to rise to the highest seat in the land, the Captain of All Councils. Become the first person other than a FirstFamilies lady or lord to be Captain. Yet you don't want to."

He sat up, his face hardening in that way that told her he was more than irritated, that hurt was mixed with his anger.

"*Potential* is not a word I care for. It has been bandied about far too often in my life, with others supplying their own definition in relation to me."

"You don't want to be Captain of All Councils."

"No. Why should I?"

"Because you would be good at it?" she asked.

He gave her a disbelieving look. "Just for that reason?"

"I don't think you're lazy. You work hard. Have worked hard, for the examination, to fit in with the nobles. To conduct yourself the way a man nobly born would."

"Thank you very much for that." He got up and pulled on his loincloth and trous.

"I'm sorry," she said.

"No, you're not," he replied, slipping on his shirt and fastening the shoulder tabs.

"You just confuse me."

Brows still lowered, face still set, he threw her a look. "In what way?"

She felt a trickle of relief. Just like herself, if Walker was asking questions, he wasn't going to walk away immediately. But maybe it would be better if she tried a different approach. "You've been a teacher. Wouldn't you have wanted Nuin to reach his highest level?"

Walker jerked a shoulder. "He will."

That hadn't worked. "You know he will."

"Because he wants his Flair, wants to be GreatLord T'Ash." Walker gave her a straight look. "That will make him happy. That's what I wanted for Nuin, for all of my charges, always, that they find and pursue the dreams that make them happy."

"What of your dreams?" Sedwy asked, but it felt as if her blood pumped leaden in her veins.

"My dreams were simple. To be a beloved part of the Family, one of the Clover boys. To teach. My dreams are gone." He faced her now. "What are your dreams?" He didn't sound as hurt or angry. Resigned.

She hurt for him but answered his question with a smile that she knew was crooked, and a helpless opening gesture of her hands. "Travel, an excellent career, a family someday. They seem to be changing." She wet her lips, knew she would trod on another shaky topic. "Change is not necessarily bad."

"No," he said. He wasn't looking at her now. "But it always must be handled, and I'm working hard at that now."

Her own words back at her. She ached. Because she'd hurt him and herself and she still wasn't satisfied. Swallowing, she murmured, "I've always believed that a person did the best they could in life."

"Which would mean fulfilling their highest potential," Walker stated.

"Yes."

"Whether they wanted to do that or not."

She was quiet, grappling with the fact that someone wouldn't want to be the best they could be, wouldn't work hard to do that.

"I had goals, and I worked toward them and achieved them. That was enough for me." He straightened blouse and ankle cuffs, checked himself in the mirror. "I look like a GrandLord." His smile was twisted. "My Family will be pleased at breakfast."

Thirteen

By the time he finished breakfast, he was set in the rut of duty. Sedwy had decided to work in her own suite. He told himself he wasn't disappointed.

So he began his new job, *GrandLord*, signing the other contracts he, Pink, and the elders thought were appropriate. He also worked on the other forms. The Application for Noble Name, Coat of Arms, Motto, Heraldry. So now he added the graphics papyrus of the Clover Celtic knot, and the motto—We Make Our Own Luck—and sent the packet to the collection box.

Then he drew his birth certificate, the Verification of Life papyrus, and looked at it, mouth tightening. Naturally he'd glanced at the sheet before when his father had stoically given the papyrus to him. He'd been born at NobleClass HealingHall with a third-level Healer attending. Everyone else in the Clover clan had been born in the compound, attended by a third-level Healer, as was every Celtan's right. The Healer had verified the birth and the parents. Uncles Pink and Mel and Aunt Pratty had been witnesses. No other Heliotropes than his mother.

There was no oracle seal, so one had not attended his birth to read his character or prophesy his future. Maybe Walker might have been spared the last three weeks if an oracle had indicated he'd experience Passage and become noble. Maybe not. But he was resolved that every other child born, starting with Trif's, would have an oracle in attendance.

The Family might be able to work a deal with Vinni T'Vine, the FirstFamily lord and an honorary Clover, to act as oracle. He made a note of that, glanced once more at his Verification of Life, reading that he was born four months earlier than he'd been told all his life. The timing would have shown him that he couldn't have been Fen's son. Then he tapped the document, adding a "return to the Family collection box after copied" spell, and sent it off with the Biography for the NobleCouncil. It had taken a lot of time and effort to make a Family tree, but they did manage to go back five generations to the first woman who escaped from the old Downwind slums and called herself Trifolia Clover.

He stared at the stacks of papyrus on his desk, as restless as a seven-year-old. In his previous job, Nuin Ash would be antsy by now and they'd take a break . . . walk down to the stream on the estate and look at it in the snow. Hell, make snow angels. Something.

Walker was stuck at this desk, and the title sat heavy on his shoulders, inescapable now. He'd have to grow accustomed to the burden.

And he should consider finding a schedule he could live with.

Sedwy opened the door. "Forms all submitted?"

"Just."

She smiled, shook her head. "I really like this ResidenceDen."

"It's an office," Walker said. "We don't live in a Residence. The Clover Compound won't become sentient for centuries."

Sedwy raised her brows and Walker rubbed his temples. "Sorry."

"Something wrong?"

He'd been avoiding the next item at the top of his box. Gesturing her to sit, he took the piece of papyrus. His request for an apprenticeship of a Clover boy at a GraceHouse had been rejected. The letter was full of thinly veiled insults. Sedwy was regarding him with those big, beautiful blue green eyes of hers, so he had to explain.

"My cuz Amos had his heart set on studying with GraceLady Lettuce, who is doing some underwater research." Walker rolled his shoulders. "Even if I somehow convinced her to take Amos on, she and her household would make him miserable." He couldn't keep his jaw from clenching. He threw the heavy piece of papyrus—overly ornate—into the deconstructor. "So that option is gone. We'll find another for Amos."

"The Hazels," Sedwy murmured.

"What?"

"D'Hazel's consort, T'Hazel, is of the Rowan Family. His Flair is associated with the ocean. He's a scientist studying tide pools. He hasn't had an apprentice for some time. I think he'll be thrilled."

Walker hadn't known any of that. Might have spent days talking to others to find that out. How could he do without Sedwy? "We would not have aimed so high."

"You need to." Her voice was firm.

Walker jerked his head at the deconstructor. "How do I stop that from happening?" He wanted to pace but figured that was a lower-class habit he needed to break. "I *know* my Flair is stronger than GraceLady Lettuce's."

Sedwy leaned back in the chair, and the sunlight angled across the curve of her bosom. Walker didn't allow himself to be distracted . . . much.

"The Lettuces have been noble since the third generation after the Colonists."

"Much longer than the Clovers."

"Yes."

"But they are weaker than the Clovers."

"Her Flair and her Family is weaker than yours."

"We'll start having more Flair."

"I'm sure you will. But there is one thing that you might do to gain more respect."

He sat up straight. "What?"

"All of the FirstFamilies have ceremonial Family swords." Her words came carefully placed. "In case of surrendering during a feud."

Walker grunted. "Sound like real weapons to me."

"They are that, too. But many other GrandHouses and GraceHouses, even some established right after landing, don't have Family swords. Swords count."

Walker grinned, knew it was fierce, didn't care. "And I know the best weapons crafter in the world, T'Ash."

"T'Ash," Sedwy agreed.

As if he'd heard his name, the scrybowl pulsed insistently with T'Ash's colors and a tune that Walker had just decided he couldn't live with.

"Here," Walker said.

T'Ash was scowling. In the background, Walker could hear Nuin screaming. "Your cuz was supposed to be here, taking care of Nuin by now."

"Travel from Gael City is slow. He was on Family business. I told you that, T'Ash. You need to learn to discipline your son."

"He has his mother's eyes," T'Ash mumbled. "I can't look at those wet eyes and . . ."

"Take him on an outing to the stream . . . Nuin's FamFox is thinking of denning there in a while."

T'Ash pushed away from his desk. "All right." He bent a stern look on Walker. "We need to talk to you tonight after the open melee at The Green Knight."

Walker hadn't been intending to be pummeled that night at the fighting salon. "We?"

"Your allies; we're meeting."

Dread coated Walker's stomach. "All right." From the corner of the eye, he saw the deconstructor with a bit of the rejection letter sticking out. "I'd like to speak with you, personally, too."

T'Ash smiled. "Fine. Later. I need to take my son for an excursion." He signed off.

When Walker faced Sedwy again, her brows were raised once more. Not in rebuke this time, and her eyes gleamed with interest. "The allies. Nice." She smiled.

Walker's heart thumped hard. He'd do almost anything for that approving smile. Just how far would he go to please her?

* * *

The minute he teleported onto the pad at The Green Knight, Walker realized T'Ash had lied. There had been something slightly off about their scry. Now he stepped off the pad and used his Flair to sense everyone in the building.

T'Ash and his allies weren't in the main area. They were in a smaller room, Sparring Salon Three.

Walker nodded to the Holly cuz who stood at the reception podium, then continued across the entryway to the corridor that led to the private rooms. A couple of doors later, he was in Sparring Room Three.

"Told you," T'Ash said to the other men lounging in various poses on the rolled mats lining one wall. All of them were of the FirstFamilies. T'Ash and Straif T'Blackthorn, Walker's former employer and cuz by marriage, were heads of their Families. As was Saille T'Willow. Of the two Hollys, Holm would one day be T'Holly, and Tinne Holly managed The Green Knight. All were excellent fighters.

Walker inclined his head, keeping the new impassive expression he'd mastered on his face. His family might all be Commoners. His mother might be a weak Noblewoman, but his Family had set their hopes upon him to elevate the family to nobility. He had that duty, and that pride.

T'Ash smiled at him, and warning bells rang in Walker's mind. He knew that smile of his former employer. Challenging.

Walker straightened his shoulders. He'd challenged T'Ash before—and won. Granted it was with regard to the education of T'Ash's son. But a battle nonetheless.

"Your Flair has been tested and you've proven to be GrandLord status," Holm Holly said. "We are pleased to welcome you into the ranks of the nobility and to offer you a seat on the NobleCouncil."

"I hear a *but*," Walker said.

"When you allied with T'Ash, you allied with all the rest of us, since we have also allied with him."

Walker knew what was coming. It seemed to him that his life

had become nothing but a series of tests. He strove to forestall it. "Tinne and Straif know my level of skill."

"You haven't tested with me lately." Tinne smiled.

"Like hell. I tested last week." Walker aimed a withering stare at Straif. "And I wrestled with you *last night*."

Straif grinned and spread his hands, then said, "Man up, GrandLord Clover."

Walker snorted.

"The matches between you and the rest of us will be chosen by lot," Tinne said.

"Do I get the choice of weapons?" Walker asked

Tinne raised a brow. "Weapons? Surely."

"Blunt swords."

Tinne and his brother Holm exchanged looks. Then Tinne pushed a panel aside, revealing practice swords. He stood back for each to choose.

Sweat trickling down his back, Walker paid great attention to weight and balance when he picked a weapon. Ever since he'd decided to ask for a sword to increase the Family's status, he'd considered that if he did, the Hollys would test him. Then there were the laws of the city. A noble had to be certified to openly carry a sword. If he did this right, he wouldn't have to test again—two rules, one test. Hopefully.

Walker stood in the middle of the floor and prayed.

Fifty minutes later, Holm Holly was helping Walker to his feet after "beheading" him. Walker's mind still spun from the shock . . . and his imagination had provided images of what he'd now be looking like if the fight had been real. Holm had killed him in under three minutes—the quickest time. Walker had actually beaten Saille T'Willow, one small kernel of pride. Walker's brother, Barton, had shown up and made terrible groaning noises that had distracted him during most of the matches.

Still, Tinne Holly was nodding in approval as he walked up to take the practice sword from Walker's limp fingers. "I'll certify you as competent to carry a sword." He buffeted Walker on the shoulder. "You didn't forget everything that G'Uncle Tab taught you."

Walker grunted.

"We'll shower, then head out to the social club," T'Ash said. "Good going, Walker."

Walker's mind didn't actually settle nicely back into his brainpan until he was sunk in a deep leather chair with his fingers curved around a mug of excellent ale.

There had been some chitchat as they were led to the private room and got their drinks, but now the atmosphere changed. He became very aware of the fact that all of them had powerful rank and wealth and Flair, and most were older than he by a decade.

Tinne Holly stared at Walker, swept a hand indicating the group. "Everyone else knows that my wife and my four-year-old baby girl have received personal threats from FirstFamily GrandLady D'Yew."

Clashes between two great sets of allies in the FirstFamiles. This was bad.

"The time has come to remove D'Yew from her title," Holm Holly said. "D'Sea, the mind Healer, suspects she is lost in madness. No Healer has been allowed in her Residence for the last two years. *We* haven't seen her in at least a year."

Straif T'Blackthorn studied his fingernails. "She hasn't attended a FirstFamilies Council or participated in a FirstFamilies ritual in that time. Hasn't managed her obligatory duties of six in three years." His smile was ironic. "The same charges that were leveled against me, cuz Holm."

"You weren't mad," Holm said.

"No, just obsessed," Straif said. He shook his head. "I'm not sure about this."

"Then there's the question as to whether to declare the Yew Family dead altogether," Tinne said.

Holm said, "She'll fight this to her last breath, and she's vicious."

That statement hung in the air like thunder about to release lightning.

Continuing, Holm said, "The conservatives in the council, the generation even older than my father, remain strong. The Yews have always been conservative. We'll have to be careful of

T'Hawthorn. He has great influence, and right now he seems to be leaning toward that side."

"It's a terrible thing, removing the title from the lord or lady holding it," said Saille T'Willow. "Much better if it could be done internally, within the Family, though that is rough, too."

Willow would know that, Walker thought. He was cognizant of all the major stories of the FirstFamilies now. Willow's Mother-Dam had been mad, too, and he'd taken the title from her.

"We don't know what's going on in the Residence or the Family." T'Ash shifted in his chair, obviously uncomfortable with the whole discussion. But Walker knew his former employer. The man was dedicated to ensuring the FirstFamilies Council was a good and honorable body. With good and honorable members, unlike the strange and mad D'Yew. T'Ash continued, "Last thing I heard, she wed with GrandLord Capit Valerian. He's since died, but they have a daughter."

"Poor child, growing up in that Residence," T'Willow said.

"The FirstFamilies aren't the ones who have final say in this matter," Straif T'Blackthorn pointed out, "All Councils must vote, and that means we need more support in the NobleCouncil."

Their gazes focused on Walker. He suppressed a shudder. First-Families politics didn't get any dicier than this.

T'Willow said, "D'Yew is my enemy, too."

"Can we count on you, Walker?" Holm Holly asked.

Walker stood, met the steely gazes of the men. They could do untold harm to him if they cancelled their alliances, to his Family if they let it be known that Walker and the Clovers could not be trusted.

"I must think about the issue." He knew he wouldn't allow a Family to be declared dead. At that moment his calendarsphere popped into existence, chiming, "Daily review with Pink Clover in twenty minutes," it announced.

Stiffening his spine, Walker met Holm Holly's eyes. Difficult, but he couldn't afford to waver. "I need information. Can I see the medical reports and any reviews? Also the last events that D'Yew has attended and any votes she has cast on the FirstFamilies Council?" Sounded reasonable to him.

"Surely." Holm stood, too, offered his hand. His smile was like a shark's.

Walker clasped arms with Holm. The man's wrist timer buzzed. So did Tinne's. "Our wives are expecting us," Tinne said with evident relief. He met Walker's eyes. "D'Yew is a dangerous madwoman, Walker."

Walker remained standing until all the others except T'Ash had left. T'Ash's face was stony. "I don't like people threatening children."

"I don't, either. A moment of your time, T'Ash."

"All right."

"I need a sword," Walker said.

Fourteen

Sure," T'Ash said, just that easily. "Got something in mind?"

Walker thought of the sword in his Passage—the sword that was his Flair that he'd claimed. Nothing like he'd ever seen a noble carry, nothing like the sword that Uncle Pink wanted for show, or Barton wanted in case of a fight. T'Ash was incapable of forging a poor weapon, so it would be good. And, finally, something *Walker* wanted.

He took the papyrus and drawstick that T'Ash offered. "I'm not good at this."

T'Ash put a hand on his shoulder. "No, you had Nuin learn sketching from me. But you're good enough, just not inspired." He thumped Walker. "You're good with *people*."

Walker outlined a regular pointed shape with cutting edges, then concentrated on the handle. There had been a winged beast—neck wrapped around the hilt. Instead of a heart pommel, he made it the head of the beast. The wings angled down—

T'Ash's finger tapped at the blade. "What kind of blade is this?"

"Any kind, it doesn't mat—" Walker caught himself, smiled. "The best blade. My skill doesn't do justice to it. I'm not good with blades, so I will leave that totally in your hands."

T'Ash grunted. "Uh-huh." But his brows lowered in concentration, so he'd already shrugged off the half insult. He'd conjured another piece of papyrus, and began drawing rapidly. "State of the art," he murmured. He measured Walker with his glance, then shook his head. "Too many different body types in the Clover Family. Hard to judge. Can't forge it just for Walker, but as a race, we are becoming taller . . ."

Walker focused on trying to get the beast handle right. T'Ash was done with his beautiful blade before Walker had finished his hilt. Now he tapped his drawing, the wings. "These are the most important, looking like, um, long scales and curved down for quillions."

T'Ash stared at them. As his finger traced up from the quillions to the grip of the twined neck and the pommel, his brows went up and up. When he met Walker's eyes, his own held humor. He clapped Walker on the shoulder again. "Walker, my friend, what *were* you drinking?"

Walker felt himself reddening, couldn't help a stiff tone. "Passage, T'Ash. I had this sword in Passage."

"That explains it. I've never seen such a fantasy hilt." T'Ash gathered the papyrus, studied it. "What say I refine this the way I think you meant it to look, and what I know I can craft? Get it back to you in a coupla septhours. That do you fine?"

"Very fine." Walker offered his arm for a noble arm-to-arm clasp. T'Ash gripped hard but not with all his strength. More than Walker could have managed before his training, though. "Thank you, T'Ash."

"'Welcome. I'll let the Hollys, the FirstFamilies, and the NobleCouncil clerk know that Clover Family will have a sword and you were tested and certified to carry." T'Ash still frowned at the drawing, angling it back and forth as if that would make Walker's lines clearer. Maybe it did—in T'Ash's brain.

"Wait," Walker said.

"What?" T'Ash asked.

"Let me send you an image." Walker gestured to the chairs.

Again T'Ash's brows winged. "All right." He settled in with a grin.

Walker went back to his chair, too, leaned against the tall back. He closed his eyes and visualized being atop the mountain again, the sword needing to be claimed. The gleam of the sun on the golden handle, the beast . . . The blade was too shiny to show forging marks. He sent the image to T'Ash. It was easier than he'd anticipated to connect with the man.

"No engraving on the blade?" T'Ash asked. He sounded disappointed.

"No," Walker insisted. There had been Flair, but that wouldn't apply. The vision dissipated and he opened his eyes.

"All right." T'Ash stood. He shook his head. "Passages. Very strange things."

"Yes."

Again they clasped arms. Without another farewell, T'Ash teleported away.

Walker was left in the empty room that showed incredible wealth in every detail, a chamber where the highest of the high planned on guiding their society. He couldn't say that he felt easy or that he belonged—but he thought he could come to feel that if he continued to associate with his allies.

If they didn't throw him out of the club and cancel their contracts because he wouldn't do what they wanted him to.

He drank down the last of his ale, and 'ported to the corner of Uncle Pink's office.

Where things got worse.

Pink was there, so were his parents, and his cuz, FirstFamily GrandLady Mitchella D'Blackthorn.

Argut had told Walker he preferred to play in the courtyard. *They have a new plan. Those haven't been good for us.* Walker could only agree.

Mitchella seethed with excitement. Before he found his chair, she said, "I'm giving you a ball." She beamed at him. "T'Blackthorn Residence is *the* most beautiful FirstFamily Residence. We haven't had a fine ball for several years. It will be *the* winter ball, talked of all Yule season. With Straif's Flair, we can pull it off in four days.

That's fast, but everyone is curious about us Clovers, so I don't think anyone will send regrets. Clover colors, silver and green . . ." She stared into space.

"All the ladies of all the Families who have contacted us about marriage proposals will be there." Pink was beaming, too. And rubbing his hands.

"I don't want a ball." Walker's voice was louder than he'd anticipated and jolted Mitchella out of dreams of decorating and success. He glanced at the stacks of papyrus on Pink's desk. The pile of marriage contracts had gotten larger. The first couple of days, he and Pink had "discussed" each one, but then he'd been avoiding them. The rest of his life was devoted to being a GrandLord. He didn't want his marriage to be business.

He continued, "I especially don't want a ball if it's going to be like I'm a glittery Yule prize."

Mitchella was flushing.

"I'm sorry, Mitchella, but that's how I feel. You got to wed your HeartMate." Walker gestured widely. "Everyone else in the Family married who they wanted."

Pink scowled. "And you're having an affair with Sedwy and want to marry her?"

Walker straightened to his full height, taller if not wider than Pink. "That's my personal business. Not any Family social-climbing business."

"I think I'll be going now," Mitchella said brightly. At the door, she turned and said, "Sorry, Walker, but the invitations have gone out. A couple of septhours ago. We—I—we didn't know you would dislike the idea." She hurried from the room.

Rage splashed in his brain, turning his vision red. He shook his head to clear it.

"Walker," his father said quietly, reaching up to put a hand on his shoulder. Walker was taller than his father, too. "It could be just like my affair with Latif."

"No," Walker said flatly, shrugging his father's hand off. "From what I understand about that, neither of you were serious."

"Oh, Walker. You shouldn't have gotten serious about Sedwy. You know she loves her career. And she travels," Fen said.

Walker found himself clenching and releasing his jaw muscles. Bad habit. New bad habit. One that was visible. He'd think about that later.

Pink sat behind his desk. His manner was calm, but Walker knew he was flustered from his high color. He said, "I grant you that Sedwy Grove is the daughter of a former Captain of All Councils, but D'Grove's influence isn't major. T'Reed, the financial wizard, has expressed interest in marriage between you and his Daughter'sDaughter. And Sedwy's reputation is smirched and will always be so."

"She was used!" Walker said.

"Doesn't change appearances," Pink retorted.

"I won't make an alliance based on what you want."

"No? What will you do? Leave? You'll never leave the Family, Walker. Never shirk your responsibilities."

"And you think you can control me that way?" Walker jutted a chin at the papyrus. "I'm sure that you will need my signature on any contract, my willing permission for any marriage."

"Don't issue ultimatums to me, boy."

"You were the one who began the escalation of this argument."

"Don't you see," Pink said, his eyes clear and matching Walker's gaze. "The higher you look for a bride, the more solid the marriage, the more solid our status as a Family. You know as well as I do that people resent us—Commoner and noble. You owe this to us, to your Family."

Walker wanted to say that his allies were already the best, but he couldn't, not now when he didn't know they'd stay his allies.

"No," he said. He wanted to teleport away, had the energy to do so, but that would be another strike against him in this battle with his elders. "No."

He went straight to his rooms, stripped, and put both his fighting clothes and his new, rich casual clothes in the cleanser, trying to keep his mind blank. Under the waterfall he acknowledged the threats on two levels. The one with the nobles gnawed at his gut, the one from his elders shot splinters into his heart.

When he entered his bedroom, he was dismayed to see that Sedwy wasn't there. He yearned for her. But he also wanted to keep this new mess with the nobles to himself.

He didn't want to share with her. Why?

Because she'd want him to go with that crowd?

Would she really?

He didn't know.

Sinking down onto the bedsponge, he stacked his hands behind his head and stared at the mural of his ceiling—the deep blue of the night sky and the discreet sparkle of the galaxies that wrapped around Celta. Closing his eyes, he questioned himself, his relationship with Sedwy.

Did he love her?

Yes, but he wasn't comfortable talking to her right now about the problem with the nobles.

If they'd been wed, would he confide in her?

Yes. So he had a conundrum. He didn't trust her to take his side right now. But if they'd both committed to marriage—and he could visualize that, wanted that—he expected that they would be a unit. They might be at odds with each other, but they'd present a united front to anyone else. He felt that.

The difficulty was getting from here to there. They had some problems to work out. Probably on her side, too.

And that conclusion made him feel worse than he had with his friend T'Ash and his parents.

A knock came at his sitting room door and he rose, snagged a robe, and shrugged it on. He opened the door to a smiling Sedwy. She wore a lounging robe, too, and held a wine bottle and two glasses in her hands. "So how did your first meeting with your allies go?"

"I survived it," he said lightly.

She laughed as he'd meant her to. Her mother would be in the older contingent, might not know what T'Ash and the others were planning.

"I met T'Willow for the first time." He took the bottle and glasses from her. Going over to the sideboard, he uncorked the bottle and poured the wine. It shone a deep red, the color if not the consistency of blood. He cleared his mind of the meeting, cast his thoughts back to the sword testing, and grabbed the feeling of triumph.

Smiling, he offered her the glass, made sure their fingers touched as she took it. Her eyes gleamed. Then he tapped her glass and grinned. "To being awarded the right to carry a sword."

"Fabulous!" She lifted her wine in a toast to him and drank. The wine made her lips darker. "Let's recapitulate," she said as she sauntered over to the couch.

It occurred to Walker that the large furrabeast couch hadn't been broken in with lovemaking. Yet.

She sat and the robe fell open, revealing a leg all the way to her hip. His breath clogged, he inhaled enough to be able to drink, though the wine lay flat on his tongue. Licks of fire sped through him, hardening his body. He dragged his mind back to the topic. "Recapitulate?"

Sedwy laughed low, shifted a little so the top of her robe gaped. Walker's gaze went from her leg to her cleavage. Very satisfying.

She wiggled her fingers, and he caught the motion and looked at them, then at her face again, and smiled.

Holding up her index finger, she said, "First, you weather Passages and develop a strong Flair." She raised another finger. "Second, your Flair is one that the councils prize and may lead to you becoming Captain of All Councils." She smiled at him and let her gaze slide over him, short brown hair to arched feet. She could see him as the Captain. He had the innate dignity, and he *listened*. He'd only appear more thoughtful and wise as he aged. Yes, in a few decades, she wouldn't be surprised if he was elected to the highest office. Her heart picked up a beat. So sexy in a quiet way.

"Third"—she ticked off on her ring finger—"you passed your written exam. Fourth, you're allies with the greatest up-and-coming group of nobles. Fifth, you'll give your Family a sword, and the status that comes with it, and can carry a sword yourself." She set down the glass and now her hands were open and too empty. She hopped off the couch and lunged toward him, sliding her fingers into that hair, bringing his mouth to hers. Just before she kissed him, she stopped. "GrandLord Walker Clover, you have done your

Family proud. You will raise them to the highest level." She pressed her lips on his and tasted them, the droplet of wine that had lingered at the corner of his mouth. Wonderful vintage. Incredible man.

She let her body lean against his. Was pleased that his arousal was strong and evident. Her own body readied for sex. This time they'd take their time. This time she'd explore him with her hands, maybe her mouth. The notion had pleasure shuddering through her, or maybe that was his hands as they caressed her bare bottom. Very, very nice.

Sensational.

His scrybowl lilted, and when he didn't move—couldn't move because he was exhausted from three bouts of sex—Uncle Pink's voice came as the man left a message in his cache. "Walker, Mitchella has forwarded me the guest list for the ball. Come get it in the morning, please."

Sedwy stretched, and since she was next to him, she rubbed against him. He appreciated the touch of her body against his but was beyond sex by now.

"A ball? Hosted by your cuz Mitchella D'Blackthorn? That should boost your Family, too. The Clovers are really on their way."

"She and Pink are inviting all the people who are interested in marriage contracts with the Family," Walker said baldly, waiting for her reaction.

Her eyelids lowered, and her smile remained, so he checked the bond between them. She wasn't as calm as she seemed. Good.

She rose and picked up her robe. Before she could don it, he stood and took it from her and gathered his own. Throwing them over one arm, he held out his hand. "Come to bed with me, Sedwy."

Her gaze was cool, but she clasped his fingers. "How many statements of interest have been received for you, Walker?"

He shrugged as they crossed from the sitting room into the bedroom. "None that *I'm* interested in."

"How many? I believe I heard your father boast that T'Reed would like you to marry one of his Daughter'sDaughters."

"Maybe." He picked Sedwy up and spun her around until she was laughing and twining her arms around his neck. "But Walker likes Sedwy Grove."

"I want a figure, Walker," she said, amusement lacing her voice.

He dropped her on the bedsponge, followed her down. "I don't know a current figure."

"Aha." Her fingers found his ribs, tickled.

He gritted his teeth and claimed her hand to nibble on the fingertips.

"Last known figure of marriage proposals, Walker?"

"Nine, perhaps. Or maybe ten. Not all were FirstFamilies, of course."

She sighed and he could feel her shake her head. "Of course not."

Pulling the covers over them, he drew her close. "Stay with me, Sedwy."

"For tonight," she murmured, and he knew she was slipping into sleep.

"And I heard that you had an excellent research offer in Chinju."

"Oh." She yawned. "Yes, it's quite magnificent. All I could want."

He hoped not.

That night, he dreamt of climbing the mountain and claiming his sword. But when he wrapped his fingers around the grip, it seared his hand and he couldn't let go. The flesh itself melted away, tendons curled and snapped as they burnt, and his very bones charred until his black skeletal hand held the sword.

Cheers came from the Family, watching him.

Sedwy shook him awake. "Walker, you're having a nightmare."

"Yes," he said starkly and buried himself in her.

She was wet and welcoming, and her mouth and hands pleasured him.

Everything would turn out all right.

Perhaps.

Fifteen

Later the next morning, while he and Sedwy worked together in his office, the girl he'd sent to pick up the list from Pink strode importantly into the room, announcing, "I have reports from the Hollys."

"Thank you." It was a large packet, and Walker was glad of that. He'd have time to figure out how to divert the nobles' intentions or find a solution.

"And here's cuz Mitchella's guest list for the ball. Lots of people are coming! Will it really be ready in three days?"

"I think our cuz is a very efficient and impressive woman," Walker said, pulling papyrus from an envelope. There was a list of FirstFamily rituals and council meetings and a roll call. That shouldn't tip Sedwy off that anything important was going on.

It wasn't so much that he thought she'd tell her mother. As far as he was concerned, she could do that. He simply had the feeling that Sedwy wouldn't be pleased to know that he was considering alienating his new allies.

"Sedwy, do you really think Mitchella can get a ball together in three days?" asked the girl.

"Yes, of course," Sedwy answered. She'd been staring at him but now switched her attention to the girl. "Mitchella is an expert planner. She's done wonderful balls before."

"But she doesn't have that much Flair. Not nearly as much as Trif or Walker."

"That's true, but her husband has great Flair, and, of course, she can also draw from the Residence. The Residence has seen many balls over the centuries."

"Oh, yes. Thank you."

"You're welcome."

Walker looked up from thumbing through the pages, none of which had D'Yew's name on them. "Thank you for the delivery."

"You're welcome." Another bright smile and a wave of the hand and the girl was gone.

Sedwy scanned his face. Her brows dipped and a line appeared between them. Then she propped her chin on her hands. "There's something you aren't telling me." She watched him for another moment or two, then sat straight. "You're concerned about your allies. What's wrong?"

Just what he didn't want to discuss, but he met her gaze steadily. "You do know that I will be my own man, don't you?"

Her smile faded, her eyes grew serious. "I wouldn't have it any other way."

He still felt that she accepted that idea in general but would disapprove of what he planned on doing in specifics.

"Honor is important."

Expression frozen, she stared at him. "I know that more than you understand."

He dipped his head. "Of course."

They looked at each other.

"The Hollys asked you to do something you're unsure of," she said slowly, puzzling it out.

"Yes."

She fiddled with a writestick. "I don't have to tell you how important allies are, especially these allies."

"No."

Inclining her head, she said, "Very well." But she sounded doubtful.

"What if I told you that I have an idea about how I can stay my own man, keep my honor and my allies. Would you trust me?"

She studied him, then nodded. "Yes."

He smiled. "Good."

Yet over the next three days, Walker still saw doubt and shadows in her eyes. A few septhours before the ball, he met with his allies in the social club again. And he brought with him the prophet, Vinni T'Vine.

"Walker?" asked T'Ash.

Walker smiled slightly, sincerely. "The FirstFamily histories and stories I learned are still floating through my mind."

"And?" prompted Holm HollyHeir.

"I considered the circumstances of the last prophecy of the previous GreatLady D'Vine."

They all went immobile. The former D'Vine had spoken the prophecy just before a terrible tragedy, worse for the FirstFamilies than the Black Magic Death Cult.

"Her words regarding Ruis Elder were not heeded." Walker put a hand on Vinni's shoulder, squeezed in support, though Walker thought he was less poised than the prophet. "I asked GreatLord T'Vine if he had been consulted in this matter regarding D'Yew."

"I haven't been," Vinni said. No one met his eyes. "It's a bad precedent to declare a FirstFamily dead. I don't like it. More, I would strongly advise against that."

"And D'Yew herself?" snapped Holm.

There was a long moment's silence. Then Vinni said softly, "I suggest you table the matter for, say, three months."

A chill whispered through the room like death's voice itself.

"Three months," Saille T'Willow repeated flatly.

Vinni nodded.

"Good idea," T'Ash said, a little too loudly. He gestured to the sideboard bar against the wall. "Want a drink, Vinni?"

Vinni smiled and walked to the liquor cabinet. "Sounds great."

Holm Holly looked at Straif T'Blackthorn. Straif strolled over to Walker as the rest of the men eased into a more casual group. "Clever maneuver, Walker. Well done."

"Thanks." Walker wanted a drink himself but wasn't going to get one unless everyone else drank.

"I didn't like the idea of stripping D'Yew of her title but thought it had to be done," Straif said.

Walker grunted.

"Would you have voted for that?"

No harm in being truthful. "Yes."

"And worked with us in the NobleCouncil?" Straif pressed.

"Yes." Though Walker might not have worked as hard as the others would have wanted.

"But our group would have been solid in declaring the Yew Family dead. And you wouldn't have gone along with that, would you have?"

Walker met the man's blue eyes, wanted a drink all the more since his throat was dry. "No." He looked at the others. "All of you know and should remember how important Family is." As the words pushed from him, they fell into the pause of silence. Every man's stare locked on Walker. He stood stiff, didn't show that sweat was trickling down his spine. He'd need more bespelled shirts if he was going to face off with nobles.

He repeated what he said. "All of you have had experiences that made you value your Families. You should remember that."

Holm nodded, lifted a short, thick tumbler with beads of condensation on it toward Walker. "Touché, Walker Clover. You have a point. You're right."

T'Ash grunted. His gaze met Walker's, then glanced aside. "The Captain of the FirstFamilies Council and all the councils, T'Hawthorn, has announced a special session of All Councils. The afternoon of Yule, of all times. You can pick up the Clover ceremonial sword in the Guildhall then."

"Fine with me." Walker smiled and made it sincere. "So how many of you are going to the ball at Straif's tonight?"

This time T'Ash growled before saying, "Every last one of us. Our wives insist."

Walker grinned and got a small glass of whiskey, toasted them. "See you later."

"They won't ever underestimate you again," Vinni T'Vine said as they teleported onto the pad in the Clover Compound's courtyard. Vinni had often fought and tumbled and played with Clover youngsters in previous years, and knew the area well. A smile curved his mouth, too. "And neither will the older generation, nor mine." He buffeted Walker on the shoulder. "Better prepare to be a moving force in the NobleCouncil, maybe even Captain of All Councils."

Walker refrained from asking whether Vinni had *seen* such a future for him. "Just what I always wanted."

Vinni raised his hands, and bottles of ale smacked into his palms, translocated from somewhere. He handed one to Walker.

"Walker, you're a natural."

Walker entered T'Blackthorn Residence with Argut and Sedwy. He was proud to have her on his arm. They'd arrived a good twenty minutes before the ball, but Clovers were rarely late.

Argut said, *See you later, FamMan. Drina the cat is holding a big Fam party. All sorts welcome.*

I'm going too! Lucor squeaked.

They'd already heard about this several times on the glider trip over. Sedwy chuckled. "Do you want me to take you upstairs?

Fams only! Lucor insisted.

Private party, Argut said. Gently he set his teeth on the scruff of Lucor's neck. *I will take him up.*

"Thank you," Sedwy said. But she'd tensed. Walker took her arm again, and they both watched as the young fox carefully mounted the stairs.

When Argut was out of sight, Walker returned his gaze to the great hall. And saw Pink, in formal clothes, standing before them. No other guests were there, a footman stood at the end of the chamber with the door open. "Greetyou, Walker. Greetyou, GrandMistrys Grove," Pink said with an air of determination.

An alarm buzzed in the back of Walker's mind. He'd miscalculated. He'd planned on enjoying the ball with Sedwy, being courteous to other women, but spending some romantic time on the terrace pressing his suit with her.

Pink said, "We'll be expecting a decision, Walker."

"No."

Pink's gaze narrowed at Sedwy.

Walker put his fingers over Sedwy's. "I'll see you in a bit, Pink."

"You're supposed to be in the receiving line," Pink said.

"The longer you talk, the longer it will take for me to get there," Walker pointed out. "Now I'd like to speak with Sedwy alone."

Pink glowered at them both, then stalked away. Walker drew Sedwy away to a lovely salon. He closed the door behind them, turned, and took her hands. "Stay with me."

"You have other obligations tonight," she said.

"I didn't mean just tonight." He lifted both her hands and kissed them, one after the other. "Stay with me."

"I . . . Let's not talk about this now, tonight."

"It's what I want, Sedwy, you must know that."

She swallowed. "I hadn't thought about it."

"No?"

Her lips pressed together, she glanced in the direction of the ballroom. "I'd like to see how I'm treated, whether the scandal around me has diminished."

"That doesn't matter."

"You're sure?"

"Yes. We can overcome all." He kissed her fingertips. "You've obviously succeeded in your latest venture to turn a Commoner into a Nobleman."

She relaxed a little, her eyes warm. "It wasn't a difficult task."

"That's what you say; others might not. Come, I want to dance with you. Let's enjoy the ball." If there was anything he'd learned to do with his Flair, it was to judge the mood of a room or an event. And he was discovering how to act to influence people, change the mood. His pleasure in Sedwy's company, the support and respect of all the Clovers, could do that for her. He was sure there'd be a time to lead her to the terrace and kiss her . . . and cement their relationship.

* * *

The ball had been a strain for Sedwy. Most particularly watching Walker dance with other women. It was fascinating, his manner was so smooth, his smiles genuine, his conversation easy. Yes, he could go very far.

Sedwy continued to receive strange looks.

Finally she went for a break to a suite that had been set aside for the ladies. She was the only one there. She soaked up the quiet a bit, then left the chamber.

Halfway down the corridor toward the ballroom, Pink Clover stepped from a room. "I'm glad I found you here," Pink said.

A tingle of dread shot through her. "I don't think you just *found* me here."

His smile was cheerful, a nice Commoner salesman smile. "No, you're right. I wanted to talk to you."

"About Walker."

Pink nodded. "About Walker and you. I want you to leave him alone."

She thought of the tenderness in Walker's eyes. "That's not what Walker wants."

Pink rocked back and forth on his heels, jerked his head toward the ballroom. "How many times were you snubbed in there?"

"A few." But not as often as she'd been three weeks ago, and not by people she cared about. She'd had genuine conversations, had seen welcoming smiles.

"You'll always have scandal attached to your name," Pink said, almost gently. "You know how high Walker could rise—to the very top, the Captain of All Councils. But can he do that with you by his side?"

All the talk about ambition between her and Walker, her own attitude, came back to strike blows to her heart.

"He's charted his course, would you drag him down?" Pink cleared his throat. "And there's more. Walker needs a good, supportive wife."

Sedwy glared at Pink. "No one has supported Walker as much as I."

"He needs a woman who will make his career *her* career. Someone who'll entertain. Someone he can talk to and rest with. I've known the boy all his life, and you aren't the woman for our Walker."

"I think you don't understand Walker's needs," she said.

"And I think that makes two of us. Know this"—Pink paused heavily—"we don't believe you're the right woman for Walker. Not me, and not his parents. You want to ask them?"

She recalled all the worried looks that Nath and Fen had sent her way lately. Sedwy's mind whirled. If the Clovers didn't accept her as a wife, they could make Walker's—and her—life completely miserable.

She drew on her haughtiest manner, stared Pink down. He fidgeted, looked aside. "You aren't the woman for our Walker," he repeated. "Would you put him in front of your career?"

"Yes."

Pink shook his head. "You say that now, in the first flush of infatuation. I know you have had offers to research in foreign lands. Walker wouldn't be able to get away to do that with you."

"The councils aren't in session all the time. They have breaks." But even as she protested, she knew that whatever arguments she put up, Pink would demolish. There was always an answer for everything.

A woman turned into the corridor from the ballroom. Fen. She stopped behind Pink. "Do you love my son, Sedwy? Enough to overcome all the trials of life together?"

Sedwy hesitated and the silence stretched. Yes, she loved Walker, but *was* it enough? Especially enough to fight his Family on a daily basis?

"I think you should leave as soon as possible," Fen said.

Another blow.

"Tonight," Pink said. "Now." He jerked his head toward the ballroom. "There are women in there who'll fit Walker and the Family better than you."

Fen's expression crumpled into sadness. "I know you had an excellent offer to research towns in Chinju. That you were excited about it." Her gaze pinned Sedwy. "That you were considering it."

"You should leave. Now," Pink repeated.

Walker's mother put her hand around Pink's biceps and tugged. "Come along, Pink. Sedwy knows what she needs to do—for Walker and the Family and herself." Fen's gaze met Sedwy's own, slid away. "Better a quick, clean break, don't you think?"

They faded into the shadows down the hallway.

Sedwy blinked. She thought she had a black hole where her heart should be, and painful devastation radiating from it. The older Clovers were right. She doubted herself, what she could give to Walker. She *had*—did—want that Chinju job. She should do the right thing.

Walker, can you come to the terrace? Sedwy's mental touch caressed his mind. He smiled and excused himself from the small group of nobles with whom he'd been talking about parenting.

The party was going well. He'd danced with Sedwy twice, and then watched her mix and mingle. People were willing to be charmed by her, set aside the scandal of the past. Every now and then he'd followed in her footsteps to a clique or two and gently reminded folk that scandals hit every Family.

Yet as he neared the terrace, his steps lagged and apprehension slid along his spine.

He strode through the weathershield across the open doors to the terrace and turned toward her before his eyes adjusted to the night. When he saw her, he stopped, and everything inside him clenched.

"Going somewhere?" he asked. She had her knapsack ready and was dressed for traveling, and Lucor's carrier was on her hip.

Sixteen

"You don't need me," Sedwy said.

The idea that she was so wrong and didn't know it stabbed through him. "I do."

She shook her head, though she didn't take a step down the terrace.

"What if I told you that I'd work to become Captain of All Councils for you?" he asked. He'd already decided that he would have to aim for that job. It was the best way to protect his Family, to be at the top, to be a power. Alliances or not, newly made noble Families had to be safeguarded just as much as any other newborn, and that was now his job.

Sedwy stared at him, eyes wide in the dark, and the emotions in her eyes as shadowed. "Pursuing a career to please someone else is not wise."

He inclined his head. "That's very true." He wanted to hook his thumbs in his belt, but the stupid clothes didn't have a good belt. "Why are you leaving me, since I *do* need you?"

Again she shook her head. "You don't."

He strode right up to her, so their toes touched, well within her personal space. "Yes, I do. I need you and I love you. But that's not enough for you? My qualities aren't something you want in a husband?" He let anger bleed into his voice, then stepped back, gestured widely to the staircase down to the grounds, the whole world beyond. "I can't give you what you want?"

She remained silent and it goaded him beyond bearing. "Or maybe you're just running away again. That's what you do, run? After the fiasco with the Black Magic Death Cult, you ran from Druida, didn't stay and stick out the rumors, the gossip, the rough times."

Shock widened her eyes now, gasped in her breath. He'd hurt her and hurt himself by hurting her, and what kind of a man was he to do that? Not a decent one. "I'm sorry. I shouldn't have said that."

"No," she said thinly.

"Do you love me?"

When she didn't answer, he turned on his heel and left to return to the too bright lights of the ballroom and people he didn't want to see and things he didn't want to do. Nothing new in that.

Sedwy doubled over with the pain. He'd been so hard.

And so right.

And whatever ambition he might or might not have, he was a strong man that didn't run but accepted his responsibility. He stood up to adversity.

She hadn't been strong. At twenty, all her hopes and dreams, even her judgement and concept of herself had been destroyed. It had been easier to leave, to abandon her study of the dark side of Flair and return to the study of people and culture.

Now she'd let Walker's Family run her off. That wasn't strong. That wasn't the person she thought she was. Wasn't who she wanted to be. She loved Walker and would fight for him and their love against all odds every damn day.

Walker needed a drink and time to compose himself. He left the ballroom for the suite that had been assigned to the men. There were plenty of nobles laughing and noisily conversing, and that sure didn't suit his mood. So he poured a couple of fingers of whis-

awkward, but she lifted her chin. "Or he can come with me to Chinju. I could use a good research assistant. And a husband." She inhaled deeply and took Walker's hand, stared into his eyes. "I love Walker and I want to marry him."

"I love you," he said. "I accept. I want you as my wife. You and no other."

Mitchella swept down upon them, smiling. "I heard that. Let's announce the news. I'll order champagne and prime the musicians for a good drum roll."

"No," Walker said. "We are separating ourselves from the Clovers."

"What?"

"Argut and I are leaving with Sedwy to Chinju. Tell Straif that I'll send notice to T'Ash to submit alliance contracts to Pink, Ilex, and Trif Winterberry as regents for their child." He tilted his head. "Now, we've been too long here, the emotions too high, people are becoming aware of a scene. That's not good for the Family. Sedwy, love, can we teleport to D'Grove's?"

She wrapped her arms around him. "Yes. I'll contact the Chinju authorities and let them know that we'll accept the job."

"No!" Pink ordered.

"You have nothing to say about this," Sedwy said.

More Clovers were gathering, Walker's parents and siblings. She stared at Fen. "I love Walker and we *will* have a life together."

We will have adventures! Argut yipped. His tail waved.

Dragging Nath with her, Fen crossed to them, met Sedwy's eyes. "I heard you say that you love my son and here you are standing by his side through a bad time. That's what's the important thing. Blessings upon you, then. A mother's blessing."

"And a father's," Nath rumbled.

"You can't let him go!" Pink insisted.

"The decision is theirs," Fen said, her voice shaky.

"Went too far, Pink. Never know when to stop pushing," Barton said. "So now you have a decision to make. For the good of the Family. You accept Sedwy as Walker's bride or not? Let Walker really be the Head of the Household or not? Bend or break, Pink?"

Pink closed his eyes. He rubbed his face. "She's not—"

key into a short, heavy crystal glass, nodded to the others, an stepped back into the hallway.

Pink caught Walker's sleeve, pulled him down to an alcove.

"Good thing she's gone," Pink said.

Walker understood it all. He spun on his uncle in fury. "You talked to her, didn't you? Told her not to stay with me."

"It would be wrong."

"I'm done with you," Walker said. He drank the whiskey, saw nowhere to put the glass, and translocated it back to the bar. There was a crash of glass. He ignored it.

"What?" demanded Pink.

"I. Am. Finished. With. The. Clovers. T'Vine has consulted with Trif. Her second child has good Flair, the babe can be the next GrandLady."

"You can't leave us!"

"I can. You've pushed me too far, Pink. I was willing to give up my career and everything else for you and the Family. But I won't give up Sedwy."

"She's given up on you."

Hideous pain. "That may or may not be true. But I can't forgive you for your interference."

"She isn't the right woman for you. She doesn't love you."

"Stop. I don't want to hear your defenses and rationalizations. It's over with me and the—*your* Family. My cuz still hasn't arrived to take a job with T'Ash. I can hire on with him."

"You wouldn't."

"Yes, I would. Plenty of room to stay at the Ashes, too. Goodbye, Pink. I'll translocate my personal belongings from the compound to T'Ash's Residence. If my parents wish to speak to me, they can come by tomorrow."

Argut, we are leaving NOW!

There was a rush of air, then Argut growled at Pink.

Walker said, "Let go of me because I'm 'porting on three and I really wouldn't care whether you got hurt coming with me or not. One, a new name, two, a new place—"

Ready! Argut said.

"Wait, Walker, beloved." Sedwy stepped forward. She felt

"We'll be leaving now." Walker set his arm around her waist. The scent of him came with the gesture, and she knew, then, that everything would be all right.

"Send us your direction," Mitchella D'Blackthorn said. Her husband strode up and gathered her close, too.

"I'll take care of the alliance contracts," Straif said. His gaze flicked to Pink. "Doubt we'll continue them. Leave them for the next generation."

Eyes bulging with horror, Pink stared around him. His mouth opened and closed. He shook his head, swallowed hard, gazed at Walker. "Walker, stay. Stay as the Head of the Household. I won't interfere again, my Vow of Honor."

Leaden silence fell, expanded. Everyone waited on Walker. Sedwy sent loving support and acceptance along their bond. *I will accept any decision you make. We will pursue our careers together.*

We can stay or go, Argut added.

Walker dropped a kiss on her temple. *Together.* Finally, he said, "I accept your Vow of Honor on this matter."

Pink sagged, his shoulders shook.

"What's going on here!" demanded his wife, bustling up. Her gaze swept over the expressions of the group. "Oh, Pink." She tsked and shook her head. "Come on, let's go home. You'll feel better there."

"It's not my home."

"Oh, for the Lady and Lord's sake, a'course it is. You just messed up. It'll be all right in a month or two. Blessings on you, Walker and Sedwy. We'll be leaving now. See you later."

"Later," Walker said. Sedwy wasn't the only one to hear the lilt of amusement in his voice.

The whole party eased.

"So, Walker, gonna let me dance with your betrothed?" asked Barton.

"No."

"I need to prompt the cook and the musicians," Mitchella said. She hurried away, and the others followed.

Sedwy turned in Walker's arms to look up at him. "My offer for you to come with me to Chinju was a true one."

He smiled. "I know." He brushed his lips with hers, looked down the corridor that still thudded with the rapid steps of his relatives on the carpet. "But my path doesn't lead that way. What of your offer to marry me?"

"Not negotiable. You promised."

He laughed, then kissed her until all thought vanished.

Champagne and gleeful triumph still fizzed in her veins when they teleported home to Walker's bedroom.

She undressed him, caressing his skin, feeling his muscles, curving her hand around his sex, and making him shudder.

Soon they were on the bed and slowly, slowly, he slid into her, and she delighted in the sheer pleasure of loving him. Her mind began to dim as they moved together. Their passion built, spiraled high, and she saw a bright coil of gold.

Walker gasped. "What the hell is that?"

She laughed weakly, tears escaped her eyes. She held him tight. "Golden bond," she said thickly, barely able to speak. "Heart-Bond. Walker, we're HeartMates."

He reared back. "What!"

She arched and didn't answer with words but let the gold bond link them. She twined her arms around his neck and lifted to kiss him. Small kisses around his mouth, along the line of his jaw, then strongly on his lips. One last press of her mouth on his, swiping her tongue along his lips before she lay back. Tears continued to slip down her cheeks. "We grew, Walker. You and me. Both of us."

His fingers twined with hers. "Together. We grew individually, and as a couple, and we grew *together*."

"Until we became HeartMates for each other."

He closed his eyes. "No one can ever separate us now."

She grabbed him again. "No one could ever separate us before."

"No, but there will definitely be no lingering doubts about our marriage, that we're right for each other." He smiled and her heart squeezed.

"Marry me today," he said.

"Yes."

"Now let's claim that HeartBond."

Ecstasy had never been so exquisite.

It was the morning of Yule, and all preparations for the evening ritual and the longest night were ready. T'Hawthorn, Captain of All Councils, had called a special session to be held in the new addition of the Guildhall, a huge auditorium room that would hold all the councils—Commoner, Noble, and FirstFamilies—as well as three hundred spectators.

Just before Walker and Sedwy, with Lucor on her shoulder, and Argut left for the meeting, he checked his personal scrybowl and the Family cache for any viz or papyrus messages from the Heliotropes.

Absolutely no word from them.

Complete silence.

He shouldn't have been hurt, but he was.

Evergreen garlands with tiny ornaments and spell-lights draped along the walls, the scent pervasive and reminding him of every Family Yule in his past.

Music filled the air as Walker and Sedwy entered the chamber. The stream of nobles kept their pace dignified. Walker suppressed the urge to tug at the thick gold border edging his long, full sleeves. Real gold thread had been used.

They reached the thickly cushioned chairs and sat. Walker let a breath sift from him. This shouldn't be too difficult. He'd already proved that he could claim a sword.

As soon as the last noble was seated, T'Hawthorn, the Captain of the FirstFamilies Council and, thus, All Councils, stepped to the podium. He was medium-sized man a little older than Pink, and intimidating with his very reserved manner. But when he smiled, he had charm.

"Welcome, Yule!" he shouted.

"Welcome, Yule!" everyone yelled in return. And with the

greeting, the acceptance that today was a holiday and one of the most important days in his life, some of Walker's tension was relieved.

It also helped that Sedwy continued to link hands with him.

T'Hawthorn spoke a little about their culture and Yule, their society, and serving in the councils. He kept that bit short, for which Walker was thankful. Then he announced each new lord and lady, some of whom were replacing relatives who'd retired or passed on. As the ceremony continued, Walker realized he was going to be called last.

He regulated his breathing and leaned on his connection with Sedwy and the serenity she was sending his way.

Finally, T'Hawthorn looked at him and smiled. Sincerely, as if one of the highest sticklers of the FirstFamilies was happy to see him and have him in the councils, something that Walker hadn't anticipated.

"It isn't often that we invest in a noble who has been raised from Commoner class to Grand status, based upon the power of Flair alone."

The room hushed.

"Nor is it often that the person raised actually tests to claim a sword."

Tension wound tighter and tighter in Walker. Was all this necessary? He arranged his robe so he could rise and walk to the podium to pick up his sword, the sword of the Clover Noble GrandHouse, without stumbling and falling.

"And." T'Hawthorn paused significantly. Not one whisper, murmur, comment. "I am pleased to announce that this individual has such Flair that indicates he can serve Celta in the highest capacity. A Flair for people that we of the councils have been waiting for and will treasure."

Walker's mouth fell open. Heat flooded his face, burnt at his neck. He *knew* everyone in the whole room was looking at him now.

"I am pleased to welcome Walker Clover as GrandLord Clover, the first of his Family, as a member of the NobleCouncil."

There was applause, but it was drowned out by a huge wave of music that filled the room. Sedwy stood and yanked on Walker's arm. Right. He was supposed to stand up and go down to where T'Hawthorn stood next to a long, wicked sword propped against the podium. Lady and Lord. Why did Walker put himself through this?

For his Family.

Sedwy kissed him on the mouth.

For Sedwy. Who was now a Clover for him to love and protect.

The din of the music roared in his ears, but the beat of it helped him keep pace as he strode along the aisle. Other lords and ladies smiled and nodded to him. Then he headed carefully down the stairs to the lectern and the deadly-looking fantasy sword. The Clover sword.

T'Hawthorn still smiled. Didn't make him any less intimidating to Walker, but he couldn't show that.

Walker felt approval rolling in from the crowd, the music was still too loud for any voice to top it.

T'Hawthorn offered him a heavy belt and scabbard in Clover green. While Walker was rebuckling his belt, T'Hawthorn picked up the thin, well-crafted blade. One glance told Walker that T'Ash had spared no effort in crafting it. Sharply double edged with a fuller groove. Etched on the blade was *Pride of the Clovers* in fancy lettering.

T'Hawthorn balanced the blade on both palms, offering it to Walker. As soon as he touched the blade, Flair sang up his arm, percolated down his nerves, spread into his blood. This was a weapon, indeed. His gaze went to T'Ash, who was sitting in the front row, arms folded across his chest, smiling. Walker inclined his head to his old boss, a man he respected and who had given his Family such a gift.

Walker slid the sword into the sheath. T'Hawthorn gestured and the music stopped.

Then Sedwy teleported to Walker, wrapped her arm around his waist, and a huge cheer went up, pounding on his ears louder than the music. Shouts, whistles, and he looked toward the public section. There was his Family.

Every one of the Clovers, down to Trif's newborn.

They were all standing and yelling and cheering him.

They were his to love, as was Sedwy.

And he was theirs, and hers.